JILLIAN,

A DAKOTA HUNT NOVEL

Book One

Book One

DEB D. DONOHUE

Deb D. Donohue
www.flourishingpenpublishing.com
Revised Edition 4: May 2024

Dakota Hunt and Private Detective Dakota Hunt are trademarks of Deb D. Donohue and Flourishing Pen Publishing, LLC.

ISBN 978-1-7359371-3-7 (Paperback)
ISBN 978-1-7359371-4-4   (E-book)

Cover design by author.
Cover images by artists, legally purchased by author.

1

Jillian,
March 18, 1977

One moment after making a senseless, hasty decision, my life as I knew it had vanished, replaced by a terrifying, living nightmare. Tears streamed down my face and my lips trembled, as I whispered to myself, "What have I done?" I shook my head in disbelief and screamed with such ferocity, that even the birds must have taken shelter. But no one heard me.

It was a blustery cold Monday afternoon and gusty winds were pelting icy rain across my face, stinging my cheeks, but I didn't care. I figured I'd be able to take care of things and still get home before the storm arrived in full force. On that fateful day, I had arranged to buy tickets for an event that I had been planning for months. The concert tickets were sold out, so I was very excited that I was finally able to find someone who had a few to spare. The concert at Englishtown Raceway in Old Bridge, New Jersey, was to be an eleven-hour concert on September third, including The Marshall Tucker Band, New Riders of the Purple Sage and The Grateful Dead. I wanted to surprise Dakota with the tickets, since he loved The Grateful Dead and I thought it would be fun to go on a road trip to see the show and camp out nearby. I have always loved flute music and was intrigued by The Marshall Tucker Band, who I was really looking forward to hearing and seeing.

Asani Shabina, a girl in one of my classes, set up the meeting with a guy named John, who supposedly was a friend of her boyfriend. That should have been the first red flag, but my stubborn will which urged me to get a hold of those tickets, prevented me from considering my safety. I jogged across the school campus, searching for John in a gray truck wearing an Aussie hat. As I searched for the truck, strong winds howled, wafting my long hair across my face and wet, thick snow began forming clumps on my eyes blurring my vision. I buttoned my winter coat, pulled my hood over my head and wiped the icy snow from my eyes as I trudged on. Suddenly, an enormous raven swooped down over me and began circling above my head. A frigid chill ran up my spine and a loud shriek escaped my mouth as I observed the mysterious bird's behavior. I watched attentively as it perched on a light post and seemed to be glaring down at me. Could it be the same raven that we saw yesterday I mused? I snickered, but then suddenly recalled Mom's wise words about the raven and

2

I gasped, shaking my head, feeling silly that I was so completely unnerved by a bird.

I was too excited about getting tickets to the concert to allow anything to prevent me from doing so. Since school was over for the day, cars and pickup trucks were everywhere, but I finally noticed a gray truck fitting the description so without hesitation, I jogged toward it. The window was down, so I leaned over the side of the truck and asked the guy if he had the tickets. He hesitated which I thought was odd but then he smiled widely, which comforted me a bit, then said we had to go get them from a friend of his. I didn't think that would be a problem and he seemed to be friendly enough, so I threw caution to the wind and jumped in the truck. But right after I closed the door, I felt dreadfully anxious and I began scrutinizing everything in an attempt to comprehend what the problem was. Suddenly, a frigid gust of wind slammed against the truck and I shrieked.

The driver chuckled and told me to relax. He said his name was Jim and informed me that it would not take long to get the tickets. I stared at him, suddenly feeling entirely distressed as I recalled the description of the guy Asani told me to look for. I noticed his dark, shifty eyes and then it struck me like a bolt of lightning jolting my brain. He was not John and he was not wearing an Aussie hat. He wore a red ball cap and had a shady, malevolent disposition, causing suspicion and anxiety to completely overwhelm me.

I was sure I had made a mistake, but it was too late. My hands began shaking and adrenaline rushed through me as I struggled to get out of the truck, but he sped away before I could open the door. I felt nauseous as I caught a glimpse of myself in the sunshade mirror. I noticed that my face had lost all color and I hardly recognized myself in my reflection. What I saw was a frightened, pitiful girl, who had just realized that she was in serious trouble. My heart pounded when I tried to unlock the door, but he had engaged the child lock preventing me from releasing it. I screamed at the top of my lungs and fear consumed me. I began thrashing and kicking, trying desperately to get someone's attention as we drove by car after car, but no one seemed to notice my distress.

I felt ashamed and reckless for not heeding the warnings from Dakota, the raven and Mom. I began trembling and wailing, then my fear turned to rage. I screamed at him to stop the truck and let me out, but he just chortled in such a sinister way that my entire body shook hysterically and my lips trembled while tears streamed down my face. Suddenly, my intuition, which had slyly neglected me earlier returned, revealing that this morning may have been the last time I would see my family.

2

Jillian,
The Day Before

When I awoke, I was drawn to my bedroom window, immediately enchanted by a crimson and tangerine sky. It was Sunday, our family day and I was excited to share time with everyone after a busy week of school studies and sports activities. My belly growled as the delicious aroma of cinnamon French toast wafted through my bedroom. I quickly put on my soft, fluffy robe and slippers and skipped down the stairs to the kitchen. Mom, Dad and Dakota were already up enjoying freshly brewed coffee. I kissed Mom on her rosy, warm cheek. "Good morning, all of you early risers." I poured a cup of coffee and moseyed to the window to enjoy the gorgeous, glowing sunrise peeking over the mountains.

Dad joined me with a wide smile and glittering, jade eyes. "Jillian, what do you have planned today?"

I put my arm around his brawny torso, hugging him firmly. "I thought I'd go snowshoeing up the Peace Trail with Ginger." She's one of our sweet, mild tempered golden retrievers who loves to run freely, chasing squirrels and chipmunks. "The mountains and evergreen branches are coated with fluffy, glistening snow, which makes me think of a scenic greeting card, so I think I'll sketch the landscape."

"That sounds like a pleasant idea. I'd offer to go with you, but that stack of wood won't chop itself. An icy spring storm is on its way which will blow through with fury sometime tomorrow, so I want to be prepared."

Dakota lazily ambled over to join us. "I'll go with you for a while and then I'll come back and help with the firewood."

"I'd like that, if you can keep up with me." I raised by brows and laughed.

"Oh, you're on! A race up the mountain will wake up my lazy bones. I haven't snowshoed in over a month, since we've had one storm after another raging through. The snow must be over six feet deep up there by now."

Mom chimed in with a singsong voice, "Sounds like you will all need full bellies. Maisy brought over some delicious maple syrup to drizzle over the French toast. Grab a plate and help yourselves."

I smiled with delight when I noticed a crockpot of cinnamon stewed apples. "Yummy, my favorite breakfast. Mom, you're the best." I hugged her tightly.

She cupped my face, noticing my cheerful, appreciative eyes. "You look especially happy today,

Jillian. What has you so enthused?"

My surprise for Dakota was on my mind, but I wanted to keep my plans undisclosed for now. "Oh, this lovely day has me feeling energetic and cheerful. Since a storm is on its way, I want to enjoy every minute outdoors until then." I felt tears form in my eyes. "I love you all so much and I've been feeling exceptionally grateful lately. Maybe after our hike, I'll help carry the firewood inside and then we could all play in the snow." I gazed at the sleds out on the deck and smiled, recalling fun filled family days when Dakota and I were young.

Mom, noticing that my attention was captivated by the sleds said, "I haven't been on a sled for a while and I envision an enormous, fat snowman being creatively sculpted in our near future." She pulled a carrot out of the fridge and pointed to the charcoal in the wood stove. "Let's see, how about charcoal eyes and shiny, green buttons down his front."

Her joyful enthusiasm was enticing prompting me to join in her merriment. "I have an old straw hat and a long colorful scarf to make him look homey and jolly." We all laughed while enjoying the delicious, syrupy French toast.

Dakota pulled a shapely twig out of his pocket. "I picked this up this morning while walking with Ginger and Cinnamon, thinking I might whittle it into something. How about a cheerful mouth? I could also carve out a pair of wooden boots." He chuckled.

We all sounded like a bunch of giddy children, which I loved. My heart fluttered, as I remembered days not long ago, when Dakota and I played in the snow for hours. After a while, we would head inside to warm up and I recalled how toasty the wood stove felt as we warmed our frozen limbs. Mom would bring us cups of hot cocoa with baby marshmallows floating on top. I had no intention of ever allowing my inner child to disappear. I thought, just because we have to grow up doesn't mean we can't continue to feel light hearted and spirited.

After the dishes were washed and put away, Dakota and I prepared for our hike. I found myself humming "Morning Has Broken", a sweet, peaceful song by Cat Stevens, while we bundled up in warm winter gear and stuffed our backpacks with water, deer jerky and fruit. I slid my sketch pad and colored pencils into the front pocket and we headed out. I felt elated thinking about enjoying such a beautiful day with Dakota. We had both been so busy with schoolwork and chores that we really hadn't spent any quality time together. I adore my brother and we always laugh and talk about everything under the sun. I wondered how many other siblings were lucky enough to consider each other close friends and I prayed we would always stay connected within our hearts and souls.

As we journeyed up the snow packed trail following Ginger's scampering lead, I grinned at the sound of my boots crunching in the thick, icy snow. I glanced at Dakota, noticing a solemn expression on his face and wondered what was on his mind. I have always been able to sense something troubling Dakota and he, likewise. I'm sure it has everything to do with being twins, but the closeness we share is uncanny. The main difference between us, other than the fact that we are opposite sexes, is that I perceive others differently. I tend to be a little more optimistic, especially concerning the character of others, and more inclined to trust people even before I get to know them. Dakota thinks I'm naïve and worries about my safety. He tends to be much more wary of others until he has a chance to learn more about them.

Dakota is definitely a positive thinking person, but he quietly watches the mannerisms of others and listens to their choice of words before accepting that they mean no harm. Because we are half first nations French native heritage, he has confided in me many times concerning teasing and harassment from other kids. I researched our ancestry years ago and learned that my great grandmother was an Irish woman, who probably passed on our jade eye color gene. My great grandfather was mostly French from the Auvergne-Rhone-Alpes Mountain area which borders both Switzerland and Italy, so we are quite a mixed breed of people.

Anyway, Dakota is the type of person who stands up for himself and our family and often fights back rather than cowering to another's deviant, cruel behavior, but the teasing surely bothered him. I, on the other hand, have never allowed myself to feel uncomfortable about who I am. I prefer to just laugh and shrug it off.

I stopped to rest and rub Ginger's back by a large boulder outcropping. "What is on your mind Dakota?"

His striking, jade eyes showed concern and his mouth drew downward at the sides. "I can't explain it, but I have a strange feeling that something gravely dreadful will soon occur. I don't think it has anything to do with our hike today, but something other than a dreadful winter storm is on its way."

"Oh, Dakota, you worry too much. Let's just enjoy our hike together." Just then, a dark, swiftly moving bird caught my eye. "Hey, look at that magnificent raven circling above the evergreens." The stunning bird spread its enormous wings wide as it gracefully glided with the gusty air currents.

Dakota and I observed the raven as it soared down, shadowing the snowy path in front of us, then perched on a high, blue spruce branch. It began bobbing its head and vocalizing, "Kraaah, kraaah." The bird's striking, burnt umber eyes seemed to be scrutinizing us intently. I kraaahed back and reached out toward it with a piece of jerky, snickering, wondering if the crafty creature would fly down and scoop it out of my hands. Of course it didn't, so I placed the jerky on top of the boulder and slowly backed away, eager to see the raven accept my offering. I handed a piece to Ginger, hoping she would not bark and scare the bird away. Dakota and I sat still, observing the bird as it paced back and forth on the branch. Then it suddenly lifted off the bough, swooped down clutching the jerky with its long, curved talons, then swiftly glided back to its perch. The raven bobbed its head, keeping one eye on us while it hastily devoured the tasty snack. Ginger let out a soft whimper as she gazed up at the raven.

I wanted to clap but I figured I would frighten the bird, so I whispered, "Your welcome my fine feathered friend." I giggled softly.

Dakota chuckled. "It's remarkable how wild creatures trust you. The deer sip water from the pond right near you while you tend your gardens, people flock around you and birds perch nearby and engage in conversations with you." Right on cue, the raven vocalized again. We laughed as we gathered our packs and continued snowshoeing up a steep, slippery slope.

We suddenly found ourselves on top of a deep snow mound, instantly sinking up to our knees. Grunting and breathing heavily, we managed to lift our heavy, cumbersome snowshoes out of the deep, icy mound. Dakota said, "Whoa, let's make our way around this heap. There is another trail ahead with shallower snow that will lead us through a dense growth of evergreens to the top of the ridge." He chuckled. "Look, Ginger is already heading that way instinctively knowing her legs would sink in the deep snow." We both laughed heartily. "We'll just follow our brilliant, canine trailblazer. The view of the mountains is spectacular from there, so maybe we can rest for a bit and you can sketch while I scout around."

As we trudged up the steep grade, I observed the raven following us from above. "I think our peculiar friend is enjoying our company."

"You've done it now. It probably wants more jerky." Dakota guzzled some water, then squirted some out of his canteen for Ginger.

I held my hand over my eyes to block the intense sun, while I observed the mysterious raven gliding with the air currents above us. When we reached the ridge, I detached my snowshoes and removed my sketchpad and pencils from my pack. As I got comfortably situated on a flat-topped boulder, I caught a glimpse of the raven perching on a fir tree branch below. I was thrilled to have him be the subject of my artwork. I began silently sketching the bird, capturing his serene demeanor and his elegant, long plume of feathers. The peace I felt within me, enveloped me completely, as I breathed in the fresh, cool mountain air.

After completing my sketch of the raven, I observed

Dakota just below the fir tree where the raven still calmly rested. I began sketching him as I reminisced about our past. Dakota was hiking down below with Ginger searching for small branches to whittle. He has worked with wood ever since he was a child and his creative skills have developed masterfully over the years. When he was a young boy, he would hike around in the mountains near our home searching for just the right branches of aspen and evergreen trees that he could whittle into various forms. As he became more skilled, he began carving magnificent bowls, sculptures and picture frames, spending weeks on each piece, carving, sanding and oiling the wood. We all loved his creations which Mom and Dad displayed on walls and shelves. One of my favorites was a beautiful coffee table that he carved out of a large burly tree that had fallen in the woods, bringing it back to life in another form.

I was pleased that Dakota stayed in one place long enough for me to capture his tall, muscular stature as he carved a small aspen branch with an intense, fully engrossed expression. My sketch soon portrayed such character and beauty that I felt butterflies in my belly. Ginger was sitting beside Dakota, so I quickly sketched her shape and penciled in her silky soft, copper fur and large, melty brown eyes. I added spruce and fir trees framing the picturesque scene and stood back to admire my work. I was delighted and felt like this sketch of Dakota, Ginger and the raven was one of my finest and I would cherish it forever.

Dakota trudged up the slope, grinning as he held the branch up high. "Doesn't this look like the long peace pipe that Grand used to smoke?"

A delighted smile crossed my face. "Oh, I see it. The stump on the end curves upward into a bowl shape. That's really cool." I felt my mouth curl downward and a sorrowful feeling shrouded my heart, momentarily disrupting my cheerfulness. "You know, I miss him terribly. It's been a few years since his passing, but I think of him often as if he is still here with us."

"Yeah, I miss him, too. He was always so pleasant and comforting to be around and always seemed to have the energy to work and hike with us, right up until his last days. I remember him the day before he passed, sitting out on the front deck smoking his peace pipe, appearing as if he was experiencing deep reflection. I sat down beside him, silently waiting for him to speak. When he did, he turned toward me, holding my gaze with intense solemnity and said, 'You must watch over Jillian always. She isn't concerned with the unknown and will need protection in the near future.'"

"Wow! I wondered why you have always felt the need to watch over me."

"I promised him I would and I tried to get him to explain, but he did not elaborate. I don't know if he meant protecting you in general or if he perceived that something or someone harmful would cross your path. That's also why I felt troubled earlier. I have dreams sometimes about that day, where I see and hear him saying those mysterious words and I wake up sweaty and feeling anxious. I hate the unknown and I realize that fate is out of our hands but I will continue trying nevertheless, to protect you when I can." He put his arm around me. "Just watch your back and try to be suspicious of anything out of the ordinary." The raven suddenly shrieked, fluttered his wings and began agitatedly bobbing his head. Startled, Ginger barked and whined. The raven abruptly lifted off the boulder and swirled upward, soaring out of sight. We both gasped. "It's as if the raven reacted to what I said. That's peculiar."

"Hmm, what a strange bird." I narrowed my eyes and began to feel concerned but I inhaled deeply, shook it off and attempted to lighten the atmosphere. "Okay brother, I will try to be more aware of my surroundings." I realize that maybe I am a bit naïve, but I'm not usually careless. I showed him my masterpiece. "You, Ginger and the raven are my bodyguards, so how could anything life-threatening happen to me." I smiled although uneasiness loomed in the forefront of my mind.

"Hey, that's really remarkable and thanks for capturing my fine-looking, muscular figure." He smiled wide and chuckled. "Well, let's head back. I want to help Dad chop the firewood."

The trek back home was peaceful and mostly downhill, so we were able to move with swifter speed. The only sounds we heard were the crunching of our feet on the snow and gusty winds howling through the trees. I pondered the promise to Grand that Dakota revealed earlier. I felt lucky to have such a caring, compassionate brother and I began to feel excited about my surprise for him. I smiled, controlling my breathing as we trotted down the path. My snowshoes were heavy with thick clumps of snow, so I stopped to shake the snow loose, then trudged ahead, determined to catch up with Dakota. He turned to witness my fortitude and laughed heartily. "Your stamina is admirable, but I'm afraid my muscular legs are much more powerful than yours are."

"Hah, watch this." I picked up my pace, caught up to him and managed to stay right behind him. We arrived at a short stretch of our path where the snow thinned out to only a few inches deep, but quite icy. We took off our cumbersome snowshoes, replacing them with strap-on cleats and continued down the path to our backyard.

Dad glanced up from his work. He had the bar-b-que fired up which was releasing the delicious aroma of smoked elk. Ginger sprinted ahead anticipating a delicious treat. Dad handed a small piece of meat to her, chuckling while she devoured it. "You're just on time for elk steaks. Yamka made her delicious spiced coleslaw and baked rosemary, red potatoes."

My belly grumbled as I ambled up the steps on rubbery legs. "Whew, what a workout. We had an amazing day and I'm absolutely starving. I'll go wash up and find out how I can help Mom."

She was in the kitchen, humming a lively tune while scooping the warm, whipped potatoes into a serving bowl. I wrapped my arms around her and a contented sound escaped her mouth. "Did you and Dakota have a good time?"

"Yes, in fact it was quite enlightening."

"Oh, and how was it enlightening?"

"A mysterious, enormous raven joined us for a while." I showed her my drawing. I didn't want to worry her with Dakota's concerning revelations, so I quickly changed the subject. "Everything smells so good. I'll set the table."

Mom faced me, her compassionate eyes lingering on mine. "Oh? A raven visited you? Ravens choose carefully who to visit. The raven reveals a sign that you might need guidance for a reason only the bird may have knowledge of. You have a mystical aura that the bird is attracted to. The fact that it spent time with you means that it has chosen to share its intuitive nature with you, to help you see what is not obvious."

I pondered this information and wondered what in the world I will need help seeing. The uneasiness I felt earlier while listening to Dakota, returned. "Well, the beautiful sable bird was absolutely enchanting, although I'm not sure what guidance I'll need."

"You may begin to understand if you encounter the raven's presence multiple times. Pay particular attention to your surroundings for a while." She smiled at me, although I noticed her eyes welling up.

"Oh, you and Dakota worry too much. I'll be mindful and will stay alert but you know me, I don't frighten easily and cannot live, worrying about something dreadful that might cross my path." I kissed her on her cheek and dried her tears with a cloth napkin.

Dakota and Dad strutted in laughing, with savory elk steaks on a platter. We all sat down and enjoyed our delicious meal and festive conversation. After lunch, we all rested lazily in comfortable, plush lounge chairs in front of the warm, wood stove. I got up and held four fingers to my forearm. Dakota snickered. "Charades?"

I nodded and began animating my thoughts. I pointed to myself, then patted my heart, then pointed to the three of them. Mom guessed right away. "I love you all." I smiled and sat down. We played for an hour, sometimes laughing hysterically. The mysterious words and occurrences I had heard and experienced earlier, had me feeling puzzled and concerned, so I really needed to laugh and spend quality time with my caring, compassionate family. After a while, Mom stood up and said excitedly, "Let's go sledding. I must exercise my stiff legs." I snickered and trotted after her.

Dark, gray clouds were moving in and the temperature had dropped to twenty-two degrees, so we all bundled up in warm coats and gloves and dashed outside to play. Mom and Dakota had first dibs on the sleds, so Dad and I had fun rolling the snow into massive balls for our snowman. Once we were finished with its stocky shape, I ran inside to find its adornments and facial features. I skipped down the stairs just as Mom was making her way to our bulging, silly creation. She clapped her hands and laughed as she began to scoop out holes for the carrot nose and eyes. I gazed at her while she joyfully decorated our portly snow statue. I've always loved a cute snowman and I recalled one year not long ago, having fun searching for ornaments for our Christmas tree. We found at least a dozen snowmen in different shapes, sizes and colors and joyfully hung them on the tree. I smiled at the cheerful memory.

Dakota worked on the wooden boots and I stuck on round river rocks in a nice, straight row for buttons. Mom tacked on green buttons for the eyes and then topped him off with my old straw hat. We all stood back admiring our artistic work. Dad strolled out of the garage with a corncob pipe and wedged it into his mouth. "I figured we'd have a wise grandfather snowman." He chuckled. "Now, see there? He looks as if he's our welcoming family member." We all laughed heartily. I thought of Grand again, grinning as I gazed with teary eyes at our dear, winter guest. I wished more than anything that he and

Grandmother were still here with us enjoying our delightful family day.

I laid on the ground and began swishing my arms and legs, carving out the shape of a snow angel. Mom joined in my merriment, both of us grinning and giggling. Ginger and Cinnamon sprinted over to join us, barking with excitement as they rolled and pounced in the fluffy snow. I could not recall having so much fun and I did not want the day to end. I would remember this day for the rest of my life.

3

Dakota
March 18, 1977

As I strolled across the football field, I spotted Jillian climbing into a dark gray truck across the parking lot at Red Spruce High School. I thought it was odd that she would be leaving school with someone else because we had arranged to walk home together with plans to help Mom. I bolted toward her, but the truck sped away suspiciously fast. There was no way I could catch up to the truck, so I stopped, frozen in my tracks, feeling stunned and confused.

Fierce winds raged and icy rain pelted my face. Fear and anxiety overwhelmed me and my heart hammered in my chest as I began to imagine several sketchy scenarios.

I dashed toward a group of kids huddled together in the parking lot. Breathing hard with alarming desperation in my voice, I asked them if they happened to notice Jillian or the gray truck. I described her, but none of them recalled seeing her in the lot. I dashed into the main building and asked the teachers and anyone else I saw, if they knew where Jillian may have been headed, but no one had spoken with her about her plans.

Feeling frustrated and puzzled, I realized I had to go home immediately in case she showed up or called the house phone. I pulled myself together, turned on my heels and literally sprinted all the way home. When I arrived at the house, I flung open the door, located Mom and began frantically rambling on about what I had witnessed. Mom tried to calm me down, so that I could explain my concerns coherently. She stayed amazingly composed and called a few friends who Jillian sometimes hung out with or studied with, but no one offered any information that could alleviate my discomfort. Mom grimaced, but didn't seem as worried as I was yet, because after all, we were fifteen years old and we both had social lives. It's just that it was Dad's birthday and we were going to help Mom set the table and prepare for a festive family dinner. Mom had baked Dad's favorite cake, chocolate with layers of chocolate pudding inside with powdered sugar and walnuts sprinkled over the top. The scrumptious cake baking in the oven tantalized my senses, but I had a difficult time feeling cheerful. I felt deeply within my heart and soul, that Jillian was in serious trouble.

When Dad came home from work, I re-counted what I had witnessed with as much detail as I could recall.

He stood silently listening, absorbing my sincerity, then briskly walked to the phone and dialed 911. He reported her missing, but the police informed him that they couldn't do much about it until she was missing for over twenty-four hours. They said, "Teenagers go off with their friends having so much fun that they neglect to call home and then surely enough, they show up the next day." Dad was irritated and angry and continued to urge the police officer to record his report anyway and at least call around to cars on duty, to keep an eye out for the truck and any girls walking around alone. They finally agreed to file the report and alert all officers on duty to keep an eye out for her and the gray truck. Dad and I drove around for a while, but we couldn't find any sign of her or the truck.

It was getting late and Jillian never came home. I was so worried and upset that I could hardly eat. We all choked down dinner and cake pretending that everything would be okay. I could sense that Dad was dreadfully concerned as well, but he didn't want to upset Mom, who thought Jillian would walk in any minute, apologizing profusely and everything would be okay. We were all contemplating silently, each of us in our own way. I normally love the sound of silence, but that night, it was deafening.

My shoulders sagged as I wearily trudged down the hall to my room and flung myself onto my bed. The ceiling seemed to draw closer as I stared up envisioning the mysterious, enigmatic scene. A flood of tears clouded my vision and guilt, like toxic shame devoured all sense of self-worth. If I had only been there five minutes earlier, I would have prevented her from getting into that mysterious truck. I felt like half of me had been ripped away and tossed into a savage parallel world with an extremely frightening fate intended.

As twins, we were always very close, sharing delights, adventures, sorrows, fears and pain. I felt that until Jillian returned, I didn't deserve to be happy, because I failed to protect her like I always had. Lately, I have been affected by visions, which usually occur during vivid, mysterious dreams, often involving our insightful grandfather and a peculiar raven. I believe the dreams are significant messages, puzzles for me to solve, which infuriates me to no end. In the dream, I recalled Jillian and I being followed and observed by a large, mysterious raven while hiking in the mountains the day before, but the connection or significance of the bird has not yet revealed itself.

I finally realized that sitting around moping and doing nothing was pathetic, so shoving my self-loathing aside, I began motivating myself to begin my own thorough investigation. I had been interested in enlisting in the police academy after graduating from high school to train to become a detective, so I figured I would try to think like a detective would. I began strategizing and planning a trip that I knew might last for months or even years, if that's what it took to locate Jillian and bring her home.

4

Dakota

After a few days, the police were finally working more diligently to find Jillian. They assigned a detective to her case, Myles LaSalle, who was genuinely concerned. He was a close friend with Dad and met us at our home to talk with us, promising he would do everything he could to find her. He ran her photo on the news and in the local papers, which Dad planned to continue doing until we discovered what happened to her. We talked with various school authorities, women's shelters, hospitals, you name it. We provided a detailed report including photos, her description, the location at the time of her disappearance and everything else we thought would be helpful to the police detectives. We published articles in the local papers of not only Colorado, but also in all surrounding states and we made sure the FBI understood that we believed she was abducted but so far, no one had found or turned in any information or clues to her whereabouts. The only clue we had was my account of what I had witnessed that earth-shattering day that I will never forget as long as I live.

Miles, along with Dad and I, believed that someone would eventually recall something or a clue would surface that would lead us to Jillian. She was intelligent, confident and even though she could be too trusting, I just couldn't figure out why she thought that getting into a vehicle with someone she didn't know would be okay. Dad and I both believe, she may have been a victim of sex trafficking, but we haven't been able to prove that theory yet. Mom and Dad have tried diligently to remove the belief from my brain that it was my fault to no avail. I alone, have taken on the annihilating burden of her mysterious disappearance, because it was my fault. I failed to protect her as I promised and I knew I would not be able to forgive myself until I discovered what happened to her. I felt my eyes well up and I shook my head in shame as I recalled the serious face of my Grand and the ominous words he spoke, only a few days before his passing.

Jillian had a very outgoing, adventurous personality and was always going off by herself, hiking in the mountains without a care in the world. It was not that she was unconcerned about possible threats to her safety, but she trusted people and the environment surrounding her. Jillian believed that most people would not intentionally harm another and were inherently good, compassionate and caring. Whenever she experienced a hateful or malicious outburst or action by someone, she just felt that they themselves were troubled and were projecting outward, possibly as a cry for help.

I, on the other hand, believe most people are egotistical, hard-hearted individuals who don't give a darn about how they behave or how their actions or words could harm others. I had to fight, with all of the strength I could muster, to gain the respect of others. Kids and even some adults are cruel and seem to find pleasure in harassing and criticizing others. I taught myself to scrutinize people and I only feel comfortable with those who pass my assessments. When I'm alone, I prefer a quiet atmosphere to reflect on my own behaviors and experiences or to contemplate my upcoming journey. If I don't create this balance, I find myself caught in the sticky cobwebs of my mind from past entanglements that continue to resurface, causing frustration and anger. With my family and other kind hearted people, who I allow into my small circle of trust, my inner compassionate nature spews out as if a lid held tight from pressure has just been removed.

As I sat on the porch swing, staring out into a gray, cloudy sky, past images and thoughts of Jillian resurfaced as clearly as if she was still here with us. Jillian had many interests and hobbies which kept her happy and occupied. With her sketchbook in hand, Jillian would walk to a local park or hike in the mountains, finding quiet environmentally diverse settings that moved her in some way. She loved to draw landscapes and anything beautiful in nature that she felt some kind of connection with. Most of her artwork depicted at least one life form, surrounded by its own intrinsic ecosystem. She would sit for hours watching a wild animal, for instance, which would move about, fully engrossed in its search for sustenance. Jillian would observe the animal's behaviors, its vocal outbursts or its ingenious ability to outsmart its prey and then she would capture the animal's nature in her drawings. She planned to attend Colorado State University to study landscape design and had been preparing her portfolio for years.

I clenched my teeth and squeezed my fists firmly, suddenly perceiving that if Jillian was snatched by a malicious criminal, she would be cheated out of the life she loved and dreamed of. I shook my head in disgust, feeling my eyes well up again. Then she suddenly appeared, standing right in front of me with her hands held out to me. When I reached for her, her image began to fade. She fell to her knees and her mouth appeared to be vocalizing, but I heard no sound. As she faded away, I could feel her soul grasping for me, then for a split second, I heard a faint cry, a terrified cry. I spun around to see if anyone else had seen the vision, but I was alone. Water gushed from my eyes and I screamed, emptying my lungs into the air, begging for the spirits to help Jillian escape from the clutches of evil and guide her home.

I drew in a deep breath and dried my eyes with my sleeve. As I gazed into the distance beyond the evergreens, I could see her faint figure, twirling in the garden. This time, the vision was merely a memory, my mind desperately longing to see her as she once was. Jillian was a friendly, compassionate young woman who laughed a lot, spoke softly, yet confidently. She saw the beauty in everything and everyone and she could light up the darkest room in seconds flat with her charismatic, cheerful nature. I instantly pictured Ginger and Cinnamon who loved her and followed her everywhere. Jillian trained the dogs to pick up sticks and twigs and drop them near the wood pile to use for kindling. She would throw their favorite ball as far as she could and watch them race to see who got there first, which always made her laugh.

I pictured Jillian working tirelessly in her splendid floral gardens with Mom. I would help them with the heavy bags of mulch and organic compost, but the planting was Jillian's project. Her favorite flowers were purple and white calla lilies, symbols of passion, wisdom, loyalty, rebirth, faith and purity, sublime ideals that she valued. She said that she loved the elegant beauty of the bloom, with its sturdy, velvety, trumpet shaped petals. Jillian would plant them interspersed with Colorado mountain wildflowers and clusters of bright orange poppies. Her gardens were like masterfully created works of art, gorgeous, natural landscapes which trailed along a peaceful, trickling creek that meandered around boulders and in between evergreens, aspens, maples, plum and apple trees. Jillian believed that her thriving, lovely gardens needed rest during the winter and would come back more beautiful than ever the following spring.

I smiled as I recalled the cool, autumn days when we would rake up the colorful leaves, piling them as high as we could and would then jump in the middle of the pile, laughing hysterically at the crunching sound of thousands of crispy leaves. After dinner, our whole family would often sit on the deck admiring the stunning, deep burgundy sugar maples and fiery golden aspens shimmering against blue-gray autumn skies.

Tears filled my eyes and anxiety began to completely overwhelm me. Thoughts of Jillian seem to have transformed into haunting memories which frightens me, because it's only been a few days since her inexplicable disappearance. My mind seems to be leading me down a dark, mysterious path where nothing but evil lurks in the shadows. I began to perceive that my disheartening fate has been determined and the mysterious path intended for me will lead me on a long arduous journey, which I must prepare vigilantly for.

5

Dakota
1979-1994

Two mournful years have gone by and I find myself unceasingly grief-stricken. I thought that time would subdue my heartache and painful memories, but the day Jillian went missing still seems like yesterday. Many times, when I felt so distraught by her disappearance, I left home for days, hunting for her which included another round of attaching posters on storefronts and city social boards. I placed fliers on car windshields and walked around for hours showing her photo to everyone I passed.

I have tried to cope with Jillian not being around by thinking about the many treasured experiences we shared, things she liked and images which constantly flash in the forefront of my mind. I thought of the peaceful sound of a bubbling, flowing river, the pungent scent of wildflowers, the sweet taste of mangoes and avocados, which were her favorite fruits. With these pleasant thoughts easing my pain and anxiety, I began to smile, but a mere, sheepish smile, because only moments later, my mind reverted back to questions like, why her and why did I not protect her as I promised I would?

I tried to picture our happy, cheerful family the way it was before Jillian fell victim to the clutches of an evil, malicious, unidentified shadow. I walked outside and gazed at the arched, stone bridge that Dad and I built for Jillian, so that we could stroll over the creek and enjoy the beautiful landscape below. It's winter now and piles of fluffy snow have blanketed the gardens and the creek has iced over. The branches of enormous deep green and smokey blue spruce trees, covered with thick clumps of snow, seem to be drooping as if they too are weeping.

I trudged down the porch steps and through the deep snow with no direction in mind. I realized that I had to shake myself out of the depression that I had allowed to consume me, but how could I, knowing Jillian is out there somewhere, possibly suffering and terrified? I turned around and gazed at our family home. Dad and our grand, Jonoche, built our two story, heavy timber and stone mountain home in 1960, two years before Jillian and I were born. The house has an open interior great room and kitchen plan with a high gabled, exposed wood roof and tall, full glazed windows and doors that open onto surrounding exterior wood decks. From every side of the home, there is a breathtaking view of the majestic, Rocky Mountains adorned with evergreens and aspens. Fond memories of our childhood in our comforting family home will always have an enormous place in my heart.

I closed my eyes, envisioning Jillian's masterpiece floral landscape in the spring. From the deck at the front and side of the home, in my mind, I enjoyed the delightfully scented, colorful landscape and I recall the sound of a trickling creek below. A tranquil, serenity surrounds me while a variety of colorful birds, deer and elk sip cool water from the creek. Entirely overwhelmed, I suddenly choked back an uprising outburst and drew in a deep breath. When I opened my watery eyes, I noticed Mom observing me from the window, so I shook off my burdening sorrow and headed back to comfort her.

I have always been dedicated to my family and with Jillian gone, I spend quality time with them whenever possible. Mom believes either we will find Jillian soon or that out of the blue, she will arrive back on the doorstep with a tremendous story to tell. She tends to the gardens, planting lilies that our neighbors and friends continue to give her every week, which is her way of caring for Jillian. She spends several hours a day in Jillian's room, sometimes weeping and sometimes arranging her things as if Jillian is coming home any minute. She'll never give up hope, because she believes that Jillian is being protected by God and the spirits.

Dad seems to be coping with Jillian being gone because he and Myles continue to work on her case, communicating daily. They often come up with ideas and possibilities, sparking bursts of momentum which have only led to more false hopes as they investigate another dead-end clue. We all sense her presence, but like a shadow without its subject, luring us toward her, but discouragingly, just out of our reach.

The following day, I decided to draft out a plan, which I would follow for the conceivable future. I have already graduated from high school and have decided that the first thing on my list is to drive around the country searching for Jillian. I plan to enlist in the police academy when I turn twenty-one, which is in four years, but my detective training begins now. I have been reading books about investigative practices, skills and how to enhance my intuitive nature. I have always had an eye for detail and have already begun documenting things that I see and hear, filing them away in my brain. I believe this is the journey cut out for me, which will soon lead me to Jillian. Mom and Dad understand why I have to do this and Dad offered to go with me, but I feel that this is a journey meant for me only, possibly to subdue the guilt and grief I hold deeply within my heart and that I express so blatantly on my face. I have forgotten how to smile and I cannot recall the last time I laughed.

When I began my journey, I continued to check out women's crisis centers, hospitals and police departments in Colorado, Utah, Wyoming, Kansas and New Mexico. Basically, I have searched in every state surrounding Colorado, which has taken several weeks so far. While walking through a hotel lobby one day, I glimpsed a photo of a turquoise ocean wave on the front of a travel brochure out of the corner of my eye. I reached for the brochure, recalling Jillian's interest in vacationing on a beach and body surfing the waves. She said that she wanted to tour California by driving up the coast, stopping to explore all of the little beach towns along the way, so I packed up my truck and drove to California. Of course, I knew she would not just suddenly leave home on her own to live near the ocean, but I thought, what if she escaped her captors? Where would she go, if she was afraid to come home? Anyway, I wanted to cover all bases, so I spent a little time in every beach town, searching, posting flyers, talking to the local people and authorities. I began my journey in San Diego and drove all the way up through Oregon, which took about a month and a half. Some days, I just sat on the beach, staring out at the ocean, wishing I would see her swimming or walking up the beach smiling and giggling. But if I'm being honest with myself, I can only envision the ghost of a young woman, which as time goes by, seems to fade despite my continuous efforts to keep her image in the forefront of my mind. I could never forget her, but her voice and her laugh seem more like echoes bouncing around in my brain, each echo more distant.

I was watching some horrific news in a hotel room one night and was overwhelmed by the amount of chaos around the world. The last news story that night was about the Hanafi Siege in Washington, D.C., where three buildings were seized by twelve Hanafi Movement gunmen, who took 149 hostages.[1] That story really spooked me, because I started wondering if Jillian was being held hostage by some radical group and was possibly involved in some terrifying predicament. I started feeling confused, my eyes welled up and I couldn't eat or sleep, so I packed up and drove home.

Four years later, I joined the Denver Police Department as planned, completed my training and began working with a seasoned detective, specializing in abduction cases. We often worked with detectives from other states, tracking dangerous sociopaths and criminal organizations who were involved in human trafficking and other sex criminal activity. I kept hoping that I would find the criminal responsible for Jillian's abduction, but no clues had surfaced yet.

After ten years of investigative experience, I left the Denver P.D. and began my own private investigative practice. I traveled around the country hoping to run across some kind of connection to Jillian, while working on cases along the way. After a year of concentrating my investigations on casinos around the country, I found a clue that seemed more hopeful than anything I had come up with for the past seventeen years. I had been in contact with the FBI who received an anonymous tip about a group of young women who were rescued from a sex trafficking ring, operating in a casino in Wisconsin.

One of the women rescued revealed information about a girl named Dalila, who had joined their group involuntarily, seventeen years ago. Dalila apparently escaped with another young woman named Julia Ivanov. She had also mailed a letter to the FBI, informing them of more young women being held against their will as well as information about the criminals responsible. To my dismay, Jillian's name was not mentioned, but my intuition screamed at me to consider that it was her, since the timing was exactly the same. The man who was responsible for the women was Ray Giordano, although he was not at the casino at the time of the bust. The FBI finally caught up to Giordano, arrested and interrogated him, but released him due to lack of evidence of his direct involvement. Frustrated, I spent several more years working on clues and searching for the man, which eventually led me to a casino in Oklahoma. Something about that casino continued to lure me back, several times a year and I could not for the life of me figure out why, but was bound and determined to find the connection.

I again, posted requests to the public in papers and on the news, to keep an eye out for her and to call the number listed. I answered call after call following every lead, but people who felt sure they had seen her, were mistaken. I was able to locate the women they described, but none of them ever turned out to be Jillian.

I had visited with Mom and Dad one evening and during dinner, Mom suddenly glanced at Dad and me and said, "Jillian is being protected. I feel her presence." Dad and I stared at her with wonder and hope. I felt my face turn pale and clammy and my heart thrummed rapidly. I got up and began pacing back and forth, my eyes filling with tears. We discussed my latest dead-end leads and what my next plans were, then retired for the night, each of us lost in our own hopeful illusions.

That silent, moonlit night, I tried diligently to remain peaceful in order to stay focused and organize my thoughts. When I finally drifted off to sleep, I had a bizarre dream involving my grand, Jonoche, which usually means the dream is more of an insight into something which will soon occur. In the dream, I saw a woman with flowing waist length, sable hair standing by a large boulder outcropping, surrounded by flowers. Her glistening eyes were gazing into Jonoche's, while he spoke with her. I sprinted toward her, calling her name, but when I arrived at the boulder, she was suddenly farther away, her image fading as I ran after her. My legs became rubbery, no longer supporting my weight and I fell to my knees, gasping for air, my eyes and mind befuddled. When I regained clear sight, a large raven swooped down in front of me, startling the breath out of me. Then as quickly as it appeared, it soared out of sight. Then, I caught a glimpse of the woman walking away, so far on the distant horizon that she was nothing more than a mirage.

I woke up in a cold sweat, breathing heavily. I closed my eyes again and tried to relax completely, hoping to slip back into the dream so that I could find some kind of landmark or a clue to her location. I believed that Jillian's spirit was trying to communicate with me, if I could only concentrate without self-doubt impeding my ability to remain focused. I tossed and turned for the rest of the night, overwhelmingly distraught that I hadn't been able to find her after all of these years.

6

Jillian
1994

It's been seventeen years now since I was abducted. Until 1991, I didn't remember much after getting into the wrong truck, although I felt sure that I had missed out on many years of my life. When I did begin to remember, nothing made sense and my thoughts whirled in a pool of confusion and discombobulation. I recalled parts of my life, particularly certain events that happened right after I was abducted, but nothing before that, until recently. I still can't remember where I came from and I feel absolutely certain that I had a past life that is quite different from the disturbing life I've been living. Lately, I have been trying desperately to piece together what happened to me after that terrifying, fateful day.

I have been informed that I was continuously drugged for months, which I guess, explains my memory loss. I had never taken drugs before, I felt sure of that and certainly not heroin, which seemed to melt my brain, leaving me feeling utterly helpless and entirely immobile, not to mention continuously nauseous. By 1991, there were fourteen years lost somewhere.

I remembered the driver of the gray pickup, telling me that his name was Jim, but maybe that was a lie, too. He drove to an old, red warehouse in west Denver. I recalled trembling with fear and anxiety and I felt cold and helpless. He told me to get out of the truck and follow him into the warehouse where he had the tickets. When I said that I would prefer to stay in the truck, he growled at me like a wolf, a ravenous predator, who recognized I was easy prey. With a deranged, scowling demeanor, he stomped around to the passenger side of the truck with fury in his eyes. I was trembling so uncontrollably that I could barely move or function. I frantically locked the doors and moved over to the driver's side of the truck, but he had taken the keys. I panicked and fear seized my mind as I held the door as firmly as I could, but he was much stronger and I realized I was in serious trouble, dreading what might happen next. He jerked open the door and grabbed me by my arm so powerfully, that I thought he had dislocated it from my shoulder. I swung at him, kicked him and let out an ear-splitting scream, but no one was around to hear my cries. I continued to kick and scream as he dragged me into the warehouse and threw me onto the floor. He then punched me so hard that I saw stars and then, nothing. I must have blacked out, because I have no idea what may have happened next.

When I awoke, I was somewhere unrecognizable and my arm and face ached with piercing, unbearable pain. My face was so swollen that I could scarcely see out of my tear-filled eyes. I felt woozy and incoherent as I tried to look at my arm which was bruised with needle marks. I realized then that I had been drugged. I tried to focus, glancing around the room, presuming that I was in a hotel room. I was so dizzy and nauseous that I felt like I might lose my stomach violently, then I passed out again.

I awoke one morning feeling anxious and befuddled, comprehending that I had lost time again. I wondered if maybe years had passed, because my surroundings looked different, I felt different, older, worn-out. Just seconds before I awoke, I had been dreaming that I was ice skating on a lovely, little pond surrounded by beautiful evergreens. I was gliding and twirling and laughing, but then the scene changed and I was sliding uncontrollably. The ice began thinning, then suddenly cracked and I almost slid into a gaping, slushy hole. Then, I fell hard and smacked my head on the ice.

I glanced around, confused, dizzy and not quite sure if I was dreaming or unconscious, then I slowly began to understand what really happened. I had recently slipped and fallen on icy pavement, somewhere unrecognizable. I forced myself to think, challenging myself to recall as much as possible, to no avail. Where am I? My dream seemed more real than what I awoke to. I wondered if I was near home in the first part of the dream, which seemed familiar and comforting. My head pounded and extreme nausea and wooziness returned with such intensity that I could only lie still with my eyes closed. I forced myself to relax to minimize the pain and anxiety, finally falling asleep.

When I awoke sometime later, there was a woman sitting next to me on my bed holding a cold, wet cloth on my forehead. I asked who she was. She was astonished to learn that I couldn't remember her or anything else at the moment and was concerned that I probably had a concussion. She said her name was Julia Ivanov and informed me that we were good friends. She also told me that she discovered me on the ground after slipping on the ice. She, along with another man named Ray Giordano, who I learned was our boss, carried me into a hotel room at a casino, where a nurse or someone with nurse training attended to me. I glanced around the room, noticing a red door and ugly, red carpet and drapes. The color red felt unsettling to me and nausea and anxiety overwhelmed me again.

Julia disclosed that Ray was our handler. I didn't understand this. What did that mean? I was horrified to find out that my job for the past seventeen years, had been to care for a number of young women who worked for Ray as courtesans, mostly at casinos. Nothing seemed right and I knew I did not belong there. I felt certain that this could not be my life and I realized that I had lived the past seventeen years in some kind of drug induced oblivion. I did not know myself at all and began feeling discouraged and enraged.

Determined to figure things out, I asked Julia how I met her? What happened? Why don't I remember anything? She told me that Ray escorted me into a hotel room one day at a casino in Atlantic City. As a warning, Ray forced Julia and the other girls to watch as I was injected with a drug that made me limp, blank minded and sleepy. She revealed that they continued to drug me until I was addicted and pacified and that they did the same thing to her. I was horrified by her words and completely distraught that I couldn't remember who I was and where my family lives. I was traumatized by what Julia was telling me and figured the memory loss was a dreadful side effect of the drugs, but I was resolutely determined to recall my past life at all costs. I began to wonder if I had devised my own mental block somewhere in the deep recesses of my mind as a coping mechanism.

As the days flew by, I continued to remember bits and pieces of my more recent life, from 1991 to 1994. I asked Julia to tell me more about our past so that I could try to sort things out. She looked unsure because she didn't want to agitate or frighten me again, but she nodded and began telling me in chronological order, the main events and our movements over the past seventeen years.

"After a couple of weeks of drugging you, Ray backed off on the doses until you were coherent and could walk around. He asked you questions and realized that you couldn't remember who you were and where you came from. He liked you. I mean, he really liked you. He took advantage of your memory loss and decided that you would be his girl."

"His girl? What, what do you mean, his girl?"

"Ray told you that you were his girlfriend and that he was sorry that you didn't remember, but not to worry because he took very good care of you. He made you his assistant and told us your name is Dalila. Is that your name? Do you remember?"

"Ummm, I, that doesn't sound familiar. Dalila.

Dalila. I don't think that's my name."

"Well, maybe you will remember soon. The rest of us were very jealous of you at first because you didn't have to work as one of the ladies of the evening. That's what he calls us. You took care of us and you made sure we had what we needed. You took us shopping and bought us whatever we needed, nice clothing and shoes, a few pieces of jewelry, feminine products and other toiletries. You took us to a clinic and made sure we had birth control and condoms. We all talked with you when we had problems and it was your job to make sure we were okay, for the most part. Some of us are okay with the work, but there were those who sometimes quarreled with Ray and that never turned out well. But you," she hesitated, "you have always come to bat for us. You are the only one that Ray listens to."

"Why have you continued to put up with this? Why haven't you tried to escape such a nightmare existence?"

"Are you kidding? Ray and his super thugs would kill us if we even tried to escape. They did kill one girl who tried to leave, Rosa." Julia narrowed her eyes, suddenly taking on a furious demeanor. "They tortured her and beat her to death in front of the rest of us, just to show us what would happen if anyone else tried to escape. The bastards!" Tears filled her eyes. "What they did to Rosa was so horrible that we are all terrified to do or say anything that would upset or aggravate him in any way. We all have been completely submissive, preferring to accept the type of life he has chosen for us rather than experiencing living hell followed by a terrifying, agonizing death, and you should, too."

My stomach was in snarly tethers and I felt woozy

again, but I was determined to stay strong and learn as much as I could. I knew right then that I would escape somehow, but it was vital that I remembered who I really was and where my family lived. I wondered who the other girls were and where they came from. "Julia, what happened to you? I mean, how did you end up here, that is, if you are okay talking about it?"

"Well, I'm okay talking about it now, because I've been dealing with it all for many years." She breathed deeply. "I was living in Moscow with my sister when my parents died in a car crash, leaving us on our own. We weren't doing very well, always hungry and barely making the house payments, which were 21,670 rubles. That's 344 U.S. dollars. We had some savings left to us by our parents and we were both working at local shops, but not earning very much. We didn't want to lose our home, so we were forced to rent it out. Of course we couldn't live on the streets, so we decided to go to America. I met a man who promised me that we could work on a ship in exchange for free travel and he said he would help us get our green cards to work in the United States. He said there were many jobs on board the ship to pay for our way, like cooking and other galley duties, cleaning cabins and doing laundry for the ship workers. I made arrangements for my sister, Natalia and me and we boarded the ship the following day."

"In March of 1976, we were on our way to America, but we didn't get any of the jobs that the man had described." Her watery eyes lowered, gazing warily down at her trembling hands. "We, we were shoved into cabins where nasty, cruel men took advantage of us in every way you could think of. We were raped and beaten, sometimes by many men at the same time." She began to speak louder with fury in her voice. "We had to do this, many times a night. We were treated like whores, spit on, kicked, punched and thrown into a filthy room with many other women. Before we were taken to the men's cabins, a bad-tempered, revolting man would open the door and throw buckets of water over us to clean us up for our jobs. It was so horrible, so horrible." Julia was crying uncontrollably.

I put my arms around her and hugged her closely. "I'm so sorry. I shouldn't have asked you. I see that it's hard for you to relive what happened." I began weeping as well. "I'm so sorry, Julia."

Julia sniffled, breathing in deeply. "I'm okay. It actually helps to talk about it because it helps me to remember that the worst is all behind me now. But, but." Her voice trembled, barely getting the next words out. "Natalia was killed. A very cruel man on the ship abused her so badly that she died from her injuries." She slid down on the floor and put her head in her hands, sobbing. "I miss her. I loved her so much. It was all my fault. We were so happy when we boarded the ship, believing the man and dreaming of living in America, a free world, or so we thought. It was all my fault and for that, I will never forgive myself."

"Julia, what happened to you and Natalia was not your fault. People have been boarding ships to come to the U.S. for hundreds of years. There was no way you could have known what that despicable man had planned for you. You were hopeful like anyone would have been."

"Yes, hopeful and look where I am now. When I finally arrived in New York, many other girls and I were herded off the ship like cattle. Two of Ray's men were there to take us to a small motel where we were allowed to shower and rest. One of the men was Hydro, who is still here now. Early in the morning, Hydro woke me up and forced me to have sex with him. He was disgusting. I couldn't imagine when the hell would end and I cried for days.

"Ray's men forced us into a van transporting us to Atlantic City, to a casino there. I had to accept being a whore in my new role in life, here in America. I couldn't figure out how to get away. I planned to on a few occasions, but there never seemed to be a good, safe time, because we were always watched. For eighteen years now, I have dressed in evening gowns, lingered around wealthy gambling men, drinking vodka and going to bed with them. Most of the men treated me nicely but every now and then, I get stuck with a real bastard who hits me and is dreadfully violent with me." She turned to me and smiled, drying her tears with her sleeve. "You have always taken care of me and the others when we are treated roughly. For this, I am forever grateful."

I held her eyes intently with my own and exclaimed with unwavering resolve, "I don't care how dangerous it is, I'm getting out of here and you're coming with me!"

She protested, "Dalila, no, don't even try. In fact, I don't think it would be a good idea if you tell Ray that you are beginning to remember or that I disclosed all that I did. He told me to watch over you, to make sure you were okay. You must pretend that you still have amnesia."

Ray was away and there was a rumor among the girls that he was rounding up more unfortunate, innocent girls and he did. Four more girls showed up later that day, shattering my heart into tiny, grief-stricken pieces. I could not tolerate seeing them experience years of barely living as gloomy, lost souls in dreadful lives as I have for too many years. I knew I had to escape and find a way to save them all.

I appreciated and agreed with Julia's discerning words. "I understand and that makes sense, at least for now, but you must tell me more to help me recall my past."

Julia drew in a deep breath while staring intently into my eyes as if she thought she might spot a bit of weakness. After a silent moment, she proceeded. "After a few months, Ray moved us to the Falcon Casino in Wisconsin in June of 1977, where we worked for a few months. He then had us driven to Las Vegas to work at various casinos there. I guess they moved us around a lot, so that no one suspected that we were being held against our will, slaves of the revolting sex trade. What I think was interesting, was that we often returned to the Wild Cat Casino in Oklahoma, where Ray has some kind of business connections. The last time we were there, I overheard him talking with some men about a partnership at the casino." She sighed, shaking her head. "It's now, September 18th, 1994."

"Hmmm, that is interesting." I filed the information in my mind under R for revenge. Someday soon, Ray Giordano will pay for what he has done. I am so disappointed that a substantial portion of my life is just gone, but maybe it's better that I don't remember such an atrocious past. "Uhm, so, did I work as a prostitute?"

"No, you are Ray's woman. He won't let any other man near you."

"Well, I guess that's a relief, but what about Ray? Is he nice to me? I mean, I don't recall how he treats me."

"He treats you nicely, believe it or not. Maybe because you haven't been able to remember your past, you have not questioned your situation in life since you have nothing else to compare it to."

"Yeah, maybe, but I'm not only questioning it now, I'm taking back control of my life come hell or high water. Julia, we're getting out of here. Even though I don't know where I'm from, yet anyway, I'll come up with a plan. Are you in?"

"Well, I don't know. Dalila, it's just too dangerous. If we are caught trying to escape, you know now, that we will suffer an atrocious, unbearable fate. None of the girls have even tried to escape since Rosa tried. We have been frequently warned that we will be tortured, killed and that our families will suffer the same. I don't have any family left, but I'm sure you do, don't you?"

"I... I don't know. Wait, he knows the locations of our families? He knows our addresses and real names?"

"I don't know, but maybe. He has our ID cards and our passports. I had a passport when I came here from Russia, but he took it from me and told me that my new job here in America was to work for him and would no longer need it."

"Does he have an office here or a safe where he keeps his books, money and maybe our ID's?"

"I actually thought you would know more about that than I would."

I tried desperately to recall observing Ray's clandestine actions to no avail. "Well, I'll be attentively watching from now on." I prayed that I could be convincing like a seasoned actress without being overly dramatic.

I was suddenly startled by a clatter at the hotel door and Ray entered the room. A medium height man with dark, spiky hair, wearing a blood red collared shirt ambled in. With a gruff, boisterous voice, he bellowed, "Well, look who is sitting up, pretty as ever. Good morning, Dalila."

I pretended to be incoherent and groggy and continued to review over and over in my head, the things that Julia revealed. I knew with absolution that I would escape this living nightmare and would discover who my family is and where they live as soon as possible. When I feel that I am safe from the clutches of Ray Giordano and he is no longer a threat to my family, I'll go home. My eyes welled up, threatening to gush over and I wanted to scream at the top of my lungs, but I resisted.

That night, I had another mysterious, bizarre dream involving an enormous raven and when I awoke, I somehow began to comprehend that I had altered my own fate by allowing myself to naively make a catastrophic, careless decision. Right then, I vowed to never allow such recklessness to influence my thinking.

7

Jillian
1994

I began to remember more and more each day, although I pretended otherwise. Julia was right, he treated me kindly, even though he was a manipulative, controlling man who was obviously used to people following his orders with no questions asked. My head still throbbed from the fall on the ice, but the pain was becoming less intense and the dizziness had diminished considerably. Ray asked me to take the girls shopping, because he planned to move us again, to another state, another casino. I realized that my only chance of escaping might be here and now, before we leave again, comprehending that I would have to move fast. I had been working on a plan

49

to get to his files and discover everything I possibly could about my family as well as for the other girls. I hoped I'd be able to succeed in convincing them to escape with me, but could I trust them? Would any of the girls allow fear to overcome them so completely that they might impulsively destroy my plans, plunging me even deeper into despair and doom? I shook myself, vanquishing the self-doubt and weakness that I felt creeping into my mind, threatening to diminish my determination. I began watching Ray closely, praying that I would witness him accessing his files, if he had them in the hotel room.

The next morning, I donned my disguise, which consisted of an auburn wig and dark brown contacts, which Ray insisted that I wear to protect myself, although I understood the real reason. My eyes are a striking, deep jade color, which surely would be noticed. I took the girls shopping but unfortunately, Hydro stayed with us the entire time. Julia said they called him Hydro because of his preferred water torture methods of punishment when any of us got out of line. I shivered at the thought. We bought the things we needed, then Ray's limo driver picked us up at a side, less popular entrance. When we returned to the Casino, Ray was gone and I knew this was my chance to escape. I decided to confide in one of the casino owners, even though I was terrified that he would report me to Ray and that would be it. I'd lose his confidence and then what?

I trotted to the casino offices, luckily finding the manager, Charlie Nevins, in the hallway. I informed him of our situation perceiving that at first, he didn't believe me. He said that Ray Giordano told him that he was vacationing with his family and friends and would be visiting his casino often. He played in high stakes poker games and spent a lot of his money gambling, which of course was extremely lucrative for Charlie's casino, so he didn't ask questions. I didn't believe him, sensing that he knew what was really going on, but I had to take a chance. I finally convinced him to help me or at least look into it promptly. I asked him to review his videos and make copies of the ones showing Ray's party along with all previous transactions, especially the large ones. I needed all sorts of evidence. He said he could not be involved in anything illegal that could disrupt or damage his business, but he finally agreed to do it.

I went back to my hotel room to think, to strategize. My stomach was fluttering and my heart was hammering furiously. Ray was still not back from wherever he'd gone to, so I took a chance and rummaged through the desk in the hotel room, searching for anything that I could keep or copy as evidence. Where were our files? Where were our passports and IDs? I finally came across a ledger where a bunch of random numbers were listed. I found the hotel safe in a closet and tried some of the numbers. Nothing. I rummaged through more of his papers and then, there it was. I just had a feeling, because my eyes kept returning for some unexplained reason, to the name of a casino in Oklahoma and a four-digit address for the establishment. I had also heard Ray speaking about the casino to one of his partners, now sensing that the place must be important to him. I dashed back to the safe and tapped in the number. The safe opened and I whispered, "Yes!" I quickly rifled through the files and dumped out a gray bag and lo and behold, there was my ID with my photo. I stood frozen in my stance, gazing at my real name. My name is Jillian Hunt and my address is in Evergreen, Colorado. Tears filled my eyes and emotional anxiety began to overwhelm me. I whispered, "Stay strong Jillian Hunt." I sniffled, dried my eyes with my sleeve and continued to quickly search through the files.

A list on top of the files revealed the names of all of the girls, our families and addresses, so I quickly removed the list and all of the girls' files and ID's. I narrowed my eyes and spoke quietly in a vengeful tone, "You don't need them anymore, you pathetic pig." I grabbed my ID card, shoved it in my pocket along with Julia's passport and put the others into a plastic bag. I then folded up some newspapers and shoved them into the gray bag to replace the passports, praying that Ray wasn't going to check that bag any time soon. Large stacks of money and a handgun taunted me, but I figured if Ray were to open his safe, he would most likely be after his money or the gun. I thought about taking a few bills, but then decided that it would not only be reckless, but I did not want anything to do with dirty money, so I closed the safe without touching it. Excited and breathing heavily, I ran down the hall to Julia's room and divulged what I had done. "We are going to escape this hell, right now."

I had to move quickly, so I jogged back to Charlie's office and asked him if he had been able to gather any information or at least videos of Ray's movements at the casino. He delighted me with an enormous smile, though a sour grimace followed. "I'm embarrassed to say, I believe you are right. I have copies of all of Mr. Giordano's movements since he arrived at the casino. The videos show you and quite a few other young women, sometimes gathered around him and sometimes showing him having conversations with men, followed by what appears to be a deliberate companion arrangement. As I reviewed the tapes, I saw that in many instances, the women eventually retired to the rooms of some of my guests for the evening. I of course, do not condone this kind of behavior, however, whether or not men take women to their rooms for the night is their own business. I believe this might be the type of information you were hoping to find."

"Yes, it certainly is and I understand your concerns though, I am not interested in your guests. I just need the tapes as proof that Ray coerces the women to work for him. I also need the names and as much information about the men in Giordano's group as you can give me, please."

Charlie breathed in deeply, then slowly exhaled with his eyes closed. "Okay, here is a list of names including Mr. Giordano and a few men that booked rooms at the same time, who were also shown many times on tape in the company of Mr. Giordano. In this package, you will find copies of two weeks of his gambling and dining transactions. It shows money he won and money exchanged into cash. I don't know if that helps, but that's all I could come up with." He gave me the package and told me that he absolutely needed to have his name and guests out of it.

"Charlie, thank you. I am leaving right now, with as many of the girls as I can. I will not ever mention you. Ray is not here at the moment, so we have to leave now if we have any chance of escaping his notice. Please show me the backdoor exit or is there a way out of the building from here?"

"Yes, follow me." He showed me a private rear exit to a parking lot. I glanced around, quickly formulating a plan.

"Give me fifteen minutes and call a taxi to meet me here. Would you do that, please?"

"Absolutely. I'll wait here until you return. Miss Dalila, I'm sorry this happened to you, but I will do anything you need to help you get away safely. Also, if anyone shows up inquiring about you, I will not divulge that you have ever been here." He paused, clearing his throat while glancing at the security monitors. "You must know that I see the man, who I have heard called Hydro, at a blackjack table right now with a couple of girls. Be careful."

"Oh, damn! Uhm, excuse me, Charlie. Okay, thanks. I'll be back as quickly as I can." I ran out of the office and down a hallway that led to Julia's hotel room and knocked on the door, praying she was still there. I called out, "Julia?" She opened the door and I anxiously shoved passed her into the room, quickly closing the door. "Julia, let's go, now. Gather a small bag of your things. We don't have much time. Hydro is down in the casino with some of the girls. Do you know what rooms any of the other girls stay in?"

"Dalila, this is crazy."

"We don't have time to argue. Do you want to get out of here or not?"

"Yes, but…" she hesitated, then nodded her head with a weary, frightened expression. "Okay. While I gather a few things, you go try room 118 and 120. Four girls stay in those rooms."

"Hurry!" I dashed out of the room and knocked on both doors. There were no answers. I tried again. Nothing. Discouraged, I jogged back to Julia's room and knocked on her door again. Julia met me at the door with a small travel bag. "No one answered either door, but we have to go anyway. I will send help for the others as soon as we get out of here."

Julia followed me down the hall and down the stairs to Charlie's office. Charlie said the taxi driver was on his way, then escorted us out of the back door to the parking lot. I gave him a trembling hug and smiled with quivering lips. He gave me $300 and told me to take it with no questions asked. I agreed reluctantly and promised him I would repay him as soon as I could.

The taxi arrived and we quickly got in. I heard the desperation in my voice as I sternly uttered, "Drive away, now."

"Yes, Ma'am. Is everything okay?"

"We'll be fine, but we have to get to a bus terminal quickly."

"Yes, Ma'am."

"Oh, I have to stop at a mailing center on the way."

The taxi driver thought for a minute and then typed an address into his computer. "Ah, yes. I see that there is a mailing center within a few blocks of the bus terminal. I would be happy to make the extra stop."

"Thank you." I was planning quickly and feeling quite anxious. I wanted to mail the information to the FBI as soon as I could. I did not think it was wise to tell them my name, just in case Ray retaliated by harming my family in some atrocious way. I decided to lay low for as long as I could, maybe under a false name. I said quietly, "I will call myself Lily." I turned, noticing Julia's pale face and slumped, shivering shoulders. "Are you okay?"

Her eyes were downcast and she appeared to be on the verge of breaking down with fear and anxiety. "I'm just so afraid. What if he finds us?"

"Not going to happen. I have a plan." I dried her tears from her cheeks and smiled. "You must change your name. Hmmm, what about Cassia for you? It means, cinnamon, spicy." I laughed, trying to lighten the tenseness. "That fits you and call me Lily."

Julia snickered. "Cassia. Okay, I like that. Lily, where are we going?"

"As far from here as we can. I've been thinking, it will be much more difficult for Ray to find us if we head into the mountains. There is a small city in Montana that I read about called Butte."

The taxi driver interrupted them. "Ma'am, we are being followed. Do you know anyone who drives a black Suburban?"

I flung my head around and gasped. "Hydro! Drive faster. Lose him."

"Okay, I'll try." He sped up weaving in and out of traffic, but the car suddenly screeched to a stop at a red light. I glanced through the rear window, observing Hydro hastily getting out of his car. He then bolted up to the door, grasping at the lever and began pounding on the window.

I screamed, "Go! Run the light if you can safely." The driver had to wait until a car passed and then he gunned it. "Turn there." The driver turned the corner as I watched Hydro run back to the Suburban. Can you quickly find another way to the bus terminal?"

"Yes, I know the area well. Who is that man?"

"He is a very dangerous man." I hesitated. "If he catches us, he'll kill us."

"So, you two are running from this guy?"

"Yes. We have been held against our will for many years, but we just managed to escape."

The driver's eyes widened and an offensive guttural sound escaped his mouth as he shook his head. "Oh, my heavenly father." He turned to us with moist eyes and a comforting, concerned expression sculpted his face. "You seem like nice girls. I have daughters and I would not want them to run into that kind of trouble. Don't worry, I will help you, but if you are running away from that man, he will probably check the airports and bus stations for you. I have an idea, if you trust me."

"Oh… I was in such a hurry that I hadn't considered that they might check the bus stations. You're right. What's your idea?"

"You two were to be my last riders for the day. My taxi terminal is not far from here. What if I park the taxi and drive you in my car? I heard you say Butte, Montana. I live north of Madison, which is west of here and on the way toward Butte. Do you trust me?"

I stared into his kind, mocha eyes for a few seconds, then glanced at Julia, who was nodding her head. "Okay, yes. I have a feeling you mean no harm. Hydro will now also be looking for your taxi, so this is a good plan. But we need you to promise that you will forget our names, forget that you helped us. Tell your company that your ride did not show up at the casino, that way your company won't have a record and you won't find yourself in trouble."

"My name is Alexander. You can trust me and that's

a good idea. I never picked you up." He continued to weave through the neighborhood and finally turned down a busy main street. "My terminal is only a few blocks away. It will only take me a few minutes to check out with my company."

"Thank you, Alexander." Both of us said at the same time. When we reached the taxi terminal, he drove up next to his green Pontiac. I had a good feeling that everything would be okay.

In less than ten minutes, Alexander was back at the car, jumped in and headed speedily down the road. "The mailing center is not far from here, if you still need to go."

I glanced up, finding his eyes in the rear-view mirror. "Yes, please." I took out the gray bag containing all of the passports and put them into the package that Charlie had prepared for me. I had asked Charlie to write the address for the FBI on the package to make it easier for me. I included a letter describing in a few short sentences, what the package contained. In the letter I wrote:

To the FBI,

Included in this package, you will find passports and information about twelve young women and two extremely dangerous men who kidnapped the girls and have been holding them against their will for many years. Ray Giordano is the man responsible for their plight. You will find these men and the girls at the Falcon Casino in Wisconsin. Please hurry! Please help these women find safety and arrest the criminals. Also, Giordano may possibly be located at the Wild Cat Casino in Oklahoma.

Sincerely,

A freed woman.

When we arrived, I nervously looked around and not

seeing any problem, I hurried in and mailed the package, sending it anonymously as a same day delivery, praying that my message would be received in time to save the girls from any more suffering.

8

Jillian
1994

Alexander drove Julia and me as far as he could, which was to a bus terminal in Madison. From there, we planned to travel to Butte, Montana to find a place to stay and to look for work. He asked, "Are you sure you will be, okay? I feel uncomfortable leaving you here. In fact, I know of a nice hotel right near the bus station. Why don't you stay there and rest for the night? Your bus will not be leaving until six o'clock in the morning, or that's when many of the buses leave. It will be a long drive to Butte, something like 1,360 miles. I have driven there several times, because my wife's family is from Missoula, which is a bit further west, so I know the Butte area well."

"Yes, thank you. That's a good idea and I'm exhausted. Do you know anyone in Butte? I mean, we will be looking for a place to stay and will also be looking for jobs."

"Well, let's see. It's a small city, but you will be able to find an affordable hotel quite easily once you are there. As far as work, there are museums and many tourist shops. As you probably already know, Butte is known as an historical mining town. I'm sure you could find work in one of the shops."

"Thank you. I love working with flowers, so I hope to find work in a garden shop." I felt a perplexing expression cross my face, realizing that I had just remembered something about myself. I whispered, "Do I like flowers?"

Julia met my eyes and smiled. "Your memory is beginning to return."

Alexander said, "Oh, well in that case, I have a contact for you. My wife has a good friend who owns a garden shop. I will call her and tell her to expect you." He wrote down the address and handed it to me. The names on the paper were Chrys and Nicholas Jensen.

"I am so grateful for your help." Alexander smiled compassionately, then drove us to a hotel and waited until we were checked in. My eyes welled up as I hugged him, feeling exhausted and completely overwhelmed, but relieved that we had successfully escaped our living nightmare.

Julia and I entered the room and collapsed on the beds. We were both so exhausted after the day's events that we could scarcely speak and neither of us were hungry for dinner. I called the front desk and asked for a wake-up call for five a.m. I could sense that Julia was worried, but I would talk with her in the morning.

When we awoke, I asked Julia how she felt. "I'm okay. I'm just concerned that we will be tracked down. Aren't you afraid for our lives?"

"I have a feeling that everything will work out fine. Remember, call yourself Cassia instead of your real name and don't forget, I'm Lily. When we get there, we will look for work. We have to earn money until we figure out what to do next but for now, let's just take one day at a time. I'm so happy that you decided to come with me. I feel much more confident with you here."

"I don't know how I could ever thank you enough for basically forcing me to go. I was just so afraid of being tortured. I'm not afraid of death, but torture is a whole different terrifying beast." We hugged each other and continued to get ready for another day of adventure in an unfamiliar area of the country. We walked to the restaurant next to the hotel to grab something for breakfast to take with us and hurried off to the bus station, bought our tickets and boarded the bus to Butte.

Once in our seats, I sighed with a gigantic breath of relief. I felt excited, yet tremendous concern lingered. I thought of my family, who I wanted so badly to go home to, but I knew with absolution, that I could not risk putting their lives in danger. It had been so many years since I was abducted and I still didn't remember them, but now and again, sudden flashes of what I believe are memories, appear vividly in my mind. My intuition informs me that they haven't forgotten me and have not stopped searching for me. I promised myself I would return when the time was right. My eyes welled up and I began breathing, short anxious breaths, tightening my lips. Am I doing the right thing? Should I just gamble on the notion that Ray might leave me and my family alone and just go home now? I recalled the last time I threw caution to the wind, I lost everything. No, I cannot allow myself to put them in danger. I dried my tears with the sleeve of my jacket and donned a fierce determined face, mustering up all of the strength I could manage.

Were my dreams real somehow, maybe memories sneaking back from the dark recesses of my mind or were they mysterious puzzles that I had yet to decipher? The night at the hotel, I dreamed that I was strolling through a field of flowers with an exquisite looking elderly man with a long, white beard and flowing white hair walking next to me. He held my hand and stated that I would return home soon, but then the dream changed. I was splashing my face in a cool stream in the mountains, magnificently high, majestic, snow-capped mountains. There were lovely purple and white flowers beside the stream and I could see a heavy timber home beyond. A woman with long, silver hair, who was tending the garden stood up and stretched out her arms toward me as if she was asking me to come to her. Suddenly, I awoke in a daze and felt goosebumps rising up on my arms. I wanted to go back to sleep and dream of the woman again. I whispered to myself, "Was she my mother, calling for me to return home?"

My eyes welled up and I laid in the bed for at least ten minutes as tremendous sadness crept over me. I wanted to remember so badly. I somehow recalled that I loved lilies, so I decided to send lilies to my family every spring and summer depending on the type and blooming month.

I wanted them to know that I was alive and well, but I would not try to go home for a while for their own protection.

When Julia and I reached Butte, we booked a room in a local hotel for the night. It was still early enough to call the number that Alexander had given me for Chrys and Nicholas Jensen. But first, I had an important errand to run. I told Julia that I would be right back and headed down the road to a floral shop that I noticed on the way into town. I ordered three potted lilies to be sent to the address on my ID card. I asked the woman at the shop to check to see what colors of lilies were available. She spoke with someone at a shop in Evergreen, Colorado who said they had butter yellow lilies and amethyst calla lilies. I selected the calla lilies and had them sent anonymously, paying cash. The woman asked who the flowers were to be sent to. I smiled, delighted to say my parents' names aloud. "Mr. and Mrs. Hunt." The woman's narrowed, questioning eyes lingered on mine, then without another word, she smiled and completed the transaction. I thanked her and left the shop.

I prayed that the people at the address were still my family, realizing that after seventeen years, my family may have moved somewhere else entirely. I wanted to let them know that I was still alive, but not yet comfortable enough to try to communicate verbally. I thought, If Ray did go to my home, my folks could at least assure him that they had not seen or heard from me for many years.

I sauntered back to the hotel room with an enormous smile plastered across my face and called the Jensen's. A friendly, baritone voice answered, "Nicholas Jensen."

"Hello. My name is Lily James. A friend gave me your number to contact you when I arrived in town."

"Yes, we've been expecting you. Are you here in Missoula now?"

"No. We stopped in Butte until the nine-a.m. bus leaves tomorrow morning. The bus ride was long and uncomfortable, so we decided to rest at a hotel here for the night. I had a few errands to run as well."

"Well, instead of taking the bus, why don't we come pick you up? We drive into Butte twice a week to pick up supplies that they don't sell here in Missoula. It's only a two-hour drive. We could leave early in the morning and pick you up at the hotel around ten after we run our errands. Would that work for you?"

"Oh, yes. That would be wonderful. We are both very grateful that you are willing to help us."

"Don't you worry. We understand the details of your situation and Chrys and I talked it over, agreeing that we would like to help you get settled. Our children are all grown and have moved away, so we have several spare rooms for guests. We'll talk more tomorrow. Let me have the number of the hotel where you are staying and I'll call when we arrive."

I was certain that Nicholas knew that Lily was not my real name, but he didn't mention it. He said, "Okay now, we'll see you in the morning. Get some rest and don't you worry about a thing." I thought his temperament was comfortably mild and compassionate. He had a gentle, soothing voice which encouraged me to trust him. The most important thing right now is to feel safe and just know that everything will work out fine.

When I reviewed the conversation with Julia, she was

skeptical and feeling nervous. "What if these people turn us in? What if they lied to you?"

"Not going to happen. Julia, I may not have my memory back yet, but I feel the need to follow my intuition and I believe we will be safe with the Jensens. Nicholas spoke calmly and compassionately and I trust them. I truly believe the hell is over. Julia, you wanted to come to America to find a good job and a live a happy new life, so please have faith. This is what you've been longing for, right? I'm not saying there won't be hardships to come, but not like the hell we've endured for so many years. Our lives are about to change in acceptable, pleasant ways, I can feel it in my bones. You helped me make it through many terrible days of illness and confusion, so let me help you now."

"Yes, of course. I'm just not as brave as you are." She sighed. "Okay, I will try to have faith. I'm exhausted and emotionally drained. Please wake me up early, so that I have time to shower."

We were ready in the morning when the Jensens arrived. The hotel desk clerk called our room to let us know our guests were waiting in the lobby. When we entered the room, we were immediately greeted with hugs and pleasantries. Julia glanced at me with tears flooding her eyes. The kind faced woman with sparking blue eyes, turned toward us smiling warmly. "I'm Chrys." She directed her attention toward me . "You must be Lily. I'm so happy to meet you." She then turned toward Julia.

I quickly introduced her. "Chrys, this is Cassia, the sweetest girl you'll ever meet." I smiled at Cassia with a wink.

Chrys put her arms around both of us. "Onward and

upward." Their evergreen Bronco was parked in front of the lobby. While Nicholas drove, Chrys asked, "Now, what do you girls need? You only have one small bag each, so you'll need some clothing and all sorts of things. You think about it and later on today, we'll go shopping. We both took the day off to help you get situated."

I put my hand compassionately on her shoulder. "Thank you, Chrys. We could pick up a change of clothing and a few things, but we plan to work for a week or two and then we will have enough money to buy a few more things and to pay you rent until we can find a place of our own."

"Nonsense." Nicholas bellowed. "You are welcome to stay with us for as long as you like. There is plenty of room for you and don't go on about buying one day of clothing until next week. Chrys will make sure you get what you need. In fact, you might want to go through the dresser drawers that are in the guest rooms. We have two daughters who left behind a dresser and closet, each filled with clothing. They were about your sizes the last time we saw them, so you might find some things that suit your liking."

Chrys said cheerfully, "We'll sort it all out. Lily, I heard that you have an interest in gardening."

"Yes, Ma'am. Do you think you might have a job for me?"

"I sure do. A gal just recently left to have her baby and she won't be back for several months. There is plenty of work anyway, you'll see. How about you, Cassia? Are you interested in working with flowers as well?"

"Well, I'm afraid I don't have much experience with gardening, but I can learn until I find something else to do.

I would like to work in a restaurant eventually. My family owned a restaurant in Russia and my sister and I prepared and served delicious Russian cuisine. I am a very good cook and would like to own my own restaurant someday." She drew in a deep breath and sighed. "At least that's what I dreamed of when I decided to come to America."

"I know just the place." Nicholas chimed in. We have a good friend who owns Babak's Bakery and Deli market. She is a delightful Russian woman. We'll meet with her to see if she could use some help."

Julia's eyes widened. "I would love to meet with her. To get to know and work with some people from my country would make me so happy."

"You, see," Chrys said delightedly, "it will all work out."

When we arrived in Missoula, Nicholas accompanied Julia into Babak's Bakery to meet with the owner, who was delighted to converse with her and hired her on the spot. They also had a room for her in their home. Julia jumped at the chance. She sauntered out to the truck, gave me a huge hug, grabbed her bag and began to get out of the Bronco. She turned back to witness my watery eyes and thanked me again for helping her escape. "We'll stay in touch and meet for lunch as often as possible." She also thanked Nicholas and Chris for their kindness and generosity. I felt like I had only known Julia for a short while, but for the past few weeks, we were each other's sole trustworthy companions. I was overwhelmingly grateful and happy for her and yet I felt alone and vulnerable without her. I gulped in a massive breath of air, dried my tears and smiled, summoning all of the courage I could manage.

The three of us headed toward the Jensen's home, which I was happy to learn, was not far from the bakery. As we traveled uphill on a long, windy driveway, a magnificent heavy timber and stone home revealed itself in all of its grandeur. My eyes stayed transfixed on a large deck, which spanned the length of the front of the home. It seemed familiar even though I had never been there before. Beautiful gardens flourished below and my eyes began to water again. I felt so tremendously fortunate to have met the Jensen's, thanks to Alexander.

9

Dakota
1994

Lofty, light gray clouds drifted in front of a pale, blue autumn sky and stunning, golden aspens shimmered in the gentle breeze. Our neighbor friends visited us earlier this morning with a truck load of white calla lilies, golden spider and oxblood lilies, which Mom, Dad and I had just finished planting and would be the last until next spring. We were enjoying the view of the gorgeous garden on the deck, when I noticed that Mom's smile had diminished and a few tears spilled from her eyes. She held my eyes with her own. "I feel her presence today, more than usual. I can't explain it, but I sense that she is safe from immediate harm, although someone dangerous lurks in the shadows." She dried her tears and turned to me. "I think it's time to renew our search efforts with vigor and fortitude."

Dad put his arms around her, hugging her gently. "I believe you're right. I received a call from Myles this morning, informing us that the FBI has been investigating a mafia ring which they suspect are responsible for numerous abductions and trafficking. They received a tip from an unknown source about a group of women who were forced to work as prostitutes at various casinos including a casino in southwest Oklahoma. Apparently, when the authorities arrived, the group had somehow vanished. The FBI has been working diligently to track them down and have intel on two of the men involved. A few weeks later, they received an anonymous letter along with a package of passports belonging to a group of women being held against their will at a casino in Wisconsin. They arrested two men and thankfully, rescued ten of twelve women, two unaccounted for. I was so hoping that Jillian was among them." His eyes welled up and he shook his head revealing sorrow and disappointment. "The authorities were able to extract information from several of the young women about Ray Giordano, the man responsible for their plight but unfortunately, he was not there at the time of the arrests. I have deliberated on this for hours and have come up with several scenarios where Jillian could be involved. The one that concerns me the most and I pray that it is not the case, is one where Jillian and another woman were taken as hostages by Giordano, who has still not been located."

"Dad, we don't know that Jillian was with the group. I mean, we all appreciate their efforts but aren't you and

Myles jumping to unsubstantiated conclusions?"

"I'm pleased that he continues to provide us with updates on every possible lead. Have you come up with any new information?"

I narrowed my eyes and stood by the railing, gazing down into the empty void where happiness used to exist in my mind. From the day I began my own investigative practice, I have been deeply involved with abduction crimes, hoping that a clue in Jillian's case would emerge. I turned to Mom and Dad, holding their eyes intently with my own. "Ever since we received the update from Myles, I have been diligently tracking a few extremely suspicious criminals who could possibly be involved with this Ray Giordano creep, but I haven't discovered a connection yet. I've been searching around the country for criminals who are known to be involved in the sex trade and have recently solved several cases, which has given me renewed hope. I'm trying to remain positive that we will find her and I, too, have been feeling her presence lately. It's as if her situation has recently changed, I can't explain it either, but," I held Mom's hand, "I feel certain as well, that she is alive and as well as can be considering her possible circumstances. I would like to stay in touch with Myles concerning this group he spoke about."

Dad nodded. "Yes, we will meet with him." He forced a smile. "We must believe that Jillian has managed to keep herself safe from danger. She is a grown woman now and I believe her weaknesses of the past will prove to be the drive she needs to alter her own fate. I have deliberated on this matter and have prayed for this to be true."

Mom smiled as she gazed at the colorful lilies that

seemed to display cheerfulness. "I will continue to pray that our beautiful, charming girl will come back to us soon and she will bring joy back into our lives once again." Suddenly, an enormous raven soared above us, then perched itself on an evergreen branch. She grinned, "See, the raven knows." I couldn't help but chuckle.

The following day, Dad and I flew to Wisconsin and met with Myles and an FBI agent at the casino, with the intent on gathering as much information as possible. I felt anxious, but optimistic that we would learn that Jillian had been there. We talked with the owner, Charlie Nevins as well as with the entire staff, showing them an aged progression likeness of Jillian, but no one admitted seeing her. The rising hope that I had been feeling, suddenly diminished, replaced by frustration once again. I thought for a minute that I had detected some recognition from the face of a casino host when she twitched her left eye while glancing at the photo, but she denied seeing her as well. I wondered why she and the others might lie so I continued to question them. If Jillian had been there, wouldn't they prefer for her to be rescued rather than any other scenario where they thought they should protect her?

Something didn't feel right and I knew that I had to continue to investigate further, even though I was not certain that we were on the right track. Myles was able to obtain a copy of the security video tapes, which only went back three months. Dad reviewed them while I drove around stopping to question taxi companies, hotels and other casinos in the area. An FBI agent had already searched the security tapes at the airports and bus terminals and again posted information about Jillian's disappearance on news bulletins. Dad thought he recognized Jillian in one of the casino tapes, but after careful scrutiny, we came to the unfortunate conclusion that the woman in question was someone else. Her hair had an auburn shade and her eyes were dark brown, nothing like Jillian's long, ebony hair nor the stunning, deep jade color of her eyes.

We all sighed, utterly discouraged as the light in our hearts faded. We would never give up, although Dad had a menacing, intuitive feeling that crept into the forefront of his mind, that now was not the time for her to come home. I agreed, sensing danger lurking in the shadows, possibly nearby. Several times lately, I have felt icy prickles racing up my spine while walking around our property. I have observed Sascha's ears, often perked straight up, her tail and stature standing at attention as she too, hears or senses some threatening presence prowling around. I have chosen to dismiss the mysterious feeling, since we often have wild critters wandering around the area, but I still cannot shake the feeling that something ominous requires my absolute attention.

10

Dakota's intuition was correct, yet there was no way for him to know that a mysterious, sinister presence was watching, lurking, stalking. Giordano had the Hunt's home staked out, cleverly rotating his men, who were always driving different vehicles. On two occasions, Giordano himself, hid in a cluster of trees near the front of the home and observed Yamka working in the garden. The first time was in 1994, two days after Jillian escaped. He intended on storming the house, taking Jillian back and killing anyone who got in his way but since she had not returned, he couldn't. Instead, he watched, waited, his fury mounting as the days passed slowly by. He just could not understand why Jillian hadn't gone home. One of the reason's he loved her was the fact that Jillian was intelligent, perceptive, not like the other girls who continuously sucked up to him for drugs and money. When he discontinued his force-fed drug regimen, she began to refuse the drugs until her body finally purged itself of all debilitating traces, though she did what he asked of her anyway, seemingly respectful and loyal to him. He figured her memory had been destroyed or at least impaired by the drugs, so he allowed her to remain sober and continued to observe her for any hint of defiance, noticing none.

Giordano actually fancied her moxie, though he was entirely astonished that she had managed to escape. He believed her loyalty was genuine, so he wondered if her memory had returned. When Giordano discovered how complacent Hydro had become, derelict in his duty to watch over the girls, he shot him point blank, right between the eyes. After the FBI had completed their interrogation, they released Giordano with no substantiated evidence to hold him. He immediately packed his car and headed to the Hunt's home to exact his revenge on his audacious, ungrateful woman.

For the next six years from time to time, Giordano or his men would observe the Hunt family at their home, hoping to finally discover that Jillian had returned. Recently, in the spring of the year 2000, he parked on the street across from their driveway and began trudging up the hill toward the home when suddenly, the dog began barking with terrifying ferocity as he leapt off of the porch and bounded aggressively toward him. Giordano bolted back to his car and sped off. He believed that the dog was acting extraordinarily protective and wondered if Jillian had finally returned, so he hired several local thugs to continue watching the family for the next few weeks. When his men had no news of Jillian to report, he called them off and reluctantly decided that his concentration was better served on his newly acquired casino club in Oklahoma.

11

Jillian and Julia
1994 - 2000

Things have been working out very well for Julia and me and we meet regularly for lunch. Julia has become an amazing cook and often asks me to taste her most recently created recipes, which are always delicious. She has been deliriously happy now that she is no longer haunted by the horror, grief and despair of the past twenty-three years of her life. She has made many new friends and has been dating a dashing, kind man that she really loves. Grigori Mikhailov strolled into Babak's Bakery one day and all but literally, swept her off her feet. She wholeheartedly expressed, "His dazzling smile and boyish charm lured me into his tender, compassionate heart and when I gaze into his golden sparkling eyes, I see and feel his gentle soul intertwining with mine." She smiled so widely with such gratitude and blissfulness that I almost cried, entirely overjoyed for her happiness, although I wished the contentment was my own. Grigori secretly revealed that he plans to propose to her soon. Julia has become a poised, self-confident, kind woman with a delightful sense of humor, so extraordinarily deserving of such happiness. Whenever I feel a bit gloomy or troubled, I make arrangements to spend some quality time with her and I walk away feeling light hearted and optimistic again.

I have cheerfully lived and worked with the Jensens for six years now. To alleviate some of my concern and fear about Ray and his thugs locating me by my real name, Nicholas and Chrys agreed to call me Lily Jensen. They said they love having me around and have treated me like I am part of the family. They have helped me through some very difficult times and care deeply for me, which I am eternally grateful for.

I am always alert to the surprises that emerge within myself, which I feel certain, spring from my past. Within the first few weeks working with Chrys, I recognized that I have a natural ability with anything that grows in the earth, a truly remarkable green thumb. Every seed or plant I touch blooms beautifully, thriving for prolonged periods of time. At first, I thought maybe it was because I often sing to the trees and flowers while watering and tending to them, though I can't help but wonder if many years ago, I worked with plants. I don't think my memory is completely damaged or blocked, since I have skills, certain learned behaviors, likes and dislikes that pop up now and again, often to my complete amazement. I found myself instantly motionless in my tracks while on my way into the kitchen this morning, when I caught a delicious whiff of something very familiar. Chrys had grilled French toast with stewed cinnamon apples and I recognized that sweet, spicy aroma. After tasting the mouthwatering, syrupy sweetness and the varying textures of crispy toast and soft apples, I suddenly realized that the meal might have been a favorite from my past.

I often wonder if the memories of my young life at home will return when my obstinacy ceases to prohibit me from going home, based on an assumption that I believed to be true years ago. Once a month, I check in with a therapist who persistently urges me to consider going home, suspecting that my memory will fully return when I do. She may be right but I still have dreadful, foreboding thoughts of Ray Giordano whirling in my mind, knowing that he could someday harm my family or show up at my new home here and destroy my life all over again. However, I have felt relatively safe here in Missoula under the protection of the Jensens. I continue to pray that Ray will finally be apprehended by the FBI and I will then feel safe enough to go home. I believe that Chrys and Nicholas will understand when I'm ready to go. I will always stay in touch with them and will visit them regularly. I breathed in deeply, exhaling with my eyes closed tightly in an attempt to restrain my emotions. "As soon as it's safe," I said to myself.

12

Giordano
2000

Ray Giordano and his partner, Andrea Marino, set up the Wild Cat Casino specifically as a front to launder money and traffic women and all sorts of contraband. They so far have been successfully able to throw the authorities off track by keeping several sets of books and by cautiously and inconspicuously coming and going. Marino had secretly built a tornado shelter with an alternate exit tunnel below the office portion of the building, so that they could covertly disappear with no one the wiser. The hidden door located in the back of a supply closet, leading to a narrow set of stairs to the basement, remained undetected by the FBI, who had stormed the casino on several occasions. The two sly criminals had so far managed to conceal their corrupt business dealing from the rest of the casino staff, thereby presenting an upstanding, legally profitable business.

Marino dealt with the interchange of contraband, while Giordano handled the women. His standard practice was to have girls picked up and transported to the casino temporarily and would then decide how they were to be worked and where. More than twenty teams of men were scattered around the country, picking up young women from bars, shopping malls, dark, shadowy rest areas, schools and parking lots at large stores, theaters and sports events.

Giordano hired immoral brutes to manage the girls, often feeling agonized and infuriated by the loss of Dalila. She did her job so well and he missed her desperately. Every now and then, he flew into Denver and hired a limo driver to drive by her home, hoping to see her again. He knew she would eventually return and he would be ready.

Even though six years had passed, his love for her had not faded, but what had recently become disturbing to him was that his vengeful intentions were beginning to diminish. On one occasion, he observed a woman who he believed was her mother, tending a beautiful garden, which self loathingly warmed his heart. He decided that he would not return, though he would have one of his employees stop by every now and then with instructions to pick Dalila up if she was spotted. He not only wanted her back, but it was mostly a matter of principle. She had defied his orders, broke into his safe absconding with all of the passports and one of his finest girls and alerted the FBI who released his women, temporarily ceasing his operation. He was surprised that Jillian had not taken his gun nor any of his money, which was hastily cleared out of his safe by one of his men, who fled undetected as soon as he learned that the girls had escaped. Eventually, Giordano was located, interrogated, arrested and finally released, but he was observed, tracked and persistently harassed by the authorities. She had to pay for her disobedience one way or another.

Giordano planned to use another casino in Nevada as his major, centrally located base for his organization, since he had noticed that in the past few years, the FBI were somehow aware of his ventures with the Wild Cat Casino. He had observed a couple of men exhibiting awkward, imposing behaviors rather than the typical gambling and imbibing behaviors similar to the rest of the guests, therefore, he turned the table a bit and began spying on them. The information about the casino had been kept confidential so he assumed Dalila had overheard him talking with his men and tipped someone off. As infuriated as he was, he was also a high stakes man of chance delighting in the prospect of participating in a dangerous cat and mouse game, one that he believed he could master. Being well aware that undercover agents were lurking around the casino, he made it a top priority to keep tabs on all of his guests. He was no fool and played along with their games, although he made it clear that he was on to them.

Giordano felt sure that the authorities would lose interest after a while and move on to other criminal organizations and then he would once again master his trade, operating at full capacity, right under their noses as he had for many years. After all, he thought, there are so many beauties out there who don't know what to do with themselves and naively look for opportunities to leave their homes. Many girls foolishly flaunt themselves, searching for men to latch onto and carelessly drown their miseries in alcohol and drugs making themselves easy targets. They need me to rescue them, he mused, flashing a sinister grin as he sat pompously in his plush leather office chair, contemplating his next moves.

13

Jillian
2000

This Christmas season has been a special time for me. I've been spending a lot of time with a tall, handsome Irish man named Liam McKinney for several years now. He has an adorable shock of red hair, hazel eyes and a charming personality. When I met Liam, I decided to confide in him right off the bat which was really difficult, because I thought that opening up to him would surely scare him off, but it didn't. He is one of the few people, other than Nicholas, Chrys, Julia and Giordano who knows my real name and the location of my family. I love Liam dearly and he, likewise.

We spend a lot of quality time together, often

laughing hysterically while hiking, camping, fishing and working together on his Ranch. Liam owns seventy acres of cattle grazing land in the mountains just northeast of Missoula, Montana. He lives in a rustic, two story log cabin near an eight-horse stable, a barn with free roaming chickens, turkeys and sheep. I love to help him gather fresh eggs and milk the cows.

Liam has been working diligently on plans for our new mountain home on a gorgeous site, near Seeley Lake with a cluster of evergreen trees on the north and west sides and a spectacular open view of the mountains to the east and south. A lovely, meandering tributary of the Blackfoot River flows below the site, creating a peaceful, splashy, bubbly sound, when the cool, fresh water flows over boulders and pebbles. We hike to the site often and I enjoy sitting by the lake, observing bald eagles soaring with the air currents above herds of grazing bighorn sheep, bison and antelope. I feel at home here in the mountains particularly among the wild animals and can't help but wonder if I had lived in a similar environment in my past life in Colorado.

Liam was delightfully excited and as giddy as a school boy right before he proposed to me. While gazing at the magnificent view on the site of our future home, he kneeled down on one knee and gazed into my eyes. Tears trickled down my face as his gentle, glistening eyes held mine with such love that I could hardly bear the moment. "Lily Jillian Jensen, will you make me the happiest man alive by becoming my wife and agreeing to live the rest of our glorious days together in love?"

"Oh, yes, my dear, sweet Liam, I will." The occasion seemed surreal, as if it was a scene in a dreamy romance novel. He slid a stunning, shimmering diamond and emerald engagement ring on my finger as droplets of tears turned to a cascading flow. I was over the moon as I realized that I was experiencing another new beginning; a hopeful, joyous beginning with the love of my life. I looked forward to years of new adventures with Liam, including reconnecting with my Colorado family.

I felt truly fortunate that Liam chose to love me, knowing I had lived a humiliating, shameful life even though it wasn't my choosing. He sees the beauty and compassion in my soul and marvels at my seemingly inherent ability to create, design, draw and my curious knowledge of plants and flowers. Chrys, Nicholas and Liam have succeeded in helping me achieve self-confidence and contentment rather than wallowing in insecurity and self-loathing.

I assumed I'd be alone until my passing, doubting that any good man would ever share any time at all with me until Liam strolled into my life. The men I have met, who I can recall anyway, have been arrogant, egotistical, over confident men who were too proud to love someone who wasn't born with wealth, title and highly educated. I noticed however, that many of those men, after several years of turning one woman down after another, were still single and lonely.

Liam is an extremely hard working, educated man who achieved a dual construction and business degree and is a self-made millionaire, although remarkably unpretentious and prudent about his holdings. Most of his fortune is invested in land and his ranch. I believe he may have chosen me because we fell deeply in love long before he mentioned his wealth. Liam presents himself as a man who generates a median income, who lives in a humble abode and who certainly never flaunts his wealth, which is one of the reasons I adore him. I don't care at all about monetary fortune, but rather a cornucopia of love, joy and companionship.

I also had a surprise for him, but I was extremely nervous, questioning how he might respond. I inhaled a deep breath, placed his hands in mine and led him to an area off of the planned master bedroom. "This could be our baby's room." With glistening eyes, I flashed a cheerful, toothy smile as I waited for his response.

An enormous, wide smile crossed his face and he laughed wholeheartedly. He then picked me up and twirled me around as he exclaimed, "That's wonderful, Lily! Whoopee, I'm a father." We danced around our future home, staking out areas for every room while excitedly discussing future events.

When we returned home, Nicholas and Chrys insisted on planning a small wedding and a festive reception in their spectacular floral back yard. We hung baskets of colorful lilies, lilac and lavender from the covered porch and tree branches. One of the highlights of the day was when Nicholas strolled with me down the aisle, while I held Liam's glistening eyes adoringly with my own. The wordless melody of "Annie's Song", a sensuous song of love and passion, by John Denver filled the air around us. I almost lost it completely when Liam picked up his guitar and tenderly sang the lyrics to me. I did everything in my power to compose myself in my lovely lace gown, but my legs weakened and tears filled my eyes. At that moment, I felt like the luckiest woman alive and nothing else mattered.

During the reception, I melted in his arms as he twirled with me around the room, while Nicholas and Chrys sang and played our song, "Harvest Moon", by Neil Young, on their guitars. The song is extremely moving and I don't think I observed a dry eye in the crowd including my own. I knew without a doubt in the world that Liam and I would always be in love and that we would share a caring, affectionate life together that most only dream of.

For the next seven and a half months, we were blissfully busy with plans for the baby and our new home construction, which we finally completed at the end of August. I stood back, excitedly admiring the large gabled roof supported by heavy timber and stone columns, which hovered over the extensive front deck. The cedar deck surrounds the home on three sides, providing a covered porch area from the walkout basement below. On the south side of the home, large windows face an exquisite majestic view. Liam built a spiral staircase leading from the deck to a flagstone paved area below, which surrounds a soft grassy play area for our baby. I worked with Liam, designing a long, curved driveway which meanders through boulders, trees and natural gardens.

Chrys, Nicholas and several other friends, including Julia and Grigori helped us move in. Nicholas fastidiously built a splendid cherry crib and Chrys and I worked daily on a lovely quilt with soft sage, evergreen and lavender colors. Liam surprised me with a skillfully detailed, wooden rocking chair, which I love swaying in while humming joyful tunes to the baby, who will be arriving very soon. I thoroughly enjoyed every wonderful moment that pregnancy offered, often cradling my belly while swaying and singing to him or her. I felt so very thankful that my child bearing years had not slipped away and deliriously happy that our healthy child was growing peacefully in my womb. I could sense that he or she was warm and comfortable and I knew with absolute certainty that I would protect my child at all costs. I learned my lesson with such severity that I prayed that naivety and carelessness ceased to exist.

As my due date drew nearer, I began feeling more and more sentimental about my real family. They should be able to experience the young life of their grandchild and I felt that I may be doing them a tremendous injustice, by preventing them from being a part of this extraordinary time of my life. I still didn't remember much about my family, although if my dreams were not just dreams, but were my memories struggling to surface, they were still there in Colorado, longing for me to return. I often feel a closeness to someone other than my parents and I have struggled many times to recall who it might be.

I love my family here in Missoula and my work in the garden shop and flower fields, but I desperately wanted to stop living with the fear that my family could be on the receiving end of Giordano's wrath. My eyes welled up while rocking the baby as I thought, what a dreadful tragedy.

Rather than wallowing in self-pity, for the health and well-being of our baby, I made a solemn commitment to myself to truly feel joy and appreciation for the loving, compassionate people currently in my life. I began singing a lullaby with several high and low tones and with light and heavy voice inflections. I closed my eyes as I sang about rain drops tapping away like a piano, the sweet hum of violins, the swish and echo of winds mysteriously reverberating across the strings of a cello. It was a lovely tune and the baby fluttered in my belly as I sang and rocked. After a few minutes, I nodded off and began dreaming again of the same elderly man with flowing white hair, his arms outstretched, walking toward me through a field of flowers. As he gradually approached, I could see his gentle eyes smiling along with his mouth. Then, he turned and gazed toward a stream where two small children, a little girl and boy were playing. The children appeared to be twins, both with striking, deep jade eyes and shiny, ebony hair like my own. The little girl's long, cascading hair whirled and bounced around her as she giggled and frolicked among the flowers. I heard her calling out, "Dakota, come catch me." Then the white-haired man turned to me and held my gaze as he whispered something I couldn't understand."

I awoke confused at first. "Dakota." I closed my eyes again, hoping that my mind would slip back into the beautiful dream. I whispered to myself, "Dakota looked just like me. If my dream was actually not a dream, but instead a memory, then Dakota could be my brother." I closed my eyes again and tried to relax hoping I could remember more. I rocked slowly for a while longer, but nothing else surfaced. I felt unbearably discouraged but nevertheless, I felt hopeful that my memory would fully return someday soon.

Another month, overflowing with daily chores and activity flashed by. On a glorious, sunshiny morning, on September 18, I had a beautiful, healthy baby girl. Autumn has always been my favorite season of spectacular colors and cool, crisp breezes and I absolutely adore Chrys, so I felt it was only fitting to call her Autumn Chrysanthemum McKinney. Liam has been such a perfect husband and father, remarkably generous with his time and always making sure that we are both comfortable and content. Autumn seems to feel relaxed and calm when I rock and sing to her, just as I did when she was snuggled up in my warm, liquid womb. I believe that she understands how peaceful and grateful I feel which reflects back to her.

A few days ago, I almost had myself convinced that I should pack my bags and drive to Colorado, but again, a menacing feeling that the time to go had not yet arrived, continued to derail the idea. Nevertheless, I thought deeply and meditatively about my family, hoping and praying that they could somehow feel my presence and my love for them.

14

Dakota
2000

I awoke one morning entirely overwhelmed by deep, reflective thoughts of Jillian. I instantly dressed and drove to my folk's home to discuss my feelings with them and to brainstorm my next plan. When I arrived, Mom walked briskly toward me and tucked my arm in hers, practically tugging me toward the kitchen where Dad was sipping coffee at the table. I suspected they both had similar perceptive thoughts on this mystifying morning. "You, too?"

I poured a cup of coffee and sat down, glancing at Mom, who captured my attention with her beckoning, anxious eyes. "Jillian longs to come home but something concerns her, therefore she will not, although I feel her phenomenal presence and she is tremendously happy."

She smiled widely, although I noticed a tear trickling down her cheek. I leaned over and hugged her tightly. Dad cleared his throat, "Ahem, excuse me. She has been going on like this ever since she woke up early this morning. Thoughts of Jillian have been keeping me awake at night as well and I am at my wit's end struggling to figure out what we should do to reach her and where we should continue our search. Our country is just so damn enormous. Myles has continued to thoroughly investigate every town and city in Wisconsin and has widened his search in a westward direction as I requested, with no clues surfacing at this time."

"I believe we will come up with new leads soon and I perceive as you do, that Jillian is alive and well. I am moving my investigations west as well, beginning in Cheyenne, Wyoming, where I am following a lead in another case. I plan on thoroughly combing through Wyoming, Utah and into Montana, a territory which could possibly take years to cover efficiently." I sipped my coffee and turned to Dad. "If I discover any hopeful clues, I'll head home and pick you up and we'll continue together."

Dad nodded as he sat back in his chair, then stared up as if something on the ceiling caught his eye. He then drew in a deep breath, exhaling with downcast eyes. We talked for another hour, then I headed home to pack my bags for an extended northwest journey. My current client, Jebb Peterson, had contracted my services to investigate the disappearance of his daughter, Jessica, a young woman who was last seen at an RV camp in Cheyenne, so as always, I will combine the two cases.

After several months of searching and scrutinizing every RV camp I could locate as well as every possible clue from Cheyenne to Sheridan, then to Yellowstone, Jackson, Green River and back to Cheyenne via I-80, I finally discovered an RV camp near Rock Springs, where an unruly bunch of campers caught my attention. I parked my pickup truck and moseyed cautiously toward the group, following a sudden impulse prompted by my compelling intuition, which urged me to investigate. As I approached the raucous group, I noticed two women who appeared to be distraught and in the company of several inebriated men. A chill surged through me as I tucked my Sig Sauer into the back of my jeans. A tall, brawny man stood, staggered toward me and bellowed, "This is a private party, so turn around and head back where you came from."

I nodded, faking my exit while recalling the description of Jessica. I hastily called 911 and asked for reinforcement. Then a young woman matching her description suddenly shrieked, "Help, come back." A heavy-set man who was sitting beside her, abruptly smacked her, knocking her to the ground.

With gun at the ready, I bolted toward them, shouting, "Move away from the girls now. The police are on the way." As quick as lightening, I unsheathed my knife and precisely flung it toward the advancing brute.

He shouted as the blade impaled his thigh dropping him to the ground with a jarring thud, "You son of a bitch. Shoot the bastard!"

Another man bolted out of the RV firing wildly, not seeing his target. I had ducked behind a cluster of evergreens while observing the scene. Thankfully, I heard the sound of sirens approaching as I unsheathed another knife which was strapped around my right calf. The man on the ground continued shouting, "Shoot him, damn you." He attempted to stand, but his rubbery legs gave way and he landed again helplessly on the ground, arms flailing while nasty protests spewed from his mouth.

Another shot was fired, though from a distance. I witnessed the man bolting from the scene in the opposite direction as the deafening sound of sirens drew nearer. With arms raised, the two young women sheepishly ambled toward me. "Please, help us."

I sheathed my knife, while holding my gun pointed downward in my left hand. "It's okay, I'm here to help you. My name is Detective Dakota Hunt." I called Jessica's name, hoping I was correct, that she was indeed my client's daughter. I explained that I had been hired by her father to search for her. With tear-soaked eyes, she placed her trembling arms around me as she wept. After a minute of allowing compassion to dominate the occasion, I waived the other timid young woman to us. As she cautiously walked toward us, I called Jebb Peterson and let him know, I had located Jessica and would be on our way soon. I glanced at the other girl with a concerned expression. "I don't believe you are here voluntarily either."

"No, I was kidnapped at the same time, from the same RV camp where Jessica was. We had just met and were just walking around, talking, when those creeps forced us into their RV and drove away." Her voice trembled as she continued, "My parents must be freaking out. I'm sure they called the police."

I held her eyes empathetically. "What's your name?"

"Rebecca. Can you call them for me?"

"Absolutely." I asked for her number and called her folks, while the authorities arrived at the scene. I informed them that the police would be holding Rebecca in protective custody. I then introduced myself to the police, described my charge and the details of the incident, as they arrested the injured criminal. Another police team immediately sped off in an attempt to catch the fleeing offender.

The officer eyed me with suspicion. "Who threw the knife?"

"I did, right after he fired his weapon at me multiple times. I wasn't interested in killing him, only hindering his ability to kill me and escape. I didn't care to leave the girls here unattended, while I chased the other idiot down." I smirked, although I decided it would be wise to maintain a helpful, pleasant disposition. "I have also been searching for another young woman and would like to interrogate that bastard, if you can give me a few minutes with him." The policeman asked me a few questions, then escorted me to the perpetrator. I grilled the man until I finally believed he had no knowledge of Jillian nor Ray Giordano.

As I moseyed back toward the young women, I once again felt utterly defeated. My eyes welled up, but I hastily dried them with my sleeve and glanced toward Jessica and the policemen. "This young lady's father is frantically waiting for me to bring her home. I'll provide you with a detailed report and then please allow us to be on our way." The two young women exchanged information, hugged each other while simultaneously crying and laughing, then said goodbye.

After concluding my business with the authorities, we headed toward Cheyenne. I glanced at my reflection in the rear view mirror, observing a miserable, dispirited, discouraged man, who had failed once again. Grandfather suddenly entered my mind and I sheepishly grinned. Even though I had failed to protect Jillian so long ago, I felt certain that Grandfather would not have blamed me for her devastating plight. I truly believed that I was on the correct course in life and would never alter my path until Jillian's return. I smiled at Jessica as we made our way toward her anxious, shaken father.

15

Jillian
2008

The years have flown cheerfully by as our little family blooms and prospers. Autumn has grown into a lovely, friendly grateful girl with an insatiable appetite for learning. She loves school, reads incessantly and draws beautiful scenes of our home surrounded by flowers and colorful, leafy trees. She enjoys helping me work in the gardens and fishing with Liam, which delights him to no end. Today, I've been sitting on the hill above the lake thinking about how happy we all are, while observing my two sweethearts below. They talked while casting baited lines, often chuckling when a trout nibbled, causing ever expanding ripples in the clear, blue water. My eyes welled up as my thoughts suddenly shifted to my Colorado family and I wondered what they might be doing at this very moment. I've been feeling extraordinarily sentimental lately, longing to bring them back into my life.

Even though I promised I would not concern myself with Ray and his business of abducting young women, I have been searching for articles lately, concerning the sex trade, hoping to see that he has finally been detained and is suffering in prison. I thought of the hundreds of girls who may have fallen victim to his sinister clutches and I cringed, wishing I could have helped them somehow or prevented them from experiencing a dreadful fate.

A light, cool breeze silenced my mind as an exquisite raven soared above, then circled around us, gliding elegantly with the air currents. I instantly felt as if I was reliving a mysteriously fleeting moment from some time, long ago. The raven seemed like a familiar friend, a spirit or an omen. I wasn't sure which, although I recalled the raven being present in my dreams many times in recent years. I felt certain that the significance of the wild bird was noteworthy and I wondered if it had something to do with my past. I realized that my longing to reconnect with my family could be causing my brain to conjure up some kind of mystical, false discovery, so I dismissed the scene as a mere coincidence.

As the months and years flew by, I discovered myself reflecting on family topics more attentively. I realized that it is my duty, my love and devotion to the people who love me, to bring our two families together, however, I will not put any of them in danger. My mother, father and brother, Dakota, who have been revealed to me in my dreams and who I absolutely believe have continued to search for me, deserve my attention. I at least wish for them to understand that I am still alive, so I hastily drove to a floral shop and ordered some lilies to be sent to my Colorado family, once again anonymously.

16

Dakota
2008 - 2018

Almost all of my employment and past time endeavors since Jillian went missing, have been geared toward finding her. I should feel proud that I have succeeded in almost every effort and venture, but I don't because I have still not solved her case. I thought I was close to finding her many times, but the clues always seem to fade away to nothing.

Ray Giordano has somehow managed to allude the FBI for all of these years. They may have given up on him, believing they have more significant targets to concentrate on, but I surely have not. For a while, I figured he may have left the country, but it's more likely that he decided to live and work underground along with thousands of other despicable criminals. I felt my skin crawl as I thought about the scum and filth that swarms and skulks among the shadows of every major city in the world. I continue to pray that young people take every possible precaution, especially while in public places, in order to have a fighting chance of living safely.

Chevyo and I have continuously followed up on all leads including making regular visits to the casino in Oklahoma, where the FBI once suspected Giordano of having ties to in some way. The owner of the establishment obstinately states that he has no knowledge of the man and even after several thorough investigations in the past years, the authorities have found nothing connecting him to the business. I believe otherwise and know that through resolute perseverance, I will eventually catch him off guard and discover the truth.

Thirty-one years have passed since Jillian's disappearance. Mother describes me as a ruggedly handsome, compassionate man, although now in my mid-forties, white streaks in my once healthy, jet-black hair, frame lines of weariness, grief and distress on my face.

Most of the time I have a mild, pleasant disposition, but if someone crosses me, I realize I can be quite intimidating and I absolutely despise myself every time I allow myself to unleash the wrath that I usually keep so well restrained. I consider myself a very spiritual man, believing that people are protected if they live with love and compassion, however, I struggle with my faith in God, who has never shown any interest in guiding Jillian home. However, the slightest trace of faith in God remaining within my heart, reveals that he has been protecting her and keeping her safe from harm, where ever she is.

I was born with a heightened intuitive nature as well as the ability to connect with spirits of enlightened beings such as my grand, Jonoche, which has provided me with the ability to persevere and maintain steadfast convictions. I do feel that I am on the right path in life, which is to do everything possible to take down vile sex criminals and rescue young women and children who have suffered unjustly. What I struggle with the most is that I have always believed that everything happens for a specific reason as warnings or messages for us to ponder, often encouraging us to consider an alternate path or direction. But if that is true, then what possible reason could there have been for the abduction of Jillian, who was such a gentle, naïve soul? If her life was entirely expunged from existence to teach me a lesson, what a tragic, dreadful means to the discovery of some minor warning or message in comparison. No, that just doesn't make sense. I have painstakingly tried for many years to feel light hearted, but doom continues to loom in my heart and soul and I am still burdened with unrelenting grief.

While relaxing in my cabin, I thought of my folks who still reside in our cozy family home in Evergreen with their golden retriever, Sascha. I felt grateful that they have continued to maintain and care for our home, because I have many treasured memories of our time there that I could never allow to fade. My last thought for the night was that our childhood home will always be a warm, safe, welcoming family home, waiting for Jillian's return.

When I awoke the next morning, a tremendous idea whirled in my mind until I finally figured out how to act upon it. I had been trying diligently to figure out how to get help from more people so that my chances of finding clues leading to Jillian would be much greater. After breakfast, I spoke with a veteran trucker friend who had often shared his open road adventures with me, when I began to put the pieces in place. A remarkable way to have eyes all over the country, would be to run a trucking company with drivers searching in every state, nation-wide. Without hesitation, I decided to build and operate a Denver, Colorado based trucking company, hauling refrigerated food and would use the company trucks, drivers and resources to track down sex traffickers.

I figured my freight business would bring in enough income to cover the costs associated with the criminal tracking division of the business and would provide a way to be strategically placed around the country where sex trafficking is prevalent. In this way, my team could track the movements of various trafficking organizations with greater success.

I decided that my trucks would be deep green, the color of life, renewal and harmony and an enormous raven in flight, symbolizing strength, freedom, wisdom, intuition and protection would be depicted on the trailers. I was delighted that I had been able to find many dedicated drivers with exceptional skills and all who were committed to tracking criminals. Most of my drivers had either served with various police forces or were retired military veterans, who felt a sense of purpose continuing to assist and protect the people of the U.S. in this way.

My team joined TAT; Truckers Against Trafficking and coordinated with the FBI, Homeland Security and local police forces throughout the U.S. and Canada. My company soon became profitable from the hard-working efficiency of the team, delivering food across the country. We also began to achieve significant results in our tracking work leading to the arrest of several sought-after sex criminal organizations. Even still, sadness has continued to consume me, sometimes with overwhelming, debilitating intensity.

It's now the year 2018 and ten more grief-stricken years have passed and still no sign of Jillian. I hunkered down one morning researching and collecting data concerning the sex trade dilemma in the U.S., And began reading audibly to myself. "The International Labor Organization estimates that there are approximately 4.8 million people trapped in forced sexual exploitation globally."[2] In another article I read, "The National Human Trafficking Hotline, operated by Polaris has received reports of 34,700 sex trafficking cases inside the U.S. from 2007-2017."[2] "In 2017, the National Center for Missing and Exploited Children estimated that one in seven endangered runaways reported to them were likely sex trafficking victims."[2]

I felt nauseous and my head began to throb but I continued reading, trying to formulate a plan for my drivers. "Some victims are lured into sex trafficking with false promises of a job, such as modeling, dancing or other nightclub jobs or work in casinos. Victims of sex trafficking can be U.S. citizens, foreign nationals, women, men and children. Many who are targeted by traffickers include runaway and homeless youth, victims of domestic violence, sexual assault, war and sometimes social discrimination."[2]

As I prepared for my drivers to convene at the Denver truck terminal for a meeting outlining our new crucial mission, I found myself feeling concerned about how the drivers might respond to work that could be much more dangerous than I bargained for. The work of my Dakota Hunt Transport team is about to become invaluable as part of a large task force, combating major sex trafficking criminals and syndicates. I didn't want to put them in harm's way, but I began to realize that there will be times when they may find themselves caught in dangerous situations.

I then thought about two of my drivers, who were currently in Central Texas, Rhys MacAllister and Nash Chavez. I began to have an uncomfortable feeling that something dreadful was about to happen. Over the years, I have learned to remain alert when my intuition kicks in, which is often right before a significant event occurs. I decided to call Rhys to find out if they were okay.

Rhys MacAllister is a robust, fine-looking Scotsman, six feet three inches tall, with wavy copper hair and hazel eyes. He speaks with a delightful, sing-song Scottish accent and is by nature a jolly sort most of the time, although he can be very serious and focused. He is a retired police officer as I am, who wanted to tour the country while still earning a living, so he began driving commercial trucks and has for over twenty years, including ten years with my company.

Nash Chavez is a Portuguese young man of twenty-nine years, who has been Rhys's co-driver for almost three years. He speaks fluent English, Portuguese, French and Spanish and has been extremely helpful on many occasions when translation was needed.

Rhys and Nash were tailing a semi refrigerated rig in central Texas. The suspicious gray truck with a red logo, stopped at a rest area just south of San Antonio. Rhys and Nash observed as a woman and two men climbed out of the truck and trotted to the back of the trailer. Rhys was instantly alert as one of the men opened a cargo door and the woman climbed into the trailer. This doesn't normally happen since most loads are sealed from the shipper and not meant to be opened until the driver arrives at his receiver.

A moment later, the woman climbed out of the trailer followed by a group of girls. The woman was apparently escorting the girls to the restroom. It was eight p.m. and a dark, moonless night, but Rhys could see well enough under the rest area lights to notice a gun tucked into the back of one of the men's jeans. "Nash, get Dakota on the telle and let him know that we are going to track the truck further to see where they go."

I was just about to call Rhys when my cell rang. "Hey, Nash. Is everything okay out there?"

Nash described the suspicious truck and the situation they were witnessing, while Rhys counted the girls. "Tell Dakota, there are eight girls, possibly from Central American countries." Rhys thought that if they could get near the drivers, maybe Nash could understand the language they were speaking.

"Keep following them and in the meantime, I'll relay the information to Chief Hank Demarka, who is heading up road operations for our team. Send some photos including the plate if you can. Obviously, we don't want them alerted to your presence, so be careful."

"Aye." Rhys got out of the truck and quickly took photos of the truck and trailer. The men were still at the back of the trailer, so he was able snap plenty of shots. He then hid behind another truck to snap a few more photos of the group, who were on their way back. He observed them, meticulously ingraining into his head as much of a detailed description as possible. When one of the men suddenly turned around, Rhys quickly ducked, then bolted in between the trailers and climbed back into his truck. "I don't think he saw me," he whispered to himself. He sent the photos to Dakota with a message: "I hope you can see enough to be helpful. One of the Jimmys is tall with blonde, shoulder length hair and is sportin' a gray leather jacket and black jeans. The other one is medium height, black hair, sportin' a red plaid shirt under a black jean jacket, who looks to be of Central American origin. The woman who took the girls into the restroom has dark hair, tied back in a ponytail, stickin' out of a gray ball cap. She's wearin' gray jeans, a red sweatshirt and gray trainers. I think she may be Central American as well, but not sure."

When I received the message, I texted back, "Good work, Rhys. Keep me updated and call me the next time they stop. I'm hoping Dirk can send a few men down there to help you, but tail them for now."

Nash said, "Well, at least they were willing to let their captives have a bathroom break."

Rhys said thoughtfully, "Yeah, I'm surprised they did, because it seems risky to me. I mean, we've been able to witness quite a bit."

"I wonder where they are headed? They could be trying to get as far out of Texas as they can. This ought to be very interesting."

"Okay, they're leaving. I'll follow them until my hours run out. Get some sleep so that you can take over in a while. I'll stop and fuel when they do and I'll get you up then."

"You've got it." Nash went back to bed, but he couldn't sleep right away. He was too anxious. Some of those girls looked really young, he thought. Forcing himself to relax, he finally closed his eyes and drifted off.

After six hours, the truck they were following stopped to fuel. Rhys's plan was working. He woke up Nash and got out to fuel next to the other truck. He watched them carefully while he was cleaning his windows. The driver of the other truck was headed toward Rhys, so he threw some trash into the bin between two of the fuel bays and decided to try to talk with the man. Rhys said, "I sure like fueling when most of the drivers are sleeping, no long lines. Where are you headed?"

The man glared at him and snarled, "North and you best mind your own business."

As he walked away, Rhys said, "Yeah, I'm headed east, out of Texas." He didn't want the man to know he was tailing them and hoped that would throw off any suspicion. "Damn!" He said under his breath. He was hoping the guy would give him a hint as to where they were headed but of course, that was just a long shot.

Nash was climbing out of the truck when he observed the creep walking into the store. He said, "Rhys, I'm going in for coffee and if I'm lucky, I'll be able to snap a clear photo of that dude in the well-lit store. Do you want anything?"

"No, thanks. I plan to sit up with you for a while to help watch that truck. I have a sandwich in the fridge for dinner. Make sure you high tail it back here as soon as that bloke walks out."

"Oh, I'll be on his tail, don't you worry."

While Nash prepared his coffee, he glanced over to the cooler area where the man was picking up some sodas. He pulled out his phone, ducked around the corner and snapped a photo. "Gotcha." He said, quietly to himself. He dashed back to the coffee bar, finished up and went to the counter to pay. The man walked up behind him, while Nash paid for his coffee. He then pretended to be interested in a flashlight beside the counter to get a better look at him. He noticed a long, inflamed crimson scar on his cheek and eerie black eyes. Nash felt a chill run up his spine.

The man spoke to the clerk, "Gimmie two packs of American Spirits." His voice was gruff, but higher pitched than Nash was expecting out of such a large, burly man.

Nash headed back to the truck and logged on the truck sat-com as the current driver. He observed the sinister man climbing into his truck, then took off behind him. "Check this out." He gave his cell phone to Rhys to view the photos. "The guy has a gnarly scar on his face and creepy, black eyes."

Rhys sent the photos and description to Dakota along with their current location. "I'm hoping we can successfully follow the bampots to their final destination. I'd like to park as close as we can when they stop, so get ready for a possible dodgy skirmish. If they back into a building dock instead of another rest area, I'll find a way into the building. I bet they plan to unload the product and the girls at the same time and possibly abscond with the girls in other vehicles, which I plan on preventing at all costs."

They followed the rig to a private cold storage facility

in Oklahoma City. Nash parked the truck a block away, then Rhys bolted up the side of the building. The truck driver backed into a dock as Rhys turned the corner. He stayed hidden for a few minutes, observing the two men and the woman as they hastily walked through the receiving door. He decided to try to enter through the same door. Luckily, it had been left ajar and there was no one at the receiving desk, so he stealthily made his way toward the dock, managing to stay out of sight. Rhys hid in between some warehouse product shelving, while observing the criminals escorting the girls from the trailer. Rhys filmed the entire scene, which would be indisputable evidence that the sinister group were guilty of human trafficking, as well as transporting humans illegally in a commercial trailer along with pallets of product. He tried to discover the contents of the boxes in an attempt to determine whether or not they contained contraband. Then, several men began unloading the pallets, but they were not opening the boxes. He decided that he was already pressing his luck, so he quietly crept back toward the door.

Nash had already called Dakota and the National Human Trafficking hotline number when Rhys entered the building, describing the situation. Rhys sent the film immediately to Nash and Dakota and quickly texted, "Call the police now. I don't know if I can get back out without being spotted. I'll try to act as if I'm interested in hauling product for the company, but it could get messy fast if they notice me."

Rhys observed the group of girls being led down a hallway and through a red warehouse door. As quietly as he could, he crept to the receiving door and opened it.

"Hey you, stop!" Boomed an enraged voice.

Rhys was sure the man would grab him or worse, shoot him, so he tried to remain calm, pretending to be unaware of what had just occurred. A bit choked up he said, "I'm looking for the manager. I'm an owner operator and I'd like to know if yer looking for someone to haul yer products."

The man shrieked, "How did you get in here?"

"I just walked through the receiving door, but I didn't see anyone at the desk, so I was just about to leave when you showed up." The man dashed hastily toward Rhys, grabbing him by the arm. "Hey, let go of my arm. There's no reason to get huffy."

"How long have you been here?"

"Like I said, I just walked through the receiving door a second ago. Why are ye grabbing me?" Rhys swung at him, landing a solid punch to his gut. As the man doubled over, Rhys threw another punch. The man tried to swing back, but Rhys kicked his leg with full might, knocking the man to the floor. He bolted toward the door, managing to open it, but the man grabbed his arm again before he could get out and pointed a gun at his head. Rhys raised his hands. "Okay, I get it. I guess you don't need any help."

Both men froze, staring each other down. Sirens were blaring outside. "Mierda!" The man roared. "Move!" He pushed Rhys toward a hallway with the gun to his back, opened the red door and shoved Rhys down the hall. The man bellowed to his comrades, "I caught this dude snooping around in the warehouse. He claims he's looking for work, but he may have seen something and now the police are out there." He shoved Rhys up against a wall with the gun to his head. "What did you see? Did you call the police?"

"Nae, nae. What are you talking about? As I said, I'm looking for work. What's going on here?"

Just then, they heard loud voices and the door flew open. Three policemen stormed in with guns raised. Rhys shouted, "They're armed!"

The man turned and fired his gun toward the cops. "Stop right there or this man dies." Rhys elbowed the man in the gut with all of his might followed by a blow to the back of his neck. The man fired his gun aimlessly as he dropped to his knees. Rhys kicked him with brutal force, causing him to drop the gun which slid across the floor. Two of the officers pinned the enormous blonde thug down while another officer called in for back up.

An ambulance and two more police teams arrived and stormed the building. Three officers caught two men shoving a group of girls into a van in the back of the building. "Freeze, now!" The two men turned and fired. The officers fired back and hit one of the men while he was attempting to make it to the van door. The other offender kept firing until he ran out of ammunition. The policemen took a chance, while the man was trying to reload his gun and kicked it out of his hands. They cuffed him and quickly escorted him to the police car along with another, who was badly injured and bleeding profusely. When an ambulance arrived, a police officer directed the medic, "Strap him to the gurney. I'm riding with you to the hospital, because I'd like to see if I can make the bastard talk."

Another officer made his way out of the warehouse with one of the criminals in hand cuffs. He bellowed, "How many more of your buddies are in there?" The man snarled at him. "You either answer my question or you're going down for the whole thing."

The man laughed. "The only person I'm talking to is my lawyer."

The officer laughed, "Good luck with that. You're not getting out of this one. Too many witnesses, you idiot." He read him his rights and slammed the car door, locked it and ran back into the building, gun at the ready.

Rhys was moving toward the door with another thug in front of him, his arm twisted back in a debilitating strong hold. He shouted, "There's a woman in there wearing a red sweatshirt and dark hair under a ball cap. She's one of the criminals who transported the women in the semi-trailer. She must still be in the building and she's probably armed."

The officer radioed to one of his comrades. "Search the building for a woman in red, probably armed." Two officers entered the building through the front office door, while the others searched the warehouse.

Another officer assisted Rhys, clutching the perv by the arm. "I've got him." He glanced at Rhys, "You come out with me. I need your statement with as much detail as possible." He shoved the scowling offender into the police car.

The thug turned toward Rhys and growled, "You son of a bitch, I'll get you!"

The cop shouted, "Shut up. You'll get no one where you're going." He closed and locked the doors, then briskly strode to the group of terrified girls. "Are any of you hurt?" He gazed at the frightened, exhausted faces of eight young women, hearing whimpering.

One of the girls pointed to another, speaking

Spanish, "La Senorita esta herida. Estomago."

The officer knew enough Spanish to figure out the word estomago. The young woman had bruises on her face and her arms were folded across her stomach. "Stomach?"

She looked up, "Si, malo."

The officer asked, "Do any of you speak English?"

A girl who appeared to be about fifteen said, "A little."

The officer said, "My name is Sergeant James. What is your name?"

She replied, "Mi nombre es Maria. Hmmm… The bad man hit her when she tried to run away. He said to all of us, esta es una advertencia, Hmmm, a warning, and if we tried to run, he would kill us."

The officer asked, "Are you well enough to ride to the hospital without an ambulance?" The girl who spoke English translated to the wounded young woman. She looked up with a painful grimace and nodded. "Okay, please help each other into these two vehicles and we'll go to the hospital. We will have the doctors examine all of you to make sure that you are okay. We will have an officer there who can translate and will help you get safely back home." Maria translated as the officer escorted the women to the two SUVs.

Six criminals were arrested including the missing, unscrupulous woman, who had been hiding in the back of the warehouse. Rhys and Nash gave a full report of what had occurred and were told they could leave. As soon as he received the call about the traffickers, Dirk Hays, the FBI agent responsible for Rhys and Nash, had contacted the Oklahoma City local police department to fill them in concerning the role Rhys and Nash were playing in the operation. He told them to fully respect the truck drivers and allow them to assist the authorities.

Rhys and Nash climbed back into the truck and rolled toward the terminal in Denver. Neither of them spoke, for quite a while. Finally, dreadfully concerned Nash turned and glanced at Rhys. "Dude, you could have been killed, but I'm glad you're okay. You are, aren't you?"

Rhys grunted, "Aye. That minger missed me by a tad." He grazed my arm. It's shite, but nae danger, pal."

Nash shrieked, "Do you need to go to the hospital?"

"Nae, I'll be fine." I'll lay down for a bit though. Call Dakota and fill him in, would ye? Let him know when we'll be arriving at the terminal."

Nash called me and described the details of the event. I was extremely concerned and attempted to get Nash to agree to drive Rhys to a clinic to no avail. Nash gulped, only half way believing his own words, "We're fine. That's why we're out here, right? Just doing our jobs. Rhys's a bit roughed up and was grazed by a bullet, but he refuses to go to a hospital, you know Rhys. I helped him clean up and bandage the abrasion and he's back there sleeping now. We should be rolling in around nine in the morning."

I questioned Rhys's decision to not go to the hospital, but I backed down, assuming that if Rhys was severely injured, he would make his way to a clinic. "Okay. I'm concerned, but I'll deal with it when you get here. I'll call Dirk and discuss the situation. You two join the meeting when you arrive and then take off for a while. We'll meet in the lounge at ten o'clock."

17

Dakota

While I was waiting for my drivers to arrive for the meeting at the truck terminal, I thought about the recent event with Rhys and Nash. I am now more than concerned about what I am getting my team involved in and have thoughts about backing out of the work. Suddenly, the hairs stood upright on the back of my neck and a chill dashed up my spine. "Oklahoma." I instantly thought of the Wild Cat Casino and realized I hadn't yet heard any news concerning criminal activity associated with the casino. It was time to pay them another visit. Ray Giordano may still be operating there and I intend to trap the bastard if he is. I clenched my fists, feeling my face redden with anger and frustration. I said quietly, "He thinks he has thrown the authorities off course for good, but I have news for him, I'm still here."

I called Dad and asked him to reach Myles, who had continued to make routine visits to the casino, posing as a regular guest. "Ask him if he has time to run down there for a few days. I have a feeling that Giordano might show up sometime soon." I eagerly discussed the recent bust in Oklahoma City, letting him know that I suspect that the men who were arrested may work for Giordano. He said that he would accompany Myles and report back as soon as they could find out any significant news.

Several driving teams had arrived during the past few hours of the morning and were finalizing their paperwork. There was quite a buzz around the terminal with everyone trying to guess what the meeting was about. I rarely arrange for my drivers to be at the terminal all at once and I planned to hook up the teams still out in various parts of the country to a conference call.

Cheynne Demarka was my newest recruit and would be my new driving partner. I had picked her up from the airport earlier and was just about to give her a tour of the terminal. I met up with her in the dispatch room. "Well, I see you discovered the heart of our operation." I beamed, proud of our accomplishments so far. I showed her the comfortable, spacious offices, a full kitchen with a large dining table, conference room and location of the restrooms. "On the second level there is an entertainment drivers' lounge with leather sofas and lounge chairs, dining tables, two large shower rooms and a spacious laundry room. There are also three lodge style bedrooms with private bathrooms for the drivers who stay out on the road for long periods of time and who don't live nearby."

Cheynne said, "It's nice to feel comfortable when you have to stop for break away from home."

"Exactly, that's the idea. Brooke Macfie, one of our remarkable drivers, helped me design it. She drew all of the construction documents and helped me through the daunting permit process as well as construction management. We are like one big family and I want everyone to feel comfortable here."

"You are really fortunate to have so many drivers that have other skills and qualifications. I heard about the five drivers that are military veterans and about three that are retired police officers such as yourself. It's comforting to be working with a team that can provide some protection and have been trained to deal with criminals."

"Yes, that's why I truly believe we will be successful with our criminal tracking efforts. Most of the drivers also have other skills and abilities unrelated to defense or driving. For instance, several of my drivers helped build the terminal, which was actually really enjoyable and entertaining. Rhys sang Scottish tunes and Blake whistled nearly the whole way through construction. After we finished working almost every day, Jake would start up the barbecue and grill halibut, salmon or wild game. What a treat that was." I smiled at the memory, feeling extremely grateful. "Cheynne, I'm elated that your Uncle Hank wants us to join his task force. This is a project that I pray we can manage safely, because if our work is successful and the company proves to be an asset, I'm hoping the work continues for years."

"Oh, I think our work will be invaluable. The way you have your teams organized now, covering various parts of the country is already working. Hank reviewed the last few years of your work with me and I'm impressed and excited to join your team."

"I'm happy to have you on board. I have been itching to get back out on the road, because I really hate being cooped up in the office. I've been driving long-haul loads about twice a month and I sometimes help my local drivers deliver loads, but somebody has to over-see things around here. I just hired a remarkably qualified guy, Chris Ruby, who will manage the terminal while I'm out on the road. I'll introduce you to everyone at the meeting. Afterwards, we will be heading to Georgia with a few stops along the way. We're delivering in Macon and then there's a truck stop I want to check out. Yesterday, a call was made to Atlanta P.D. reporting a suspicious black Chevy Blazer. A pervert was knocking on truck doors, possibly drumming up business for five or six women seen in the vehicle. That same vehicle was seen by Brooke last week. I'll tell you more later. Grab your things and get set up in my truck. It's the dark green truck with the bear hood-ornament, parked on the west side across from the main door. Number 2018. I'll meet you all in the lounge at ten thirty."

Cheynne was surprised and amazed at how much room there was. She made her bed on the top bunk, put her folded clothing in the cupboard and food in the refrigerator. She was delighted to see that Dakota kept a tidy truck. She thought, after all, the truck is a mini home away from home. The truck was clean and his belongings were neatly stowed away.

Most of the driving teams have convened at the terminal and I connected the drivers that were still out on the road to a conference call. "I'll start by saying, great job.

I'm thrilled that we have begun to make a real impact on the human trafficking dilemma here in the U.S. We are being noticed more and more by law enforcement agencies and other organizations, who feel that we can provide an invaluable service, assisting them in the capture of some of the most heinous criminals in the country. Our next mission is going to take a lot of focus and good communication."

I sipped my coffee and continued. "I'd like to introduce you to Cheynne Demarka. She'll be joining our team for this mission and hopefully, she has an interest in staying on with us. She worked with the U.S. Forestry Division in Washington for twelve years doing search and rescue as well as wild animal protection and management."

Cheynne said, "Hello. I look forward to meeting all of you and I'm also really excited to join your team."

"Cheynne's uncle, Sgt. Hank Demarka, with Atlanta P.D., has been tracking a massive ring of sex traffickers who are also involved with drugs and assault weapons. He has discovered several rendezvous points so far between Texas, Oklahoma, Missouri, South Carolina, Georgia and Florida. We have to cover a lot of territory. This operation might be even larger than we know at this point, so Hank is bringing us on board to not only keep our ears and eyes open, but to play an active role in hunting and tracking perpetrators down. We will be working with an FBI task force who have gathered tremendous amounts of information, but they of course want to get to the ringleaders. They suspect thirteen kingpins so far and many others, possibly all handlers.

"As most of you know, Blake served in the military

both in the Navy and the Marine Corps for thirty-two years. He has experience in decoding messages, computer data, research and boots on the ground during the Gulf War and was involved in many other missions in the Middle East. Since we have five military veteran team members and three retired police officers, the FBI is interested in adding us to their task force."

Blake said, "Most of us received our official recruit info yesterday."

"Great. That means we now have eight team members who are licensed to carry and use firearms when and if needed. If you find yourselves in a situation that you are not sure how to handle, call me and I'll decide if the situation requires communication with Dirk and his men or local P.D.s. Cheynne and I will be rolling to Atlanta, where we will meet with Hank along with some of you who will also be in the area. An enormous quantity of criminal activity has been going on lately in South Carolina and Georgia, so be prepared."

Cheynne said, "Large truck stops are prime targets for sex traffickers and unfortunately, as you all are aware, some truckers are considered part of the problem. There may be thousands of lonely truck drivers out there who don't get to go home often enough and some don't really have a home to go to, so they may seek company. But, since there is now much more information out there about trafficking, more truckers are realizing that many of these women are involuntary slaves and thankfully, the drivers are choosing to call the NHT hotline number instead of inviting the women into their trucks."

I nodded to Cheynne, then addressed Nash and Rhys. "You will be covering a massive territory in Texas, but I'd like for you both to take time off since you were just involved in a horrendous, though successful bust."

Rhys said, "I'm fine and I don't need time off. We only have a week before the Christmas holiday, so I say, let's keep rolling until then." Nash agreed.

I glared concerningly at them both and sighed, "Okay, but Rhys, you go get that shoulder checked out at the clinic and then you can leave. I want a professional medic to assure me that you're okay. You both found yourselves in a dangerous situation and as much as I think our work will prove to be invaluable to Dirk's task force, I don't know if I could ever forgive myself if any of you get killed. I hope you all understand the possible consequences of working undercover like we will be. If we are identified, we could find ourselves targets. Traffickers will want us out of the way as soon as they can possibly manage it. Do you all understand?"

Everyone spoke up with various comments, basically saying that they understood and were still in no way deterred. I turned my attention again to Rhys. "Okay, then when you are ready, you are to check out several truck stops and rest areas that Dirk has planned for you. I will be sending you an email with the locations. There have been quite a few calls to the NHT hotline about shady activity along I-35 from Laredo, heading north through Texas and into Oklahoma. I also want you to check out casinos, particularly the Wild Cat Casino which is not far north of the Oklahoma state line." My eyes narrowed as I looked down, feeling my gut wrench. "The FBI has tracked a tremendous amount of corrupt activity coming across the U.S.-Mexican border, moving through Texas."

Rhys said, "I wonder if trafficking from Mexico will

slow down a bit with all of Trump's 'Round-Up' and deportation activity as well as the building of his wall, although, that might make it worse for a while." Rhys scowled. "Traffickers may be trying to work up as much business now as possible before an upsurge of border searches takes place. I still believe there are payoffs."

"You're probably right. Okay, next discussion. We are all hooking into a 'Go-To-Meeting' at eleven thirty eastern time, December twentieth, with Hank. That gives us two days to get our loads delivered and shut down for the meeting. All deliveries are scheduled around this meeting, but I will be in contact beforehand so that we are all prepared. Please record what you hear. Here is a pre-briefing; Hank has been informed by the FBI, that women and contraband are being picked up in various places in Texas including Laredo, Galveston and Corpus Christi and also along the South Carolina, Georgia and Florida coastal areas. In the past two months, two ships and several small boats were captured by the Coast Guard with women and contraband off the coast in Texas. On one ship, the guard found several shipping containers with young women locked inside. Most of them were very sick and badly roughed up. Laredo has so much corrupt activity that it horrifies me to think about it. These women are forced to ride in not only hot, dry vans, but also in reefers in between pallets of refrigerated foods." Everyone gasped and murmured.

I was feeling hopeful that Dad and Myles will find out that the criminals recently arrested work for Giordano and will finally have a reason to arrest him. I plan on being able to interrogate him myself. I couldn't shake the feeling that the shady character knows where Jillian is or at least, maybe he will be able to confirm that she was there in Wisconsin years ago.

I swallowed and continued, "For those of you who haven't heard about our recent bust yesterday, Rhys and Nash tracked a reefer semi rig from central Texas to a private cold storage facility in Oklahoma City. They worked out a plan to get into the building and assisted in capturing the traffickers and the rescue of the young women." I reviewed the highlights of the bust. "Rhys acted bravely, but you all need to understand that he was injured and he could have been killed. I would of course prefer Dirk's men along with the local authorities to handle the arrests, so that you all aren't put in harm's way, but the group may have escaped if Rhys hadn't acted without hesitation. Use your best judgment. I'm not interested in you guys performing as vigilantes. We all need to be team players. Call the local authorities and call me, so that I can help in every way that I can before you decide to take criminals down yourselves."

Rhys said, "I'm not likely to let the bampots get away with innocent girls. Dakota, I do understand what you're saying, but I sure hope we can get help sooner than we did out there. Local officers arrived before it was too late, but I felt that until they arrived, I found myself a bit of a chancer. Those manky traffickers are being interrogated as we speak and hopefully, one or more of them will sing to save their own arses. I mean, one of the main objectives is to find the big mental mingers behind the scenes who are controlling the operations, right?"

I said, "Yes and anything we can do to prevent the offenders from escaping is top priority. Our jobs have just become much more dangerous, so if any of you have concerns, come see me or call me. Thanks to Rhys and Nash, eight young girls were rescued and will be returning to their homes or somewhere safe. This event, the massive bust in Houston and the one just recently in Orlando are the reasons the task force has been able to identify the trafficking routes that we are to cover. The task force has been tracking movement and shady activity all around the country, but we will be given certain territories that we are to cover for the next few months when we meet with Hank. I may move you all around a bit so that you don't have to stay in the same region for too long."

Cheynne said, "For those of you who didn't read about those recent busts that Dakota just mentioned, there was a human trafficking prostitution sting called 'Operation Cross Country', in north Houston near the Woodlands, which included seventy-five arrests and recovery of five trafficked victims including a minor. You can read about that one in the Houston Chronicle.[3] The second bust Dakota mentioned is the case in Orlando, Florida, Polk County, where undercover detectives arrested 103 people in an alleged prostitution and human trafficking operation. You can catch up on that one online in the Orlando Sentinel.[4]"

I added, "I believe the men arrested in Oklahoma City are a small sector of a larger operation and it's possible that the pervs that Brooke awoke to last week are as well."

With hackles raised, Rhys spun his chair to face Brooke. "Whoa, what happened?"

Brooke sighed with a grimace. "We were parked at a small truck stop for the night, off Georgia I-16, when I was rudely awakened by a loud bang on the door. I was a bit disoriented, in sleep mode and thought it might be the truck stop employees trying to collect parking fees, but boy was I wrong. I cracked my window to hear what the creep was saying and a heavy-set Hispanic man asked me if I wanted a bone in me. What a sick bastard! I'm sure he was surprised to see a woman come to the window. I told him to get lost and not to bother me. I also mentioned my co-driver who was trying to sleep, because I wanted the creep to know that there was someone else in the truck with me. I pulled the curtain back across the window and peeked out to scope out the scene. There was a dark gray Chevy Blazer with five or six women inside, so I figured the guy must have been drumming up business for them. I called the hotline number and Dakota."

I drew in a deep breath. "That's one of the reasons Cheynne and I will be visiting that same truck stop."

Rhys's concerned eyes lingered on Brooke's. "Will you please stay away from shady truck stops? What if he aimed a gun at you and tried to climb into the truck?"

"Rhys, I appreciate the concern." She blushed crimson. "But I have my bodyguard with me. Look at him. He's huge and mean looking."

Blake chuckled, "You better believe it Rhys, I'll look after her, don't you worry and anyway, have you seen Brooke spar in the Dojang? Whoa, look out, she's tough."

"Good to know. I guess I had better watch out for the lass." Rhys grinned at Brooke coquettishly.

Rhys and Brooke had been flirting with each other for almost a year. Rhys was hoping to eventually get Brooke to go out on the town with him, but since they drive different trucks and are rarely in the same state at the same time, getting to know each other has been challenging. Brooke thought, I hope Rhys will be at the holiday party, because I'd sure like to get to know him better. She grinned back with a girlishly shy, blushing face.

I couldn't help but smile at Rhys and Brooke, then continued. "Remember, don't let the perves you are tracking notice you. I believe that most traffickers think that truckers are customers, so most likely, they won't suspect you are onto them, but still be careful. It's not our job to apprehend them unless you are sure you can do so safely and if backup is on the way. Okay, let's roll. Pick up your load manifests from Rich."

As everyone headed out to their trucks, I asked, "Cheynne, would you please grab that clipboard? I'll need you to drive first if that's okay with you. I have a few calls to make. Our trailer is number 5318, south side of the lot. Please hook up to it and I'll meet you at the gate. Can I bring you a coffee for the road?"

"Yes, please. Just black. I have coffee cream in the fridge." She gathered her things and headed to the truck.

Human trafficking, involuntary servitude, is the third largest criminal activity in the world. Forced labor, domestic servitude and commercial sex trafficking; Slavery.

Victims are often beaten, starved, forced to work as prostitutes or to take jobs as migrant workers in restaurants, factories and agricultural fields with little or no pay.

A nonprofit group fighting sex trafficking on the nation's highways issued an appeal that truckers and shippers train their employees to recognize and report suspicious activities and instances of human trafficking.

"Truckers are the eyes and ears of our highways and they see things that most do not."

TAT is based in Colorado. TAT has teamed up with law enforcement agencies and truck companies and through their efforts, they have freed 100's of human trafficking victims.

By Feb 11th, 2016, truckers had made more than 2,250 calls to the 24-hour National Human Trafficking Resource Center (NHTRC) 1-888 373-7888 hotline number reporting suspicious activity at truck stops, rest areas, casinos, motels and adult X-rated stores and clubs. Over 612 likely human trafficking cases were identified involving 1,133 victims. [5]

Homeland Security Investigations (HSI) urges people to call their tip line:

1-866-DHS-2-ICE (1-800-347-2423)

18

Dakota and Cheynne

Cheynne was thinking about Dakota while waiting at the front gate. She had met Dakota at a TAT conference and afterwards, they shared dinner together and talked for hours. Neither Dakota nor Cheynne had been dating anyone in the past few years and were both feeling a bit lonely. Dakota felt that someday, he would find a woman he truly cared for when the time was right After just one day with Cheynne, he began thinking about her. They had seen each other again at a meeting with Hank DeMarka in Georgia, when she inquired about Dakota's trucking team and asked Hank if there might be a place for her on the team. Hank chuckled and told her he would speak to Dakota and see what could be arranged. She was delighted and felt hopeful.

Cheynne really admires Dakota for what he has so far accomplished. She whispered to herself, "He's tall, handsome, has the most captivating deep green eyes and the most compassionate disposition of anyone I've ever met." Cheynne is very aware of facial expressions and mannerisms of others by nature. During the meeting earlier, there were a few moments here and there, when she sensed something troubling Dakota. On the two previous occasions when she had spent time with him, he had been friendly, confident, energetic and compassionate, but she noticed a sadness in his eyes then as well. She would encourage him to open up to her soon.

Cheynne is a tall, attractive woman with waist length, sable hair and bronze eyes. She loves to run and perform Tai Chi movements for exercise and hopes to persuade Dakota to join her in her exercise routines. Even though she likes Dakota very much, she is afraid to reveal her feelings, at least not yet. She realizes they will be working together on an extremely significant project, so staying professional will be necessary. She also hopes he shares her feelings, since they seemed to have some close connection that she couldn't yet explain.

"Okay." I drew in a deep breath as I climbed into the truck. "Oh, good. Looks like you're set up here. If I need to move my stuff around to make room for your things, let me know."

Cheynne said, "I'm good. This Peterbilt is amazing. I've never driven a truck with so much room in the sleeper area. I made some delicious meals for both of us and there was plenty of room for everything in the fridge. There are also fruits and other snacks in the bin here, so please help yourself."

"Hey, I'm liking our team already. Thank you."

"I love to cook and I can't eat the fatigue causing junk food that the truck stops sell."

"I agree. I usually bring leftovers from home, but I haven't been home for over a month. Sometimes I cook here at the terminal, but I've been so busy lately that I haven't stayed on top of my meal prep, so I do appreciate it. Please use the terminal kitchen whenever you like. I also like to bar-b-que sometimes, so maybe we can team up when we get back and cook up a storm."

I entered the receiver address into the navigation system. "Okay, head out toward I-70 east. I'm going to make some calls." I spoke with the other teams that weren't at the meeting and then sipped my fresh, cinnamon spiced coffee.

Cheynne asked, "Hey, if I could pry a little, what is your story? I see a little sadness in your eyes."

"Oh, it shows?"

"Maybe not to others, but I noticed."

I sighed with a grimace. "Well, I witnessed my twin sister, Jillian, climbing into a pickup truck a long time ago and she never returned. I recounted the tragic details of Jillian's disappearance and explained how I have tried to locate her ever since that fateful day.

"I'm so sorry. How devastating that must have been for you and your family."

"My family and the detective on the case, Myles LaSalle have been extremely troubled and concerned that her case has never been solved, which is why I have dedicated my entire life to the pursuit of traffickers, who I truly believe abducted Jillian. Every time I locate sex criminals, I interrogate them, hoping to find clues to Jillian's current location. Once the internet and Facebook were invented, I posted her photo and her story developing quite a following for a few years, but my following faded away after a while when there was just nothing else to report."

Cheynne asked awkwardly, "Have your parents continued to look for her as well? I mean, are they still around?"

"Oh yes, of course. Chevyo, my dad is a retired Army Officer. He called in some favors and got Jillian's information added into as many databases as possible and he continues to post articles in the newspapers. He often drives around for days at a time, searching casinos, hotels, bars and so on. Chevyo also believes that she may have been snagged by traffickers, but we don't talk about that idea around my mother for obvious reasons. Jillian's body has never been recovered, so she must still be alive, at least that's what we want to believe. No reports about an unknown woman's death that match Jillian's description have ever turned up. My mother, Yamka, fell apart when Jillian went missing but after a while, she began to realize that Jillian wasn't coming home, at least not yet. She believes that Jillian has been protected and that there is a very good reason she hasn't returned."

Cheynne said, "I sure hope we can find her now that we will be working on the task force."

It took me a minute to respond and I felt my frustration mounting. "Yeah, damn it, I know she's out there. If I could just..."

"Dakota, have faith. I know you do, or you wouldn't continue to search. I'm all in and I'm here because I want to help in every way that I can. I have heard of too many women from all backgrounds who have been forced to work as female escorts. I'm certain that most of them are threatened, so they feel that they can't leave. Night club and casino owners deny that women are working as prostitutes in their establishments and they say if there are any, they have no knowledge of them." She paused, "Well, I want to help you find Jillian."

"Thanks, Cheynne." I felt my anxiety diminish by sharing my story with her. "Chevyo learned from Jonoche, my grandfather, how a person's spiritual nature can guide one's thoughts and behaviors in very intuitive, harmonious ways. He also studied theology and figured out how to incorporate various religious beliefs into one main spiritual ideal. He believes that no matter what God one believes in and no matter what religious faith one aspires to is good, as long as it is a harmonious, compassionate, loving faith and that one practices that faith on a daily basis. He also believes that people should use their spiritual, loving nature to guide them in everything they do. It works for him and it has not only kept him strong, but it has kept him on a very positive course through life."

I cleared my throat, "I believe that way, too, but sometimes it's difficult for me. Some days, I feel so frustrated that I find myself yelling at God for allowing my sister to be taken away from us." I paused for a minute. "I have to admit that for a long time, I lost faith in God almost entirely, but I have recently begun to pray for his guidance and for her safe return, even though it has been over forty years. I just have a feeling she is still alive and well, but has been afraid to return, like you mentioned, because she has been threatened. If that is the case, what a horrible tragedy." Cheynne stayed quiet. She must have understood that I needed to talk it out. "I also understand that you all, my entire team, care a great deal. Jake and Chris have similar passions for our quest since they both have had someone important in their lives go missing as well. We are all in. Our main mission is to help take down as many of the trafficking syndicates as possible and of course, some of us have our own personal missions, to find someone we love no matter how long it takes."

19

Dakota

Cheynne and I were making headway across I-70 toward Kansas. The weather was drizzly and quite cold, twenty-six degrees, but luckily, the polar vortex was supposed to bring frigid temperatures mainly in the northeast, probably not affecting climate across our route toward Georgia. However, I was concerned about a few of my teams working in the northeast, so I called Rich to arrange for the teams to head south toward Georgia.

As soon as I hung up with Rich, my cell rang. The caller ID showed Jake's number. "Hey, Jake." He was excited and rambling on, out of breath. He said he was following a dark gray SUV and a dirty white commercial truck that he suspected were traffickers. He said he witnessed four men leading a group of women from a casino boat that was docked in Myrtle Beach.

Jake said excitedly, "The circumstances of what I witnessed aren't good. I was parked near the boat docks after grabbing some seafood for lunch and noticed an abusive, sinister situation. Some obnoxious, burly men were escorting a group of women off the boat toward the gray SUV when one of the women broke away from the group and tried to run. One of the men wearing a gray Fedora hat and black leather jacket, grabbed her by her hair and yanked her back toward the group. He slapped her pretty hard. Then, I watched them hastily shoving some of the women into the truck and the rest into the SUV."

"Could you see how many women?"

"I counted twelve. I tried to read the plates, but they took off too fast. The SUV is leading the other truck, which is about twenty-four feet in length with a lift cargo door. The plates are smeared with mud, so I can't see them, but I snapped a few photos. I'll have Zach send them to you now. There is no sign on the truck to identify it. They are headed northwest on highway 501. I'll follow them for as long as I can. Should I call the local authorities?"

"No, I'll call it in to Hank right now and let him figure out who to put on this. That's a lot of women and we need to help them but we must have back up, so for now, keep tailing them while we formulate a plan to take them down. Cheynne and I are ultimately headed to Atlanta, but we won't be there until Thursday, so call me again if you need immediate help. Jake, for God's sake, please don't get involved like you did on that last one. I pulled this team together to help the law, not to take it into our own hands."

"I know, damn it! But Dakota, you know it ticks me off to no end when the bastards get away. And I know some of these 'good ole boys' down here turn the other cheek. I also believe they are getting payoffs, so who can we really trust? I mean, I can't prove it yet but I've been working down here for long enough to know that something is just not quite right, so let's not have a kerfuffle, eh?" Jake is from Canada and sneaks in a few comical slang words on occasion to lighten the mood.

"Have you been in touch with Sheriff Sauer again?"

"No, I don't like the way that hoser responds or rather doesn't respond. It's like, nothing is important to him and he has an, 'I'll check it out when I have time' attitude, so I don't even want to involve him on this case. Last time I talked with him, he said he had a team working the area 24/7 but if that's true, where are they? He really screwed up the last one which is why I got so involved. I know he let them get away and I'm sure he was paid off."

"Jake, you are a warrior in every sense of the word, but we need you to stay alive. I'll get a hold of Hank right now and let him know what you are on to. He will decide who to bring in asap. Both Hank and I have contacts in a few of the casinos down there, so maybe it's time to bring them on board."

Jake yelled, "They're turning off 501, only a few klicks in front of me! I'll call you back."

"Jake, Jake! Damn it. He worries me."

Cheynne said, "Zach is with him. He won't do anything too crazy with him in the truck, right?" Zach

Kahale is a young Hawaiian man of twenty-six years and is quite impressionable. He is one of my newest recruits who joined the company, because he'd been concerned about the growing sex trafficking issue in the Hawaiian Islands. He decided to move to the mainland U.S. to gain some experience and eventually will return to the islands to help the people there as well. I purposely teamed him up with Jake hoping that Jake would slow down a bit and think more rationally before acting on Zach's behalf.

With exasperation, I replied, "I don't know. I sure hope not. Hank will need to send some backup quickly or things could go sideways very fast. Jake can be a loose cannon. He just hasn't trusted any law enforcement ever since Sauer screwed up a major investigation that he had been conducting for months."

Cheynne asked, "Who is Sauer?"

"Hans Sauer is one of the local patrol officers on the coast of South Carolina, who Hank has been investigating. Hank is also fairly sure that Sauer has been receiving money to turn the other cheek, specifically on the Riverboat Casinos, but they haven't been able to prove it yet. They call him Riverboat Sauer. He's notably a really dirty cop."

"Oh, I haven't heard about him. Hank briefed me on quite a bit, but he failed to mention Sauer."

"No worries. We'll be learning a lot more at the meeting Thursday." Hank finally answered the call. "Hank, Jake is tailing two vehicles near South Carolina, highway 501. He tracked them from Myrtle Beach where they disembarked from a riverboat casino." I relayed the details from Jake. Hank, I'm worried about Jake. I don't want him attempting to handle this operation alone."

"Okay Dakota, I'm on it. I know who to call and don't worry, it won't be Sauer. Call me back if you hear more from Jake. I think they may be planning to hit all of the casinos in the area, which seems to be a current pattern. Dirk has been working on gathering information on a massive casino ring including South Carolina, Georgia and Florida. I'll get a hold of him now and I'll call you later to fill you in."

"Thanks, Hank."

Dirk Hays is the FBI agent in charge of the task force partnering with Hank DeMarka. He has been working in the sex trafficking division for over ten years and has collected a substantial amount of information on sex criminals. He has an extensive network of agents working around the country and has arrested hundreds of mafia members, johns and pimps but he of course, wants the crime syndicate principals. They are much more difficult to locate and track and in many of his cases, the top organizers have either eluded him or after being arrested, were able to get off due to the lack of evidence involving them directly. Dirk is extremely dedicated and has an unstoppable will to bring down sex traffickers and other sex criminals including cyberstalkers, johns and pimps who use the internet to abduct and exploit young women and children.

Kate Lindt is Dirk's partner, who has no tolerance for sex criminals and has an extremely serious demeanor. Dirk, Kate and his other comrades have already made tremendous progress here in the states, but sex trafficking continues to be a colossal problem across the world. In spite of our tough restrictions entering the U.S., traffickers continue to infiltrate the states from many other countries including Canada, Mexico, South America, Russia, the middle-east, Pakistan and other Asian and African countries. Dirk and Kate's mission is to stay on top of the problem, take down as many sex criminals as possible and save the unfortunate victims. I have immense respect for Dirk and feel that his task force team, which now includes my team, can locate and take out enough of the main sex trafficking organizations to make a difference.

Cheynne asked, "What's up with Jake?"

"Jake, hmmm, where to start. He's okay. He's just passionate about our work. A good friend of his disappeared a long time ago but he thinks, like I do, that he'll find her while tracking sex criminals. I met Jake Losato at a TAT event in Colorado. He was a flatbed driver working all across the country and being compassionate about the trafficking problem, he was looking for a way to get more involved. He was my first recruit and since he has a similar story, we share a common interest."

Cheynne was listening intently, yearning to learn more. "How were you able to find all of your drivers, especially the ones who were okay with the trafficking work?"

Jake called a few trucker friends including Chris O'Conner, Mack O'Donnell and Ian Mulloy and told them about my truck company and my interest in TAT and convinced them to join the team. I also called a few trucker friends including Rhys MacAllister, Blake Nevins and Brooke Macfie, invited them to dinner and convinced them to join as well. They were all excited, especially when I told them I was planning to build a new terminal and could offer extra pay for their help. We worked on the terminal day and night until it was complete on June 18, 2009.

Then in July, 2013, I was reading articles about the national 'Uniform Crime Reporting' program and articles on Sex Trafficking, by The Nevada Trucking Association who were addressing truckers and the general public to be aware of the forced sex trafficking issue and how truckers could help.[6] That's when I decided to place my drivers all over the country by using a few good load brokers to keep us in business."

"It's such a courageous and ambitious plan and I understand how it could be really ideal for our new mission. Since many of your drivers are police or military veterans, they have the necessary skills and experience to take on such an endeavor."

"Right and I appreciate that their skills aren't being wasted. I mean, driving is tough work and delivering food and medical supplies is absolutely vital to our economy and the welfare of the people of our country, but to give these guys a job in which they can use their special skills as well is tremendous. There are many military veterans who struggle to find suitable employment after serving."

"Yes, I understand and appreciate that as well."

"Jake had already been familiar with PACT - Ottawa, Persons Against the Crime of Trafficking in Humans, since he is originally from Canada, so he was able to offer some valuable experience. He had been running in and out of Canada and Alaska for years and also has a fishing cabin up in the Yukon Territory."

"Cheynne smiled. "He must have some amazing stories."

"Oh, you bet. He used to unload and park his rig for a week or two to either hunt or fish depending on the season. He had just come back from one of his Alaskan trips when I met him at the TAT event. He has an extended cab, longer than mine, with a larger refrigerator/freezer. He pulled out a large box of Dungeness crab, salmon and halibut and told me to take as much as I wanted. I knew right then that we'd get along just fine. Speaking of more exciting events, I'm bringing everyone in between Christmas and the new year for a week of entertainment, rest and relaxation at my mountain cabin. It's our bi-annual event, so you'll get to know everyone, that is, if you can come." I have always liked planning special events for my drivers to help promote some kind of healthy activity to balance their lives with the intense work that the team is involved in on a daily basis.

"Oh, nice. That sounds invigorating. I really like Colorado and I plan to move here on a permanent basis. Most of the people I know from Washington have either moved away or we just lost contact. My uncle is the only relative living in the U.S., but I don't care for Georgia. It's too hot and humid."

"I agree. I prefer a drier, cooler climate and I can't even imagine not living in the majestic Rocky Mountains. When I'm home in Evergreen, I wake up to an amazing view of the surrounding mountain peaks, which takes my breath away every time. Almost every morning, I brew some delicious, strong coffee, wrap myself up in a blanket and sip my coffee out on the deck often enjoying a tangerine and cherry sunrise over the mountains. That's my daily quiet time, when I prefer not to think of anything other than how grateful I am to be living right then and there. I pray every morning for my health and well-being and that I will continue to be shown the path and journey that will lead me to Jillian. I also pray that I can be shown the way to rescue and help others in need find peaceful, safe lives. I believe that we are all here on this earth for special purposes and that it is our duty to find out what that special purpose is. I believe mine is to live with compassion for others and to find these life destroyers and take them down. That's why I'm extremely dedicated to my work and hope I am making a difference somehow. Okay, that's my sermon for the day. I don't mean to sound self-righteous and believe me, I have my not so good moments, but I keep trying."

I was hopeful that Cheynne would move to Colorado so I said, "I bet you'll love it here and I would be happy to help you find a nice home." I had a very good feeling about her and I have enjoyed being around her immensely, even though it had only been a day. I discovered myself smiling more often, feeling calmer and less anxious when I'm with her. I'd been a single man for most of my life other than a few casual relationships with women who just didn't prove to be the companions I longed for. But, Cheynne? I wondered if she could be the woman I had been waiting for. I smiled shyly, noticing Cheyenne observing me and I felt my face turning warm red.

She grinned back. "I loved hearing your sermon. I believe as well that we are all here for a special purpose. I feel so content when I am doing something to help others. What you were describing about your quiet time in the mountains makes me think of happier days to come."

20

Cheynne had just crossed the Colorado-Kansas state line. "Did I hear you say Brooke is from the northwest as well?"

"Yes. Brooke has lived in Colorado, mostly west in the mountain areas for the past fifteen years. She also lived in Alaska for a while and has some really interesting stories of her time there. For the past four years, she had been working diligently to get her son through college, until he graduated just recently. She was just about to quit driving to pursue other types of work, when I mentioned we were going to be hired for some really dedicated work as part of a task force combating sex trafficking. She is extremely disheartened by the amount of sex criminal activity in the country, as we all are, and really wants to help, so she's probably going to stay with us for a while longer, especially since Rhys has shown such an extraordinary interest in her."

"Yeah, I caught that at the terminal." She chuckled. "I have been planning on touring the Alaskan mainland within the next few years and anticipate enjoying all of the little towns and the rich history associated with each area. I'd also like to hike in Denali and fish for halibut and salmon, so I'll have to get some tips from Jake and Brooke before I go."

"Well, if you want some company, I would love to go with you. In fact, Jake and I have talked about planning a fishing trip for a couple of years. He knows where to rent cabins and boats and probably where to find the big fish." I chuckled.

"Hey, I would love that. Let's plan it. You said this Christmas holiday break is a bi-annual vacation, so let's go to Alaska this summer."

"I think that's a great idea. Just wait until Jake finds out we're serious about it. He won't stop grinning." I observed Cheynne grinning as well and wondered what she was thinking. I had been interested in learning more about her background ever since I met her. "Do you have family other than Hank?"

"Yes, in fact, I have family in the Yukon Territory, Canada. When you mentioned that Jake has a cabin there, I was thinking what a small world it is. I wonder if he knows my brother, Micco DeMarka, his wife, Sylvia and their two kids, Daisy and Skye. I have thoroughly enjoyed visiting them every year since they moved up there. They used to live in Vancouver, but Micco was fed up with the working conditions at the Vancouver Port, so he packed up and moved the family to the Yukon six years ago, which they love. Micco teaches sled dog racing and also leads fishing tours on the Yukon River in the summer. Sylvia opened her own restaurant as a chef extraordinaire, specializing in seafood and wild game cuisine and boy can she cook."

"You know, Jake is going to want to talk with you about that."

"Yes, I figured as much and I look forward to it. It would be fun to stop and visit Micco and Sylvia on the way to Alaska. You'd love them. We could always rent a Jeep one way, play around and then drop it off in Anchorage and fly back if we don't have enough time for the round-trip drive."

"I like the way you think. Most of my employees are also friends and they join me on vacation time, unless they have other family obligations and some of them bring a few family members. The more the merrier." Thinking about Cheynne's situation, I asked, "Do you miss Washington and your work there?"

"I love the Snoqualmie area, which is remarkably majestic like the Rockies are. I never grew tired of gazing at the mountain views. Severely harsh, stormy weather blows in with fury in the winter, but I loved my work. The search and rescue work was incredibly dangerous, but I learned how to carry the right equipment, wear the appropriate clothing and respect mother nature. I worked and lived basically off the grid at times for twelve years, trudging trails, pulling sleds with supplies and sometimes injured people, who thought they could climb the mountains, not as prepared as they should have been."

"That's also the case here in the Rockies. Many

people come to Colorado thinking they can hike around in the mountains without adequate clothing, water and food. They don't bother to do some research to find out what safety precautions they should take. They don't think about the daily possibility of storms, wind, lightning or injuries. Search and rescue teams are often on the trails trying to locate people who have gone missing." I chuckled. "There is a really funny read and quite an informative book by Geno Kennedy from Rollinsville, Colorado, called, *Welcome to the Mountains – Now Behave*, that I think you'll enjoy.[7] The book is filled with Geno's humorous wit in describing what happens to people who come up to the mountains without being prepared. I have a copy in the drivers lounge at the terminal and I give a copy to everyone who visits my cabin."

"I saw that book on the coffee table when we toured the terminal. I flipped through a few pages. You're right, it's super funny."

I felt relaxed and grateful to find myself in good humor. I chuckled, "So tell me more about the Snoqualmie area and your family."

Cheynne thought about her family often. She missed her parents and wished they were still around. "I was born in Snoqualmie Valley and lived there for most of my younger life. My parents passed away in an avalanche years ago while running their sled dogs. They were hauling food and supplies from the market on Snoqualmie Valley Trail, near Lodge Lake on Snoqualmie Mountain, which is in the North Cascade Range of Washington State. Apparently, they were almost down a steep slope when an avalanche caught up with them and buried them." Cheynne frowned and her eyes welled up. "They were found in the early evening when a team from the forestry division, who were scoping out the avalanche damage noticed three of the sled dogs frantically digging in the snow. The three dogs were rescued, but my parents and the other dogs didn't survive."

"Oh, I'm sorry. That's devastating. I can't even imagine how I would feel if that happened to my folks. I've driven through the Valley and over Snoqualmie Pass many times. It's quite beautiful, but in the winter as you mentioned, it's quite treacherous and I have seen the aftermath of some horrific, fatal truck crashes on that pass. Well, I'm sure you really miss your folks."

"Yes. That's also the main reason I had an interest in working in search and rescue, but I had to force myself to move on. In the past couple of years, I had been feeling that was time for a new journey. I haven't experienced much of the rest of the country, so I really look forward to our work and seeing the beautiful areas outside of the northwest. A year ago, I noticed an ad in the paper for truck driving training, signed up and after a month out with a trainer, I was ready to drive solo. I've done alright, although when I met you, and Uncle Hank reviewed your upcoming operation with me, I was not only intrigued but excited to jump on board. And the country is as beautiful as I'd hoped. It's over populated in some areas especially in the east, so I have chosen Colorado."

"Well, I'm truly delighted that Hank put you in touch with me. I was concerned that I would never see you again." I felt myself smile flirtatiously.

I noticed her face turn crimson. "I love my uncle. He has always looked after me and he thought we would work well together and you know, I believe he was right."

"I agree." My cell phone rang and I noticed Brooke's name pop up on the screen. "Hey, what's up?"

"We've been thinking of you. Cheynne seems like a real darling and I think she's sweet on you." Brooke, as well as my other employees have been hoping that I would find someone special for quite a while now. She often teases me all in good fun, but hopeful for me.

"Oh, you think so, huh? Did you call just to harass me?" We both chuckled. My drivers often call to chat, especially during long hauls.

"No, actually, Blake just talked with Jake. I guess he's onto something that is becoming more urgent."

"Okay, thanks. I'll call him." I laughed again.

Cheynne asked, "What's so funny?"

"Oh, just Brooke. I really like that woman. She's the mother hen, always concerned for all of us." I thought about her situation and hoped she would stay on. Brooke is important to me and my team, because she has a compassionate, caring nature and promotes a lively, confident cohesiveness for the team.

I called Jake. "Hey, what's going on?"

He answered excitedly, "I just received the strangest call from a mysterious woman and I don't know who she is, but her voice sounded familiar. She said to follow the trucks and that they were going to hit another casino in Savannah. I guess Hank and Dirk are right, but how did she know? Weird. She also confirmed that Sauer is dirty. She said that she took a picture of Sauer getting paid off when the traffickers disembarked the river boat with the women. I hope she's planning on turning that over to Dirk. It's about time for that idiot to get what's coming to him. Anyway, the woman hung up before I could ask who she was. She called right after I left the river boat casino, as if she was surveilling us and obviously, she knows who we are. Does Dirk have an agent tracking these guys?"

"I don't know, maybe so. I'll call him and will find out if he knows who she is and get back to you. Where are you now?"

Jake said he was tailing the two vehicles, heading toward I-95. "We're almost to Florence. I wonder if they will be heading south to Savannah like the caller said. I want to keep tracking them."

"Okay, good. We're headed toward you, so maybe we'll meet up, if they stay for a few days down there. With any luck, we'll be able to find out who they work for. I'll call you back."

I called Hank, gave him an update and asked him if he had a woman working down there on his team or if he knew of any woman working for Dirk who was given Jake's cell number. Hank said, "No, I don't. Did she identify herself?"

"No. She informed Jake that the perps were headed to a casino in Savannah, but then hung up. Hank, I'm going to call Dirk. I'll let you know what he says."

Dirk answered immediately as if he was expecting the call. "Dirk here."

"This is Dakota. Do you have a minute?"

"Yeah, sure and just so you know, I have a few men on the way to intercept Jake, possibly within the hour."

"I just spoke with him. He said he received a call from some woman who seemed to know about the two vehicles from the riverboat. Do you have someone stationed down there?"

Dirk said, "No, did she give a name?"

"No." I reviewed the conversation I had with Jake and mentioned that she snapped a photo of Sauer getting paid off.

"Hmmm. I think it might be the same woman who calls in every now and then, always from a different location and always from a non-traceable phone. It's a mystery. She calls in providing information about traffickers and has always been right, but I have no idea who she is. At first, I thought she might just be some bystander who happened to see something strange going on and called to report it, but she calls in several times a month. My fear is that she is a vigilante sort which could be a nightmare, but I haven't heard of any situation that has gone awry involving her."

"Wow, that is mysterious. Jake says the two vehicles are near Florence and wonders if they are headed down I-95 to the casinos in Savannah like the woman suggested. I have him tailing them until you tell me otherwise."

"That's good. You know, we've been after Hans Sauer for years and haven't been able to nail him, but if the woman sends me that photo, we just might finally be able to take him down. Let me know if Jake receives another call from the woman."

"Will do." I called Jake back and re-counted Dirk's information about the woman who calls him and to let him know that help is on the way.

"I hope she does keep in touch, but I wonder how she got my cell number?"

"Yeah, that's odd, but she must be tracking sex offenders as well, so that's advantageous. Let me know when Dirk's agents catch up with you and keep me updated." I sat still, contemplating, sensing that Jake could find himself smack in the middle of a dangerous situation and I felt anxious, since I couldn't be there to help. I would remain in close contact with him.

21

Sarah

I am Sarah Beaulieu, a resourceful woman in my fifties, who will stop at nothing in order to guarantee that sex criminals receive the punishment they deserve. I have been tracking sex traffickers ever since my best friend, Grace Nadeau, mysteriously disappeared and have been searching for her ever since that fateful night in the dance club. Grace, Jake and I were close friends in high school in Edmonton, Alberta Canada. We were three peas in a pod, usually accompanying each other everywhere. We enjoyed some exceptionally memorable experiences together in northwestern Canada.

Jake and I unfortunately lost contact, so I had also been searching for him for many years, when I finally discovered that he was working with Dakota Hunt

Trucking. I discovered Dakota's company at a TAT convention, did some research and was thrilled to learn that Jake was listed as an employee. I decided to track Jake and the team, perceiving that we could help each other with the trafficking work. I am quite savvy with computer research, although I work with a highly skilled computer genius, Trevor O'Casey, who helps me find information quickly and efficiently. Trevor was able to locate Jake's cell phone number and also found out through a source of his, that Dakota's trucking team had recently begun working with FBI agent, Dirk Hays, on a special task force.

I have mastered the art of disguise, which I cleverly utilize to inconspicuously spy on sex criminals. My mission in life is to take down every sex trafficker I can manage and every nasty, twisted John who buys child sex videos or photos online. I am relentless and will stop at nothing, even if I have to do something illegal to take them out, which I often do. For the past five years, I have been tracking what I call 'The Casino Coterie' and have managed to get close enough to the owners, to spy on their behaviors and activities. Recently, after days of planning and careful preparation, I creatively disguised myself and rescued some naïve young women, who found themselves entangled in a corrupt casino manager's devious sticky web. The despicable criminal was immediately arrested and charged with sex trafficking and child pornography.

I have been able to work in my preferred profession, because I am luckily financially independent after inheriting a large sum of money when my parents passed on, sadly, one after the other when I was in my teens. Not having any family left nor any attachments to a specific place, I choose to live on the road in my RV to be ready to go at a moment's notice.

I have been working in Washington State for the past few weeks, although lately, adverse winter weather conditions have been making road travel difficult, so I have decided to head toward the southeastern states. Trevor and I had been gathering information on current trafficking activity in the east, when he discovered some information about a group of handlers that were moving women on and off the river boat casinos in South Carolina. I smiled slyly, as I began to organize my next mission, which will be to swiftly and cunningly terminate the criminal operation. I began to formulate a clever plan while driving through the country, although in order to pull it off successfully and safely, I realized I would need the assistance of a few others and thought of Jake.

My RV is completely decked-out with everything I could possibly need for work and comfort. Before leaving, I studied my project board, which is one large section of wall, covered with maps, showing my planned routes, areas that I will be thoroughly scouting around in and lately, the current locations and routes of Dakota's drivers, which Trevor continuously monitors. I also reviewed the names and photos of sex criminals as well as names of missing young women, which unfortunately and to my dismay, are numerous. I have lists and pinned locations of every X-rated store, adult club and casino in the country, which I reviewed, highlighting the ones in the southeastern states.

I organized all of my equipment including listening devices, computers, cameras, binoculars and tracking equipment, then connected with Trevor who helped me download the computer programs I would need to set up surveillance and online searches without being tracked by the Feds. I had already been assisting Dirk Hays covertly, by calling in anonymous tips with the locations and activity of sex criminals that I wanted nothing to do with.

It took three and a half days to get from southeast Washington to my first planned casino stop on the coast of South Carolina. I parked my RV in the lot at the riverboat casino where Trevor had tracked a group of suspicious men reported to be in the company of twelve women. I quickly disguised myself as an elderly woman, packed a suitcase and ambled to the front desk in the casino where I purchased a state room ticket. After settling in, I closed my eyes and inhaled deeply in order to focus on the devious, risky scheme that I had ingeniously concocted, feeling fairly confident that I could carry out my plan flawlessly.

I pocketed a tracking device and sauntered down to the casino deck, where I pretended to be interested in gambling. I scouted around the room for my main target, who I quickly noticed among a sizable group gathered around a craps table. He was a large man, wearing a gray Fedora style hat, standing in between a sizable group of young women who were dressed quite suggestively. The women did not appear to be enjoying themselves and I observed several frightened faces. I detected one woman in particular, a young Asian woman, whose eyes darted around the room, frantically searching for someone to notice her. I did, though discreetly. I then observed Fedora speaking quietly to some of the women, who began mingling among the players. I noticed two women walking toward the upper stateroom deck with intoxicated, obnoxious men. I wanted so badly to intervene, but I couldn't blow my cover. I sighed and whispered to myself, "All in good time."

I worked my way toward Fedora and slipped a dual listening, tracking device into his coat pocket, then carefully walked on by. "I pray you lead me to an advantageous rendezvous with your superiors, you old fool," I whispered quietly, then snickered. I sipped some white wine while observing them for a few hours, until Fedora and the remainder of the group retreated to their staterooms. The boat would be back at the dock early in the morning, so I moseyed back to my stateroom and set my alarm for six a.m. I wanted to be up way before the group was, so that there would be no chance of slipping away without my noticing.

When the boat returned to the dock, I detected Sergeant Hans Sauer standing at the ramp. I hastily pulled out my camera and began filming just as Fedora handed Sauer a small, gray bag, about the size of a stack of bills, I figured. I thought that even if the bag wasn't enough proof that Sauer was receiving a payoff, proof of his guilt would be evident just by meeting with the thugs when they disembark with the girls.

I furtively followed the group down the ramp, while observing the men as they escorted twelve women toward an SUV that had just pulled up behind a small commercial truck. I scrutinized the scene, hoping to find other people working in positions of authority. I saw none, then suddenly to my surprise, I noticed a semi-tractor trailer with a familiar logo parked across the street from the boat docks. I felt my eyes widen, momentarily shocked as I peered through my camera and zoomed in close. "My God, it's Jake," I whispered. "It must be." I couldn't make out the company name since the trailer was positioned at an angle to my line of sight, although I was very familiar with the enormous raven logo painted on the sides of the trailer. "It's definitely him," I chuckled, "and he hasn't changed a bit. He's still devilishly handsome with wavy brown hair and warm, melty mocha eyes." Then I noticed that he was watching the group as well.

I whirled around, noticing swift movement from the corner of my eye and set my camera to video and began filming. One of the girls suddenly bolted. "Go, go! Damn!" I watched as Fedora caught up with her and slapped her viciously across her face. "You bastard, you lose because you're on film." As they were walking briskly back toward the truck, I glanced toward Jake, realizing that he had witnessed the incident as well. "Whoa, he's getting out of the truck. No, Jake." I continued to monitor him when he suddenly stopped and stood by his truck, inconspicuously observing. Fedora shoved the girl toward the others and quickly herded them into the vehicles. I dashed to my RV and waited until all of the women were in the trucks, then decided to call Jake. I watched as he climbed into his truck and began following Fedora's group.

I desperately wanted to reconnect with Jake to get to know each other again and most of all, I wanted to tell Jake about my work. Even though I was certain he would keep my presence and work a secret, I was afraid he might inadvertently blow my cover. "Not yet. I just can't take any chances." I wasn't sure that I ever wanted him to know about the illegal, risky, daring things that I sometimes have to do when dealing with criminals. I don't attempt to take the perverts down myself, but I have some very crafty ideas that I keep in a tidy bundle under my hat.

As I followed Jake's truck, I summoned the courage to call him, but I would do so anonymously. I figured out how he could help me on this mission and considered that if all goes well, we could continue working together on future pursuits. When I was at the casino, Fedora was conversing with one of his cohorts and I overheard I their plan, so I breathed in deeply and dialed Jake's number. When Jake answered, I said, "Follow the trucks. They are headed to the casino in Savannah. Hans Sauer is dirty and I have proof." He asked who was calling, but I quickly hung up, not wanting to stay on the line too long.

I planned on staying behind Jake's truck at an inconspicuous distance for as long as possible . Since I put the tracker in Fedora's pocket, I could keep tabs on him and if the vehicles turned down roads that Jake wasn't allowed to traverse due to semi restrictions, I'd be able to get him back on track.

I have always felt like a feral cat, hunting my prey, when I'm on to a sex criminal. It's my game, but I find it really frustrating that the authorities often take too long to arrive at the scene. The FBI wants to track the syndicates for lengthy periods of time in order to find the main organizers and as many key people as possible which is understandable, but I have to save the victims immediately. Of course, the despicable criminals must be arrested and punished accordingly, so Trevor and I always supply the FBI with all of the information we discover.

As I followed Jake, I felt a chill rush up my spine as I thought about the enormous amount of trafficking currently occurring in the southeastern states, particularly in Georgia. I recognized irrefutably, that there would be a considerable amount of work for me there in the near future.

Operation Safe Haven

"Federal Authorities arrested 29 people across eight states Thursday on sex trafficking charges in a sweeping operation called Operation Safe Haven.
Five of the arrests were in Moultrie, Georgia led by US Immigration and Customs Enforcement (ICE) and Homeland Security Investigations. (Coordinates the movement of Hispanic females throughout the country) [8]

Operation Cross Country

"Nationally, 120 suspected traffickers were arrested and 84 minors were recovered in Operation Cross Country."
Included is a report where 60 people were arrested and 4 children were recovered in Georgia during an FBI led operation that focused on child sex trafficking." [9]

22

Dakota

Cheynne had just passed Salina, Kansas. With eyes at half mast, I whispered, "I'm headed back to the sleeper. Try to make it to a truck stop seventy to eighty miles east of Kansas City and I'll take over. Please answer my phone and wake me up if something urgent comes up."

"You've got it."

A couple of hours later, Mack O'Donnell, another of Dakota's drivers called. He described the situation in North Dakota, although he mentioned that there was no urgent matter and that he mainly wanted to check in with him. She was tickled by his Irish slang manner of speaking and wasn't sure she understood a few things he said, but she got the gist of what was going on. She would relay the message to Dakota after his rest.

Strong, gusty winds had been hurling icy snow across the road and ice was beginning to cake up on the windshield making it difficult to see clearly. She had the windshield defrost set to high heat, but the storm was relentless. Cheynne thought she would pull off if she wasn't able to drive out of the worst of it soon. To lesson her mounting anxiety, she decided to listen to comforting music, so she inserted an earbud and located a file of favorites including "Reelin in the Years" from Steely Dan's first album, *Can't Buy a Thrill*. She loved the jazz fusion, soft rock blend of music, finding it soothing driving music. When Cheynne finally reached a truck stop at the end of her allowed driving hours, she was exhausted from the tremendous focus.

When I felt the truck come to a stop, I ducked out from behind the sleeper curtain with my backpack. "I'm headed to the shower. I'll be back in about twenty minutes." Cheynne informed me of Mack's call. "Is everything okay?"

"Yes, he said he was just checking in."

I observed the blizzard from the window. "Whooo! You must be exhausted."

"Yes, I will probably fall asleep very soon, but I'm sure I'll still be awake when you get back, so I'll fill you in on Mack's report then."

Ice was beginning to build up on the pavement as I walked toward the truck stop building. I thought about the severe weather around the country and began to worry about my drivers as I do every winter. When I returned from my shower, I asked, "Okay, what's up with Mack?"

"Apparently, Mack and Chris have been tracking something monstrous in Williston, North Dakota. He reports that large travel vans transporting young women have been arriving in the nearby truck stops and motels in the area. Two women, at different times of the night, knocked on his door to solicit, one of them looking really young. He asked them questions like, were they alone or were they transported there with other women and where from? As well as, who was handling them? I guess they got spooked and left, but not before he asked them if he could help them get somewhere safe. The women refused and apparently just moved on to other trucks, so Mack decided to stay and scope out the scene for a while. He took some photos and notes.

"Okay, I'll give him a call." Mack answered right away. "Hey, what's going on up there? Cheynne explained the gist of it."

He gruffly exhaled audibly. "There are hundreds of oil field and fracking site workers here including fracking water haulers and oil tankers, who seem to be attracting the attention of sex traffickers and possibly drug cartels, according to some of the locals. The traffickers are acting the maggot, so we think we should hang out here for a few more days and see what we can find out. I've been scheming up a plan so that we don't handle this arseways."

"Okay, I'll let Dirk know, but keep me posted. I'll hold off on finding you a load back to Denver for now, but there is a severe winter storm heading your way from Canada, so I'd like for you to head south before it reaches you. I have a feeling that the traffickers in that area will stick around for a while and Dirk most likely has some of his investigators working up there now. I'll get back with you after I talk with him." I liked giving my drivers something fun to think about every now and then, since our work is often extremely intense. "Are you planning to come out to my cabin this year?"

"Aye. We'll have a whale of a time." He chuckled, then said, "I talked Chris into coming as well and you know what that means."

"That's terrific." I laughed heartily, foreseeing lively music and dancing along with boisterous merriment filling my home. "This will be Cheynne's first Dakota Hunt Trucking holiday. I think she'll have a blast."

"Aye, we'll have to get the lass out on the sleds."

"Call me tomorrow and let me know if you find anything out. If you witness any of the women headed toward vehicles other than trucks, take some photos and try to get the plates. Be careful and watch your back, buddy."

"No worries, pal."

They hung up and Cheynne asked, "So, tell me a bit about Mack and Chris. It will help me wind down a bit before I sleep."

"Well, to start with, Mack is a jovial, tall, brawny Irishman with copper hair and beard and stunning sapphire eyes. "He is an extremely hard-working, twenty-five year trucker veteran and one of my best friends, who I trust with my life. He really likes working on my team and feels very compassionate about helping me find Jillian. Mack has hauled everything you could think of including oil tankers, flatbeds and fracking water trucks. He is also a retired Army Officer, which makes him invaluable to our trafficking work. Our drivers with either military or police training are now licensed to carry firearms and are qualified to take more aggressive action when we come across criminals. He is from Missoula, Montana and has a lot of experience driving all over the northern states and across mountainous regions. Since he lives in Montana, I plan loads for him up there whenever he wants time off."

She snickered. "Mack's accent is quite amusing. I didn't understand a few things that he said earlier."

"You should hear Mack, Chris, Ian and Rhys conversing when they get together. I understand one out of every few words especially after they've had a couple of beers on their time off. Anyway, Mack knows the industries up north well. He also has a few investigative contacts who he reports to when he collects enough info and who are now working directly with Dirk."

"Oh, I've been curious about those types of connections."

"Mack's co-driver is Chris O'Conner, forty-six years old from Dublin, Ireland. He's what I would call a tall, strapping lad with strawberry blonde hair, hazel eyes and has a light hearted, good-humored personality. He relocated from Ireland when he was twenty-two after graduating from Trinity College in Dublin, with a degree in computer science. Chris has lived and worked in the U.S. for twenty-four years including many of those years with the Oregon police department. He's fast and efficient at searching the internet for anything and anybody. Mack has to keep an eye on Chris though, because he's a loose cannon, like Jake. He would prefer to do vigilante work, but we finally convinced him into helping our way, at least for now."

"Oh, boy, both Chris and Jake."

"Yeah, but their passions about the work motivate them to find the creeps that abduct women and are on board with our project. I'm not sure I know Chris's whole story, but he followed his ex girlfriend from Oregon to North Dakota about six years ago. I guess you could say he was stalking her, but not with mal intent. They apparently had some heated argument and split up. He observed her putting her luggage into a ford pickup with an unknown dude driving which really pissed him off, so he followed them. He must have somehow been inconspicuous, because they didn't discover him tailing them the whole way. I'm sure he installed a tracker on her phone without her knowing."

"He just happened to have equipment like that lying around?"

"Chris is really into all of the latest technology and is a computer expert, hacker genius. He doesn't discuss what he has done with that, but I'm certain that since he used to work with the police department, he isn't involved in any sort of criminal activity, although I'm not sure I ever want to know the extent of his capabilities. We run a legal service for law enforcement and it has to stay that way for obvious reasons. He's just extremely good at finding out info that isn't in the mainstream. He has some facial recognition software that we use to update Jillian's photos every year, which he posts all over the internet.

"Chris lives in the Columbia River area in Oregon, which is where they were when his ex-girlfriend got into the unknown truck. After following them for a while, she just vanished one day. Surprisingly, he lost track of her and is concerned that she may be mixed up in some sort of shady business with the guy. His worst fear is that she was taken against her will and maybe held somewhere or forced into who knows what. Anyway, he hopes he can eventually discover what happened to her, while working across country with my team." I frowned, suddenly thinking about Jillian.

Cheynne yawned audibly. "Excuse me I'm fading."

"Well, you should sleep now. I plan to make it to a truck stop in Monteagle, Tennessee. That's not far from the Georgia state line, about 615 miles, so you'll have plenty of time to sleep. We'll deliver our load in Dalton, then head toward the truck stop off I-16. We'll talk about that when you wake up. Sweet dreams." She nodded and closed the sleeper curtains.

As I was driving, I began to plan how I would renew my search for Jillian. I had been sorting out all of my old research materials lately, concerning her disappearance. I just had a feeling that a thorough new search might lead me to some kind of clue to her location, especially if it turns out that Giordano is back in the picture. I thought about her strong-willed, determined nature believing that she would fight, plan and eventually escape, even if it took forty-one years. That thought made me cringe.

23

December 19th, 2018

While driving cautiously through severe winter conditions, I thought I should check up on Jake and Zach. "No news is often good news," I whispered. A few minutes later, my cell rang.

"Hey, mate, it's Ian." Ian Mulloy is good natured, friendly, dedicated driver from Ireland, recruited to the team by Mack.

"Hey, what's up?"

"We're headed into North Carolina. Is there an update with Jake?"

"I was planning to call Jake when I noticed he was on sleeper mode with Zach behind the wheel, although the last time we spoke, he had been tailing the perps toward I-95. Dirk believes the group is part of a casino circuit ring. After you deliver your load at the distribution center, I'll have you head down toward Savannah. Blake and Brooke are headed that way as well, so Jake and Zach will have plenty of help and Hank sent two under-cover teams from Atlanta, who should be in South Carolina by now. Hey, listen to this. Jake received a call from an unknown woman, who seemed to know where the group was headed. She apparently followed the group of twelve young women and several men onto the riverboat in South Carolina and overheard their plan to head to Savannah. I'm sure she is following the group as well."

"Boyo. So, the lass might know Jake?"

"It appears so. It's a mystery at this time. Dirk has also received calls and tips from a woman, who he thinks might be the same. Her leads in the past helped Dirk locate and bring down a few significant syndicates. He's concerned that she might be a vigilante, because on one of the busts in the Seattle area, several women escaped with an unknown person, while the authorities were occupied with several dangerous criminals. Dirk thinks she may have been the one who rescued the women, because it was her tip that led us to the scene. In any case, the mysterious woman has remained elusive."

"Well, mate, keep me informed and I'll let you know when we are in South Carolina."

We ended the call and I dialed Zach. He answered on the first ring. "Hey, I picked up right away so that the call wouldn't wake Jake up. He was pretty keyed up earlier, but he finally wound down and realized that he wouldn't be much help if he didn't get some sleep."

"Where are you guys?"

"We tracked the perps to a motel and I parked on the

side of the road, close enough to see the room they checked into. Hopefully they'll rest until sunrise, but I'm afraid to fall asleep in case they move."

"Do what you can, but don't worry. If they slip away while you're resting, we'll be able to pick up their trail at a casino in Savannah, unless Dirk's agents arrive before then."

"Okay, that makes me feel better."

"Call me if you need anything. I'll be driving for the next nine or ten hours, so if I don't hear from one of you, I'll call you at sunrise."

24

Sarah

I arrived at the motel where the group stopped to rest for the night. I scoped out the scene noticing Jake's rig parked along the side of the road just beyond the motel, then immediately called Trevor. "Hey, I know it's late, but I need your help. You mentioned you have a friend who rents passenger vans in South Carolina. Can you reach him?"

"Yes. On it. I've been tracking you, so I called my friend earlier and filled him in about the group and location and asked him to be on stand-by. What else can I do?"

I thought for a few seconds. "I'll head down the road to a grocery store parking lot, where I'll need to leave my RV. Can you have him meet me at the lot in a van large enough for me and twelve women?"

"I'll call you right back." Trevor called his friend, Mike and told him what Sarah needed.

"You bet. I have a very reliable driver on duty that I can dispatch. He's also a bouncer at a nightclub, so he's physically capable if you need his help. Trevor, do I need to have him armed?"

Trevor replied instantly, "It would be a good idea, since you know a bit about Sarah and you know that whatever she has planned could go sideways."

Mike said, "This guy lives on the wild side, but he's also exceedingly cautious. He knows how to be inconspicuous, usually moving well below the radar. He's your man."

"Okay, good. Sarah will be parked in the grocery store lot in a large white RV. She'll fill him in on her plan on the way." Trevor sent Mike the location of the store, then asked, "How long do you think it will take him to get there?"

"I'll get back to you in a few minutes." Mike hung up and called Dale Savoy and gave him the scoop.

Dale said, "Hey man. No problem. I need a little excitement. What kind of backup do we have, just in case."

Mike disclosed a bit about Jake as well as the two under-cover agents who were on the way. "Sarah is a well-paying client, so do what you can, but keep me posted."

"On the way."

Mike reported back to Trevor, who said, "I owe ya big time, Mike. Thanks. I'm sending you a link that you'll need to forward to Dale. It's imperative that he clicks on the link and downloads it immediately. Once it's installed,

I'll be able to track him to coordinate with Sarah. And tell him that once he's no longer needed, he can delete the program. That will make him feel more comfortable about doing it. I have no interest in his private affairs."

"Got it." Mike sent Dale the link and discussed Trevor's tracking program with him. "Are you okay with that?"

"Yeah, no problem. I trust you." Dale downloaded the link and quickly installed the program into his cell. He instantly received a ping from Trevor with a message:

"Tracking. Good luck. Sarah is prepared for your arrival. ETA?"

Dale replied, "ETA, fifteen minutes."

Trevor called me with Dale's ETA. I thanked him, feeling tremendously grateful that we worked so well together. "Things may happen fast, so stay alert as always."

As soon as Dale arrived, I locked the RV and jumped in the van, disguised as a lovely, curly blonde with large, rose-tinted glasses, a long, sage green cape draped over dark blue jeans and high heels. As I was fastening my seat belt, I heard Dale whispering, "What the hell is she thinking? She plans to confront some thugs dressed like that? Oh, boy. This ought to be very interesting."

I snickered, introduced myself and quickly reviewed my strategy. "Of course, we may have to improvise. Things don't always work out according to my plans, but we'll figure it out." I flashed Dale a devious grin. "Here is a can of mace. Keep it handy." I opened a pouch with several syringes with just the right doses of Ketamine, which is basically an animal tranquilizer, and put them in a concealed pocket in my cape. I then placed a can of mace in the other pocket. I noticed Dale observing me with obvious astonishment. "Here's what I want you to do. When we get to the motel, park at the end of the lot, not too far from the white commercial truck, which is parked in front of a motel room. I plan to flatten the tires of two vehicles, then figure out a way to get the attention of the men detaining twelve young women. Did Trevor fill you in about the group?"

Dale said, "Four perverts are holding the women captive in the motel, right?"

I narrowed my eyes, feeling anger rising, fueling my courage. "Right, and we're going to take them down. When you see the girls run out, I need you to help them get into the van as quickly as possible. If anything goes awry, you'll see a semi-truck parked across the street with an old friend of mine on standby, who will help us if needed. As soon as the girls are safely in the van, we'll drive out of there like bats out of hell and I'll call my FBI contact responsible for the two agents who will be here soon. When we return to my RV, I'll head immediately to a safe house. My trucker friend will guard the thugs until the authorities arrive. Well, that's the plan anyway."

He said, "Wow, okay. Lady, you are one gutsy broad. Do you have a gun or something? I mean, those traffickers aren't going to allow you to just walk away with the women."

"I do, but I don't plan on using it. I'm not the killing sort. I have methods of dealing with these perverts without committing murder even though they surely deserve it. My job is to get the girls to safety, however, it's important for the authorities to be there immediately after I leave, that is, to arrest the creeps."

"After you leave?" he asked. "You mean, you don't work with the authorities?"

"No. I assist in the capture of every heinous sex criminal I possibly can, but I cannot reveal my identity. By the way, I hope I can trust you. You don't speak of the situation, you never saw me, you've never seen my RV, got it?"

"Yes, Ma'am." Dale said sincerely. "I'm here because I want to help. My lips are sealed."

"Okay, good." Sarah continued to prepare as they got closer to the motel.

25

Zach was starting to drift off when he saw a van pull up and park next to the motel. Earlier, he and Jake had observed the group of men and women entering two motel rooms. They ingeniously let the air out of the tires and wiped the smeared mud off of the plates. Jake took photos and sent them and the location of the motel to Dakota who forwarded the information to Dirk.

A moment later, a woman got out of the van and briskly walked toward the truck and SUV. She stood transfixed for a few seconds, noticing the flattened tires, then turned and glanced at Jake's truck. "Well, aren't you clever." She whispered to herself.

Zach wondered if she saw him. "Jake, wake up.

Something is going down." Zach opened the sleeper curtains to make sure Jake heard him. He did and was on his feet in a split second. He peered out of the window and observed the woman heading toward one of the motel rooms where two of the men detained six women. He hastily put on his shoes and jumped into the passenger seat.

"Did she get out of that van?" Jake pointed.

"Yes, and there is a man in the driver's seat. She is either working with the perps or the authorities and if the latter, it looks as if she is going to confront the bastards alone. She must be half out of her mind and did you notice her clothing? I wonder if that's the woman who called you."

Jake observed, curiously. "You might be right. Roll down the windows so that we can hear what's being said." Jake was prepared to assist her immediately if needed. "Call Dakota and tell him what's going down. I think we need Dirk's men here now." They watched the woman knock on the red motel door. The enormous man who Jake and Zach observed with Fedora earlier darkened the doorstep like a massive shadow, ominously hovering over the woman.

He gruffly asked what she wanted. She pointed to the tires and lured him over to look at them.

Jake said, "Oh, shit! She just sprayed him with something. Maybe pepper spray? What? Holy bejeesy! She just injected him with something." Jake and Zach watched the large man fall to the ground, landing with a thunderous thud. "She's going up to the door again."

They heard her say in a shrill, southern voice, "Hey, I was checking into my motel room and I noticed that man there on the ground. It looks like he's having some kind of attack. Do you know him?" They continued observing the scene as the sinister man shoved abruptly passed her to see what the problem was. As soon as he knelt down beside the man, the woman injected him with another syringe. He glared up at her, trying desperately to grab her, but he seemed to be paralyzed and fell limply on top of the man on the ground. Then the woman shoved open the door and told the girls to get out, quickly and quietly and run toward the van. The driver opened the doors and assisted the girls into the van.

Jake jumped out of the truck and bolted toward the motel room. The woman whispered, "Go hide by the stairwell. I have to help the others and I need you to prevent the man in the hotel room from running if he tries to."

He did what she said, observing the woman with incredulity and admiration. He thought, who in the hell is this nutcase? She's obviously half out of her mind. But he was just as pumped up as she was to help the women escape and get to safety. He watched as she approach the second door. Jake figured she must have seen them arrive earlier since she knew what rooms they were in.

A disheveled, burly looking man came to the door and bellowed, "Yeah, what do you want?"

Another man stood behind him staring at the woman, then said insolently with a devilish grin, "Oh, look what we have here. A knockout broad here to join our little party." The two men laughed and started to grab her, but she swiftly maneuvered away from them and sprayed them both with pepper spray. The men shrieked, blindly swinging their arms as they both awkwardly approached her. She kicked one of the men in the crotch and sprayed them both a second time. Jake punched the second man in his gut several times, while the woman pulled out a syringe and quickly injected it into his arm while he fell to his knees. He glared at her then suddenly dropped like a rock. The second man was still fighting with Jake. Dale sprinted to help him take the thug down, while the woman quickly escorted the rest of the girls to the van.

Zach helped Jake and Dale wrestle the thug, who was proving to be a fiercely, challenging adversary. After a mighty blow to his head, the man fell backward into the motel room and tried to grab for his gun, which was on the table by the door. Jake noticed the man was the one wearing a Fedora, who hit the young woman the previous day and who seemed to be in charge of the group. He elbowed him in the face while Zach swiped the gun off the table with his leg and then kicked the bastard in the gut. As he fell to the floor, the woman tased him, then she injected him as well. He slowly stopped moving, paralyzed, while his infuriated eyes glared malevolently into her own.

The woman turned toward Jake, pointing to one of the men. "Hurry, drag that one over there and tie him up with the other two. Then help me get this idiot into the back of the van. He's coming with me. Please stay with the other three until the Feds arrive. They should be here shortly. You can tell them that I took one of the bastards with me, because I need some information from him. I will drop him off at the police department in Atlanta when I'm done with him. And Jake, thanks for your help." She smiled widely. "You should wipe your prints off of that gun and lay it next to one of the bastards."

Jake stood frozen in his stance, staring after her, amazed and puzzled that she knew his name. Sarah entered the hotel rooms to search for passports and anything else the girls might need. She noticed a bag on the table containing twelve passports, keys and another gun. She grabbed the passport bag and a suitcase with women's clothing and quickly exited the room. She tossed the gun next to the paralyzed men on the ground, then removed their wallets and snapped photos of their drivers' licenses. She then threw the wallets on the ground and sprinted toward the van.

Jake called after her, "Wait, who are you?" The van speedily disappeared into the night, leaving Jake entirely awe-stricken. "Damn!" Jake yelled. "Zach, get Dakota on the line. Tell him we need help asap. He sprinted to his truck and pulled out some rope from his outside hold compartment. As he was tying up the men, the authorities finally arrived, lights flashing and sirens blaring. People were coming out of the motel rooms to see what was going on. Jake said under his breath, "Jeez-em-crow! I thought Dirk was sending undercover agents." One of the men on the ground was staring up at him, but couldn't move. "Ah." Jake whispered. "She injected them with a tranquilizer."

The agents jogged toward Jake to help him with the criminals. Jake recounted the details of the scene including the actions of the mysterious woman. He informed them that she had injected them with some kind of tranquilizer. He said with amazement, "She was able to get all twelve of the women into the van along with one of the perps and drove off with them."

"I'm sure she didn't mention her name or where she was going, right?"

"No. I asked her but she bolted to the van and they sped off. She's an eccentric, gutsy woman, I can assure you."

"Did you get a look at the van and the plates?"

"White passenger van with tinted windows and the plate was FLZ-4 something." I took photos of the perps, their vehicles and the plates." He showed his cell phone to the agent. I already sent them to Dirk Hays. I was also able to get some good shots of the men shoving the women into the motel rooms, so hopefully that'll be enough proof that the men are traffickers. I also have photos of the group as they disembarked a riverboat in Myrtle Beach."

One of the agents trotted toward an approaching police car and spoke to the driver anxiously. "There is a white van headed south with a woman, a male driver and twelve victims, who were just rescued. The woman seems to be responsible for the rescue, however, she also absconded with one of the perps." He gave him the partial plate and description of the car. "Go!"

Zach showed his phone to the agent. "I also snapped as many photos of the scene as I could until Jake needed help.

The agent scrolled through the photos. "Oh, this is good. You were able to capture a video of the fight, the women running out of the rooms and our mystery woman. Both of you, send those photos to Dirk and to my cell." He gave Jake and Zach his number.

Jake called Dakota, quickly recapping the significant details. "We're both exhausted, but we want to get out of here, just in case whoever those men are working for have other goons in the area."

"I agree and I hope none of the men arrested noticed your truck and trailer. You're not too far from Atlanta, so head west on I-20 and shut down once you are across the Georgia state line. Get some rest and call me in the morning."

Dakota called Dirk. "I'm sure you've been informed of the situation with Jake."

"Yes. Reports have been flooding in by my men and the South Carolina local P.D. I would like for Jake and Zach to write down every detail they can possibly recall as soon as they have a chance. I'm driving down there to interrogate the perps in the morning. But, Dakota, damn. That infuriating woman took off with all of the victims. I need proof that the men had the twelve women in captivity. I have the photos, videos and testimonies of everyone involved with the case, but no victims. I hope she calls in."

"I know. I was thinking about that as well. She is probably afraid that you and other sectors of the government will force all of the women to return to their homes including the ones who are from other countries. Dirk, you are well aware that some of the women fled their countries or even homes in the U.S. because of unsafe or abusive conditions. They are the victims and should be helped with compassion. There are so many divisions in the fight to combat sex trafficking, but which ones actually help the victims once they are rescued? Don't get me wrong, I don't agree with the methods of this vigilante woman, but it seems that her main objective is to rescue the women and make sure they are safe from these predators. She also mentioned that she plans to drop the perp off at the Atlanta P.D., downtown precinct when she's done with him."

"What we need is for her to at least send in a recording of all of the girls' testimonies and their identities for the record. I have an APB out on the van that they drove off in. Hopefully, we can figure out who this woman is and where she has taken the victims. And Dakota, you know we have victim protection divisions set up to help the women. We also hope that some of them can help us identify their captors, even though most of them will not talk because they're afraid of retribution." Dirk was receiving another call. "Hey, Dakota, hold on." He clicked over to the other call. "Yes, Dirk here. You what? Who? Wait, help me out here. Please, give me your name. We are on the same team, so work with me. You're sending it to…. Wait, damn it!" The caller hung up. He reconnected with Dakota. "Guess who just called?"

"Our mystery woman."

"Yep. I'm happy to say that at least she understands the process and get this, she said she knows who the men we arrested were working for. She definitely intends on giving us the information we need to prosecute them. To my surprise, she also sent me photos and a video of our friend, Hans Sauer in the company of the perps. I'm delighted to say that his police career as well as his lucrative little side endeavor is all over."

"That's good news. Jake has been at his wits end dealing with Sauer. He has believed for years that Sauer was a dirty cop. What a son of a bitch. I wonder how many young women have been abducted, tortured and abused because of that perverse idiot."

"Yeah, one more idiot behind bars, where he'll quickly discover the meaning of retribution. The woman said she is sending me a package within the next 24 hours and expects us to detain the bastards until I get it. I mean, I will, of course, but without solid proof, there is only so long that I can hold them and I guarantee, they are flight risks."

"Well, hell, Dirk. Even if they lawyer up, you have enough proof to detain them for at least a few days. Have faith. I have a feeling she will give you everything you need. She obviously wants to make sure these perverts are off the streets.

"Dakota, I can't thank you and your team enough for your help. It's encouraging to have you on board and you're right. I'll check out the package before I jump to any more conclusions. Have a thorough talk with Jake. Maybe he'll recall something about the woman that will help us locate her. I'll talk with you tomorrow."

26

Dale hastily drove the van toward the grocery store parking lot managing to avoid being detected by the authorities, who they figured may have been trying to locate them. Sarah said, "When we get back to the store lot, help me get the girls and the pervert into the RV, then you take off immediately. Park that van inside a garage or somewhere out of sight, maybe remove the plate and don't drive it for a while. In fact, you might want to report it stolen."

Dale flashed a confident smile and said, "I've got that covered. Before I left, I took the registered plate off and replaced it with an old one that was lying around for years. I'll have the van painted when I return to the garage."

"Well now, aren't you smart? We should definitely keep in touch. I might need some help here again sometime." Sarah handed him an envelope, thick with cash.

He nodded, "Thank you, Ma'am. You know how to reach me." Dale pulled into the grocery store lot and helped Sarah get Fedora and the girls safely into the RV, then Sarah sped off immediately. As she drove, she addressed the girls, "Don't be afraid, I'm your friend and I'm going to help you get to safety. Do any of you speak English?"

One of the girls replied, "Yes, Ma'am, I do. My name is Anna. I'm from Columbia."

Sarah could speak a little Spanish and French fluently, but the girls appeared to be from various countries and she wanted to be certain that they understood what was going on. "Anna, would you please speak with all of the girls and find out who can understand either English or Spanish?"

"Yes, Ma'am." Anna discovered that there were seven girls who spoke Spanish, two U.S. Americans who spoke English and three from the Philippines. "Jasmine understands some English and can translate to the other two girls from the Philippines."

"Perfect. Anna and Jasmine, tell the girls that we are going to a safe house to stay for the night. We will get to know each other in the morning and will figure out how to get you all back home safely then."

Jasmine relayed the information, listened to their responses, then said, "Sarah, the other two girls from the Philippines don't want to go home. They said they have made a long journey on a fishing boat and were promised good jobs here in the U.S. The condition of their homes is not good and they are afraid to return after such a long journey." Sarah observed Jasmine searching her eyes for compassion. "I don't want to go home either. The men who you found us with promised us work but obviously, they were not good men. They lied and forced us to do unspeakable things. For five weeks, we have been taken to different casinos, hotels and brothels. They abused us, sometimes severely and they told us if we didn't do what they said, we would be killed and dumped into the ocean to be eaten by sharks."

Sarah gazed at her, empathetically. "Jasmine, you are the one I saw, who tried to get away at the riverboat aren't you?"

"Yes, it was crowded so I thought I could get away, but I tripped and the man wearing the hat grabbed me and slapped me very hard."

"I saw that. You are a brave girl. We will get that bruise checked out at a clinic that I work with. Tell the girls that I will be talking with each one of you and together we will figure out what to do."

Sarah always had a plan. She has helped many girls find safe places to go both in the U.S. and in Canada. On three occasions, she was able to get a few young women back to Central America to their families, but would only take them home if their home life was safe. Many girls find themselves involved in risky situations in the U.S., as well as in other countries, so they either try to buy their way into the U.S for refuge or they may be fleeing from disturbing situations in their homes and end up getting kidnapped.

Sarah has also helped young women many times who

were working as prostitutes, who wanted to get out of the business and into better lives. Some women worked as prostitutes only because they felt they had no other option. Some had served time in prison for petty crimes and found that they could find no work when they were released, so they turned to prostitution. But most of the girls and young women that Sarah helped were abducted and trafficked.

She felt elated that she was able to discover who the men they captured were working for. She had overheard Fedora talking with someone named Giordano on the phone, while on the riverboat. She suddenly recalled previously doing research on a criminal named Ray Giordano years ago, so she called Trevor to find out if he could be the same man. While he searched through the files, Sarah decided to take Fedora with her and would force him to talk, one way or another.

She figured it was time to get even. She had also sent the photos of the men and their IDs to Trevor earlier and was waiting for feedback. He called her back quicker than she had anticipated. "Trevor, did you receive the photos and did you discover any recent activity or information concerning Giordano?"

"I have my database running now. I'll let you know the minute I discover something."

"Thanks, Trevor. I also need for you to prepare a package with the photos, IDs and every bit of info you can find about the criminals and any possible connections. I will be dropping off the package at the Atlanta P.D. along with Fedora when I'm through with him. I am now sending you copies of some of the girls' passports, although I withheld the passports of the girls who don't wish to return home. When we have enough evidence to convict the perverts, send it to Dirk Hays. I will be recording the testimonies of the women and will send that to you to include in the package."

"Got it."

Next, Sarah called a Rabbi friend, who serves as a middle man in locating safe homes for young women who don't want to or can't go home. A woman answered. "Rabbi Ike Ezekiel's office. How can I help you?"

"My name is Sarah and I would like to speak with Rabbi Ezekiel, please." The woman put her on hold.

Ike Ezekiel serves God at the Temple of Faith and Refuge. He was one of only twenty-eight Jewish refugees who were allowed to disembark the infamous M.S. St. Louis in Cuba in June of 1939. During World War II, the MotorSchiff St. Louis was a German ocean liner known for carrying more than 900 Jewish refugees from Nazi Germany, who intended to escape the Holocaust to disembark in Cuba. They were denied permission to land by the Cuban government headed by President Federico Laredo Bru. The passengers purchased Cuban visas in Germany and all but twenty-eight were revoked. The refugees had to await their turns to qualify for and obtain immigration visas before they were admissible to the U.S. Ike and his family were a few of the lucky ones, who had been able to obtain U.S. visas.[10]

Captain Schroder headed for the coast of Florida only to be denied entry by Roosevelt, advised by Cordell Hull, the Secretary of State at the time. The U.S. Coast Guard surrounded the ship making sure no one escaped. The St. Louis was denied entry into the U.S. and Canada as well and forced to return to Europe. Not all of the refugees were taken in when the ship returned. Some passengers managed to get visas to countries like Holland, France, Great Britain and Belgium, but many were forced back home to Nazi occupied territories. Many died in transit and many others were sent to death camps where they were ultimately killed during the war. As Sarah recalled the hideous story, she cringed while considering how many tragic, cruel, egotistical, decisions had been made throughout history causing the catastrophic suffering of millions of innocent people. In 2012, the United States Department of State formally apologized to the survivors of the ship, but it was too late for so many hopeful people.[11]

Ike Ezekiel and his family as well as Leon Joel, the great uncle of singer songwriter, Billy Joel and 24 others, settled in the U.S. Sarah loved Billy Joel's music and felt grateful that his uncle had been accepted into the states as a refugee. Ike had been so grateful that for over seventy years, he has helped anyone arriving at his door hoping for refuge. He is now a very old man, but she prayed that he lives on for many more years.

After several minutes, Ike finally picked up the line, "Sarah, how are you?"

"Zeke, I'm fine. Do you have a moment?"

"For you? Anytime. How can I help you?"

"Well, I just helped twelve young women escape from a perilous situation and I need a few places for them to stay. I'm taking them to House of Flowers for the night, while I sort out what needs to be done." Ike and Sarah have several homes which are inconspicuous safe houses, covertly named and strategically located around the country. House of Flowers is near Charlotte, North

Carolina, about 150 miles from her current location. "I may know who is behind this trafficking faction. Trevor is checking into it now. If I'm right, we are going to bring down a dangerous, pompous, fat cat."

"Sarah, please be careful. I worry about your involvement with dangerous criminals."

"I know you do, but I will be working with a team of professionals who will be handling most of the dangerous work."

"Okay." Zeke hesitated, "I have a new confidant who has been taking in women in need. I want you to meet her. She is not Jewish, but neither are you." He chuckled. "Her name is Reverend Angelina Lavoie. She is connected with St. Faith's Anglican Church in Vancouver, B.C. Her affiliate motto is 'Compassionate Support Advocacy and Referral Services for people in need or crisis.' I have a feeling that she will be an invaluable friend, source, partner, etc. You will have to travel a bit further to get your girls there, but I think you will find it worth your while."

Sarah pondered his words. "How did you find out about Reverend Lavoie?"

"Through my network. You're not the only one who has secrets. Sarah, I am getting old. I have been searching for new confidants for you to connect with in case I should have to retire this old body to be with God."

She didn't like hearing Zeke talk that way, but she understood and was happy that he was thinking of her and the work she engages in to help women in peril. She wrote the information and address down and would call Trevor to have him verify the location of St. Faith's Anglican Church. Even though she was intrigued and felt hopeful about the prospect of having a new source, her eyes welled up and she swallowed hard. "Who will help me with our current safe houses in case you move on to higher places?"

"I'm working on that. I believe I have encountered a young man whom I can trust, a new devotee to the Temple and to our cause. He came to me hoping to work specifically with people in need. I will let you know more about him after I work with him a while longer. You go ahead and get your girls to safety and call me back to let me know what you think."

Sarah reluctantly ended the call with Zeke, then called Trevor, giving him the details and address. "Call me back as soon as you can. I'll be at House of Flowers. Do you have any information about the men yet?"

"Yes, I was just about to ring you. The guy with the Fedora is Lorenzo Russo, the boss man under Andrea Marino. I found that connection because Russo was arrested with no conviction due to lack of evidence for kidnapping and sexual assault in 2017. Andrea Marino sent his lawyers to get him out of it. I discovered something about one of the other thugs, Matteo Costa, who also has a connection to Marino. It seems that Marino is in business with a guy named Ray Giordano, an old guy, with a few convictions and a small amount of jail time. He was always released instantly, most likely by a few corrupt lawyers and judges, conveniently lining their dirty pockets. Giordano may have been involved with the disappearance of some young women in 1994 and again in 2004 and another slippery, short jail stint way back in 1977, but nothing was proven. He was released, then he disappeared for eighteen years."

"Yes, thanks Trev. Keep working on it. Find out

where Giordano's and Marino's last known locations were and any connections to other businesses, nightclubs, casinos and so on. Drop everything in my computer folder and I'll let you know when we have enough to send to Dirk." She instantly thought of Dakota Hunt and recalled discovering that his twin sister had been abducted about forty years ago and that the poor, disheartened man has continued to search for her ever since. It seemed likely that Ray Giordano was the criminal responsible for her disappearance, since he had been accused of being involved in the trafficking of minors from Colorado and Utah at that time.

"Uh, Sarah? What are you going to do with Fedora? You need to get him out of there."

"I'm taking him to Gray Hall. He will talk or he won't be a very happy man." Gray Hall was an old condemned warehouse in South Carolina that Trevor and Sarah had set up to interrogate perverts like Fedora.

"Sarah, you can't do the interrogation yourself. It's too dangerous. I'm sending Jimmy."

"Okay. I really hate that kind of work and I still have a lot of work to do to take care of the girls. I'll call you when we get there. I also promised Dirk that I would drop him off at the Atlanta P.D., so when we are done with him, Jimmy must make a plan to get him there."

Sarah ended the call, then dialed Dirk's cell. As soon as he answered, she quickly spewed out that the group of men arrested in South Carolina work for Ray Giordano and Andrea Marino and that she would make sure he had all of the evidence needed to take them down. He tried to get her to identify herself and pleaded with her to work with him, but she hastily ended the call.

As soon as she hung up with Dirk, Trevor called back. "Your pal, Andrea Marino, hangs out at the Wild Cat Casino just across the state line in Oklahoma. I discovered that he is the owner and a major shareholder and Ray Giordano runs one of the nightclubs in the casino."

"Trevor, how could I ever manage without you? Hugs." She hung up and immediately rang Jake.

"Hey, who's calling me so early?"

"Jake, listen to me closely. The Big Kahuna behind the South Carolina ring is Andrea Marino. He owns the Wild Cat Casino in Oklahoma. He has a partner named Ray Giordano who runs one of the nightclubs at the casino. He might be part owner of the casino as well. Giordano was involved with the disappearance of several young women back in 1977. He's some old guy now, but I would like for you to follow up on that lead. I just have a feeling about him, since Dakota Hunt's sister went missing at the same time. Can you get there asap or find someone on your team to go check it out? Dirk is now aware of the two creeps, but I just learned about the casino. Maybe you or whoever gets there first can go hang out in the club and see if you can find out if he's there." Before he could say anything, she hung up.

Jake sat there with his mouth open. "Oh, my, God." He said to himself. His heart hammered and his eyes welled up as he thought of Dakota. He said to himself, "This is the lead on Jillian's case that we've been hoping to discover for over forty years."

27

Dakota
December 19

I had just finished fueling in Chattanooga, Tennessee just north of the Georgia state line. Cheynne leaned out of the window and told me that Jake was on the line. I jumped into the truck and picked up the phone. "Hey, buddy, what's up?"

Jake spoke excitedly, "Is Rhys somewhere near Oklahoma? Our mystery woman just called and told me Andrea Marino is the kingpin behind the group we just took down. She said he owns the Wild Cat Casino in Oklahoma near the Texas state line. Maybe we could get lucky and find the bastard there, eh?"

"Okay, I'm on it. Did she say whether or not Dirk

knows yet?"

"He is aware of Marino, but not that he owns the casino in Oklahoma."

"Well, I'll call him. I don't want anyone on my team trying to handle it alone. Head to Atlanta and stay in touch."

"Hey, Dakota?" Jake was choked up and not sure how to tell him. "The woman said there is another thug who partners with Marino named Ray Giordano. She said he runs a nightclub at the Wild Cat Casino. Giordano was suspected of being involved with the disappearance of some young women back in 1977. I was just thinking…"

"Holy Hell! Jillian?" My heart suddenly hammered in my chest and my eyes began to well up. "If only, Jake." I couldn't speak.

"I know Dakota. Let's move fast."

I immediately rang Dirk. The call connected with Kate Lindt. I gave her the location of the casino and told her I was sending one of my drivers to the casino. Kate said, "I think sending your driver to the casino is good, but Dirk will want to take the lead on that. He's been after Marino for years. I'll have him call you as soon as he gets in."

"Okay, thanks, and Kate? Marino has a partner, Ray Giordano, who may have been involved in the disappearance of my sister, Jillian, back in 1977. We just received that tip from our mystery woman caller. It's possible that he could be at the casino as well as Marino. If we find him, can you have him brought to Georgia for interrogation or would he have to go down in Oklahoma?"

"Oh, Dakota. I know about Jillian's case. Since the

FBI has been searching for Marino for so many years, I'm sure we can transport him anywhere we want to with no problem."

"Good. You might have to put me in restraints so that I don't kill him, but I have to talk with him."

"I'm sure that can be arranged and without restraints. Marino and Giordano will be spending days with our interrogation team, but first things first. Let's go get him and let's just pray he's there."

We ended the call. I thought about the situation and then made a quick decision to contact Rhys. He answered within a few rings, "Hey, Dakota. What's up my man?"

I filled Rhys in on the remarkable good fortune and arrests in South Carolina. "I just received word from Jake, that our mystery woman discovered that Andrea Marino is the man who the traffickers work for and who may be at the Wild Cat Casino in Oklahoma." I also told him about Ray Giordano. "Where are you?"

"Crivvens, Pal! We're in Wichita, Kansas headed toward Oklahoma now. We won't be able to get to the casino for another four and a half hours, but Dakota, this sounds more hopeful than anything we've come up with concerning Jillian in years. Ye might want to have Chris run a check on him."

"Good idea. Hopefully, if Marino and Giordano are really there, they'll stick around for a while. That casino is one of your planned stops anyway, so head there and in the meantime, I'll be able to work out some back up. I'm looking forward to interrogating Giordano. In fact, maybe I should fly out there and deal with him myself."

"Whoa, Dakota, let me handle this for now, since I'm not far. Does Dirk know about your sister?"

"I'm sure he knows she went missing, but I haven't talked to him in detail about her. Dammit, Rhys! This is Jillian we're talking about. If Giordano knows what happened to her, I need to know."

"Dakota, on the way. Sit tight and talk to Dirk. I'll call ye back soon."

I was understandably anxious about the possibility of finding out what happened to Jillian and I thought I should call Chevyo immediately, but then I realized that if I called my folks too soon, they would get all worked up and I wanted to find out more first. I was feeling exhausted over all of the recent turbulence, but amazed at the progress the team was making. My team had accomplished more this year than we had over the past five years. I thought, maybe Rhys was right. Maybe all of the illegal roundup and deportation events have stirred things up. Maybe these traffickers were making mistakes, bringing young women across the borders quickly before the border searches become more thorough.

Thinking of Jillian, I called Rhys back. "Rhys, when you get to the casino, I want you to look around for Jillian. I know you might think I'm crazy, but we are locating and tracking so well, that I just have a feeling that she will turn up very soon. And maybe, if we catch Marino, we can make him point to Giordano. Sometimes, when these mafia types get old, they become the scapegoats. Giordano must be in his seventies by now."

"Dakota, I don't think you're crazy. Over the years I have learned to appreciate your extraordinary intuition and Pal, I also believe we might have some luck in locating her in light of what we now know. Let's get Chris working on it again via the internet. In fact, why don't we send out a possible age progressed photo of Jillian on the news and on every internet site possible."

"Thanks, Rhys. I'll get him going and I'll work on Facebook."

28

Dakota

For the past few hours, I had been awake in the sleeper anxiously reviewing articles on the latest search and arrest activity and other steps recently taken to combat sex trafficking in the U.S. Trafficking has been for decades, in a crisis state of affairs, but the problem seems to be too colossal for any government to take it seriously. I believe that numerous private organizations must be set up to assist our country's social care and security programs. People want everything to be done for them by the government, but it's painfully obvious that the population of our country is too numerous for our government to handle everything efficiently alone. I feel that my team has been making exceptional progress and I envision a country where many more courageous, skilled individuals have grouped together such as we have, finally eliminating trafficking as a profitable business option.

I read:

"The San Francisco Chronicle reported in 2006, that in the twenty first century, women, mostly from South America, Southeast Asia and the former Soviet Union, are trafficked into the U.S. for the purposes of sexual slavery."[12] Again, these traffickers are choosing to transport people here to the U.S., so we all should ask ourselves why? Then we must change our thinking about what are acceptable living standards for a country with over 300,000,000 people.

"A 2006 ABC News story stated that, contrary to existing misconceptions, American citizens are also coerced into sex slavery."[13] I sighed and expressed audibly, "My God, does the media actually think that Americans don't realize this?" Maybe, people choose to have children, but then do not take the responsibility to educate and protect them, therefore, many adolescents associate themselves with groups of others who are experiencing similar problems. Deviant behavior, the heavy use of drugs and alcohol as well as sexual promiscuity are common insecurities, often caused by discontent and are usually cries for help. Sex criminals seem to be able to spot such weaknesses in young people and have been answering their cries, which has led to our current catastrophic state of social affairs.

While trafficking organizations exist, millions of innocent young people will continue to be plucked from their lives, like wilted flowers and will suffer tremendously. What makes me furious and continues to baffle me, is that

Jillian was educated although unfortunately, she was a naïve victim who must have simply made a serious, unexpected mistake during a momentary loss of mindfulness. She was not at all interested in drugs or alcohol and I know this to be true with absolute certainty, because we confided in each other regularly, discussing and working through troubles and difficult issues together. Jillian was a genuinely content, joyous person, uprooted from her life unwillingly and possibly maliciously according to my confounded intuition. I wish I didn't have the ability to sense anything out of the ordinary so that the suffering I endure every day would surely be diminished. My eyes welled up and I felt sorrow and anxiety beginning to overwhelm me once again. The only thing over all of these years that has relieved my unbearable torment has been my continuous efforts in the battle against sex trafficking and my adamant will to locate Jillian.

I read: "The Bush administration set up 42 Justice Department task forces and spent more than $150,000,000 on attempts to reduce human trafficking. But since the law was passed, the task forces have only identified 1,362 victims of human trafficking since the year 2000 which is nowhere near the 50,000 or more per year the government had estimated."[14]

President Barack Obama referred to sex trafficking as "Modern Slavery." The U.S. continues to fight slavery, involuntary servitude in the most hideous form. He stated in an announcement on September 25th, 2012, concerning Efforts to Combat Human Trafficking at Home and Abroad:

"It ought to concern every person, because it's a debasement of our common humanity. It ought to concern every community, because it tears at the social fabric. It ought to concern every business, because it distorts markets. It ought to concern every nation, because it endangers public health and fuels violence and organized crime. I'm talking about the injustice, the outrage, of human trafficking, which must be called by its true name, modern slavery."[15]

I completely agreed with Obama's statement and will repeat a few sentences as a mantra in my meetings and dealings with government organizations. *"It ought to concern every person, because it's a debasement of our common humanity."*

Then I read: "U.S. Immigration and Customs Enforcement (ICE) arrests nearly 2,000 human traffickers in 2016 and identifies over 400 victims across the US."[16]

I wish the governments of every country would work much more diligently to eliminate sex slavery. Just wishful thinking, because I have read that many countries recognize it as a profitable trade, whether or not they condone it. I recorded statistics of the countries with the most colossal quantity of sex trafficking. India is at the top of the list with approximately 14,000,000 victims followed by China with over 3,000,000 victims and Pakistan with over 2,000,000 victims. Russia, Ukraine, Thailand, Bangladesh, Africa, U.S., Mexico and Philippines are listed in order respectively. I shook my head in disgust, perceiving that the world will never be able to prevent sex crimes, no matter how dedicated many of us are, but we can continue to hunt, track and imprison as many of these heinous criminals as possible and do much more to educate and protect our loved ones.

I realized I had been occupying my brain with reports

and statistics to avoid going ballistic about the possibility that we may have found Jillian's captor and all I could do was stand-by. I printed the editorials and put them in my journal, along with the articles I have been collecting since the day Jillian went missing, praying for a day like this to arrive. I called Dirk again, finally getting through. "Dirk, I'm sure you know that my sister was abducted many years ago and since we finally have a new lead…"

"Yes, I got your message. Dakota, I'm headed there now. My flight leaves in one hour. I understand how much finding Jillian means to you, but I must insist that you and Chevy sit tight and stay away from our investigation physically, for your own safety. I assure you that I will do everything in my power to locate Giordano. If he's there, we'll force out every scrap of information possible, right before we take him down, you have my word."

"Thanks, Dirk. I owe you and please call me with an update if you discover something hopeful. I have a team on the way to the Wild Cat Casino who should be arriving within a few hours."

"Okay, good, but Dakota, you don't owe me anything. You and your team have already accomplished more within a week than I could ever have hoped for. Since Jillian most likely has been hiding out because of Giordano, we'll broadcast his arrest and figure out how to find her. I realize you want to fly out there with me, but for your own safety, sit tight and allow me to handle it for now."

29

Dakota

I called Dad to find out how he and Mom were doing. "We're fine, but I need to talk with you if you have a few minutes?"

"Yes, of course."

"You should know that we have been receiving calla lilies from an unknown sender. I have tried to track them every time we receive them, but they have always been sent from various places. Multiple floral shops were always involved in the orders which were paid for with cash and sent anonymously, therefore, there is no information about the original sender." I heard Dad inhale deeply and I instantly felt the hairs stand up on end. "I finally managed to track the last order to Montana, although again, sent anonymously."

I stood, frozen in my stance, my mouth agape and heart thrumming. "Dad, they must be from Jillian, which means she's has been sending us the message that she is alive and well."

"Yes, I think they might be, which is why I called you. We have been receiving them every spring along with many others for about fourteen years."

"What? Fourteen years? Why didn't you tell me this years ago?"

"I have wanted to for some time now, but I have been investigating it with no leads. At first, I just figured our neighbors were sending them in honor of Jillian and had no reason to consider otherwise. When I finally tracked this last order to Montana, I just had a feeling that we should look into it right away. I also had a mysterious dream last night, quite different than the dreams about Jillian that I've had ever since she went missing. A woman with long, ebony hair was walking with Jonoche in a garden surrounded by mountains and was clearly holding a cluster of lilies. I know you are well aware that when your grandfather appears in my dreams, they are usually messages, which I then consider prudently until I identify the significance. It is no coincidence that I had the dream right after tracking the order of lilies to a shop near Butte."

"Jonoche." I sat silently for a moment, contemplating. My grandfather was a very spiritual man who often had visions which always led to something significant. "When was the last time you received lilies other than the ones you just received?"

"Late summer of this past year. Yamka has never questioned who sent them, although each time she receives purple lilies, she flashes a sweet, perceptive smile. I can't help but wonder if she has believed that some of the lilies were from Jillian for all of these years. Dakota, she is out there and quite possibly ready to come home. I'm planning to go to Butte myself and have considered hiring a private investigator to re-open her case, someone in the area who could follow up on the lead immediately."

"Dad, I have just recently discovered a solid lead which is being followed as we speak. Ray Giordano, who I have asked you to keep an eye out for at the Wild Cat Casino, has finally been linked with the disappearance of several woman back in the late seventies. He may be there now, or at least that's what we are eager to discover."

"Holy timbers! I should fly there now, then on to Butte."

"Dad, please don't. Rhys and Zach are headed to Oklahoma now and will be meeting with Dirk. If they find anything out, I'll let you know. We must let them handle it for now until we have more information to go on. A mafia criminal named Andrea Marino, owns the casino and is assumed to be Giordano's business cohort. If either one of them are there, Dirk and Rhys will confront them, most likely resulting in a dangerous situation. Neither of us should go out there anxious and excited and blow the whole operation."

He sounded a bit choked up and his voice quivered as he spoke, "I want our girl home. If Giordano is the despicable man responsible for abducting her, he must be quite elderly by now, possibly in his upper seventies. So, if he is still involved in various types of corruption, he could be a top dog in the criminal community by now and difficult to get to."

"Yes, I have been thinking about that, too, however, if we can get to Marino and Dirk arrests him, he might give up Giordano to save his own neck. Marino is going to be accused of trafficking a group of twelve young women. The traffickers were arrested and the women were rescued in South Carolina yesterday. He is going down, one way or another and I suspect he will do anything to get out of it. If we find Marino, our plan is to interrogate him until he points to Giordano. And Dad, I'm sending a team to Butte immediately. Mack lives in Montana and is currently in South Dakota, about 700 miles from Butte. They could be there in eleven hours and will begin searching the area as soon as they get there."

"Okay son, I'll try to remain patient for a while, but not for too long. I'm not going to discuss this with Yamka yet. I hate keeping things from her, but she's happy and I don't want to upset her by postulating resulting in false hopes. I will talk with her when we have some evidence of her whereabouts. A few days ago, we were at the breakfast table and Yamka asked, 'I wonder what Jillian is doing today?' I played along and said, 'Wherever she is, I bet she is thinking of you.' I gave her a compassionate hug and left the table, barely making it to the den before my emotions overcame me, leaving me feeling more discouraged than I've allowed myself to feel in many years. I thought about calling you right then. Well, it took me a couple of days, but here we are."

"We'll find her soon, I can feel it in my bones. I have to go now, but I'll keep you informed."

As soon as I hung up, I called Rhys. "Hey, where are you?"

Rhys said, "We'll be at the casino within the hour. Are

Dirk's men on the way?"

"Dirk is handling this lead himself and should be at Gainesville airport soon. He will be calling me when he lands, so check in with me when you guys arrive. Rhys, I just spoke with Chevyo. He knows about Marino and wants to help. He told me that they have been receiving lilies every year for the past fourteen years, believing that they were from our neighbors until now. You remember that lilies are Jillian's favorite flowers, right?"

"Aye, Dakota, this is huge. Why didn't he mention that earlier?"

"He wanted to investigate the leads before he contacted me. He's very good at following up on things concerning Jillian, but after getting nowhere for years, he was finally able to track the last order to Butte, Montana. He also had a vivid dream, which he believes was a sign and I don't question that. As I'm sure you recall, Chevyo and I have always been spiritually connected with our ancestors, especially Jonoche and many of our dreams have led to truths in the past."

"Yes, I respect and have faith in Chevyo's and your insightful abilities. I'll find out what Dirk has up his sleeve and if we manage to arrest Giordano, Dakota, we'll find her."

"Thanks, Rhys. Keep me posted." I sat there contemplating, desperately fighting the urge to fly to Oklahoma immediately, but I understood that I just had to be patient until Dirk and Rhys discover whether or not Giordano was even there. I closed my eyes and attempted to calm my nerves so that I could remain focused without my emotions reducing me to a hysterical wreck.

Sooner than I expected, I received a call from Dirk.

"Dakota, I'm on the way to the casino. I'll snoop around for a while, then I'll play at a blackjack table. I also booked a room so that we can talk privately. Oh, let them know, I'll be wearing an Oklahoma City Thunder ball cap and tee shirt."

I chuckled. "Well, I'd give anything to see you dressed like an Oklahoma sports enthusiast. I thought you were a Washington Wizard fan."

He chuckled. "I have a good friend who lives in Oklahoma City, who I occasionally catch a game with, so I like to support the team and there's no better way to blend in with local gamblers."

"Well, I'll let Rhys know."

When Rhys and Nash arrived, they parked the rig and casually strolled into the casino as planned. They had never met Dirk and weren't sure what he looked like. Dakota called a few minutes later. "Rhys, Dirk said he'll be at one of the blackjack tables. He's tall, mustache, wire rimmed glasses and will be sporting a Thunder ball cap and tee shirt. Keep me informed."

"Got it."

They walked around the casino until they spotted the blackjack tables, then sat down next to a man who they assumed was Dirk. The man turned, greeting them with a broad smile. "Jim, how are you, good buddy?" They shook hands. Rhys was aware that Dirk called him Jim to avoid using real names. "Hey, let me buy you guys dinner. We'll come back and play later."

"Rhys said, "Aye, sounds great, I'm starving." They walked out of the casino together and followed Dirk to his hotel room.

Once in the room, Dirk said, "We'll eat here so that

we can talk privately." He introduced himself properly. "I'm Dirk Hays and you are Rhys MacAllister and Nash Chavez, right?"

"Right you are, Pal."

Dirk laughed. "I have a great friend, also a Scotsman, who calls me Pal as well." He chuckled again. "Let's order some grub and then we'll put our heads together and strategize." They ordered steak, potatoes, salads and beer. "When I arrived, I talked with a woman at the chip exchange counter, who confirmed that Andrea Marino is here. I've already checked him out and he does own this casino. He's not getting away on my watch. He's going down for the kidnapping and trafficking of the twelve women who Jake helped escape in South Carolina. I informed one of the perps, Matteo Costa, who we arrested at the motel in South Carolina, that he would go down for the whole trafficking operation if he didn't reveal the name of his boss. He relented and sang like a yellow canary, as long as we agreed to keep him safe from Marino and Giordano. I figure, in or out of prison, he's a dead man walking, even if we agree to set him up in witness protection, although, no judge will authorize that with his record. A fairly large percentage of prisoners detest sex traffickers, because many of them have had aggressive confrontations with them over various issues. Here's my plan. We'll arrest Marino tonight and confront him. With his back to the wall, he'll hopefully lead us to Giordano. I have a team of locals on stand-by right now."

Rhys asked, "Did that mystery woman come through with evidence yet?"

"No, damn it, but I believe she will soon. She has the passports of the victims which I need asap. Believe me,

I'm thankful that she was the mastermind behind the arrests and has provided invaluable information, but she is now interfering with our investigation and the possible apprehension of a major criminal trafficking syndicate."

Nash said, "So far, she has been invaluable to our team, so if you locate her, I hope you don't have plans on arresting her. I think she will continue to be advantageous to our operations."

"You're right, I agree. I am empathetic to her cause as well, but she is a vigilante and walking a fine line."

Rhys asked, "So how do we play this? If everything goes down as planned and you arrest him, Dakota is adamant about questioning Marino concerning Giordano."

"Yes, I am, too." His cell rang. "Hang on." He saw Hank's number on his caller ID. "Dirk, here." He listened for a few minutes, then said, "Okay, terrific. Try to get him to confirm what went down." He ended the call. "She dropped the perp as promised. Hank now has Lorenzo Russo detained in lockup. He witnessed a van stopping near the station, a man was briskly shoved out, then the van immediately sped off. The scene was captured on camera, but no plates were visible. Get this; the guy had a bag tied around his neck and guess what was in the bag?"

Rhys said, "The passports."

"Yep, well, copies of the passports which is fine. She included an audio tape of the women talking about their captors and the places where they were forced to work. Also included was a note revealing her plan to take the women to safe homes. She is concerned that the government will not grant asylum to the women who don't want to go home, where there may be more danger to them, therefore she requested that we do not require them to report to the authorities. She also requested that we abstain from putting the girls at risk by alerting the borders, which means she may be planning to help them cross one of the borders into Mexico or Canada. I'm actually fine with that. It may not be protocol, but I want the criminals, not the women. If she can keep them safe, more power to her."

When dinner arrived, Dirk said, "I'm famished. Let's enjoy our meals. We'll continue to discuss the plan while we eat."

30

Sarah
December 19

I had Fedora, Lorenzo Russo, transported to the warehouse in Atlanta where Jimmy, one of Trevor's contacts, interrogated him intensely until he was able to extract as much information out of him as needed. Russo confirmed that he worked for Andrea Marino, who owns the Wild Cat Casino in Oklahoma, which is the base location of their organization. He revealed that they move many groups of women on a circuit, usually to casinos around the country, just as I had surmised. He also confirmed that Ray Giordano is Marino's partner and is responsible for the trafficking sector of the organization.

When he got as much out of him as he could, Jimmy

dropped Russo off with his evidentiary declarations, copies of some of the girl's passports and the audio tape in exchange for a solid promise that Dirk would immediately dismiss the victims.

As the young women and I made our way toward House Of Flowers, I prayed that I would receive Dirk's assurance that the girls would not be on a check list, before arriving at the Canadian border in a few days. I believed that Dirk would agree to my demands, because he hopefully has an interest in my vital, resourceful assistance. I promised I would let him know when the girls arrive at safe homes, but not the locations. I did not give him copies of all of the passports. The girls that did not want to go home would need to remain unidentified with no alerts of any sort, so that I could help them transition into new, free lives.

I hoped that Dirk was expediently and diligently investigating Giordano's syndicate before he managed to elude the authorities once again.

31

Dirk, Rhys and Nash were eating dinner, while discussing their next move. Dirk said, "As soon as we're through, get ready. Here's my strategy; I'll find the manager and let him know that I'd like to talk with Marino directly about joining a high stakes poker game, a play that has worked well in the past. Marino will want to check me out. He'll have me searched for weapons and will require seeing my cash. Rhys, you'll be close by and will have your weapon tucked in your jacket along with mine. My men will be on stand-by, all under cover and armed. If everything goes as planned, when Marino walks out of his office to meet with us, you walk up behind him and nudge him back into his office, of course with me behind you. You'll hand off my Sig Sauer and the plan will go down. My men will follow you in so that you can get out of harm's way and we will handle it from there. That's plan A. Plan B, I don't have a plan B." He chuckled. "Plan B for now is that we walk away if there is a major glitch. I checked the schedule for high stakes poker and the next game starts at 1900 hours. That gives us 45 minutes to get everyone in place."

"Whoa! Rhys exclaimed. "Ye really fly by the seat of yer pants."

"Well, we don't have any time to waste on this one. This may be our only chance to snag Marino. If he gets away, it's all over. Are you up for this, Rhys?"

"Aye. Let's go get this dunderheid."

Nash asked what he could do. Dirk said, "I need for you to be our look out for any signs of trouble, such as casino thugs headed our direction or anything that doesn't look right. Have your cell handy and you'll text Rhys if anything problematic occurs."

"Got it."

Dirk's cell rang and the caller ID showed T. Michaels, one of his agents who was playing a slot machine, while inconspicuously on stand-by. "Dirk here. Rhys and I are heading down now. Don't group together but remain close to each other, following Rhys when he gives you the signal. He's a tall Scotsman with copper hair and beard." He ended the call.

"Okay, let's head down." The three men casually strolled down to the casino and Nash split off keeping Dirk and Rhys in plain view. Dirk asked for the manager who approached him within a few minutes. "I'd like to join the next high stakes poker game. Can you please arrange that?"

The man scrutinized him with narrowed eyes, then nodded. "Follow me." He followed the man to an office with Rhys not far behind. In front of the door, he patted Dirk down to check for weapons and asked him to show him his cash as assumed. He said, "30,000 gets you in the game. More is better." Dirk showed him the money and when satisfied, the manager knocked on the door and said, "Number six for the game."

Marino opened the door and scoped out Dirk. Dirk held out his hand to shake Marino's. "Mr. Marino, a good friend of mine informed me that you're the man to see for a good game. My name is John Rivers. It's a pleasure."

Marino shook his hand cautiously with dubious, glaring eyes. He then seemed to relax when he glanced at Dirk's money. "Glad to have you join the game. I'll be playing tonight, which is quite unusual. I normally play on Friday, but I feel lucky."

Rhys abruptly stormed in, shoving the manager aside and handed Dirk his gun. The other officers bulldozed in behind Rhys. Dirk swiftly aimed his Sig Sauer at Marino's head and said with a huge grin, "Marino, your luck just ran out."

"What the hell? Who the hell are you? Are you here to rob me?" Two of the agents struggled with the enormous, brawny manager, finally succeeding in pinning him to the ground just as he pulled out his gun. A shot was aimlessly fired, smashing the ceiling light directly above Marino's head. He ducked and shielded his head with his arms. "Now hold on here, just tell me what you want."

Dirk said, "I guess you haven't heard that your man, Lorenzo Russo, is behind bars in Atlanta along with Matteo Costa and two others. They both have really pretty voices. And those sweet girls that were in his splendid care are no longer your property. So, what do you have to say about that?"

"I have no idea what you're talking about. What girls? And who is Russo?"

"Don't bother Marino. We have so much evidence that you are behind this that you're going down for the rest of your revolting, pathetic life. But there is one thing that you can do to help your case."

Marino stayed quiet for thirty seconds, contemplating. "And what might that be?"

"If you reveal Ray Giordano's location and divulge as much information as you can about his illegal activities during the past forty-one years, we might be able to make a deal."

"Ray Giordano? Who the hell is that? You guys have it all wrong. I don't know who you are talking about. You can arrest me, but I'm calling my lawyer right now."

"Come on Marino, play a little. We know that Giordano is your partner. We also require some information about a particular young lady who Giordano abducted years ago, so if you tell us where he is right now, I promise I'll go to bat for you to lighten your sentence. You might even get to keep your casinos."

Marino stood still in his stance for a minute then suddenly, they could feel and see the change in his demeanor as the angst on his face diminished. He was swiftly changing his tune just as Dirk and Rhys hoped. "That old man. What a fool he is. I should have done away with him years ago. He's the one you want and Russo works for him, not me. I don't have anything to do with any girls other than the girls I have working here, legally above board in the casino. They are nice, respectable young women who work the tables, bar and restaurant and they are on my standard business payroll."

"Okay, so where is Giordano?"

"He's up in his suite, room 350. Go get him. I'm done with that fool. He's all yours, just leave me out of it."

Dirk turned to one of his men. "Go knock down that door if you have to and bring him here." Three agents bolted down the hall and up the stairs to his suite. They kicked the door in and found an old man lying in his bed.

The man sat up, startled. "What, what are you doing?"

One of the agents said, "Get dressed, now. Marino would like to have a chat with you." He brazenly reached under his pillow revealing his gun, though an agent hastily snatched it away from him. "Nope, you won't be needing that."

"Okay, I'll go. I'm sure we can settle whatever this is without all of the fuss." He got dressed, then they hurriedly escorted him to Marino's office.

As soon as Marino saw him, he said, "It's all over Ray. They know everything about your little endeavors."

"You son of a bitch! What did you do?"

Dirk said, "Giordano, sit down." He pointed to a chair, where Ray reluctantly sat down. "We are in a real bargaining mood. You need to think hard, way back to 1977. You were involved in the disappearance of only God knows how many young, helpless women that you forced into prostitution, women whose lives you destroyed. We know all about that, but we want you to think hard about one young woman in particular. She had long, black hair and jade eyes. You picked her up in

Colorado, didn't you?"

Giordano glared at Dirk with anger, confusion, then with bewilderment as his eyes welled up and his face turned crimson. "Dalila, I loved her. Yes, I had her brought to me and I fell in love with her as soon as I laid eyes on her. I didn't hurt her. She was my girl but she escaped while I was away, back in 1994 I think it was and yes, I was furious. I had everyone keeping an eye out for her for many years, even after I quit searching. But I'm done with all of that and I'm old and dying. Go ahead, lock me up. I won't be around much longer anyway, in fact, I bet I'll be dead before my trial."

Dirk glanced at Rhys and then turned back to Giordano. "What did you say her name was?"

"Dalila, or that's what I called her. She lost her memory, so I gave her a new name. Her real name was Jillian Hunt. I swore to her and all of the other girls that if they tried to run, their families would pay. I knew her address but I never hurt her family. I went to her home and I observed her mother working in the garden. I thought about threatening her, but I wanted Jillian back and I knew that if I directly threatened the family, I wouldn't have a chance. I watched the house for days and then put a couple of my men on the task but after a while, I realized that Dalila wasn't going to return home any time soon or she would have already, so I called off my dogs."

Dirk shouted, "You stalked her mother? You sorry son of a bitch!"

Giordano grumbled in his gruff voice, "That girl made off with the passports of all of my girls and sent them to the FBI. I found that out because two days later, they came looking for me, but luckily, I wasn't there. An informant called, warning me not to come back for a while. When the agents finally managed to discover my hideout, to my disgust by the way, they interrogated me, but they had no substantial evidence to keep me detained, so they had no choice but to release me. Anyway, that girl knows her name. I'm surprised that you haven't heard from her by now, although, I suppose it's possible that her memory never did come back. She also took off with a young Russian woman named Julia Ivanov."

Rhys asked, "Where were you holding her at the time she escaped?"

"At a casino in Wisconsin."

Rhys glanced at Dirk and nodded. Dirk handcuffed Marino and Giordano and escorted them out of the building. They were shouting protests at first, but then Marino realized he didn't want to disturb his casino guests, so they pulled their jackets over their heads and remained silent as they were escorted out of the establishment.

Rhys called Dakota and recapped the incident in detail. Dakota shook his head in frustration. "Damn! Only God knows where Jillian is now. If she escaped, why didn't she come home?" He sniffled as tears streamed down his cheeks.

"Dakota, she was warned that her family would be harmed if she did. And also, Giordano mentioned that she lost her memory. At first, he called her Dalila, but then he spoke her real name. Dakota, she was in Wisconsin in 1994, at the same casino you and Chevyo scoped out. Yer intuition was correct at that time, although, it was clearly not the right time to find her, with physical threats to your family looming in her mind. And I'd bet everything I own that she fled into the mountains, maybe somewhere in the northwest. Ye feel more comfortable in the mountains, right? Don't twins feel the same about things like that? And Chevyo tracked the lilies to Butte."

"Yes, that all makes sense to me as well. I'm arranging for Mack to head home to start scouting around in Butte and Missoula. Dirk promised to put out an all-points bulletin and I've already re-posted her photo on Facebook. I'll be contacting every mountain town in Montana to start with and if she doesn't turn up, I'll widen the search. Chris is working on an aged facial photo that he will update Facebook and other social media sites with." I was so excited with renewed hope and anticipation that I could barely function. "Rhys, thanks brother. I'll find a load back to Denver for you and then you guys take a break, at least for a couple of days."

"We'll hang out at the terminal in case ye need help on Jillian's case."

"I appreciate that. I'll get back with you soon."

32

I called Dad with an update. "Dad, we got him. As you mentioned, Ray Giordano is an old man now, apparently suffering from a terminal illness and may not be around much longer, so he divulged enough to paint a fairly clear picture of what occurred at the time of Jillian's escape. He revealed that he was evidently in love with her, the gruesome bastard. I was astonished to hear that he was willing to go down for everything, but I'm sure Dirk will hold Marino accountable as well." I recapped the conversation in detail, excluding the part where Giordano had been stalking my folks. I cringed, tightening my fists as I thought about the creep lurking around our family home with his shady, malevolent eyes observing my mother. "I'll let you know what Mack learns after he searches for leads in Butte and Missoula."

"Why hasn't she come home? I just don't understand that."

"Dad, she was threatened. The girls were warned that if any of them tried to alert anyone or escape, they and their families would be tortured and killed. Jillian tragically, would want to protect us at all costs. The lilies you have been receiving are obviously her way of letting you know she is still alive and well."

"Yes, I understand that now. I bet she works at a garden or tree farm. I'll call around again immediately and will prepare to fly out there if Mack discovers any significant clue. My dream was exceptionally vivid and continues to remain in the forefront of my mind."

"Are you going to inform Mom of our latest discoveries, especially now that we know for certain that Giordano was responsible for Jillian's abduction? She will be grateful to learn that he has finally been arrested."

"I don't know, maybe not yet. I'd like to see if we discover her whereabouts first. Like I mentioned before, I just don't know if I should provide her with false hopes."

"You and I will fly out there together if Mack locates her, then you can tell Mom at that time. I'll keep you posted."

33

December 20, 2018

Cheynne and I arrived and parked at our planned shady truck stop and began attentively scoping out the scene. Sure enough, just as Brooke had described, a dark gray SUV pulled around the corner and stopped near a row of parked trucks. A burly, stocky man, displaying an ominous, boastful grin began meandering around, knocking on truck doors. I held up my binoculars and focused on the SUV and noticed people inside, although I wasn't certain they were women. "I'm going out there to speak with him. Call the NHT hotline and give them our location and a description of the SUV. Then call 911."

Cheynne displayed a look of concern. "What are you going to do?"

"I'll ask him what he's selling and if he offers women, I'll flash you a signal and I'll try to stall him."

I grabbed two knives, inserting one in its sheath on my belt and slipped the other up my sleeve. As I casually strolled toward the man, I set my phone on audio record. "Hey man, what are you selling?"

The sinister man narrowed his eyes, then flashed a wide, toothy grin. "Are you lonely?"

"You bet. I haven't been home for months. Are you saying you can fix that little problem?"

The disheveled, smug man spit a mouthful of tobacco on the ground, glanced around, then declared, "I have six lovely girls for you to choose from."

"May I have a look?"

The man opened the rear passenger door, so that I could see inside. "Only look, don't touch."

"How much?"

"That depends on how long you want the lady for. One fifty buys you one hour. If you're quick, say a half hour, I'll cut you a deal, $100."

Immediately after I recorded the monetary offer, I observed two police cars heading inconspicuously around the corner. I grinned as I pulled out my wallet and swiftly glanced toward Cheynne. "Okay, let me think for a minute. I walked up to a truck parked near the front of the SUV, observing a driver sitting in the seat and signed for him to roll down his window. Quietly, I said, "Hey man, would you pull up a bit so that you are blocking that SUV? I'm taking this guy down." The driver was an old timer who had witnessed the scene. He snickered, put the truck in gear and pulled up, trapping the SUV.

I sauntered back to the man with a wide, sly smile.

"Looks like," I hesitated while observing the policemen getting out of their cars, "it might not be such a good time."

The man suddenly spun around, entirely flabbergasted to see the authorities moving in behind him. He bolted away from his vehicle, then turned toward me as he shouted, "You son of a bitch."

With practiced lightning speed, I whipped out my knife and flung it toward the perp, purposely and expertly nailing his hat, which flew off in front of him. He shrieked as he hastily reached down and snatched his hat, pulled the knife out and attempted to throw it back with no success. It bounced off the side of a trailer as a policeman clutched his arms and tackled him to the ground. I approached them with my badge raised. "Private Detective Dakota Hunt. I followed a lead here and found this creep lurking around, marketing women." I pointed to the SUV. "Six young women are in that vehicle, obviously held against their will. I work with Sargent Hank DeMarka and FBI Dirk Hays on a trafficking task force. My partner called this in."

Another cop jogged toward us, relieving us of our burden. While maintaining austere eye contact, the policeman dialed Hank DeMarka to check out my story. I presumed he had probably worked with Hank before and was aware that he worked in the sex crime division. I heard him say, "Right, does he need to come in with me?" After a slight pause, he ended the call and the intense glare in his eyes, thankfully subsided. "He verified your story. Hey, thanks for the assistance. We've been after that elusive ass for months."

I nodded. "I'll fill out a report with Hank. I have a

video and an audio recording of the incident and everything the perv said, which I can send to your cell if you give me your number. I'll also be sending it to Hank."

The policeman grinned as he gave me his card and handed me my knife. "Your pretty good with that knife. Did you aim for his hat or did you miss?"

I chuckled. "Years of practice. If I wanted to nail any part of his body, believe me I would have, but I only wanted to spook him and slow him down a bit."

"Well, it worked. Thanks again." The cop chuckled as he strolled toward the scene.

I felt a smile cross my face as I observed the girls being removed from the SUV and escorted to the police vehicles. While sauntering back to my truck, I stopped to talk with the obliging trucker. "Thanks, man."

"You bet. I saw that guy roaming around earlier. You know, I called the NHT hotline and reported the pervert. I also saw you heave that knife." He chuckled. "Remarkable skill. I probably would have injured the creep but you barely missed his head, on purpose I suppose."

I beamed, feeling quite proud of my knife throwing skills. "Thanks for calling the hotline. I hope there are many more compassionate drivers out there reporting traffickers." He nodded as we shook hands, then backed his truck into his parking space.

While I rolled toward Atlanta, I called Hank, who answered right away. "Hank DeMarka."

"Hank, Dakota here. Cheynne and I are on the way."

"Thanks for checking out that truck stop. I have received many calls about that perp, but we've never been able to catch him. We had a stakeout there for several weeks, but he was either on to us or he just went elsewhere for a while. I had a feeling he'd be back. I think you're my lucky charm." He laughed. "Thanks again."

"Absolutely. One of my drivers had a run in with the pervert, so I made it my business to see what I could do. I guess we were lucky that he was there." I took a swig of my coffee. "We should be rolling in around 9 a.m. and a few others should be arriving soon. My drivers who are still out on the road, will be joining the meeting via teleconference."

"Right, I'll meet you in the conference room, second floor. I've arranged for a full breakfast to be delivered, complete with bacon, eggs, biscuits, fruit and coffee. Dirk flew back early this morning and has been processing Marino and Giordano and will be leading the meeting. Dakota, you must know that Dirk is planning to give you the opportunity to pry details out of Giordano concerning Jillian. He brought them both here for that reason, so after the meeting, I'll bring you down to the interrogation room, if you still want to talk with him."

"You bet I do. I've had time to calm down a bit, but I do want some time with him."

"Giordano says he's dying and doesn't mind discussing it. The whole damn thing is astounding. I have never in my life arrested a criminal who was so eager to talk. He's an old man and I guess he wants to make amends before he dies. He doesn't think he will last through his trial, so he's not concerned about anything at all. He's been giving up information all morning about the last few years of his business dealings. We now have enough information to bring down Andrea Marino and his entire organization. Apparently, Giordano has no family for any fall out to affect, although I'm certain that his main objective was to wreak vengeance on Marino for throwing him under the bus. You know, he mentioned several times that he was in love with Jillian, so maybe that's another reason he's so willing to give it all up."

"Bull shit! You don't keep someone that you love hostage. Also, he revealed that she had suffered a memory loss. I have to ask, why? I have read about the systematic forced drugging methods that sex criminals utilize, which in many cases causes severe brain trauma of various sorts, including memory loss." I tightened my fists and I could feel my blood boil and my face turn beet red. "If I find out that he did that to Jillian, he had better be in solitary confinement for his own protection because I will find a way to get to him, incarcerated or otherwise. I just hope he has some kind of lead to Jillian's current location but I guess if he did, he would have picked her up years ago. My God, Hank, it's been forty-one years. I called Chevyo and filled him in. He wanted to fly out to Oklahoma and have his way with Giordano while they were at the casino and so did I."

"Dakota, I will do everything in my power to help you track her down. Dirk already sent out an APB and has several agents focusing on her case, scrutinizing every lead previously documented. They will be concentrating diligently to discover new leads and will follow up on them immediately. He feels much more positive that we will come across something promising based on what we now know about Giordano's organization. Dirk saw your latest Facebook entry and he has one of his guys already working on a more probable age progressed photo. He's also planning to run a missing persons report on TV using the updated photo."

"That's terrific. Thank you for the help and support." My eyes welled up and my emotions threatened to gush out. I felt excited, although after so many years of searching with no results, ambiguity and hopelessness hovered in my mind. I dried my eyes with my sleeve and forced myself to think positively and remain focused. "Has Dirk mentioned the possibility of publicly declaring the arrest of Marino and Giordano as well as presenting their photos on all news channels, so that people who may have seen them together could call in with tips? I think that if Jillian sees or hears the news that Giordano has been arrested and is incarcerated with absolutely no chance of bail, maybe she will feel comfortable enough to finally come home."

"Yes, he is. After Giordano mentioned her escape in 1994, Dirk searched the old, unresolved open case files and pulled up the reports. Giordano was brought in on kidnapping charges, but was released due to lack of evidence. He wasn't there at the casino during the raid, so the FBI couldn't hold him. Dirk discovered a report from the owner of the casino who evidently helped a young woman named Dalila, no last name mentioned, and a young Russian woman named Julia Ivanov, escape. I suspect the casino owner knew her real name and covered up for her, believing he was protecting her. He called a taxi for the two women and also gave Dalila copies of videos, which were standard recordings of everything going on at the casino, as well as some other evidence of various incidents. The tapes showed Giordano and two of his thugs playing the tables, always in the company of a group of young women who were often escorted by various men to their hotel rooms. The owner also gave her a record of Giordano's transactions while at his casino. He stated in the report that Dalila had plans to send the tapes and transactions to the FBI. She did. The following day, the FBI showed up at the casino and located one of Giordano's thugs and the women, but Giordano wasn't there. The casino manager speculated that he may have been out of town, so they checked out flights and discovered that he was booked on a flight to Oklahoma. They had the airport staked out and arrested him at the gate. But like I mentioned, since he wasn't at the casino when they showed up, they couldn't hold him even though the tapes proved he had been there with the women previously. Either a good attorney managed to have the charges dropped or a corrupt judge was paid off or both."

"Wait, you said the casino owner called a taxi for them?"

"Yes, although unfortunately, no one followed that lead back then, probably because they weren't sure how many girls had been held captive and they already had quite a lot to do in dealing with the ones they discovered, along with searching for and arresting the other perps."

"Is the name of the taxi company listed in the report?"

"I thought of that, too and it's not, but the owner of the casino may still be around. If so, even though it's been many years, he may still recall what the girls looked like."

I began feeling more optimistic, but I had to move on the lead immediately. "Thanks, Hank. I'll see you soon."

I hung up and checked my driver program to see who was on duty. Chris was driving, so I called him and he answered immediately. "Hey, Dakota, what's up?"

"Chris, I need you to do some research. I just discovered a new lead in Jillian's case."

"I'm headed to a rest area down the road. I'll call you back in a bit."

"That works for me." I wrote down a list of things that I wanted to review with him. Chris has a way of connecting with several other computer genius friends who all know how to locate information quickly and can help him at the drop of a hat. I decided to try my luck and call the Falcon Casino in Wisconsin. When they answered, I asked who the owner currently is and if that same person was also the owner back in 1994. The woman on the line said, Charlie Nevins is the owner and has been for over forty years. She said he was there and connected him to my call.

"This is Charlie Nevins. How can I help you?"

"Mr. Nevins, my name is Private Detective Dakota Hunt. I'm hoping you can help me locate someone who was at your casino in 1994. As I understand, you were there at that time, correct?"

"Well yes, I was. That was a long time ago now, but I'll do what I can to help you."

"I am working with the FBI to locate my sister, who was abducted forty-one years ago and the man who held her captive has finally been arrested. His name is Ray Giordano. From what I understand, there was a group of young women working for him at your casino and my sister was one of them. I've been informed that you helped her escape with a Russian woman and for that I am extremely grateful. What I'm hoping you can recall is the name of the taxi company that picked them up and whether or not they are still operating. Do you recall any of this?"

Charlie hesitated for a few seconds before he responded. "Yes, I have never forgotten. The day I helped the two women escape was the same day I upgraded my entire security protocols. I have made it my business to make sure that no courtesans work in my clubs and that no mafia thugs are able to traffic young women here. None of that happens at my casino." He breathed heavily and sighed. "Your sister was a brave young woman. She reminded me of my own daughter and I would have done anything to help her. Her name was Dalila, right?"

"No, but I understand that Dalila is the name Giordano called her. Her real name is Jillian Hunt."

"Oh, I see. Well, I should describe her to you to make sure we are talking about the same woman. Dalila was about five feet, eight inches tall, long, sable hair and striking jade eyes, although she often wore a disguise as she did the day she left. That day, she wore an auburn wig and brown tinted contact lenses, altering her appearance considerably. She was wearing blue jeans and a purple sweater. Does either description sound familiar?"

My heart drummed and I inhaled an enormous breath to suppress my emotions. "Yes, my sister Jillian has sable hair, jade eyes and purple is her favorite color."

"Okay, well, the taxi company is still operating under the name of Emerald Cab."

"Do you happen to have the number handy?"

He paused for a minute, then recited the number. "Detective Hunt, I hope you find her. I can't even imagine how I would feel if my daughter went through what your sister must have and even worse, how I would feel not knowing where she has been for so many years. Dalila, I mean Jillian, came to me that day and asked me to help her collect videotapes and transaction information about Mr. Giordano's time here. At first, I was reluctant, you must understand, I did not want to get involved with anything that would cause me or my staff harm, but she was adamant about making her escape right then and so extremely distressed, that I did everything I could to help her. Mr. Giordano was not at the casino at the time, so I presumed that she had to escape immediately before he returned. I gave her money to help her with her travels and called the taxi for her. You know, I recall her mentioning that she was headed either to the airport or a bus station and thought she might head northwest, maybe into the mountain areas. I suggested that she take a bus in case Mr. Giordano decided to look for her at the airport. In fact, I suggested several buses to make them more difficult to track. She thanked me for the assistance and said she had a plan."

"That's very helpful, Mr. Nevins. Thank you. If you give me the mailing address to the casino, I will send you a check to reimburse you for the amount you gave Jillian."

"No, absolutely not. If you find her, that will be much more rewarding than a monetary reimbursement. Oh, in case it might help, the young woman who left with Jillian was a Russian gal who went by the name of Julia. I don't know her last name but she had dark hair, shorter than Jillian's and light brown eyes. She was about five feet five inches tall I would guess. I'm also grateful to hear that this man has been arrested. He must be quite elderly by now."

"Is there anything else you remember that would be

helpful?"

"Oh, there is something else I recall. Jillian had a fall on the ice outside the casino, I guess it was a couple of years before she made her escape. She hit her head pretty hard, so I had a staff member who had nurse training look after her. Mr. Giordano refused to let me take her to the hospital, promising that he would look after her. I believe she may have suffered amnesia for a while. She stayed in her hotel room for several weeks after the fall. I remember this because I didn't see her around the casino. At that time, Mr. Giordano informed me that he and the group of women were friends, vacationing. I had my suspicions, but the girls seemed okay and I never had any reason to suspect something off until Jillian came to me that day."

"Thank you for all of your help Mr. Nevins." After I hung up, I sat motionless for a few minutes contemplating. That's why she didn't try to get a hold of us. Maybe she didn't remember who she was and where she lived. I thought about the name they gave her, Dalila. Maybe she believed that was her name and Giordano must have taken advantage of her amnesia and made her believe she was his woman, since he admitted as much during his arrest. "That bastard!"

I reviewed the conversation with Cheynne. "That's incredible. Dakota, I know it's been many years, but this new information is extraordinarily promising."

"Yes, it is. I've tried to comprehend why I hadn't been able to discover clues like these for all of these years, until now. The only thing that makes sense to me is that in the past, the time just wasn't right and I'm realizing that there has been a very good reason why Jillian has not returned home. Since we now know that she had been severely threatened, we also understand that she had to protect her family as I would." I felt an overwhelming rush of remorse and sorrow. "The whole damn thing is utterly tragic."

I restrained my distressed emotions, not wanting to appear weak and entirely pathetic in front of Cheynne. "I'll have Chris look into the Emerald Cab's records for information about the driver. He may have dropped the girls off at a bus terminal where they possibly headed northwest."

I dialed Chris's number and he answered right away. "My laptop is up and running. How can I help."

I gave him the Wisconsin local Emerald Cab number and told him what I wanted him to research. "The casino owner mentioned that she may have taken a bus possibly to the northwest. Find out what bus services were in operation in 1994 and search records for destinations to cities in the northwest on November 18. It's possible that Jillian would assume that Giordano would concentrate his searches for her in cities not far from Wisconsin, therefore, mountain locales would be logical places to hide out." I sipped my coffee as I thought audibly. "Jillian would have paid cash for the bus, so I wouldn't think there would be a record of their names. Let's start with the I-90 route through South Dakota and into Montana. Also, see if you can find listings of floral and garden shops in Montana, since Chevyo tracked down an order of lilies that was sent to them by an unknown customer there. The last order was sent from a shop in Montana, but he was informed that the shop didn't have a way to order flowers to be sent through the internet, so they called another shop who arranged for them to be sent to a Colorado address. To make our search more difficult, the shop that sent the order didn't have a record of the original shop, nor the city. I suppose Jillian may have created that mess on purpose, so that it would be difficult to track her down, however, I have a feeling that Butte, Montana is a good place to start."

"On it. I'll call you after the meeting to let you know what I discover."

34

Dirk, Kate, Hank and my team had convened in the conference room at the downtown Atlanta police department. Hank helped me connect my other drivers to a conference call, then Dirk stood up and addressed the group. "Good morning. Please help yourself to the delicious breakfast that Hank so generously arranged." He glanced at Hank and nodded. "I can't even begin to describe how grateful I am to have you all on board with us. Our task force has already proven to be successful due to the diligent efforts of your team. He turned toward me. "Your team has within one week, brought down two major trafficking organizations and one smaller operation here in Georgia in the wee hours of this morning. I don't know if it's good fortune or you were in the right place at the right time or maybe both but either way, I hope it continues."

He paused to sip his coffee. "After doing some research into the three busts, I have been able to determine that the group that Rhys tracked to Oklahoma and the men arrested in South Carolina were absolutely tied to the Marino-Giordano syndicate. Since they both will spend the rest of their despicable lives in prison, perhaps the organization will fade away, at least for a while. We have discovered so far, that Marino and Giordano had over $60,000,000, now seized from over 18 bank accounts which means they were the top dogs supporting the syndicate financially. Unless others tied to the business have money in other accounts not known to us at this time, the remaining players will have to find another monetary source."

Dirk cleared his throat while shuffling a few papers. "I had a nice long chat with both Marino and Giordano and neither of them would confess to knowing anything about the men arrested here in Georgia earlier. However, Giordano revealed enough information to take down Marino for life. Our agents are combing through his casino at this very moment, boxing up every shred of paper, computer, video tapes, basically everything we can confiscate as evidence."

Dirk then turned his attention to me again with a serious demeanor, "Dakota, Giordano is all yours when we are done here. I understand that you want to talk with him about Jillian. He's resting in his cell now." I nodded to Dirk, clenching my teeth to prevent my fury from affecting the others.

Dirk continued, "Regrettably, Georgia has been a

major sex trafficking hot spot and thoroughfare for many years now. I'm sure you have all read about Operation Safe Haven where U.S. Immigration and Customs Enforcement along with Homeland Security arrested 29 people in 13 cities and 8 states on sex trafficking related charges. Most of the victims brought to safety were Hispanic females from Central America, trafficked across the southern border and as we know so far, into the southwest and southeastern states. There were also a few Asian girls, who could have been picked up from just about anywhere. The traffickers could be independent operators, but we believe they are most likely connected to one or more core syndicates."

He picked up a folder and glanced at its contents. "We are going to continue to track in the southeast, but I am adding two new territories to our program. Midwestern states and the pacific northwest, including northern California. Dakota, I'd like for your drivers to head west to cover these territories after the holidays beginning in mid-January, until we discover that we need your assistance elsewhere. It makes sense to me that nine trucks, three working in each territory, would be the safest and most efficient way to help us and your team, since there may be situations where backup is urgently needed. My agents are already in place in each territory and have begun investigations online and boots on the ground. You will always have someone on our task force to contact when needed, which will help you concentrate on tracking while our agents continue investigations and arrange reinforcements."

Dirk picked up another folder, sipped his coffee and continued. "These territories will probably change depending on our discoveries. I have hired other retired military personnel who have significant experience in dealing with dangerous criminals, search and rescue, internet and computer related skills, etc., who will be monitoring the territories as well as concentrated boots on the ground in several key areas. Most of them will be scouting around undercover, posing as major clients in order to ensnare traffickers, detect and expose other criminal activity along our borders."

Brooke asked, "How does our government help the victims? I'm assuming they are protected, but are safe havens provided and are the ones who cannot return home due to unsafe conditions in their home countries, being assisted in locating new, safe homes?"

"Yes, to everything you mentioned. We of course would like as many of the victims as possible to assist with our investigations. HSI grants them T-Visas, which allows them to stay and work in the U.S. in exchange for help with our investigations. We of course, assist those who want to return home."

Brooke stated, "I am opening a safe house ranch in Colorado, which should be ready to take in young women sometime in June." Everyone stirred and regarded her with surprise and bewilderment. "The ranch is located in Grand County, Colorado. I began the project this past summer and the construction will be completed next spring." She turned and glanced at me, observing my surprised expression. "I didn't mention my plans to any of you because originally the ranch was to be a women's crisis center or shelter if you will, but within the past few months, I realized that it should be much more than that. The ranch encompasses forty acres of land with a main lodge building and twelve cabins planned. There will also be a large stable for eight or ten horses, a barn for other ranch animals and a large greenhouse. My idea is to provide a fully sustainable, safe, healthy home for rescued young women to live and work temporarily, until they are ready to go out on their own. It's all still in the works and I'm hoping the government likes the idea and is interested in providing me with some funding."

Brooke glanced at Dirk, who seemed to be listening intently. "I'm calling the home Harmony Ranch, which is modeled after another ranch called Hope Ranch in the Yukon Territory, Canada. A good friend of mine, who I have visited several times in the past few years, owns the ranch. She is an amazing woman who was abducted many years ago and managed to escape her captors. She met a woman at St. Faith's Anglican Church in Vancouver, B.C. who helped her until she was able to figure out what to do. She decided to build the ranch for the same reasons I mentioned earlier. Her name is Grace Nadeau."

Startled and entirely astounded, Jake choked for a second on some fruit. His eyes welled up and his crimson face showed instantaneous anxiety. He asked with a trembling voice, "Did you say Grace Nadeau?"

"Why, yes. Do you know her?" He got up and bolted out of the room, then slid down the wall in the hallway into an anguished heap on the floor.

"Did I miss something?" She turned to me, observing my baffled expression.

"Grace Nadeau is Jake's long, lost friend, who was abducted thirty-eight years ago, two years after Jillian went missing."

Dirk said in awe, "Brooke, you are someone special,

aren't you? I will make this known and I think you can count on some government grants to come your way." Everyone was murmuring.

I held her eyes intently with my own. "Girl, we need to talk about communication. Why didn't you let us in on this before now? You know we all would have helped you and I thought you were aware of Jake's friend who went missing."

"Oh, my God, Grace? I had no idea she was the same woman. I don't recall his saying what her name was. And I was just waiting for the right time to talk to you about the ranch. As soon as my loans were approved, I hired a very good contractor who has really moved quickly on the project and I have been focusing on helping you as part of this new task force. I planned on surprising everyone at the holiday gathering, but since we have been rescuing young women already, I thought you and Dirk should know now."

Brooke realized that all eyes were on her. "If we have the ranch available as a resource, the girls will immediately have a safe place to go, at least until the government decides how they intend on handling each situation. The girls can learn to grow crops, cook, take care of the ranch animals and develop sought after skills. With professional assistance, hopefully they will be able to overcome probable nightmare experiences and begin to move on. I will be hiring psychologists for individual and group sessions and I've been searching for advice on other legal requirements to obtain the government's approval." She turned toward Dirk. "I was hoping that you might have a few contacts for me. Her bright blue, soulful, compassionate eyes held Dirk's as she waited patiently for a positive response.

"Well, I actually do and I hope many more people step up to the plate to help trafficked victims. Thank you, Brooke. We can talk more about this after the meeting."

Brooke nodded, then excused herself and briskly walked out of the room to find Jake, who was sitting hunched over on the floor. "Are you okay?"

"Yes, but Brooke, I've been searching for Grace for a long time with no leads whatsoever. I wish now that I had talked with more of you about the details of her disappearance. I guess I never mentioned her name. Brooke, I need to know where she is. I'm going to see her right away."

"Of course. I'll give you all of her contact info and I'll take you to her if you want company."

"No, I have to go alone. I want to call her though, right after the meeting."

She hugged him compassionately, then put her arm around him as they ambled back to the conference room.

Jake sat down next to me and I nodded empathetically. There was no need to say anything. I felt a lump in my throat and tears threatened to flow. I was excited for Jake to have finally located Grace and the overwhelming positive energy, provided a tremendous rewed hope, that I would also locate Jillian and bring her home soon.

Dirk said, "Jake, is there anything I can do to help you?"

"Well, I'd like to take a week off. I am going to see her right away." He glanced at me.

"You bet, buddy. Take as much time as you need. Christmas break is coming up anyway, so we can get back to our work in January." Dirk and Hank nodded. The room was suddenly quiet. The faces of everyone in the room displayed mixed emotions of amazement and anticipation.

Rhys said over the teleconference line, "Brooke, I think you just made the lad a happy camper indeed. Ye know, I would have helped ye as well if you had mentioned your plans. Jake, this is amazing news. Get on with it." Everyone clapped and chimed in with similar responses.

Dirk said, "Okay. I feel incredibly fortunate to have you all on this task force. It was obviously meant to be. In case you all were wondering, yes, you are getting paid for your work. I just couldn't discuss it with you until I got the budget approval back. I'll be sending Dakota $18,000 per month to start with, a $1000 per driver, per month, tax free. I think it should be much more, so I have been applying for grants. When I send in the reports about the progress you have been making, I feel certain that you will be receiving more than double that amount. I'll keep Dakota updated. Does that work for all of you, at least as a start?" Everybody nodded or spoke with approval. The team comprehended that the work expected of them was considerably dangerous, understanding that they would be be putting their lives on the line, but they also comprehended that it was a work in progress.

Dirk's eyes met mine. "We'll find Jillian as well. I plan to put out a nationwide statement about Jillian, if you agree. I believe that if she is still out there, she may feel comfortable about returning home now that Giordano and Marino are in jail and not getting out, ever. In fact, I just noticed an officer escorting Giordano to the interrogation room. Let's wrap up the meeting and I'll take you in there to talk with him. Does anyone have any questions about the territories?" He paused for a few seconds. "I will be sending Dakota an outline of your territories. I realize that at this time, the information I have provided is a little vague but when you return from your holiday time off, you will have much more to go on."

I said, "I'll be meeting with all of my drivers to plan who will work in each territory. It makes sense to have you all working in the areas closest to your homes so that you can easily take breaks. I'll be meeting with Chris Ruby and Rich to arrange loads back to Denver and then we'll start working in our new territories after the first of the year. I think we've all been through a lot in the past few weeks, so I'm recommending that you all go home. The winter weather will become more severe within the next few days and many of you have to traverse the mountain roads to get home, so head on out. For any of you who aren't going home, you're certainly welcome to stay at the terminal in one of the rooms there and I hope to see all of you at the cabin for Christmas." I turned to Dirk, Kate and Hank. "That includes you three as well."

Blake laughed. "He calls it a cabin." He continued to snicker. Others who had been to the home laughed as well. "His cabin is a large mountain home with plenty of room for everyone. Wear your warmest winter coat and good snow boots."

Rhys said, "Aye and don't bother driving up there without four-wheel drive."

I chuckled this time. "Yes, from the main road, you will arrive at a long, meandering driveway, but I keep it plowed. The roads on the way to my driveway are not always plowed if it's snowing so be prepared, but don't worry, if anyone gets stuck, just call me and I'll come pick you up on my snowmobile."

"Okay, guys." Dirk said. "I'll be talking with you either after the holidays or at Dakota's cabin." He put his hand on my arm. "Let's go see the arse, as Rhys would say." We walked down the hall, then Dirk hesitated and said, "I think you'll be pleased with what you find out, but I recommend holding back a bit. I'm sure you'd like to take his head off, but just try to remain as calm as possible so that you can get him to reveal everything you want to know."

"Yeah, thanks. I'll try to hold it together." I felt an icy prickle on the back of my neck, my face flushed with heat and my palms felt instantly clammy. Honestly, I didn't want to talk with Giordano. I wanted to tie him to a chair and fling knives at him, although I recognized that this might be the only chance I'll have to learn more about the countless, lengthy years that Jillian was held captive within his appalling, sinister clutches. I thought of the girls who the mystery woman rescued, feeling relieved that this monster would no longer be able to harm another woman.

35

Sarah

While the young women rested, I drove toward House of Flowers near Charlotte, North Carolina, where we would stop for the night. Then my plan was to head west across I-40 all the way into California to avoid the winter weather and then work our way toward Vancouver. I was grateful that the women were somewhat settled and calm for now.

As I drove along, I thought about my young life, specifically during that terrifying, fateful period of time when I was utterly devastated and grief-stricken. I was eleven years old when thieves broke into our home and murdered Maman. She was standing in front of me, protecting me when one of the thieves stabbed her with a knife. I bolted out of the back door and hid behind some shrubs at the next-door neighbor's house. After a few minutes, I quietly crept back to the house and cautiously peered into the windows. I heard thumping and crashing sounds as shadowy figures moved hurriedly across the room. My fingers and toes felt numb and I began to cry realizing that I would have to crawl back under the shrubs until it was safe to go back to my warm, comfortable brick house on Raven Lane in Edmonton, Alberta, Canada.

I wasn't wearing a jacket and the mid November climate was frigid with gusty winds wafting the snow around me. I recalled feeling so cold that my teeth chattered and I shivered uncontrollably. I curled up into a ball, clutching my sides and stayed hidden for at least a half hour longer until I finally mustered up the courage to go back into the house. I quietly opened the back door and listened. Hearing no sounds, I figured the thieves were gone. I was shivering and breathing so uncontrollably that I could barely walk. I trembled with fear and tears streamed down my face as I ambled on rubbery legs into the kitchen and there was Maman, lying lifelessly on the cold tile floor in a pool of blood. I was so horrified that I couldn't even scream. I knelt beside Maman and hugged her, cradling her like she was a small, frail child.

I was in a state of shock, refusing to believe that Maman was dead. My mind kept returning to the scene where Maman was protecting me, shielding me from the evil person who stabbed her. I thought, why? Why did he have to kill her? The thieves could have just taken whatever they wanted in the house and left. They didn't have to kill her. It had only been Maman and me for several years, after Papa passed away, when I was five years old. As I stared into her lifeless eyes, I suddenly realized that she was dead, too, and I was alone. I thought, what will I do? Where will I go? I wanted to clean up the mess, change Maman's clothes and put her to bed to make her feel comfortable.

I finally shook myself out of the delusional state I was in, understanding that I had to call the police. The living room was a disaster with drawers dumped on the floor, things strewn all over, cupboards open and broken dishes on the floor. I noticed that the TV had been removed from the shelf and the stereo, speakers and silver were gone. I then ambled into Maman's bedroom on rubbery legs, immediately noticing that her jewelry box was also missing. With watery eyes and reality setting in like a lighthouse beacon in a mystifying, pea soup fog, I picked up the phone and called the police.

My navigation system suddenly alerted me to my upcoming turn, momentarily snapping me out of my grief-stricken memory laden trance. I dried my tear-soaked eyes with my sleeve as I turned down a long, dimly lit section of the highway and attempted to suppress my shattered memories. The cool, moonless night was silent and still as I drove on. I soon drifted back to the scene when the police arrived, reliving the events of my nightmare past.

The police arrived eighteen minutes after I called and found me curled up in a fetal position next to Maman. The police woman asked me to sit down in the living room and try to relax so that I could explain what happened. I described everything I could, but the thieves wore masks so that I couldn't see their faces. I shuddered again as I recapped the dreadful scene when the horrible man stabbed Maman. When they were through taking photos of the house and gathering all of the evidence they needed, the lady cop informed me that I would have to go with her. I realized then, that my life had just changed for the worst, I assumed at that time. I recall feeling so alone. Everyone I loved was gone. I thought, where would they take me? The police woman instructed me to gather some clothes and a book and that I could come back in a few days to box up and take anything else I wanted. I hadn't thought of that. "Why can't I stay here in my house?" I asked her. "What would they do with all of our things, Maman's things?" She assured me that social services would help me sell the house and anything that I couldn't keep in my new home. It was just too much for me to process. I started to weep and didn't stop until we arrived at some kind of temporary safe house. They put me to bed and I cried myself to sleep.

When I awoke the next morning, there were several people sitting at the kitchen table talking about me and my situation. A kind woman asked me to sit down and she would make some breakfast for me, but I wasn't sure I could eat anything. My eyes were swollen from crying and my stomach was tied up like a gnarly ball of yarn. Another woman sitting next to me informed me that they had already located a home for me in a nice house with some caring people near my school. I peered out of the window at an entirely unrecognizable environment and felt instantly frightened. The woman tried to comfort me, introducing herself as Allison Bellamy and said she was my guardian and that she would be there for me whenever I needed her.

I was in and out of foster care homes until I was seventeen. Allison continued to be there for me the whole time, helping me manage my affairs. That was her term for selling my home and almost everything in it and setting up a trust fund that would be mine to use as needed except for a monthly amount allocated to the foster care families.

When my papa passed, he left Maman a small fortune which was passed on to me. At eleven years old, I understood the value and concerns of owning such a trust fund, so I made it clear that no one, especially no foster care family should have knowledge of the value of my wealth. Maman had explained to me that we had plenty of money to live on for the rest of our lives, but we would have to protect it vigilantly. I remembered thinking about that when Maman was killed. I wondered if someone had discovered our money and murdered her, thinking that she had it hidden in the house. We never lived like rich people, instead, we lived modestly like everyone else, because Papa and Maman wanted me to grow up learning to appreciate everything in life, which I do. I'm also exceedingly grateful that I can pursue my chosen, unconventional career without worrying about money.

Home life at the foster care families never really worked out. There was always one reason after another why they couldn't keep me. It's not that I was an unruly child, I just never really warmed up to them. They weren't Maman and Papa which I guess, frustrated them. I didn't get along well with kids at school and I was bullied until I started fighting back. I toughened up until no one would challenge me anymore but I felt completely alone, until I met Grace.

Grace Nadeau sat down at my lunch table one day in the autumn of my seventh-grade school year. She had lovely, long, auburn hair and pine green eyes and was the friendliest person I had encountered in a long time. She started talking with me as if we had known each other for years. She had a way of making me feel that she was really interested in me and never belittled me or made me feel uncomfortable and she would look right into my eyes when she spoke with me. I thought she was my angel, sent to earth to comfort me and let me know that I was no longer alone. We went everywhere together and also had several of the same classes which actually helped me turn around a bit in school. I hadn't been doing very well in school with everything that happened, but when I met Grace, I cared more. I guess, I allowed myself to live again. Maybe being around her helped me pack up my weepy violin and move on. We carried on chumming around as best pals for the next six years.

One day, Grace and I were at the Edmonton Mall, which is one of the largest malls in the world, playing indoor mini-golf and trying to be as inconspicuous as two young teens could be while spying on cute boys. A handsome, tall, dreamy eyed guy walked up behind us and waited for us to complete the golf hole. He clapped loudly when Grace made a hole in one shot. Grace turned and gazed at him and I was certain it was love at first sight. She was so delighted with his enthusiasm that she walked right up to him and asked him to join our game. He introduced himself as Jake Losato. We were three peas in a pod from then on. The Mod Squad. That's what we called ourselves, like the TV series back in the late sixties. We used to watch The Mod Squad, Wojeck, Columbo and Charlie's Angels and then create scenarios where we were the sleuths, out searching for and taking down the bad guys. And now, here I am, still searching for and taking down the bad guys.

I dried my tears after my grief-stricken stroll down memory lane and realized I was getting tired of driving so I pulled into a rest area to make plans for my night's rest. My RV was comfortable for several people to sleep in but not for thirteen. After our stop at House of Flowers, I decided to book two hotel suites at the end of each day which would accommodate everyone. I made it to Charlotte, which was a good distance considering the events of the previous day.

I reviewed my route again, thinking about the winter weather and road conditions that we might encounter. I shivered as I thought about driving through Washington, which would most likely be sleety with gusty winds and icy roads. I didn't want to detour further to the south since we were already facing about 3,000 more miles, which would take me a little over four and a half days at 700 miles per day. I thought it would be nice to celebrate Christmas with the girls so that they could experience comfort and joy after the hell they had just endured, so I wanted to get them to some kind of safe home before then.

I didn't know what to expect when we arrived in Vancouver, but I trusted Zeke. If he believed Reverend Angelina Lavoie could help me find safe places for the women, then it was worth the long-distance travel. I was also very curious with Zeke's decision to suggest Reverend Lavoie considering how far away it was. He always had something up his sleeve, some beneficial ulterior motive. I remembered him saying, "I think it will be worth your while." What did he mean by that? For whatever reason, he thinks Reverend Lavoie will be a great partner or source for help, or… I wasn't sure, but I learned a long time ago, that you trust the people who help you and truly care about you.

I thought again about Grace and Jake. I missed my two friends tremendously, but at least I have been able to be near Jake lately, even though he doesn't know I'm around yet. I will tell him soon, because I believe I can trust him with my secret. I also wanted to team up with him to search for Grace.

36

Grace
1989

It's been ten years since I was abducted. I planned for many years, then my chance to escape a living nightmare finally materialized. I lived temporarily at a safe house in Vancouver until I figured out how to move on with the help of Reverend Lavoie. I have been staring out of the window at a gorgeous mountain view for what seems like hours, just trying to recall fond past memories, although thoughts of more recent, abhorrent experiences still loom in the forefront of my mind. Recollections of frightening, dreadful events, which occurred during my captivity, continue to disrupt my joyful, grateful mood which makes me furious. For a while, I was agonizing over the disruption, but then I decided to redirect my fury into motivation. I wanted to help other girls who have suffered similar terrifying experiences.

My mind suddenly drifted back to the horror I had experienced not long ago. I lived in Edmonton when I was abducted and then taken to Seattle, Washington, where I was held captive and forced to dance at several nightclubs in the area. I was lucky that the nasty men who shoved me into their van didn't force me into prostitution. That thought crossed my mind many times. I was terrified that it would come to that but even still, they both had their way with me multiple times. I resisted, but every time I did, I was beaten within an inch of my life. On one occasion, I had passed out from unbearable abuse and when I awoke, a nasty, burly man, who's stench lingered in my nostrils and in my memories for a long time was zipping up his pants and making animal sounds like a wild boar. He glared at me with a perverse, frightening, clownish grin and I had nightmares about him for years.

I don't think I could ever forget that terrifying, fateful night. Sarah and I were having so much fun dancing, until I sauntered down the hall toward the restroom without a care in the world. The club was so crowded that you could barely walk by without bumping into someone. After leaving the restroom, I was forcibly grabbed by a large, burly man who put his hand over my mouth and shoved me to the side of the hallway. He told me that if I screamed, he would stab me and I felt the point of his knife in my side, so I didn't dare move. He stated that we were going to walk quietly out of the club and that if I didn't smile while passing the bouncer at the door, things would turn out gravely uncomfortable for me, very quickly.

My entire body was trembling and my rubbery legs barely supported me as I staggered helplessly beside the ruthless pervert. My eyes were pools of water, gushing down my ashen face as I passed through the crowd of people. I desperately glanced into one face after another, but not one concerned eye caught mine. I glared at the bouncer on the way out, hoping he would sense something was wrong and come to my rescue, but he glared right back at me with shifty eyes, laughing boisterously and bellowed, "Good night, lady."

I realized that the bouncer must have been in on the whole thing. I wanted to scream, but the burly creep still had his blade pointed in my side. Then suddenly, I was being shoved into a gray van, where other girls sat silently. I screamed as the van sped off and another obnoxious man with a ghastly red scar on his left cheek, sitting across from me, punched me in my stomach so hard that I almost lost its contents. He roared, "Shut up you little whore! If you scream again, I'll knock you out cold."

I still couldn't stop sobbing and I asked, "Why? Where are you taking us?" He just chuckled and grinned at the others. I glanced at the others, too. Did they know where we were going? Had they already been told something? One of the girls looked familiar. I'd seen her in the nightclub, so I assumed we had all been taken from there. I thought of Sarah, realizing she must be going crazy searching for me. One of the girls glared at me and put her finger up to her lips. I tried to compose myself for the rest of the ride, comprehending that the rest of them surely didn't want me making trouble for all of us.

While the van continued moving for hours, I tried to

plan some kind of escape, but my mind was whirling with fear and anxiety. Finally, the van stopped and the doors were opened. The scar faced man ordered us to follow him to the restroom. I hastily glanced around, observing that we were at a shadowy rest area with enormous, droopy oak trees, but I had no idea which direction we had traveled. Two men walked behind us until we entered the women's restroom, then one of them shouted, "Hurry up or I'll come in after you." I hate it that I can recall everything in such detail. No one else was at the rest area at that time so there was no use in screaming. While all six of us, huddled together as we ambled out of the restroom, a large camper pulled up and parked. Scar face said, "Don't get your hopes up." He chuckled in such a sinister way that the hairs stood upright on my neck and arms. "That is your next ride."

We were ushered into the RV and instructed to keep our mouths closed. "Listen very closely, because if you all do as you're told, I won't have to harm you. We will be heading into the United States tomorrow afternoon. We are all close family and friends on vacation and on our way to Oregon. I have passports for all of you." He handed out the passports. "Study the names, birth dates and addresses, because you will be quizzed in the morning. These are your new names, so get used to them. When we get to the border, the guards will check your passports and may ask you questions. You will not screw up or you're all dead. Do you understand?"

We all nodded. He continued, "There is a bag of clothing there. Go through it and change into your new casual, vacation clothing. I have taken your ID's out of your purses, for those of you who had them when we picked you up, so don't think you can pull a fast one. He tossed out sandwiches from a bag, which landed on the counter. "Eat. We'll talk again in the morning."

We made it across the border the next afternoon with no problem, but we never ended up in Oregon like scar face said we would. Instead, we were taken to Seattle, to a nightclub owned by a bunch of perverse, cruel thugs who I suspected might have been affiliated with the Seattle mafia. We were informed that we would learn to dance topless and there was a woman there who trained us. I was absolutely mortified. I had a nice-looking body, but it was not for public eyes. I have always dressed in appropriate fashion, never revealing too much, so I was embarrassed and humiliated. I felt such shame.

I learned to dance well enough to collect quite a bundle of cash each time I worked, but I had to give all of the money I earned to Max, who was our boss and a disgusting animal. I didn't have to work as a prostitute, but I had to let Max have his way with me whenever he wanted to, so it felt like the same thing. The first time I tried to resist him, he punched me until I was bruised and sore for several weeks. What a bastard! Men do not have the right to torture and abuse women, even if they provoke it, which many of us have had to do to defend ourselves from beastly, cruel bastards. I believe that it's only a matter of time before poetic justice befalls, teaching such egotists a valuable lesson, although many abusive men are merely degenerates who are too dense to learn anything and remain sadistic. Maybe it's because they loathe themselves and inflicting cruelty and pain on others is easier than solving their own problems. Sex traffickers are all sadistic degenerates, therefore, the only way to prevent them from abducting and forcing people into sex slavery is to wipe them off the face of the earth, which is exactly what must happen.

I did what the villains told me to do until I could escape. I danced and earned money for them, but I planned. I smiled and acted like everything was tolerable but for ten agonizing years, I planned. And then one day, since we were all such good girls staying in line, our captors got complacent and turned their backs for just the right amount of time. One morning, scar face had left the door to his hotel room open while he was conversing with some men. I couldn't believe my luck. I slipped in, rummaged around and finally located our real IDs in a suitcase pocket. I took Kara's and mine and snuck out without being noticed. The following day, Kara and I crept out of the back door and ran for miles. We tried to get the other girls to escape with us,but to my amazement, the rest of them wanted to stay. They were just too afraid to leave and liked the money, clothes and gifts they were given, but Kara and I seized the opportunity without any hesitation.

We made it to a busy city area with taxis lined up along the sides of the street and flagged one down. We asked the driver to take us to Bellingham, Washington, which was 89 miles from Seattle and not far from the Canadian Border. Our plan was to stay for the night in a motel, while we figured out how to find a ride into Canada.

The following morning, Kara and I were sitting at a corner table in a small diner having breakfast, when a group of young people sat down across from us. I overheard them talking about Vancouver. There were two girls and three guys, who I figured to be about nineteen or twenty years old. I heard them planning what may have been a fishing adventure. As gutsy as it was, I got up and mentioned that we were headed to Vancouver and I asked them if we could ride with them. I revealed that we didn't have much money, but could spare $50. One of the guys chuckled, displaying a wide, toothy smile and said, "Sure, the more the merrier."

Kara joined me at their table and we introduced ourselves. The bunch were friendly and having a great time talking about their adventures and what they were planning to do in Vancouver. I had a calm, reassuring feeling that we would be safe with the group. When we arrived, they dropped us off at St. Faith's Anglican Church as requested.

When we met with Reverend Lavoie, she was kind and compassionate. She immediately located a temporary, comfortable safe house for us. It was a relief to feel protected and a renewed sense of sanguinity uplifted my spirits.

After a few months of healing, both mentally and physically, I decided to build a ranch home in Whitehorse, Yukon Territory for women in need, a safe place to go to escape from the hell way too many women are forced to endure. I decided to call it Hope Ranch. Reverend Lavoie helped us get to Whitehorse and arranged for us to stay with a friend of hers not far from a lovely, scenic parcel of land which was fortuitously for sale. Kara was intrigued by the plan, which I was grateful for because I realized that I would need her help and much more. I had some money saved at a bank in Edmonton and even though the account sat unused for ten years, it was still there. The building of the ranch is currently underway and my excitement on my new life journey, grows exponentially as the weeks pass.

I discovered that vengeance was a perfect way to force my brain to move on. I had previously written down the names of the men in charge, the girls that worked for them and the location of the club on a small note pad that I kept hidden in my cosmetic bag. I had also written a detailed description of how we were abducted and where from. Once safe, I mailed it to the Seattle police. A short while later, I discovered the club was closed. I hoped the other girls had been rescued and were safe from harm and the pathetic goons were arrested, convicted and imprisoned for the rest of their wretched lives.

I've been hoping that Jake will discover me here, if he still lives in his cabin in Whitehorse. I also think of Sarah often. I tried to call her recently, but the phone number I remembered had been disconnected. Considering ten years had passed, I realized that she and Jake had most likely moved somewhere else entirely. I prayed that someday they might want to help me run the ranch, but I realized I was just dreaming of our chummy, devoted friendship so long ago. I still had to find them first and I believed that surely, they had been searching for me without giving up hope. I would continue to have faith that we would enjoy each other's company once again.

37

Dakota

I walked into the interrogation room with Dirk. Giordano was sitting slumped over the table looking resigned, defeated. I sat down across from him and said, "So you're the bastard who kidnapped my sister, Jillian, forty-one years ago. How could you do that to a fifteen-year-old girl or to anyone for that matter?"

"Mr. Hunt, I've done many things that I regret in my lifetime. At that time, I was just concerned about number one. I was a pompous ass I admit, but if it helps you to know, I loved her and I protected her."

My blood boiled and I was suddenly so furious that I could not hold my temper. I shrieked, "No, you did not protect her. I've been told that you admitted to drugging her until she lost her memory. That's not protection, that's abuse. Torture. Criminal!"

"Yes, there was that, but you should be grateful that I didn't make her work as a prostitute for me. She was lucky." He sat there smirking like the pompous ass he was.

"Lucky? Lucky? Bullshit! You stole her life. You abducted her from her family. Giordano, she's still missing. What the hell did you tell her to make her think she couldn't go home?"

He scowled and spoke in a low, gruff voice, "All the girls knew that if they tried to run, I would find them and kill them and their families. She was protecting you. And by the way, yes, I was furious with her for leaving. I searched for her for quite a while, but I would never have killed Dalila."

"Don't call her Dalila." I paced the floor realizing that I had to calm down in order to get him to talk. I leaned over the table and drew in a deep breath. "Tell me everything you know about the day she escaped."

He threw his hands up and slammed them back down on the table. "I don't have much to tell. I wasn't there when she left. I was on my way back to Wisconsin when my colleague, the dunce, called me and informed me that she ran with another one of my girls. He was too comfortable, drunk and stupid. You know that I was arrested the day after I returned, right? But the Feds had no proof that I was involved with anything illegal. Only video tapes of me being with some of the girls and records of my gambling transactions." He narrowed his eyes and snarled, "I had a very good lawyer."

Dirk glanced at me, then lowered his eyes, appearing as if he felt guilty even though he wasn't working with the FBI at that time. He shook his head in disgust. I asked

Giordano if he went to Jillian's home. He said that he did. He said that he spied on a woman who he figured was her mother tending flowers in the garden. "Such a beautiful garden. I watched her for a while, singing and smiling. She had just planted some purple flowers and then she sat beside them and sang to them. It was sweet. She was a beautiful woman, like Jillian. I couldn't harm her. I couldn't do anything to harm the woman I loved, so I eventually gave up. I just let her go."

My heart pounded ferociously and I felt so angry that I thought I might pass out. I held the edges of the table thinking I might pick it up and throw it at Giordano. I leaned over the table almost in Giordano's face. "You went to my home and watched my mother? You twisted creep!" In an attempt to regain control of my emotions, I got up and walked around for a minute, my eyes welling up.

Dirk leered at Giordano. "So you are saying, you have no idea where Jillian went? You did not kill her or have anyone else kill her?"

"No, no. As I said, I let her go."

"Did you release your dogs on her or did you hire anyone to hunt for her?"

"I had someone drive by her home every now and then but after a while, I called it off. Believe me, if I knew where she went, I would have picked her up. The reason I renamed her Dalila is because she lost her memory. She woke up one day and didn't know who she was or where she was. I took advantage of that and kept her as my own. I made her my assistant of sorts. She took care of the other girls. The only reason I went after her at all was because I was worried that she might be wandering

271

around, not knowing where to go. But then I discovered that she somehow found my safe, broke into it and took her ID card along with all of the other girls' passports." He glared at Dirk. "You Feds know all about that, since you tried to bust me. She knows where she lives and she knows her real name, if she's still alive. And if she's not, that's not on me. I didn't kill her and I didn't have anyone else kill her. As I said earlier, I just let her go." He breathed in deeply. "Look, I'm an old man. I'm dying. I don't have any excuses for my behavior. Lock me up, I don't care. I'll be dead before you can set my trial date." He leaned over the table with his hands covering his reddened, scowling face.

I stormed out of the room and leaned against the wall in the corridor, staring up at the ceiling. Dirk asked me if I was okay. "Yeah, but damn it, I just wanted another lead. I don't want that bastard to hear us. Let's talk in another room as far away from him as we can. I don't want to go back in there because I might kill him!"

"I understand. I'd feel the same way if I were in your shoes. Okay, let's go down the hall to Hank's office."

"Dirk, I have one solid lead which hopefully will help us locate Jillian. My folks have been receiving lilies from someone anonymous for years. Chevyo just revealed this recently. Purple lilies are Jillian's favorite flowers, so Yamka plants hundreds of lilies in the garden every year. When Jillian went missing, our neighbors began bringing her potted lilies for her to plant, so for all of these years, they thought all of the lilies were from neighbors."

"Wow! When did the last ones arrive?"

"Just this past summer. Chevyo said they had been receiving them more often than normal in the past two years. He began looking into it, calling the neighbors and floral shops to find out who sent them. He was able to track the last shipment to Butte, Montana. I'm sending Mack up there to ask around, hoping to discover that she's there or was there. He lives in Missoula which isn't far from Butte and knows the area well. Chevyo and I plan on going up there and may not come back until we find her."

"I'll send an agent there immediately and will get my team working on news bulletins right away. TV, newspapers, internet and any other source we can."

"Thank you. I was just about to ask you to help in that way. I would like to make a statement for the press, directed to Jillian. I think if she sees my face and hears that I'm her brother, maybe I can get her to call in. Maybe we can set up a special number for her to call. I'm not sure I want my phone number or my family's number or address publicized, but I can let the public know that she is from the Evergreen, Colorado area and that she might currently be located somewhere in northwest Montana."

"Okay, I'll work out the details. You write down what you want to say. I should be able to get this worked out by tomorrow morning, then I'll call you and let you know where to go. Maybe we can get you on the early morning news."

"Thanks, Dirk. I'll check into a hotel for the night here in Atlanta." We shook hands and I headed out to meet with my team.

38

Brooke, Blake, Cheynne and Zack were waiting for me in the conference room. I reviewed the highlights of the interrogation with Giordano and my conversation with Dirk. "I think we've all been through enough for one day. I'm booking hotel rooms for the night for all of us. I've asked Chris and Rich to locate loads back to Denver, leaving sometime tomorrow. I'm hoping that Dirk can work out my TV face time for Jillian early in the morning. If you plan to go home for the holidays, please let me know, otherwise we'll all meet up at the cabin. I plan on heading up on the twenty third."

Brooke looked concerned and put her arm around me. "Are you okay?"

"Yes, thanks. I'm just beside myself, anxious and yet

feeling hopeful that after all of these years, finding Jillian might now be possible. If Mack and Chris find anything out while they're up there, I'm going to fly up there and look for her. I would give anything for her to be home for Christmas. If that does happen, you all go on to the cabin and have some fun and I'll meet you back there, hopefully with Jillian."

Zack turned to me. "Jake is headed to the airport, so I'll be driving back solo. I plan on joining you for the holiday. My family is in Hawaii at my grandmother's home this year, but I feel like having a white Christmas. You know, Jake mentioned bringing Grace to your place, if he finds her early enough to make the arrangements."

I forced a smile. "I hope he does. I asked him to call me when he gets home and I'm on the edge of my seat right there with him. He hasn't seen or heard from Grace for almost as long as Jillian went missing, so I can imagine what he's going through right now." My eyes welled up again, my emotions continuing to interfere with my self-control.

Blake walked around the table and put his hand out to me. "Come on big guy. Let's go check into the hotel and then go have a beer. We are all going to help you find Jillian and bring her home. If she's in west Montana, Mack will find her."

I forced a smile. "Thanks. I actually have Rich searching for a load to Butte now." I breathed in deeply and dialed Mack. "Hey, buddy. How's it going up there?"

"How are you, is the real question? I was beside myself when I heard all of the commotion and good fortune at the conference. Jake, on his way to the Yukon and new leads on Jillian? How can I help?"

"Well, that's why I'm calling you." I reviewed the new information about the lilies with Mack and told him that by the time he arrives in the Butte area, I may have a couple of addresses for him to check out. I asked him to talk with all of his friends, acquaintances, shops, restaurants and as many people in the area as possible. "Are you still in Williston, North Dakota?"

"Aye, 658 miles to my front door. No problem. I can leave now, get loaded and will be there early in the morning."

"How's the weather up there? I've been so preoccupied that I haven't checked on it today. I'm hoping you won't run into a winter storm on the way."

"No worries. It's a bit snowy, but the roads are well maintained and you are well aware that I've been traversing these northern roads for many years."

"Okay, Rich has a load lined up for you. Your dispatch should reach you shortly. You'll be picking up some kind of beverage right there in Williston at 3 p.m. and you'll deliver in Butte tomorrow, open time block between 5 a.m. and 3 p.m."

"On the way. Dakota, if Jillian is anywhere in Montana, I'll find her. Keep your faith. I already know who to talk to when I arrive."

"Mack, if you do find out anything, I'll fly out there to search for her with you and we'll bring her home together. Lately, I've been releasing fragments of heart felt emotions everywhere I go, which is quite unusual for me. I believe everything happens for a reason, so what makes sense to me is that we are really close to finding out what happened to her. My faith is stronger than it's been in many years."

"Aye. I'll be prayin' and scoutin' around like Sherlock Holmes. Looks like my dispatch just came in. I'll call ye when we arrive in Butte."

I put my phone in my pocket and stood up. "All set. Let's go get checked in and I look forward to that beer." I forced another smile, hoping that my mental faculties appeared somewhat intact. "I'll call for a limo taxi and we'll ride together. The hotel is the Westin Peachtree, right down the road. Hank said the lot here is secure, so we are leaving the trucks where they are now." We all walked to our trucks, gathered our things and headed to meet the taxi.

I felt like an emotional train wreck. Anxious, concerned thoughts whirled around in my head. I was still furious with Giordano and I thought about what he said concerning Jillian's memory loss and wondered if she remembered Mom, Dad and me. I decided to call Dad to give him the update right after checking into my room.

Cheynne walked up beside me and took my hand. "Dakota, I know your faith is strong, I can feel it. There is a technique I use sometimes when I feel like I need to remain calm and focused. Have you ever tried a contemplative mantra? You know, where you focus deeply, reaching out to your closest ties, a connection that helps you feel each other's presence, sense each other and communicate with each other."

"Yes, I used to do that quite regularly. When I get to my room, I'll take a few quiet moments to settle my mind."

"It's possible that Jillian has been waiting patiently for the right time to safely find you as well. I will meet the others at the hotel café and let them know you will be there in a little while."

I stood still, delighted, though quite nervous as I faced Cheynne, my captivated eyes lingering on hers. "You are an amazing woman and I also feel a strong connection with you. I don't want to scare you off, but I just wanted you to know that. Thank you for your compassion."

Like a flash of lightning, she reached up, held my neck with her soft, warm hands and kissed me so passionately, that it made my knees buckle. She gazed deeply into my eyes. "You will never scare me away. Please forgive me for being so forward, but I feel a strong connection with you as well."

With no more said, I continued to hold her hand as we strolled, slowly back to the police precinct to wait for the taxi, I thought about what Cheynne had said. I cleared my mind and breathed in deeply, visualizing my forthcoming meditative state.

When I arrived at my hotel room, I called Dad who answered right away. "Dad, I think it's time to connect with Jonoche." I filled him in on the latest events and discussed my plans to investigate the Missoula area. "Dirk Hays is arranging for me to speak to the public and hopefully, we'll reach Jillian. Once she learns that Ray Giordano and others that worked with him for many years have now been arrested, she hopefully will feel like she can come home. After we hang up, I'd like for you to meditate with me, calling on Jonoche. I'm convinced that it's time to find Jillian, since our dreams lately have become increasingly more vivid, stronger and similar."

"Yes, I've been thinking about that as well. Let's begin." We ended the call. Dad and I meditated, each concentrating on Jillian and Jonoche. I sat silently still, relaxed though solid and stable. Thoughts of Jillian surfaced and within seconds, I began to visualize Jonoche like I had in my dreams a few nights ago, with his long, flowing white hair, standing in a garden with his hands raised toward someone. A figure slowly came into view and walked toward him. A beautiful woman with long, sable hair pulled back in a braid, took Jonoche's hand and walked with him through the garden.

He told the woman to be prepared to be with her family and to watch for them in the next few days. He told her not to be afraid and that her brother, father and mother were waiting for her among the lilies at her family home. The woman knelt down to smell a cluster of purple flowers, leaving my vision with only Jonoche remaining. He then spoke to me, "You know what to do and where to go. It's time for her to come home and she will remember soon." I tried to speak with him, but his form faded away.

I was not sure if Jonoche faded away because I began to feel frustrated that he wasn't offering more information or maybe I just needed to stay focused and work diligently to locate Jillian with the clues I had. I awoke from my meditative state, silently contemplating the images I had observed, feeling certain that I was on the right track. I then prayed to God to keep Jillian safe and to help us reconnect.

I called Dad, who answered immediately. "Son, I visited with Jonoche while he was with Jillian. He advised me to keep my faith and be ready to help you when needed. I believe we are on the right track in planning to search in Missoula, otherwise, I believe Jonoche would have redirected us somewhere else. He also asked me to wait for a while longer, before divulging what we know to Yamka. He informed me that when the time was right to talk with her, I would know."

"Yes, I agree. Jonoche also revealed that she will begin to remember soon."

"Thank you, Dad. I feel much more convinced and self-assured now. Mack is on his way to check out the addresses for the floral shops that you tracked down, so we'll let that play out. If he doesn't find her, we will go there together. Do you agree?"

"Well, I'm on the edge of my seat, you know that. I would rather go now, but maybe you're right. He might be able to narrow down the search. I trust him."

"I'll keep you updated." After ending the call, I sat still, reflecting. I began to feel relaxed, allowing my demeanor to return to my normal, calm, focused state. I splashed my face with cool water feeling energized with renewed determination and headed down to the café.

39

Jake

All I can think about is Grace. It's unbelievable that I might find her after all of these years. I am completely amazed that she settled in the Yukon Territory, not far from my cabin. I whispered, "It can't be a coincidence, because she loved it up there and she knew I did, too." The thought reminded me of the warm, compassionate feelings that I remembered having for her, so many years ago. I wondered if she hoped I would eventually find her. I had been to my cabin many times over the years, but it never dawned on me that I would find her there.

I was on the plane headed for Whitehorse, feeling anxious, but excited. There are about 160 square miles of the city and about 25,000 people living there, so I hoped it wouldn't be too difficult to locate her. Brooke had given me the address, but I was racking my brain trying to picture where the ranch was located. I remembered Grace enjoying Takhini Hot Springs, which was near acres of open land, years ago. I whispered to myself, "I'll go home to my cabin, shower, then drive my jeep to the address."

I didn't want to think about what may have happened to Grace after she was abducted. I wanted to let her tell me in her own time. I did not want her to have to relive experiences that may have been terrifying. I shivered as icy prickles crept up my spine. I shook myself and continued to plan what I wanted to say to her. I felt my eyes well up, wondering if she had been thinking of me through the years as well. I closed my eyes and tried to rest.

40

Grace
2018

The ranch has been a beautiful, comfortable, safe home for many young women for twenty-eight years now and I have loved every minute of my work here. I feel so very fortunate to have the life I have, but I still miss Jake and Sarah. I think of them both constantly and wonder what they have been doing for all of these years. I have tried many times to locate them both to no avail as if they somehow, just dropped off the face of the earth. I have been hoping to run into Jake since he has a cabin up here somewhere, or at least he used to. His address and phone number are not listed, so maybe he doesn't come up here anymore. I only went to his cabin twice when I was young but over the years, I have forgotten exactly where it was. I tried to inquire about him, but no one seemed to know him.

I met a woman earlier this year, named Brooke Macfie, who was vacationing up here in Whitehorse. She said she heard about my ranch and wanted to open one up similar to mine in Colorado. She said she works with a trucking company that hunts and tracks sex traffickers and she wanted to provide a safe place for the women to go when rescued. I was delighted to show her around. It really made me feel special that she wanted to model a new ranch after mine.

She stayed at the ranch for a week, planning, sketching, riding horses and touring around. She met with the young women who were staying at the ranch and found that they really loved being here. Some of them live in cabins on a permanent basis working at various jobs to help me run the place while others were just here temporarily, until they could figure out what their next journey would be.

We raise chickens, turkeys and dairy cows and Brooke showed a special interest in our greenhouse, because we grow all of our own vegetables, fruits and berries. I share with a few friends offering vegetables, herbs and fruits in exchange for fish and wild game, which she thought was a brilliant idea and decided to organize trade arrangements for necessities at her ranch as well.

She invited me to visit her and tour her new ranch when completed. I would love to explore Colorado and I hoped that her ranch would prove to be as successful as mine has been. I smiled, thinking about the contented, courageous young women I have gratefully been able to help.

I thought that maybe when I visit Brooke, I could look into the possibility that Jake and Sarah may be living in the states and I could begin a renewed search for them there.

41

Sarah

After two and a half long days of driving, the girls and I arrived in Barstow, California. I was very happy to have the help from two other girls who shared the driving, so that we could make the trip in far less time. I looked up Vancouver on my GPS system and figured that we had a little over 1,300 miles to go. I thought that if the girls could continue to share the driving, we could be in Vancouver late the following night. I also thought about the cold, possibly icy, mountain passes in Northern California, Oregon and Washington. That will slow us down, but I felt satisfied with the distance driven to this point. My goal was to get the girls somewhere safe before Christmas.

I stopped at a motel and booked three rooms for the

girls and one for me. We were all exhausted. My RV only has one bedroom but also a sofa, a lounge chair and plenty of room on the plushy carpeted floor. We talked about it and decided together that we could all manage without having to stop every day at a motel. The RV has a shower, toilet and sink room which would be fine.

Two of the girls said they wanted to stay in California and one of the girls, Maria, said she had a cousin living in Bakersfield, who had a good job working on citrus grove land and would be able to help her find work there. She planned to go there immediately after crossing the Mexican border but to her horror, everything had gone awry.

I was concerned, but I had no way of making them travel to Vancouver if they didn't want to. Maria gave me the name and number of her cousin. It was my responsibility to take them somewhere safe, so I informed them that if I didn't feel comfortable with the people there, I couldn't let them stay.

I called the number and a young man answered, "Hello, this is Carlos Emanuel."

"Good evening, Carlos. My name is Sarah and I have your cousin Maria Gonzales and a friend of hers, Rosa Garcia with me. They said they had arranged to visit you several months ago and are still hoping you can take them in. They also said you may be able to find work for them."

"Oh my God, yes. Yes, of course. I have been so worried. Maria and Rosa were supposed to be here months ago."

"Yes, they've been through quite a horrible ordeal, but they are safe now. I would like to meet with you before I let them stay there. You must understand, they were abducted by some very dangerous men who I helped the girls escape from and I am now responsible for their well-being."

"Oh, my God! Yes, please bring them to Bakersfield. I will show you our home, so that you will feel that they are safe here. There is plenty of room for them and I have a good friend who will help them get their work visas. When can you be here?"

"We are all exhausted, so we'll be staying at a hotel for the night in Barstow. We should be able to make it to Bakersfield around 8:00 in the morning. Would that work?"

"Yes, that is a good time for me." He gave me the address and we worked out the details.

When we arrived at Carlos Emanuel's home, he was outside waiting to greet us. His warm, coffee brown eyes welled up as he jogged toward Maria and Rosa giving them a heart-felt, compassionate hug, which made me see that the kind, good-natured man would be okay. The house was a splendid Spanish style brick and stucco home with lovely gardens surrounding it. Carlos said, "Please, come in." He introduced the girls and me to his wife and mother, who graciously put their arms around the girls and walked with them into the living room.

We talked for about twenty minutes. I asked all of the questions that needed to be asked to leave me feeling comfortable about allowing the girls to stay there. When I felt satisfied, I thanked them and headed toward the door. The girls jogged toward me and hugged me with tears streaming down their faces. Maria said, "You are an Angel of God. I will be forever grateful to you." Carlos flashed a grateful smile and shook my hand, promising they would be okay now. I held back my own tears, beamed at them and ambled back to my RV.

The other girls had their faces pressed to the windows, afraid to come out, but wanting to see if it all worked out. I flashed a cheerful smile as I climbed in. "That's a good home for them and they will be okay, I'm sure of it." The girls all talked at once thanking Sarah and feeling hopeful for themselves as well. "Does anyone else want to stay in California?" They all looked unsure, since they weren't familiar with the area. Several of them let her know that they wanted to go to Vancouver with her. None of them knew anything about Canada, but after the experiences they had just endured, they were hopeful about living in another country.

One of the girls, named Violet said, "The United States is not a safe country. I thought it would be different."

I couldn't disagree. I had seen so much filth, hatred and abuse in my chosen line of work in the U.S. that I didn't have anything positive to say back to her, but I did say, "There are good and bad things that happen in every country. Remember that. You must all be careful no matter where you go. Don't let your guard down and for God's sake, don't trust anyone until you have checked them out thoroughly. There are lovely places and people here in the U.S., but as you have experienced, there are dangerous, evil ones as well. My plan for the rest of you is to get you to a safe house either in Northern California or Vancouver. There are Social Care Programs which teach you how to be safe and the kind employees will help you find work. I may be able to help with that, too, once we are there."

I made sure the girls were settled, then headed out. I had called Trevor the night before and asked him to check into The Freedom House, a program in Northern California which opened up The Monarch House in the San Francisco Bay area, specifically for women who were trafficked. I read about the place and wondered if some of the women would be interested in giving it a try. Since the rest of the girls had just informed me that they didn't want to stay in California, I felt reluctant to mention the place. I also wanted Trevor to look further into it to make sure they wouldn't just deport the young women back to their homelands even if they didn't want to go for unsafe reasons. I called him back and he answered right away.

"Hey, Sarah, I have some good news about The Monarch House. I believe it's a safe option for the girls. I checked into the background of the company and read reports and stories from women who stayed there. It's a good, safe place as far as I can tell. They provide education, social programs, psychologists, spiritual services, clothing, food and clean, healthy rooms. They don't turn anyone away, but they only have living space available now for two girls."

"Okay, thanks Trevor. I'll talk with the girls to see if two are willing to try it out. Please email me a copy of the brochure so that I can print it out for the girls to read." I told him about our good fortune with Carlos earlier and let him know that I was now down to ten girls. I pulled into a gas station to fuel and printed out the brochure, then talked with the girls again. I asked if any of them would like to live in the Bay area to try out the Monarch Home. Two of the Philippine girls said they would as long as they could call me if things weren't working out. Jasmine wanted to stay with me to see what else we could find. "Okay, just a small detour." I figured we could be in the bay area in about four hours.

When we arrived, Trevor had already arranged for the girls to be received. He had given the employees the background details and filled them in on the rescue events. I sat down with the staff and explained my concerns about leaving them there. They assured me that they would not deport the girls or alert the Federal agencies. They said they have ways of helping the girls find jobs, obtain their green cards, visas and everything else they would need. When I was satisfied that the home was safe, I escorted the girls in and several women greeted them with open arms. An enormous smile crossed my face and I felt an overwhelming sense of joy and gratitude.

I wrote out a check for $10,000 to donate to the program. The women, of course were extremely grateful and they realized in unspoken words, that I wanted them to care for the girls there and not arrange to have them deported.

The girls hugged me, said their goodbyes and we were on our way, finally to Vancouver. I felt exhausted, but I wanted to make it at least a few hundred more miles before we stopped. "Down to eight girls," I whispered to myself.

As I drove, I thought of Dakota and Jillian, hoping that the team would be able to locate her soon now that Giordano had been arrested. I would help them at the drop of a hat, if they needed me and decided that as soon as the girls were safe, I would arrange to meet with Jake.

42

Dakota

I met with Dirk at a local Atlanta television studio. Dirk had set up the interview the night before, so that I could have a two-minute spot, live on the nine o'clock news. I had my speech ready and I appreciated that I had to be a pillar of strength so that I wouldn't lose it on live TV. The anchor woman introduced Dirk and me, then gave the public a short recap of Jillian's disappearance and reported the fact that the men responsible for her abduction had finally been arrested.

The anchor woman gave the microphone to Dirk who repeated her significant words. "Ray Giordano has been arrested along with Andrea Marino without bail. There is more than an adequate amount of evidence to prove that they are both guilty of heinous crimes such as child abduction, sex trafficking, money laundering and a whole slew of other crimes and will receive back-to-back sentencing with no parole."

He handed the microphone to me. I swallowed hard and drew in a deep breath to calm and restrain my emotions. "I am Dakota Hunt, residing in Evergreen, Colorado. I am reaching out to my sister, Jillian Hunt, with hope that she will see this news story and feel safe enough to finally come home. Jillian, I know you're out there and we all love you and miss you." The camera moved to show her photo. "If anyone has seen her or maybe you know this woman by a different name, please call. We believe her to be somewhere in the northwest mountain areas, possibly in Butte or Missoula, Montana. She may be working at a garden center or a tree farm. She loves lilies. I encourage all floral shops to call in if you have seen this woman or have taken orders for lilies to be sent to a Colorado address. Jillian, please call the number listed." I smiled awkwardly, my watery eyes revealing sorrow and concern.

The anchor woman read out the number for people to call and also flashed it up on the screen. She said, "I hope Jillian finds you. I can't imagine what you and your family have been going through." She continued to speak to the public. "Sex trafficking is slavery and it must be prevented. Our law enforcement agencies are working diligently to find criminals who are responsible for abductions like Jillian tragically experienced, but everyone can help by calling the National Human Trafficking hotline or 911. If you see something suspicious, don't just look the other way, call it in." The NHT hotline number flashed up on the screen. The anchorwoman publicly thanked Dirk and me then wished the best for us on our search.

Dirk put his hand on my shoulder. "Well Dakota, how do you feel?"

"Thank you for arranging that. I think it went well, but we'll see. Mack and Chris will be searching the area until they come up with something hopeful. I sent him the photo and information so that he can print and distribute flyers as he searches. I'll keep you informed."

Dirk said, "I'll arrange for the photo and flyer to be sent to all of the Montana P.D.s along with an APB."

"Thanks, Dirk." I shook his hand and headed back to the hotel.

The drivers were all waiting for me in the hotel lobby. Cheynne asked, "How do you feel? We watched the live news spot and thought it sounded informative and hopeful."

I blew out a puff of air. "I'm feeling optimistic. Dirk had the tape sent directly to every news station in the country. As soon as my folks see it, I'm sure I'll be getting a call. Mack is in Butte as I speak. He just delivered his load and will begin searching for her shortly. Mack knows a lot of people and businesses in both Butte and Missoula, so let's hope he finds some good leads."

Ian put his arm around me. "Hey, Dakota. My heart is with you. It sure seems like you're closer than you've ever been to finding Jillian. If needed, we'll all go help Mack find the lass."

"Here, here," all of the drivers said at once.

I shook Ian's hand. "Thanks, buddy. I'm glad you guys made it here safely. Let's all go have breakfast before we roll. The Café right here in the hotel has a nice breakfast menu. It's on me."

We toasted with fresh squeezed orange juice to finding new leads to Jillian and to Jake's great fortune in finding Grace, thanks to Brooke. After the meal, I said, "Well, let's all keep in touch on the road back to Denver. The weather here in Atlanta will be getting worse throughout the day, so I'd like for us all to roll out ahead of the storm. Chris and Rich have been working on back-hauls for us. I called him a few minutes ago and he has two loads in Dalton, one for Zach and one for Blake and Brooke. Cheynne and I'll be picking up a load in Chattanooga this afternoon. "Okay, let's roll. See you at the terminal."

We headed out on snowy, slick roads. The wind was kicking up making it unnerving to haul empty trailers, but we didn't have far to go to reach our shippers. After driving for a couple of hours I asked Cheynne to call Mack. "Thank you. I want to check in with him."

"Yeah, sure." She dialed his number and he answered right away. She put him on speaker.

"Dakota, you'll never believe what I just found out. The lass at the floral shop, who sent the last order of lilies for Jillian, talked with her a bit. She remembers her, although she said her name was Lily. What do ye think about that, Pal? And she said she lives in Missoula. The lass asked her why she didn't send the flowers from Missoula and Lily told her that it was important for them to be sent anonymously. She thought it was a bit suspicious ye see, so she recorded the sale and the address. It's yer pop's address. And she saw the news spot with you asking for help in locating Jillian. That was a good call in saying that she might be using a different name. The lass

tied it all together, ye know, since Lily was ordering Lilies."
He chuckled excitedly.

"Mack, that's tremendous. Okay, so head for Missoula and call me when you find out more."

"Aye, on the way."

I was thrilled and excited, though anxious and I momentarily thought about heading for the closest airport immediately, but I knew I had to trust that Mack would be able to narrow down the search. I glanced at Cheynne, "You might want to get some sleep. I'll make the pick up at the shipper, then you can take over. I'm wide awake now, but I have a feeling that when we switch, I'll crash hard. I have a lot to process."

Cheynne got up and gently placed her arms around me. She whispered, "It's time for her to come home. You feel it, we all feel it, so hold on to that. Jillian is out there waiting for you to find her. If Mack doesn't get back to you before you head back to the sleeper, I'll be on stand-by for you. If you run across icy roads and want to chain up, wake me up and I'll chain with you." She kissed my cheek, rubbed my shoulders and headed back to the sleeper.

I put the truck in gear and headed down the road, thinking about how lucky I was to have Cheynne by my side. I felt like a young lad again, in love but at the age to know I may have finally found my soulmate. "She understands me so well," I whispered to myself. I feel comfortable and more optimistic with her here. I have wanted to express more love and compassion towards her, but I've been so entirely dedicated to finding Jillian that I've been concealing my true feelings. I just hoped that she will be patient with me. If she really feels love for me, she will, although I won't let her slip away.

I have always enjoyed driving through the country, even in the winter. I appreciate the mountain views and beautiful old cities with spectacular architecture, such as the hundred-year-old brick and stone churches with colored glass windows and spires soaring toward heaven. Snow was falling, lightly coating the buildings and trees, but it wasn't a problem, yet anyway.

I put on my headphones and selected guitar songs. I taught myself to play guitar at an early age and I've always been fascinated with fast, energetic music. I eventually became skilled enough to play flamenco guitar songs, which are extremely moving. Ottmar Liebert and Paco de Lucia are two of my favorite flamenco guitarists who have inspired me to try to master the art form.

I suddenly recalled a time not long ago, where I was so worked up concerning Jillian, that I strummed my fingers into a flamenco frenzy, faster and faster until I broke two strings. So, I figured I shouldn't get all worked up while I needed to stay focused, so I settled on J.J. Cale's album, *The Breeze*, which is tranquil rolling music.

The roads curved and meandered like wild rivers snaking along the hilly terrain. The landscape colors were magnificent. Deep evergreens dolloped with glistening snow were interlaced with dark gray deciduous trees which contrasted splendidly against the Georgian terracotta clay. Someday I will take a year off or who knows, retire and drive around in a jeep, camping and hiking in all of the majestic areas of the country. I wondered if Cheynne would enjoy that as well. My heart fluttered and my face flushed, a feeling I hadn't experienced in many years.

After a while, Jake called to let me know he had arrived safely and that he was at his cabin. He said he was nervous, yet excited. I appreciated how he felt and hoped his plans to reconnect with Grace would work out for the best. I sensed that life was about to change in unprecedented ways and I perceived something peculiar, as if something else concerning Jillian would soon be discovered. I felt another presence, but I couldn't yet identify what my intuition was alluding to.

After I departed from the shipper, I rolled toward Denver through steadily falling snow, which was beginning to pile up on the roads. I liked being ahead of the other drivers so that I could call to warn them if there was anything ahead that they should be prepared for. I tried to remain focused, keeping my thoughts clear, believing that everything will work out as it should and a new life journey, including my sister, will begin soon. I drew in a deep breath and rolled on.

43

Jillian
2018

I was sitting on the porch swing, thinking about Liam and Autumn and how happy I've been. Liam adores Autumn as I do and we spend a lot of time camping and hiking, which I love. I feel so at one with nature and I have enjoyed a special friendship with a very mysterious raven, that must live nearby. I see the raven almost every day and oddly, the bird shows up in my dreams as well, which have been becoming more and more vivid lately. I believe that the dreams are actually my memory returning and I sense that it is now time to visit my Colorado family. My fear has diminished substantially and I have decided that maybe I don't care anymore, whether or not Ray finds me. He must be way too old to be able to harm me anymore and I cannot allow myself to prevent Autumn from visiting her grandparents. I long to get to know my family again and Liam has been extremely supportive.

Autumn has had a very contented, joyful life with many people around her who love her and protect her. We spend a lot of time with Nicholas and Chrys and Julia pops in several times a week with her tall, handsome husband, Grigori Mikhailov. I looked up the meaning of his name one day. Mikhailov means gift of God, so perfect for Julia. She deserves a good, loving man and he is. He is also the funniest man I have ever met. Autumn loves having them over for visits, because when Grigori and Liam get together, they make her laugh continuously until joyful tears, soak her blushing cheeks.

Liam and Grigori are very good friends. They go hunting together every fall while Autumn, Julia and I practice recipes that our husbands love, such as delicious Russian and Irish dishes. Liam also likes some Scottish dishes, like Haggis. I don't care for Haggis, so I learned to cook some of his favorite Irish dishes like corned beef, buttery, softened cabbage and red potatoes. He also loves seafood dishes as well as one of his favorites, roast grouse with black currant and beetroot sauce. Julia likes to cook Pelmeni which is really delicious. Pelmeni is considered the national dish of Russia. The dish is basically pastry dumplings, filled with minced meat, wrapped in thin dough. Autumn likes the dumplings swimming in a garlic soup broth.

Autumn is now seventeen years old. She has healthy, wavy, long auburn hair and jade eyes like I do and is stunningly beautiful, which sometimes worries me. I cannot blame myself for feeling that way after the hell I went through. I protect her like she is still a baby. Liam and I discussed when to reveal my past, which was an extremely tough decision to make, but I wanted her to know what could happen if she is not careful. She is so grown up, intelligent and seems to sense things that I can't explain. She has an adorable, jovial personality and yet she can be extremely quiet and contemplative at times.

I finally decided it was time to reveal that we have another family. Autumn wasn't surprised, which I thought was odd. She said, "I know. I have felt them in my heart for many years now." We wept while hugging each other and then the tears turned to laughter. She wants to go with me to Colorado and stay for a long visit.

I took Autumn to Chrys's floral shop and we had calla lilies sent to our Hunt family. I promised her that we would go soon. Liam agreed that it might be time to go without fear or concern. He didn't feel that there would be any threat to my life, since twenty-four years had passed from the day I escaped and I agreed self-assuredly.

Three months later, on December twentieth, Nicholas and Chrys showed up at our home right when we came back from shopping. Nicholas took me aside and told me that he just heard a report on the news that Ray Giordano had been arrested and was in jail indefinitely. He also informed me that my brother, Dakota Hunt, announced publicly, that he was looking for me and wanted me to call and plan to go home. I didn't see the news story, but Nicholas said there was a photo of me on the news and that they somehow figured out that I might be in Montana. They also asked for any floral shop who may have taken an order for lilies to be sent to a Colorado address, to call the number listed. He gave me the number.

Chrys and Nicholas held me while I broke down, sobbing uncontrollably. Autumn heard the commotion and trotted into the room, asking what was wrong. I asked Nicholas to tell her, because I was so emotional that I could barely speak. The haunting hell of my past had finally ended and I was completely overwhelmed with the knowledge that I have a brother, just as my dreams portrayed. Autumn gazed deeply into my eyes and said, "We're going. Pack your bags."

Chrys said, "She's right, you need to go. Your family loves you and they miss you terribly, I'm sure. You must go." Nicholas and Liam agreed.

Liam and I made plans for all of us to drive to Colorado, but he wanted to call the number listed on the news program first. I agreed, but I needed a day to gather my thoughts and promised him we would call in the morning. I could hardly contain myself. After all of these years, that bastard is finally in jail, but it's a shame that it took so long. The fact that my family would no longer be in danger, began to sink in. I now felt certain that my wonderful, vivid dreams were my memories returning. Last night, I had a similar dream about the comforting man with long, flowing white hair who was reaching out to me. He kept saying, "You must go. It's time, Jillian." I remembered asking him in the dream, "Go where?" But I know where I must go and soon.

It all makes sense now. My brother, Dakota believed that I was still alive and must have felt strongly that since Ray is in jail, it's now safe to go home. I broke down in utter hysterics, tears gushing from my eyes. I felt so happy, yet overwhelmingly emotional. Forty-one years of terror, grief, guilt and shame from being so naïve had been instantly lifted off my shoulders.

The next day Autumn, Liam and I went out for lunch at Scotty's Table, one of our favorite eateries. We frequently dined there with Nicholas and Chrys, especially during the warmer months, because they have a lovely outdoor dining area. We know all of the friendly people working there very well. While we were waiting for our meals, a tall, handsome man with graying copper hair strolled into the restaurant and sat down at a table nearby. I overheard him talking with the owner, who was showing him something and then I heard him say my name. My real name, Jillian Hunt.

44

ack and Chris had been driving around, walking into every floral shop, restaurant and gift shop in Butte showing people Jillian's photo. One woman at a floral shop in Butte was sure she recognized Jillian, but by the name of Lily. She informed him that on numerous occasions, the woman had stopped in to send lilies to a Colorado address. She said that the woman mentioned Missoula. So they immediately drove to Missoula, Mack's hometown, to try their luck there.

By the time they arrived, they were both starving. Mack said, "Let's take a break. I know a great place for lunch, one of my favorites. They parked the truck at a truck stop not far from the restaurant and walked into Scotty's Table. "The food here is delicious and well portioned." Mack and Chris sat down at a table, looked over the menu and ordered lunch. The owner sauntered to their table with a wide smile across his face and welcomed them, vigorously shaking Mack's hand. They were laughing and carrying on for a while and then Mack showed him the photo and asked if he knew Jillian Hunt.

"Oh, yes, I know that woman, but her name is Lily Jensen. She's here now, sitting right over there." He pointed to the table where Jillian, Autumn and Liam were sitting.

Mack turned in his chair, immediately recognizing Jillian, who was gazing at him with watery eyes. Mack's eyes welled up as well and he drew in a deep breath, exhaling slowly to steady his emotions. "My God, she looks just like Dakota, but much prettier." He stood up and ambled to her table, forcing a smile with trembling lips. He had listened to Dakota revealing his angst and grief concerning Jillian for so many years that the joy he felt at finally locating her was overwhelming. She stood up on rubbery legs. "Did I hear you ask about Jillian Hunt?"

"Yes, Ma'am, you surely did. My name is Mack O'Donnell. I work with your brother, Dakota, who is also a very close friend. We followed some clues that led us here to my hometown as it so happens. Dakota sent me here to find ye, lass." A tear trickled down his cheek.

Autumn stood by her mother and put her arms around her. "It's okay, Mama, it's okay."

Jillian walked around the table and held out her hand to shake his. Mack put his arms around her. "We've been looking for ye for many, long years. Your family misses ye terribly and want you to come home."

Liam stood up and shook his hand. "Liam

McKinney, Jillian's husband. We were just informed that the man responsible for Jillian's plight is in jail. We just planned a road trip to Colorado and will be leaving tomorrow morning. We all talked about it and agreed that it is indeed time for Jillian to go home or at least visit for a while until she decides where she wants to live. She also has her own home here." Liam swallowed hard, wondering if Jillian would want to move back to Colorado. He immediately decided that they would figure out a way to spend plenty of time in both places.

Jillian finally found her voice, "This is Autumn, my daughter."

Mack put his hand on Autumn's shoulder, "My God, ye both have your uncle's stunning jade eyes. A spittin' image." Autumn laughed. "Dakota will be so happy to see ye and to find out he has a niece." He chuckled heartily. "I have an idea, but we should talk a bit. Do ye mind if we join ye?"

The flood gates opened as Jillian replied, "Please, yes, come join us."

Mack called to Chris who was watching and listening intently. "Chris, grab our glasses if ye would lad and come join us."

Liam said, "You look familiar. I own some ranch land near Seeley Lake and I believe I've seen you around there."

"Aye, maybe. I own a log cabin on ten acres in Swan Valley. We must be neighbors. I'm sure I've seen ye around as well. I've lived up here for forty some years, although I drive a rig, so I'm working out of state quite a bit." Mack noticed Jillian attempting to restrain her emotions, so he put his arm around her again. "Darlin', ye've had a tough life, struggling for so many years to stay away just to protect yer family, but everything's about to change. You have many people that love and care about ye. And now ye have two families. No, three. We've been hunting for ye for so long that we all feel like we know ye, Dakota's whole trucking team." She laughed and it felt good.

Mack said, "So, here's my plan. Dakota has an amazing cabin in Evergreen, Colorado, not far from where ye grew up. Every year over the Christmas holidays, he invites yer folks and all of his employees to enjoy a week-long holiday. I'd like for you all to follow me out there." I wish we could surprise Dakota and yer folks, but we should call them as soon as possible. They have been beside themselves with the anticipation that I might find ye here and have been prepared to fly here immediately if I discovered you were."

Jillian said, "Yes, I should talk to Dakota and my folks right away. I haven't been able to remember most of my childhood, my brother or my parents. Just recently, I've been remembering bits and pieces, but I have dreams of people and places that seem real to me."

Mack reflected for a minute. "Your brother has dreams like that and he has never given up on ye, Lass. He has always felt that ye were alive and would find ye somehow. Ye know it was the lilies that led us here, don't ye?"

"I was hoping that my family would understand that I was still alive when they received the lilies. What are my parents like? If you tell me something about them, maybe I can remember."

"Yer father's name is Chevyo and yer mama's name is Yamka. They have never given up hope either. Yer mama plants lilies all around the house, because they were your favorites. Dakota says that she talks about ye as if ye are always coming home at any moment." Jillian's eyes welled up again and she cupped her face with trembling hands. "She has kept your bedroom exactly the same as ye left it. Your papa wanted to come out here, but Dakota asked him to wait to see if I could find out anything first."

Jillian dried her tears with the sleeve of her sweater. "There is always an elderly man in my dreams. He has long, white hair. Do you know who that is?"

"That'd be yer grand. His name is Jonoche. Dakota says he sees Jonoche in his dreams as well."

"Can you give me Dakota's phone number, please?" Mack wrote it down for her. Jillian looked at the number and sat quietly, contemplating. She needed to compose herself for a minute. She felt anxious and excited and her palms were sweaty. She thought about Dakota and whispered, "My twin brother, who I haven't seen or spoken to in forty-one years, feels close to me somehow.

Jillian dialed Dakota's number, nervously listening to the ring tones with anticipation. He answered, "Dakota Hunt."

"Dakota, this is Jillian. I'm here with Mack in Missoula."

"Jillian? Jillian?" He began weeping uncontrollably, then suddenly fell to the ground in a childlike heap with grateful hands in prayer.

With a trembling voice, she said, "I'm coming home and I have a surprise. You are an uncle. Autumn is seventeen years old. She has been wanting for us to drive out there for quite a while now, but when we heard that the monster was in jail, I decided that it would finally be okay."

Dakota, drenched in tears and barely controlling his

breathing, whispered with a shaky voice, "Jillian, I can't even begin to tell you how I'm feeling. Are you okay? I mean, I was told that you lost your memory and that you and our family were threatened, which is why you thought you couldn't come home. Do you remember our folks and me?"

"My memory has been coming back a little at a time, mainly because of my dreams. At first, I thought I was just having beautiful dreams but I have continued to have the same ones, more and more frequently throughout the years. I always see an elderly man with long, white hair walking with me in lovely gardens. Not long ago, the man showed me two young children playing by a creek. There were beautiful flowers all around them and a lovely arched stone bridge over the creek. The little girl called your name, Dakota. After I woke up from the dream, I believed that the children in the dream were you and me. I just revealed my dreams to Mack and he told me that the man was our grand, Jonoche. Is he still alive?"

"Oh, Jillian, I'm so grateful to have you back and for the infinite love of Jonoche. He passed away many years ago, but his spirit lives on within us. Jonoche has the extraordinary, spiritual ability to connect with those he loves from beyond his grave. He has helped Dad, Mom and me continue to visualize you alive and well.

I never believed you had passed on and my faith and bond with you have kept me aware of your existence. Jillian, since we are twins, you and I have always had a close connection with each other. I also have had dreams involving Jonoche, in fact in a very clear, vivid dream just recently, he stated that you will begin to remember and that it was time to go find you and bring you home."

"Yes, in my latest dreams, he tells me as well, to remember and that it's now time to go home. Dakota, I haven't called Mom and Dad yet, because I wanted to speak with you first. Mack suggested we follow him to your cabin, so I'd like to leave first thing in the morning. I'd like to surprise Mom and Dad, but do you think it's better to call them now? I mean, would they be even more upset if I just showed up without letting them know that you found me?"

"I think you should call them now. Mom will want to prepare and Dad would never forgive me if I didn't let him know that we found you. As soon as we figured out where your last order of lilies was sent from, he wanted to fly there and search for you."

"Okay, I'll call them now, but I don't know the number." Dakota gave her their phone number, told her he loved her and that he was really looking forward to spending time with her. He then asked to speak with Mack.

Jillian passed the phone to Mack. "So, what do ye think about all of this, my man?"

"Mack, I'll never forget what you've done for us. I don't think I can thank you enough."

"Pal, no need. You're like family to me and if the situation were reversed, ye would have helped me in the same way, my brother."

"Mack, the winter weather is stormy over the mountains. I should be in Denver tomorrow, but we need to make sure that Jillian can drive here safely. After finding her, I can't even imagine what I would do if anything else happened to her out on the road."

"Jillian has been looked after very well by her

husband, a good man named Liam McKinney. He's a strong and able man and will be accompanying Jillian and Autumn on the drive. In fact, I'm sure he'll do the driving. Since they live in the mountains, I'm certain he has a four-wheel drive and a good set of chains. I'll have them follow Chris and me and we'll stop if we need to. Don't get yer head messed up with it, Dakota. Trust that I'll get them there safely."

"Okay, please check in with me once you're on the road and again during your travels." They ended the call and Mack handed Jillian her phone.

Jillian gulped and regarded Mack. "I'm going to call my folks. I, I don't know what to say or what to expect."

"Lass, they love and miss you more than you can imagine. You'll be fine."

"Okay, here goes." She called the number Dakota had given her and her father answered on the second ring.

"Hello, this is Chevyo Hunt."

"Dad? This is Jillian. I'm coming home."

"Jillian? Jillian, hang on, I'm going to get your mother." He called for Yamka, who could hear by the excited tone of his voice that something significant had happened. She quickly trotted to him.

"What's wrong? Is everything okay?" Chevyo put his arm around her holding her eyes steadily with his own.

"Sit down next to me. Yamka, it's Jillian. They found her and she's on the phone." He put the phone on speaker. "Jillian, I have you on speaker. Your mom is sitting here beside me."

Jillian was trembling with tears streaming down her cheeks. "Mom? I'm okay. I'm coming home."

Chevyo held Yamka in his arms as she broke down

wailing with relief and joy. "Oh, Jillian, my baby. I knew you'd come home when you were ready. I've kept your room just like you left it. When will you be here?"

"We are in Missoula, Montana. Dakota's friend Mack found us at a restaurant. It's unbelievable. I feel so grateful that you all never gave up searching for me. We are leaving in the morning. We will be following Mack and his driving partner, Chris. Dakota wants us to meet him at his cabin when we get there, but we will come see you first and then maybe we can all go to Dakota's home together."

"Honey, you are saying we. Who is coming with you?"

"My husband Liam and your granddaughter, Autumn. She is seventeen now."

Chevyo said with overwhelming excitement, "Did you hear that, Yamka? We are grandparents. Jillian, we look forward to meeting Autumn and having you back home. I want you to be safe on your way here. It's quite stormy and the roads may be icy."

"Yes, I'm sure we'll all be fine. Liam is a good driver."

Yamka said, "Jillian, tell me about Autumn. Does she have your lovely, jade eyes?"

Jillian chuckled, "Yes, actually she does. She looks like both me and Liam. He is an Irish man with gorgeous copper hair and hazel eyes, so I guess it was inevitable that she was born with green eyes and lovely, wavy auburn hair. She's a beautiful, sweet, intelligent girl, Mama and she loves to help me take care of our gardens. She is remarkably skilled at drawing and painting and loves studying history, sociology and psychology."

Yamka said, "Oh, I'm so happy. You left as one and now you're back as two. Life is balancing right back out for all of us."

"Mama and Dad, Mack said that you have been receiving the lilies I sent you for many years now. I couldn't come home until I felt safe, so I sent you lilies with hope that you would understand that I was alive."

Yamka looked questioningly at Chevyo. "Did you know the lilies were from Jillian? All of these years and you didn't tell me?"

"No, honey. I thought they were from our neighbors until just recently. I went to thank our neighbors for sending us the lilies that just arrived, but none of our friends had sent any recently, so I began checking into it. Jillian sent the lilies anonymously, you see, for obvious reasons. I'm sure she was afraid for us to know where she was hiding out, is that right, Jillian?"

"Yes, that's right. I didn't want you to be harmed. I was threatened and told that my family would suffer if I tried to escape from the awful man who kept me prisoner. I don't want to talk about all of that right now. I have gotten over all of the past now, so I can talk about it with you, but not now, okay?"

Chevyo said, "Yes, honey. You can talk about it whenever you are ready. Jillian, the men who abducted you are now in prison. They won't ever be able to harm you again. Come home and we'll talk more. I have an enormous bear hug ready for you and Autumn and we'll properly welcome Liam into our family."

"A wonderful, caring couple in Missoula, Nicholas and Chrys Jensen, unselfishly took me in and have shared their lives with me for many years. The Jensens own a large garden landscape company where they grow flowers and trees all year round. I have lived and worked with them for many years now and I love them dearly, so I will always consider them part of our family as well."

Yamka spoke softly and lovingly, "Jillian dear, we'll make sure that we all stay together, including the Jensens. I have been working on your gardens every year since you went away. I have kept them beautifully planted, because I knew you would come home and now we can work on them again together."

Chevyo said, "Doll, after the holidays, I'd like to drive to Missoula to meet with the Jensens and thank them properly for caring for you all of these years."

"That would be lovely. You will like them very much. We'll all stay close as one lovely, happy family. I've felt very contented for many years now, except for the gaping hole in my heart which you, Mama and Dakota now fill."

Chevyo said, "You go on and get some rest so that you'll be ready to head out in the morning. We'll have everything ready for you when you arrive. We love you, Jillian." They ended the call. Jillian's emotions overwhelmed her once again. Tears flowed and her body trembled uncontrollably. She felt excited and yet grief-stricken about losing so many years with her family.

Liam put his arms around her. "Everything will work out well. I will make sure that we stay as long as you want and we will make regular visits.

She sniffled and tried to compose herself. "I feel so relieved and happy, but I'm completely heartbroken that my life with my family was so abruptly torn away from me. I have many times now, considered how naïve I was and have no one to blame but myself." She dried her tears, shook off her grief and raised her glass. "Here's to many more incredibly joyful days, getting to know my family once again."

Everyone cheered and Mack raised his glass. "Here, here, my good people. This is a jolly good day indeed."

45

Sarah

We finally arrived with the girls at St. Faith's Anglican Church in Vancouver. I hoped that Reverend Angelina Lavoie would be there so that we could figure out what to do with the girls, but she wasn't, although, I was informed that she would be there shortly, so I waited in the church lobby. After a few minutes had passed, Reverend Lavoie entered. She was a lovely woman with a kind face and compassionate demeanor as I was hoping. "Welcome, my dear. I understand you had to make quite a long journey to get here. Would you like some tea?"

"Oh, no thank you. The girls are waiting for me."

"Ike told me all about you. He said you needed some

help finding safe homes for some girls in desperate need."

"Yes, that's right. The girls are freshening up in my RV and look forward to meeting with you. How do you think you can help?"

"Well, I've given it some thought for several days now and I have an idea. I have a few living spaces in a splendid program with full support for the young women. We can offer guidance, education, food, clothing and a safe home until we all work out together what comes next. I also know of an extraordinary young woman who designed and built a lovely ranch home specifically for young women in need. The ranch is located in the Yukon Territory. I've been in contact with her recently and she not only has room for some of your girls, but she also has several jobs around the ranch that need to be filled. If you are interested in that idea, we can call her together."

I said excitedly, "The Yukon Territory? Do you know where it is located?"

"Yes, it's in Whitehorse. Ike mentioned that you are a Canadian. Are you familiar with Northwest Canada?"

"Yes, I grew up in Edmonton, Alberta, although I spent many summers exploring the Northwest and Yukon Territories." I thought, Whitehorse, Jake. My heart thrummed and I instantly thought of Grace. "Can you tell me the name of the woman who owns the ranch?"

"Yes, her name is Grace Nadaeu."

Rubbery legs no longer supported me, so I quickly sat down and drew in a deep breath of air. "Grace Nadaeu?"

"Yes, honey, do you know her?"

"Y… Yes. Oh, my Grace. I can't believe it, my sweet friend, Grace. I have been searching for her for so many years. I was with her the horrible night that she went missing." I suddenly broke down in a puddle of tears, overwhelmed with emotions.

"Oh, my dear." Reverend Lavoie put her arms around me. "There, there. You see? God knows just when to bring us all together. His plan may not always be understood, but our Father knows what he's doing. Let's go give her a call, shall we?"

"Oh, yes, please." I dried my tears on my sleeve and followed her into her office. She dialed the number for Hope Ranch and a French-Canadian woman answered the phone.

"Hope Ranch, this is Clare, how can I help you?"

"Clare, my name is Reverend Lavoie. I'm looking for Grace. Is she available to come to the phone?"

"Yes, Reverend. Please hold the line and I'll go get her."

Grace answered excitedly, "Hello, Reverend. What a pleasurable surprise. How are you?"

"I'm doing very well, thank you. Grace, I have another surprise for you. Are you sitting down?"

"Well, I can be." She sat down on the porch swing wondering what the surprising news could possibly be.

"I have a good friend of yours here with me. She said that she has been searching for you for many years. I am going to hand her the phone now."

"Grace?" I tried to hold it together, but my voice was trembling. "Grace? This is Sarah."

"Oh? You mean, Sarah Beaulieu?"

"Yes, Grace, it's Sarah. I have been searching for you and worrying about you for so long and now I can hardly believe I'm talking with you. I'm coming to visit you right away."

Tears filled Grace's eyes. "Oh, please, do come now. Oh, I can't believe it's you, after all of these years wondering where you were. The weather is stormy and the roads may be icy, but I hope you can come now. Oh, I have so much to tell you."

"I'm used to driving in winter weather and I have chains and a lot of help in case I have to put them on. Grace, I have some girls that I just rescued from some seriously heinous, perverts. Some may want to stay here with Reverend Lavoie, but a few of them may want to journey up there with me. One of the girls is a very good driver and has helped me drive already from South Carolina, U.S. to Vancouver. It's about 2,400 miles from Vancouver to Whitehorse, so if we share driving, we could be there in two days. Do you have room for these girls?"

"Oh, yes, most definitely. I'll have rooms prepared for you and the girls and a nice hot meal when you get here."

"I have to sort a few things out first, but we will leave soon so that we can take advantage of the daylight hours. I'll call you when I'm on the way." I was beside myself with excitement and anticipation. I composed myself and turned to Reverend Lavoie. Will you follow me to the RV and talk with the girls? I'd like to find out which girls would like to stay here and I think it will help the girls make a decision if you could describe the living arrangements and program to them."

"Of course." They walked out to the RV where the girls were quietly waiting.

"Girls, this is Reverend Lavoie. She has a few spaces

for some of you, if you are interested in staying near here. I think you will like Vancouver and the program that Reverend Lavoie has to offer."

"Hello, sweet girls. I am so happy that Sarah has brought you here. I have made it my mission in life to help young women in need such as yourselves. I think you will be very comfortable here and you will always feel safe and loved. You will have warm homes, educational programs that you can participate in and we'll help you find good jobs."

The Reverend described five available spaces for the girls to stay, with friendly people in nice homes nearby. I also discussed Grace's Hope Ranch with the girls and they all decided together who would be happy staying in Vancouver and who would go on with me. It worked out just right, because three of the girls including Jasmine wanted to journey with me to Whitehorse. I thanked Reverend Lavoie and exchanged contact information. The girls and I hugged each other and said goodbye with overwhelming emotions, then the rest of us headed out.

"Jasmine, it's a long journey to Whitehorse. I need for you to help me drive again. Are you up for it?"

"Yes." She was enthusiastic and hopeful. "I love adventures and I'm excited about living at a ranch."

"Oh, you are such a courageous girl." The other two young women, Violet and Sofia were from mountain areas in South America and were enthusiastic about the adventure as well. I printed out brochures for them before we hit the road, so that they could see where we were headed. We stopped at a shop to pick up some warm, winter clothing, jackets, hats and winter boots. Violet made some lunch for us while we journeyed on toward the great Yukon Territory. I was so remarkably thrilled to be on the way to visit with Grace again after so many years. My memories of our childhood years came flooding back and I couldn't help but smile and giggle like a school girl.

46

Jake and Grace

Jake freshened up at his cabin and headed out to find Grace. The road to the ranch meandered in between tall, snow-covered evergreen trees and along a small stream that was an offshoot of the Yukon River. Mounds of snow along the sides of the curvy drive were glistening in the sunlight, which was peeking through dark storm clouds. Jake was relieved that his flight had landed safely before the storm arrived. When he saw the Ranch, he stirred and gasped in amazement. It was beautiful. The main building was a grand, two-story lodge with a heavy timber, gabled roof and cedar decks surrounding the lodge.

As he parked in front of the lodge, he noticed a woman bundled up in a long, winter parka with a fluffy fur lined hood covering her head, rocking on the porch swing. He parked his jeep and walked toward her with mounting anxiety. The woman stood up, smiled and then froze in her stance. She looked as if she was seeing a ghost. She was, although the pleasant, haunting vision from her past moved closer and she suddenly realized the vision was real. On rubbery legs, she ambled toward him, crying out in amazement, "Jake? Is that you, Jake?"

Jake was choked up, but he jogged to her and answered, "Yes, yes Grace, it's me." He scooped her up in his arms and twirled her around the deck, weeping as he kissed her soft, lovely cheeks. "Oh, you're even more beautiful than I remembered. I've been searching for you for so many long, mournful years. Oh, Grace." He put her down and held her eyes intently with his own. Then, they embraced each other passionately, their longing for each other gushing out in a whirlpool of blissful remembrance.

"Jake, I'm sorry, I didn't mean to kiss you like that, but I'm entirely overwhelmed. Please come inside by the fire. Oh, I just knew you'd come find me someday. Of course, you know how much I loved it up here when you, Sarah and I visited your cabin so long ago. I tried to find it several times, but I couldn't find your address and you're not listed. She realized she was rambling on nervously.

"Please don't apologize. I've been craving to kiss you and hold you again for thirty-nine years." He grinned and blushed like a school boy. "When did you move here?"

"In the spring of 1990. I was lucky enough to escape to Vancouver where I met Reverend Angelina Lavoie. She is the Reverend of St. Faith's Anglican Church in Vancouver. There is a women's crisis center there, where they help young women in need. She assists women who have escaped from various abusive situations. Reverend Lavoie took me under her wing and helped me through my troubles and she helped me plan this ranch. After that terrifying fateful day and the atrocious anguish I experienced, I wanted to help other women who had to endure similar types of suffering, so I built the ranch for them. We have eighteen girls here now and three more are on the way." She studied his eyes for a moment, wondering how he might receive the news.

"Grace, this is amazing. You're amazing."

"Jake, there is a woman who has been rescuing girls from sex traffickers, mostly in the U.S. She is traveling with three young girls who were abducted by traffickers and have journeyed so far to locate a safe, warm home. She rescued them in South Carolina, something like four days ago. She is on her way here now from Vancouver, where some of the girls stayed." Grace noticed an odd look on Jake's face.

"Holy bejeesy! I work with a trucking company who have been tracking traffickers as part of an FBI task force. We just helped a mysterious woman capture several criminal perverts and rescued twelve young women from South Carolina. She was incredible. She also helped us identify a group of gangsters who kidnapped Dakota Hunt's twin sister, who went missing two years before you disappeared. The criminal who abducted her is finally in jail." Grace observed his face as he struggled to perceive the connection.

"Jake." She paused. "The woman is Sarah."

"No way. You're kidding? Sarah?"

"Yes, Sarah." Her eyes glistened with tears. "She's on her way here now."

"Huh! Wow, Grace. I can't believe that was Sarah. She has my phone number and she's been calling me providing me with tips about the traffickers, but she always hung up before I had time to trace her phone or find out who she was." He thought for a moment. "That means, Sarah has known where I have been for some time now. Wow, I just can't get my head around this. I wonder why she didn't trust me, why she didn't confide in me. I mean, I would have been able to communicate with her and we could have been working together for many years."

"She probably didn't want you to be involved in her work. You know Jake, what she does is illegal. Rescuing these girls is a beautiful thing, but it's dangerous work. The women are probably supposed to be registered and helped through legal U.S. social programs and maybe some are even supposed to be deported back to their own countries. She couldn't put you at risk. I know about these things, because I have many girls who come here that don't have proper identification and so on. If they want to stay in Canada, I help them obtain their PR green cards and I help them get their passports so that they don't have to worry about those things. But when they come here, it is risky for them."

"Yeah, okay. I'm just a bit disappointed that she felt she couldn't trust me. I have been searching for both of you for so many years, Grace. Do you know how I found you?"

"No. Oh, wait, Brooke Macfie. My friend Brooke came up here to tour my ranch. She said she is planning one similar to mine in Colorado. Yes, that must be how. She said she'd been driving for a company called Dakota Hunt Trucking and she mentioned Dakota several times concerning his twin sister, Jillian."

"Yes, Brooke just sprang the news a day ago at a conference, that she had been up here checking out your ranch. When she mentioned your name, I lost it completely. I'm grateful that she visited you or I may never have found you. She didn't know you were the one who went missing and the same woman that I had been searching for. What a small world it is. Grace, I'd like to take you back with me to Dakota's home for the Christmas holiday, if you'd like to."

"I would love to. I'll just need to work a few things out here at the ranch."

Jake's eyes rolled and he gasped. "And we have to wait for Sarah. I have to see her and talk with her."

"Yes, we have to wait. I am still in shock that you are here and she will be here soon, at the same time. This is so incredible. God works in mysterious ways. Jake, I am interested in spending as much time with you as possible." She looked into his eyes and cupped his face. "I don't want to ever lose you again." They kissed each other hungrily, with heartfelt passion.

"No chance of that, Grace." She led him to her bedroom suite, she herself surprised that she would behave like a sultry desperate woman, but she had been lonely for so long that she was hungry for intimate, human interaction. She had been carrying a torch for Jake for so many years that she had not been interested in other men. They held each other, making beautiful love for hours. Afterwards, they laughed and teased each other as they sauntered into the kitchen and opened up a bottle of wine. "This place is amazing, Grace." They laughed again at the reference. Jake began singing Amazing Grace to her. She laughed and joined in. "How sweet the sound." They laughed again after completing the verse.

"That's your song, Grace. And now you're found, in more ways than one." He held her close and kissed her tenderly. "I'm never letting you go. Marry me, Grace."

She crumbled in his arms. "Yes, oh, yes, I will marry you, Jake." He put his arms around her and twirled her around the room, dancing and laughing. I want to be with you for the rest of my life but I'd like to take it slowly, just for a while. I want to find out all about you and what you have been doing for all of these years. You could stay here with me for a while if you would like to settle down a little and help me run the ranch."

"I would really like to be here with you and I definitely have an interest in working with you here on the ranch, although I will be working with the task force team for at least six more months. We may eventually be working up here as a coordinated effort with Canada and mainland Alaska. Dakota has been concerned about young women in the lower forty-eight states for many years and we have been doing everything we can to help them. He also feels that the Alaskan and Canadian Native women, who have been viciously targeted by sex traffickers to an appalling degree, could surely benefit from many more people helping in every way possible. I bet we'll be working up here by mid spring."

"I have been reading about the inexcusable targeting of our Native Canadian people as well and I surely believe that much more can be done to help them. In fact, that is one of the reasons I was so interested in opening Hope Ranch here in the Yukon. I keep hoping other compassionate souls can find the necessary resources to open many more transitional safe haven homes for women in need. Well, I hope you do work up here soon, so that we can be together as much as possible. Whenever you and your team drive through Whitehorse, I expect you all to stop in for a hot meal and a nice rest out of your trucks. Please make sure you relay my welcoming invite to Dakota and the others."

"Jake put his warm, muscular arms around Grace, his gaze lingering on her gentle, kindhearted eyes. "Now you understand why I love you so much. I have never met anyone so sweet and generous. Speaking of generosity, I think we should call Dakota and give him the good news. He wants to know whether or not I was able to locate you. I'd also like to find out if Mack had any luck in discovering where Jillian has been hiding out. We have believed for all of these years, that both you and Jillian were alive and out of harm's way. You and Jillian are strong minded, determined women and we all felt deeply within our hearts that you would be able to escape from the clutches of your captors and you did."

Grace was listening to Jake intently and did not want to begin a new life together harboring secrets, so she made a decision to reveal her past with him. She held him closely, while reliving the tragic past ten-year period of time she was held captive. Each time Grace spoke about her painful memories, she had to endure mentally reliving the unbearable servitude she worked so hard to escape from, but she learned to appreciate renewed strength and self-confidence as her resolve. She felt proud of herself for deciding to give back rather than wallowing in depression and self-loathing. Building Hope Ranch was a remarkable turning point for her and every time she received distressed young women who lived through life shattering experiences, she realized all over again that she was doing the work that God intended for her.

When Grace finished her tales of woe, Jake wrapped her in his loving arms and held her watery eyes with his own. "Grace, I love you tremendously. Troubled times are over and I will dedicate myself to helping you replace the memories of the past with happy, adventurous, exciting experiences." He expressed his love and commitment to her which she received with equal, genuine, tender devotion. After a while, Jake and Grace lounged comfortably in front of the blazing wood stove and called Dakota.

47

Dakota

Cheynne and I finally arrived at the Denver terminal. The drive was slow travel in the stormy weather, but the plows had stayed on top of the steady snow fall. The other drivers would arrive within a few hours and I checked in with Zach, who said he was doing okay and would arrive sometime the following day. We had just walked into the terminal when my cell rang and I noticed it was Jake. "Hey, I guess you made it there safely."

"I did and I found her, contentedly bundled up on her porch swing. You are the first to hear some spectacular news. We're getting married!"

"Way to go, buddy. You sure don't waste any time."

"Dakota, I've longed for this day for thirty-nine years

and I'm not letting her get away."

"Well buddy, congratulations. So when is the happy occasion?"

"We'll be giving that some thought, but we'll know when the time is right. "Dakota, you're never going to believe what I'm going to tell you next. It's about our mysterious vigilante. She's on her way here with some of the girls."

"You're kidding. How in the world did that come about?"

"Serendipity. The most intriguing part of it is that the mystery woman is Sarah. Do you remember me telling you that Grace, Sarah and I were all friends when Grace went missing?"

"Yes, I do. No wonder she kept calling you with tips. It all makes sense now." He laughed heartily. "Oh, dude, it sounds like you have a lot of catching up to do. Bring them both here for Christmas."

"We talked about that earlier. Grace says that she has plenty of help here at the ranch and can leave for a week. I've already looked into a three-ticket flight to Denver on Christmas Eve morning, that is if Sarah can and will come with us."

"You know how I feel about Christmas. The more the merrier. Jake, you might want to have a serious talk with her first. You know I invited Dirk and if he decides to show up, she might want to conceal her identity unless she is ready to reveal her secret life to him, otherwise my lips are sealed. She's been exceptionally helpful to us and I want her on my team whichever way she wants to play the game. Dirk doesn't really need to know that she's the mystery woman, so that she can continue to assist us in her own way. Try to talk her into coming. I think she can pull it off."

"Grace and I will work on it and we'll let you know."

"Jake, guess who else is coming home?"

"Jillian? Did Mack find her?"

I smiled reflectively, feeling my eyes water. "Yes, and you might be interested to learn that I have a niece. Her name is Autumn. Jillian, Autumn and Liam McKinney, her husband, are on their way now. They're following Mack and Chris to the cabin. Jake, this is turning out to be one exceptional reunion." I felt entirely euphoric with the weight of the world suddenly lifted off my shoulders. I had to pinch myself to make sure I wasn't experiencing a spectacular daydream.

"Dakota, I'm sure you and your folks are overjoyed and utterly relieved. I can't wait to meet Jillian, Autumn and the good man who has been looking after them.. This is great news and a year to remember and celebrate. I'll get in touch with you when Sarah arrives and we'll update you with our plans."

When we ended the call, I recapped Jake's remarkable news for Cheynne. She was ecstatic for Jake and marveled at the good fortune they were all having. I said, "I'm exhausted, so let's stay here for the night and we'll head to the cabin in the morning to get things set up for everyone's arrival. I'll ask Rich to bring Zach up to the cabin when he rolls in. Rich will be delivering loads today and tomorrow morning and will secure the terminal before he leaves. We have eight more teams on their way here, all arriving tonight and tomorrow." I glanced out of the window when I heard a truck motor in. "Looks like Rhys and Nash just arrived."

I have always felt relieved when my drivers all made it safely back during adverse winter weather conditions. When Rhys and Nash ambled into the terminal, I gripped them both in a brotherly hug. "I owe you both more than I could ever repay. The effort you made in taking down Jillian's captor in Oklahoma initiated the beginning of a new era, filled with gratitude, hope and faith. With the help of you, Nash, Mack and Chris, my woeful, age-old stories and gloomy memories will be replaced with laughter and rejuvenation." My eyes began to well up. "With your continuous support, I have been able to set shame, guilt and sorrow aside, redirecting my strengths into determination and the motivation needed to take action and for this, I am forever grateful."

Rhys compassionately put his arm around me. "Brother, ye don't owe us anything. Jillian is family and I look forward to getting to know her, Autumn and Liam. In fact, I'd be thrilled if Autumn called me Uncle Rhys." He chuckled with delight.

I summarized the extraordinary events going on with Jake in Whitehorse and also mentioned that Jake would be bringing Grace and Sarah with him to join us in our Christmas reunion.

"Well, I'll be. What were the odds that Jake would reunite with Grace and Sarah at the same time? And Sarah is the mystery woman?" He laughed heartily. "That's remarkable. I'll have to say, she is one gutsy, intriguing woman. By the way, I'm not allowing you and Jake to have all of the glory. I am motivated to finally yank myself up by my boot straps and ask Brooke to go out with me. I'm madly in love with that woman and I feel the urgent need to find out if there is something there, unless I have merely imagined it all in this crazy old noggin of mine." He chuckled, smiling widely.

Cheynne snickered. "I hope you do. I have only spent time with the team for a short while, but I've already seen and heard your dalliance for long enough. Go sweep the gal off her feet." She grinned, then lifted her brows. "You do realize that if you guys start dating, she might want to keep you all to herself and ask you to help her at Harmony Ranch, right?"

"Aye, I hope she does. These old bones have been nudging me to plant my boots on the ground for a desirable change. I have been driving by life for long enough."

I said thoughtfully, glancing at Cheynne, "I understand how you feel, brother." I grinned at Rhys, quite certain that he noticed the sparkle in my eyes.

In the morning, Cheynne and I were preparing to head up to the cabin when I received a call from Mack. "Dakota, just givin' ye an update. Everything is going well. We are about 100 miles out. ETA, zero-nine hundred."

"Excellent. Cheynne and I are heading home now and will be picking up food and beverages and setting up rooms for everyone. Rhys will be tying up some loose ends and will not be far behind us. Safe travels, buddy and take care of my family."

"Aye. We'll be along soon with bells on our toes and lively tunes echoing from our hearts."

I was excited to go home. It had been the most eventful, emotional week I had experienced in many years. I was exhausted, yet exhilarated with the thought of reconnecting with Jillian and getting to know my niece. I was also interested in becoming acquainted with Liam, to make sure he was the right man for Jillian, although I had a feeling that Liam would prove to be the sensitive, compassionate man that Jillian deserves. I suddenly realized that I was still feeling like I had to protect her as I used to when we were young. I also recognized that I still had to resolve my issue of self-blame for her disappearance. Jillian has proven to be the strong, self-determined woman I hoped she would be, therefore, I figured I would be able to forgive myself over time.

I had spoken with my folks about Jillian while Cheynne was driving yesterday. They were anxious and overjoyed about having Jillian home after forty-one years of anguish and sorrow. It still didn't seem real to me yet. I breathed in several times, centering myself, calming my thoughts and feeling content with aspirations of a new life filled with joy and laughter.

48

The Holiday Event

Cheynne and I were laughing and talking while setting up the guest rooms. I glanced at my watch, noticing that the others would not arrive for several hours, so I put my arms around Cheynne and brought her to me. The fire was roaring in the massive stone fireplace, while the wind was puffing snow in swirls outside and whistling at the windows. A classical violin and cello composition created a sultry mood from the surround sound speakers. We kissed each other, slowly and tenderly at first and then our passion grew stronger, both ravenous for love and closeness. I danced with her to the bedroom where our passionate hearts intertwined for a lingering, enchanting time.

As we held each other closely, I gazed into Cheynne's

stunning golden eyes, regarding her beauty. "You are so gorgeous. You're fifty-six years old, but you look like you're thirty. Cheynne, I realize we've only known each other for a short while, but I find myself completely and unexpectedly in love with you, which seems to grow deeper every day. When I saw you in the truck for the first time at the terminal, I knew right then that I had finally discovered my soulmate. If you feel the same, would you consider exploring our relationship together to see where it leads?"

She gazed into my eyes, grinning, her face turning crimson and more lovely than it was a second before. "Dakota, are you asking me to be your girlfriend?" She laughed coquettishly, smiling widely. "We have a strong connection and I do want to be near you, sharing everything with you. I've been longing to find love like we seem to have my entire life."

I held her close, craving more, wishing we could remain wrapped in each other's arms for the rest of the day. Just then, there was a knock on the door. We glanced at each other and laughed as we quickly unraveled ourselves from the sheets and hastily dressed. I raced to the door, heart pounding with anticipation. It was Mack and Chris. "Hey mate, don't get yer hopes up just yet. It's only us for now."

"Come in. Welcome brothers." I hugged Mack and Chris with such fervor that I could barely releases my grip. The gratefulness I felt toward Mack for locating and bringing Jillian home was immeasurable."

Mack met my eyes and nodded warmly. "Jillian wanted to stop at yer folks' house first. They plan to bring the lass here in a few hours. Jillian is excited to see you as well, so don't think otherwise. She wanted Chevyo and Yamka to meet Autumn and Liam and also thought it would be best to stay with the folks. She wanted to put her things away and get reacquainted. She walked around the house, taking in every sight and scent and being at the house again appeared to be jolting her memory. Then she and Autumn walked out to the gardens with Yamka, which of course are covered with snow, but she seemed to be affected by the bridge over the creek and the view to the icy pond below. Sascha ambled up to her, sniffed her, then snuggled up to her as if she has known her for years. Jillian kneeled down to rub her back, giggling and smiling with such a sparkle in her eyes that I knew right then, the lass was okay." Mack flashed a wide, toothy smile.

As Cheynne sauntered toward us, I said, "Mack, Chris, I'd like for you to meet Cheynne."

"Well, you are as beautiful as Dakota described ye, lass. Have you been keeping this big ole' bear in line?"

She snickered and peered at me with adoring eyes. "He doesn't seem to need that, but I sure enjoy being around him."

I said, "I just asked her if she had an interest in sharing our lives with each other to find out if we are truly soulmates, which I believe we are." I beamed. "She said, she would indeed." I put my arm around her and grinned like a school boy.

"Well, okay then, congratulations are in order. I just happen to have some champagne right here for a proper toast. Why don't I go get some glasses and pop the cork right here and now?"

"I'll help you find the glasses." Mack and I moseyed

into the kitchen.

"I wouldn't let that one slip away either if I were you. It's about time you found a gorgeous, lucky lass, so that all of your kindness and generosity is not all wasted on your buddies."

"Mack, I fell in love as hard as one could fall. She is my soulmate. I can feel it in my bones and deeply within my heart. Truth be told, Cheynne helps me find the better man in me, truer to myself. It was because of her, that I quit wallowing in self-pity and she somehow sparked my internal engine to envision my strengths and confidence that had been lost along with grief-stricken memories. She's my miracle woman who came to my rescue right on time."

We hooted like happy go lucky young lads as we toasted with the delicious oaky bubbles. Mack began singing a lively Irish tune, grasped Cheynne's hands and twirled her around the spacious, lofty room. Chris then joined, dancing an energetic Irish jig. We all clapped and roared with laughter, which felt fantastic.

Chris poured more champagne. As everyone raised in salute, I expressed, "Here's to my incredibly brave brothers and to my lovely soulmate, Cheynne."

Mack raised his glass again, "Here's to papa bear, the most compassionate, generous, hard-working man alive. You deserve a good woman, mate."

"Here, here!" Everyone clapped.

I held my glass up again. "This one is for Jake and Grace. For all of you who haven't heard, he found her and asked her to marry him and he's planning to bring her here on Christmas Eve."

Mack said, "That doesn't surprise me a bit. I don't

remember him thinking about any other woman since I've known him. Good fer the lad and I look forward to meeting her."

"I have some more interesting news. Our mystery woman is none other than Sarah Beaulieu. Jake, Grace and Sarah were good friends when Grace went missing. Sarah is on the way to the Yukon Territory with three of the girls she rescued in the South Carolina bust."

"Are ye kidding?" Chris asked.

"Nope. Somehow, Sarah discovered a church in Vancouver to take the women to, which has a women's crisis division. Reverend Lavoie informed her that Grace was running Hope Ranch, the ranch in Whitehorse that Brooke visited. Sarah immediately called Grace to make the arrangements to drive up there with the girls. There must have been a few extremely emotional moments, I can just imagine. The other interesting thing is that Sarah somehow found out that Jake was working with us, tracked him down and discovered his phone number, which is why she was calling him. Jake had no idea that our mystery woman was Sarah, no idea. Apparently, she didn't want to blow her cover, so she felt she had to keep Jake in the dark for a while longer."

Chris said, "That's phenomenal. I tried to find out who Sarah was through my network. I figured she was working with someone with exceptional computer skills, but I haven't been able to figure out who yet."

I said, "If Jake brings her here, you all need to know that she will not mention her work. Dirk might show up and I don't want to blow her cover. I'd like to welcome her to the team. I happen to think her work is extremely invaluable but she is a vigilante, which is not illegal in this country, but some of the things she does are illegal. Running off with the girls to get them to safe havens is admirable, but injecting criminals with tranquilizers is risky and illegal. Dirk went ballistic when she took off with one of Marino's thugs. She had one of her comrades interrogate him until she got what she wanted out of him." I laughed. "You have to admire her. She's got some moxie and I can't wait to meet her. Anyway, we don't want to blow her cover. I want her to keep working with us and I owe her my right arm, since she gave us the lead to Marino and Giordano. If Sarah hadn't been involved, Jillian might still believe she and her family were in danger and she wouldn't be here now."

Everyone cheered and continued discussing our good fortune. "Well, why don't you boys get settled. Put your gear in your rooms and Cheynne and I will cook up a storm in the kitchen.

Throughout the day, my drivers arrived and got settled in their rooms. Delicious aromas filled the air with roasted turkey, homemade rosemary sour dough bread and blueberry pie. Everyone was having a jovial time. Brooke and Blake helped Cheynne and me in the kitchen, while talking and joking around. Mack tended the bar, concocting delicious beverages, Chris played his Irish whistle and Rhys and Ian were involved in an animated game of darts.

After a couple of hours, Dad called and I became instantly anxious. "Hey, where are you?"

"We just arrived. I just wanted to give you a heads up." My heart leaped with excitement and I hoped I could restrain my overwhelming emotions that instantly popped up as soon as Dad said they were here. I combed my tousled hair with my fingers and eagerly jogged to the door. There was Jillian, standing there with her beautiful jade eyes smiling up at me. I scooped her up in a huge bear hug with cries of joy. I grinned at Autumn, who was standing behind her and embraced her along with Jillian. I hugged Mom and Dad with watery eyes. Liam and I shook hands while walking inside my warm, cheerful home.

I pulled Jillian off to the side of the room, still feeling overly emotional. "Jillian, I've missed you so much. I feel like I'm whole again after forty-one years of grief-stricken separation."

Jillian said in a choked-up voice, "You don't know how long I've wanted to come home." She didn't want to talk about the horrible things she went through in her past life. She just wanted to have a good time reconnecting with her family. "I plan on spending as much time as possible with you, Mom and Dad, so we'll get to know each other again. We embraced each other, then dried our tears. Jillian sauntered toward Autumn. "I want to introduce you two properly. This is your niece, Autumn Chrysanthemum McKinney."

"I hugged her again, proudly. You are stunning! You remind me of your mother when she was almost your age."

Autumn laughed. "And you are just as Grandpa Chevy described. A huge teddy bear uncle. I'm so happy to finally meet my family." She took Liam's arm, locking it with her own. "And this is my Papa, Liam."

I held my hand out to shake Liam's, but we both ended up in a compassionate embrace. "Thank you for taking care of my sister and niece and welcome to our family."

"I really appreciate the warm greeting. My heart goes out to you and your folks. I have wanted Jillian to reconnect with you for some time now, but she was concerned that it was still not safe until recently. I can't begin to tell you how relieved I am that Giordano is in prison."

We both nodded as we strutted into the kitchen. "Cheynne, this is Liam McKinney. He's the honorable man I spoke of, who has been taking such great care of Jillian and Autumn."

Cheynne smiled whole-heartily and hugged him. "We are all so grateful for your care and compassion and I look forward to getting acquainted."

Jillian sauntered into the kitchen. "What is this I hear, Dakota? You met your soulmate?"

Cheynne put her arms around Jillian. "You are a dear, aren't you? Welcome home, Jillian."

I joined them with another bear hug. "I'm sure the two of you will become great friends."

Jillian pranced out to the living room where everyone had gathered, pulling Cheynne behind her. "Come on, Dakota, don't be shy. Everyone, Dakota and Cheynne are seeing each other, seriously. She peered at Mom. "I already think of her as my sister and maybe someday soon, they will make that official." Cheynne beamed and blushed crimson.

I put my arm around her as I caught Dad's eyes, nodding with a joyful, satisfied grin. "I have finally found my soul mate after all of these years. Cheynne is a very compassionate, kindhearted woman and will probably prove to be my better half."

Mom stood and hugged us both. "Dakota, I knew you would find the right girl, all in your own time. And I'm so grateful and proud of you for finding and bringing Jillian home. You deserve a good woman." She winked at Cheynne. "Welcome to our family, Cheynne."

Rhys stood up holding his glass high. "Cheers to ye happy couples. And may I be as lucky as ye are someday." Everyone cheered. Rhys placed Brooke's hand in his and twirled and danced with her around the room. I picked up my guitar and began playing a lively bluegrass tune, while others grabbed a partner and danced. Rhys held Brooke closely and I heard him say, "Will ye go out with me sometime? I think ye know I'm head over heels for ye, Lasse."

Brooke put her arms around his neck and gazed into his glistening, hazel eyes as they twirled and swayed. She pulled him to her and tenderly kissed him, then whispered, "Yes, I would love to go out with you, Rhys. I think you know how I feel about you as well." He flashed a wide toothy smile and laughed whole-heartily as he twirled her around again.

49

Grace gave Jake a tour of the ranch. He marveled at the tremendous space, thoughtfully planned with six log cabins surrounding the main lodge, each designed to house two to four people and a large recreation, education building. There was a heated horse stable large enough for eight horses, a heated barn housing chickens and dairy cows and two Quonset hut style, heated greenhouses, containing neatly planted rows of vegetables and herbs. There were also outside activity spaces and acres of land for horseback riding and grazing cows.

"The ranch is quite impressive, Grace. If you ever need help here with maintenance, repairs, company, you just let me know." He tickled her sides.

"I have a couple of full-time ranch hands, but I could

always use another, especially if it's you."

They heard a vehicle engine heading up the drive. "That must be Sarah." Grace said with excitement. They trotted to the lodge to greet them.

When Sarah saw both Grace and Jake approaching her, she shrieked with excitement. "Grace!" She opened the door. "Put your jackets and boots on girls and let's go see your new home." She jumped out of the RV and bolted toward Grace, threw her arms around her and kissed her rosy cheeks. "Grace, you darling woman. And look at what you've accomplished. I'm so proud of you and I've missed you so much."

Jake cleared his throat, "Uhm. Hi, Sarah." He smiled conspiratorially.

"Oh, what a surprise. Jake. She put her arms around him with a fond embrace. "I didn't recognize you with that enormous fur hood concealing your face." She turned to look at Grace. "You didn't tell me that Jake would be here. H…How long have you known where Grace was?"

"A colleague from work, Brooke Macfie, had befriended her and just recently revealed her location. As soon as I heard, I jumped on a plane and headed here. Sarah, it's so terrific to see you, that is, without your disguise." He chuckled.

"Oh, yes, that." She said nervously. The girls ambled apprehensively toward them. "Grace and Jake, I'd like for you to meet Jasmine, Violet and Sofia. They endured a long journey here and I'm sure they are exhausted and anxious."

Grace sauntered over to them, hugging each one compassionately. "Welcome to Hope Ranch. Let's all go inside where it's warm and we'll talk."

Sarah put her arm around Jake and talked with him as they moseyed inside. "Jake, I know you're a bit perplexed, but please don't be angry with me. Let me explain."

"No worries, Sarah. I talked with Grace in length about you and the work you've been doing. We are both completely impressed with your efforts. I think you're just about the craziest woman I've ever encountered, but the young women out there need you. I understand why you didn't confide in me, although I do wish you had trusted me." He chuckled. "That disguise you were wearing in South Carolina was pretty outrageous. I would have expected you to show up wearing vigilante style, dark, inconspicuous attire with a hood over your head. I had no idea that the gorgeous curly blonde was you." He chuckled. "Really? High heels and a southern belle accent? I haven't seen you in a long, long time, but wow, that was remarkable." He chuckled again.

She laughed. "Yes, I have to dress the part. You should have seen the disguise I wore on the river boat. I dressed as an elderly woman with tons of makeup to make me look wrinkly, glasses and a wig to boot. I wanted to be completely unassuming. I mean, who would expect an old woman to get right up close to that nasty thug, so that she could slip a bug and a tracer right into his pocket." She laughed.

"Oh, I wondered how you were able to track them. That's very clever, Sarah." He hugged her. "I just can't believe we are all together again. Let's stay in close contact. In fact Sarah, you might want to consider revealing your identity to Dakota's team, because all want to work with you. I'm not certain we would have made that bust if you weren't helping in the way that you did. You had the whole thing organized. The team will not reveal your identity to anyone, especially not to Dirk or any law enforcement agencies. Just think about it."

"Okay, I'll give it some thought."

Jake grinned. "I have some terrific news. Grace and I are getting married. I asked her yesterday and gratefully, she said yes."

"That's terrific, Jake. I couldn't hope for more. Don't let our darling Grace out of your sight. I don't want anything evil to happen to her, ever again. In fact, I am going to make regular visits here and if Grace will have me, I might even stay for a while. I've been working nonstop for many years now and I'm tired, quite frankly. So, when's the big day?"

We haven't gotten that far. We will be taking it slowly for a while, getting to know each other again and when the time is right, we'll let everyone know. If she wants a big wedding, we'll surely have it, but who knows? She might want a small gathering with her closest buds and maybe a few of her friends here." He nudged her. "Actually that's what I prefer, but I want her to be happy. We'll do whatever she wants to do."

"Yes, she deserves to be happy, safe and cared for. Did she reveal anything, I mean, like what happened?"

"Yes. I didn't want her to have to relive any of it, but she insisted that she get it off her chest so that we could go on with our lives without her haunting memories floating above her head like storm clouds ready to burst. To me, it's all over and I just want her to be deliriously happy. I'm sure she'll tell you about it, but in her own time. On another note, you should tour around this incredible place. She's providing a tremendous, necessary service and the girls love it here."

"Yes, I agree. I need warm, comforting places like this for the women I rescue."

"You know Brooke, the woman I mentioned earlier is opening up another ranch like this one in Grand County, Colorado, called Harmony Ranch. So sometime next spring, you'll have that resource available in the U.S."

"That's so good to hear. I look forward to meeting Brooke and touring her ranch." She flashed a friendly smile. "Let's see what the girls are up to."

Grace was helping the young women get situated in their lodge rooms. "They seem to feel comfortable here which makes me so happy. I'd like for you to meet Lorraine Dubois. She is a highly skilled, compassionate partner, who I could never run this ranch without. She is an amazing chef and a psychologist. The women really feel comfortable talking with her and she teaches cooking classes to any of the girls who have an interest."

Lorraine Dubois is a sweet, kind hearted French woman with a heavy accent. "Bonjour. I'm happy to meet you and it's nice for you to visit here, yes?" They shook her hand with delight. "Come into the kitchen and I'll make some tea for you. Are you hungry? I'll make some blueberry crepes."

Jake's stomach growled. "Thank you, that sounds delicious. I haven't had crepes in years."

Grace said, "Lorraine is a fantastic chef and has taught me a lot about cooking and baking." They all followed her into the kitchen where they sipped tea and talked.

After lunch, the girls retired to their rooms to rest.

Grace asked, "Sarah, did Jake tell you that he wants to bring us to Colorado for Christmas to meet Dakota, Jillian and the rest of the Hunt family? Some of his other employees and friends will be joining in the festivities as well. It sounds like it will be a really fun holiday. I haven't been to the states in a long time for very good reasons, but I'd like to replace dreadful memories with cheerful, exciting adventures."

"That actually sounds like fun. Hey, Jake, give me some details about Jillian's rescue? I heard on the news that Marino and Giordano were in jail and I also saw Dakota's news bulletin."

"Mack followed a lead to Missoula, Montana and discovered her dining at a restaurant. She had been sending lilies home to let them know she was alive, so they were finally able to trace one of her orders to Missoula. Jillian, her daughter Autumn and Jillian's husband, Liam, followed Mack and Chris to the Hunt's home in Colorado. They are all at Dakota's house now, probably having an exciting time reconnecting and getting acquainted."

Sarah cheered. "Hurray! That's so wonderful. I live for happy endings."

Grace's eyes welled up, momentarily recalling the day she escaped. "I'm really happy that Jillian is now home and by the sound of it, she's okay. I look forward to talking with her about all of the pleasant, enjoyable things she has been experiencing since her escape."

Jake added a bit of detail for Grace. "Jillian disappeared in 1977. Dakota, his family have searched for her for forty-one years, but thanks to Sarah's tips about the thugs responsible for her kidnapping and Jillian's order of lilies that she had been sending to her folks, she's safe and sound at home."

Grace's face lit up. "You know, it's funny sometimes how small the world really is. Everything is connected and people just have to follow their intuitions and study their innermost thoughts. Everything eventually comes full circle."

Jake smiled and nodded. "I also believe that. You, Sarah and I are back together again, because of entirely unrealized connections that were there for many years, unbeknownst to all of us. I guess the time was right for our paths to cross again." Jake flashed a wide, toothy smile. "Well, should I book those tickets to Colorado? We could fly out tomorrow morning and be at Dakota's cabin by early evening. We could all stay for a few days and then come back here and help Grace on the ranch. Dakota wants us to have a break, so I'm not expected to return to work until mid-January." They all talked about it and agreed. Grace's staff members would help the girls fit right in and would all enjoy a warm and cozy Christmas holiday.

Jake called the airlines to make the arrangements and then updated Dakota with the good news. He turned back to the gals and merrily said, "Well, we're booked, so pack your bags." They were all excited as they prepared for a cheerful holiday.

Sarah was a bit skeptical about being around the team as herself and not incognito, but she was used to living on the wild side. She had endured and coped with so many hardships in the past forty-three years that she felt confident and fearless. She felt like the world needed her and often wished there were more people, who weren't afraid to step up to the plate and conscientiously and diligently assist victims of sex crimes. She was proud of herself, but lonely. She had been living in her RV with no home to go to, until now, she thought. She talked about living at the ranch for a while, with Grace and Jake. They asked her to consider Hope Ranch her permanent home, an invitation in which she was overjoyed to accept. Sarah planned to continue her work and felt positive about the prospect of collaborating with Dakota's team as often as needed.

Grace, Sarah and Jake sat outside on the porch swing, snuggled in blankets, drinking hot cocoa and enjoying the beauty around them. A crescent moon peeked out from beyond the mountain tops appearing as if it were a glowing Christmas ornament dangling in the deep, ebony sky. Lovely, white icicle lights, draped along the roof eaves of the lodge and cabins and fresh evergreen boughs adorned the fronts of cedar doors. Sapphire blue, plum purple and emerald green lights, twinkled on juniper shrubs, reflecting glistening colors on freshly fallen snow.

Inside the lodge, stood an impressively tall, shapely spruce tree, adorned with white lights and colorful ornaments that the girls enjoyed decorating. They were singing Christmas carols while stringing popcorn on the tree. Grace, Sarah and Jake listened without saying a word. The message was clear; the girls felt safe and happy and were eager to experience new lives filled with peace and hope. Grace and Sarah cried tears of joy.

50

Colorado Christmas

Early Christmas Eve morning, Jake drove Grace and Sarah to the airport, parked the jeep and they all excitedly strolled across the lot toward the terminal. Grace snickered. "The Mod Squad, just like the old days." They all laughed. They would fly to Edmonton and then take a connecting flight to Denver, Colorado. During the flight, Jake highlighted the fun things they could do once they arrived at the cabin. He emphasized music, dancing, singing, cooking, eating, sledding and riding snow mobiles.

"Wait until you meet Dakota's folks. They are both a hoot. Yamka must be in her upper seventies by now, but she'll take you by the arm and waltz you around the floor like a twenty-year-old. She sees the beauty in everyone and always makes us feel welcome and comfortable. Chevyo is a tall, bear of a man, about the size of Dakota, with the kindest demeanor I have ever encountered. He has so many stories to tell, all of them either hilarious or sensational. I really love those people. Dakota has a similar demeanor and is like a brother, who I feel very fortunate to know."

The flight landed safely despite the frigid blowing snow. Jake thought there might be a chance that the Denver airport would shut down, but thankfully there were no problems. They rented a four-wheel drive vehicle and were almost to Dakota's cabin in Evergreen when Jake's phone rang. It was Dakota. He put on his headphones and answered the call. "Hey, buddy. We're about to head up the drive now. The white lights are beautiful and helpful. They appear to light up the whole stretch of the drive."

"Yes, I thought you might appreciate that. I had Mack and Rhys out there helping me put them up this morning. Ian plowed the drive and the gals decorated the Christmas tree. Come on up and join the party. Cheynne helped me make up your rooms, so all you have to do is set your things down and grab a glass of bubbly."

"Dakota, you're the man, on the way."

Dakota was standing at the door when they pulled up, then jogged out to help Jake with the bags. He greeted Sarah and Grace with delight and excitement. "Come on in out of the cold and we'll introduce everyone properly."

The spirit in the room was energetic and warm. Mack was playing lively guitar tunes while folks were mingling. Dakota announced, "Listen up, everyone. I proudly introduce Grace Nadeau and Sarah Beaulieu. And you all know my bro, Jake." Every one expressed various greetings as Rhys handed them each a glass of champagne.

Jake hugged Grace with one arm and held up his glass with the other. "Grace and I are getting married. I decided I'm not letting her slip away ever again." He brought her to him and gave her an enormous, sloppy kiss. She blushed and smiled as everyone cheered.

Jillian shuffled toward Jake. "I've heard so much about you, Jake. You and the rest of your team are truly sweet angels for working so hard to rescue women in need." Her eyes welled up as she hugged him.

"Jillian," He said with watery eyes, "I'm so very happy that you are safely back home. Your family must be relieved and tremendously excited to be able to enjoy the rest of your lives together."

"Thank you, Jake. Everyone has been remarkably sweet and compassionate towards me. Hey, come meet my daughter, Autumn." Autumn was in the kitchen talking with Grace and Sarah. "Autumn, this is Jake. He is one of Dakota's heroes that helped rescue a group of women, just recently."

"Hello, Jake."

He hugged her genially. "Wow, you are a beautiful woman, just like your mother and with the same stunning eyes. I think I'll consider you my niece, since Dakota is like a brother to me. Autumn, you now have another uncle." They all chuckled and exchanged adoring comments.

Sarah said, "Hey, Autumn. Did Brooke tell you about Harmony Ranch? I bet she would love to have you help her on the ranch if you're interested." Brooke sauntered into the kitchen at the mention of her name. She put her arms affectionately around Sarah and Grace and flashed a warm smile.

Autumn said excitedly, "I would love to help. I'm graduating in May and I've been trying to figure out what I want to do for my summer vacation. I've been thinking of studying both Sociology and Psychology as a dual major, beginning in the fall semester. And since I love riding horses, I could help girls learn how to ride and care for the animals."

Brooke was thrilled. "You will fit right in then and you will be my first recruit. In fact, I will need a lot of help right about when you graduate. I'll need help with setting things up, interior decorating, picking out furniture and a hundred other necessary chores." She shook Autumn's hand. "You're hired, my dear."

Jillian clapped her hands. "That's terrific, Autumn. We could drive you back here to work for the summer and on your spring break. Liam and I have discussed our living arrangements in detail. We plan to buy a home near here so that we can go back and forth from here to Missoula. Until then, I bet Mom and Dad will want us to stay with them."

Chevyo said, "You know you are all welcome at the family home whenever you come here. The house is half empty. The spirit of the home informs me on a daily basis that it needs some love and family running around in there. Please don't think you have to buy a home. Yamka and I would be overjoyed to have you here. Besides, we're getting old and the house will be passed on to you someday anyway."

Jillian hugged him. "I'm so proud to be a part of such a wonderful family. Before I started to remember more, every day I wondered what my real family were like. I just had a feeling that you were loving, compassionate people.

I had many dreams of life here and they were always beautiful dreams. I awoke one day years ago and my friend Julia was there beside me. Right then, I just had a very strong feeling that I belonged somewhere else. That was what motivated me to escape the hell I was living in.

Chevyo and Autumn hugged her simultaneously. "Mama, it's okay now. We are all here together. The past is over and no one will hurt you ever again. We'll all protect each other."

Jillian smiled at her through watery eyes. "See how wonderful my daughter is? She is so wise at such a young age."

Chevyo looked thoughtfully at Jillian. "You know, you were that way, too. Such a wise, friendly, thoughtful young girl and you haven't changed a bit in that regard. The only difference I see is that you are even more beautiful."

"Thank you, Papa. Everything is just as I prayed it would be." She beamed.

Brooke turned her attention to Jillian. "I need some expert landscaping advice. Would you be interested in helping me out with that?"

"Absolutely. Show me the plans and the property and I'll help you design it complete with colored sketches and a list of what we need to order."

"Oh, that's so great. I'm thinking I want a water feature, some hardscaping advice and trees that display beautiful color at different times of the year. And of course, lots of flowers. In fact, I would love to plant lilies just for you. Maybe we could all take a drive to the ranch before the end of the holiday. I'll give you a set of plans and you and I could sketch out the landscape plan, take photos and anything else that would help. You mentioned that you may stay here for a while, so you are welcome to visit the ranch whenever you like."

"That sounds terrific. Autumn will be delighted to see it as well."

Brooke put her hand on Autumn's shoulder. "Do you think you'd be interested in running up there with your mom a few times a week while on school breaks, to help me with a few things? The exterior is almost complete and as I mentioned earlier, I would like to get the interior of the main lodge pulled together. There will be contractors coming and going, but I think we could begin sketching out each room so that we can buy just the right furniture and anything else that will make each room feel warm and comfy. Jillian and Chevyo could drive out there with you." She looked at Chevyo with hopeful eyes.

"I'd be happy to. I need some kind of project so that I'm not just putzing around the house, driving Yamka crazy." He chuckled. "Truth be told, Yamka and I enjoy each other's company. I love her dearly and we always seem to have something that needs to be done around the house and gardens and I'm quite handy. If there is something that I could help with at the ranch, just let me know."

Brooke sighed. "Oh, there will be so many things you could help with. Be careful about what you ask for, because I could definitely put you to work."

Autumn said, "I really believe I'm up for the challenge. I think it will be a hoot with Mama and Grand there with us. I can help until my school starts again in mid-January and then I could come back during spring break. I'll be graduating at the end of May, so I could come back to help you finish it and maybe work for the summer. Hey, I just had a thought. Grandmama showed me some beautiful quilts that she made. Maybe she could teach me how to make quilts and we could put them on the beds. That would make the rooms feel really homey."

"What a terrific idea. I actually love to make quilts as well, but I haven't had the time to work on one in quite some time." Brooke smiled thoughtfully. "I made one with my grandmother years ago, which was a very special quilt because we worked on it together and completed it before she passed away."

Autumn dashed into the living room where Yamka was sitting by the fire. "Grand, will you show me how to make quilts? I want to put them on the beds at the ranch so that when girls are brought in, they will feel like they have a comfy, homey place to stay."

"Why sure, dear. I'll show you some quilting books and you can pick out a pattern and we'll start on one tomorrow. I have a closet filled with materials for you to choose from, a nice layout table and another one to cut on." She smiled with obvious joy in her heart. "Oh, what fun that will be." Autumn hugged her.

The group continued to laugh, sing and dance to skillfully strummed guitar songs played by Mack and Dakota. Christmas day was an eventful, jovial occasion, filled with love and hope, enjoyed by one big happy family. The year 2018 would be a year to remember.

Epilogue

Dakota and his team had an exceptionally fun holiday week at his mountain home with the Hunt family. Having Jillian home after forty-one years was a miraculous gift treasured by everyone. Yamka treated Autumn as if she was her daughter rather than her grand-daughter, but Dakota talked with Autumn about that. Autumn was two years older than Jillian was when she was abducted, close enough in age for Yamka to feel like she was her daughter, as if Jillian never went missing. Autumn understood and was okay with it. She loved the attention.

Dakota awoke, put on his robe and pulled back the curtains. The morning sky was bright blue and the snow sparkled in the sunlight. 8 a.m. on December 30, Rhys,

Brooke and Blake were at the dining table enjoying some fresh brewed coffee and talking about the previous events. "Well, good morning sleepy head." Brooke teased.

"Aren't you guys up a little early? I thought I'd be the first one out here this morning after all of the late hour libations flowing last night."

Blake said, "We were just discussing that and actually, not all of us tilted our glasses as many times as some of you did. I figure we'll be having a grand ole time on New Year's Eve so I'm taking it slowly for now."

Dakota poured a cup of coffee and sat down with them. "I've learned to pace myself around you guys, but the extra sleep was heavenly."

Brooke poured another cup of coffee. "I love wine, but I can't drink much of it without feeling horrible the next day. I'd much rather have some fun in the snow. Rhys and I are doing some cross-country skiing again this morning and anyone who wants to come is welcome"

"I'd like to go and I bet Cheynne would enjoy skiing today, too." Dakota glanced at Cheynne as she sauntered into the room.

"I heard you talking about skiing. I'm in. The clear, bright morning sky is beautiful and I hear the glistening snow calling my name."

Dakota poured her a cup of coffee. "When the others wake up, I'd like to have a short informal meeting. Dirk, Kate and Hank will be joining us tomorrow afternoon for a New Year's Eve barbecue and a few early libations. He wants to have a brief meeting before another day of festivities begins. I want to discuss his territories with all of you to see where you all want to work. I think it would be best if we are organized before he arrives so that you can ask questions concerning your territories. As I mentioned in the meeting in Atlanta, I will move you around so that you are not having to stay in the same area for too long. I know that gets boring."

Once everyone was up, Dakota discussed the work ahead and was elated that everyone was content with their territories. "Looks like we have a plan."

"All of us may all end up working in the northwest at some point this spring. I have been reviewing some information concerning traffickers entering Canada and Alaska by ship. Disturbing as it is, PACT-Ottawa has been receiving hundreds of calls in the past few months, so we may all be working in and out of Canada and Alaska mainland. Anchorage has had a tremendous amount of trafficking going on lately and since the main industries up there are tourism, fishing and oil drilling, the state is vulnerable to trafficking of all sorts. Anchorage has the highest volume of sex trafficking out of the top ten U.S. cities where trafficking is prevalent."

Dakota paused to sip his coffee. "For some mysterious reason, the Alaskan native people have been targeted to an appalling degree. I'd sure like to help in a major way. Maybe if our task force team as part of a major operation including a large group of other authorities, arrive in Anchorage and stir the pot, the criminal work of largest crime syndicates will at least be hindered. In fact, I believe that a continuous barrage of onslaughts should be planned until we figure out who the major criminals are and take them down."

Brooke gasped, "They must be furious. I for one, want to help as soon as possible but if I can't because of my work at my ranch, I pray you guys are able to go up there and take those creeps down.

Cheynne had been reviewing the trafficking issues in Alaska. She looked up from her computer. "I agree Brooke, I'm ready to go, too. I just read an article on missing and murdered indigenous young women in Alaska, which seems to be taking place mainly in Anchorage.

Dakota said, "I have a feeling that Dirk is going to change our territories so that we can focus our work in Canada and Alaska and all states along the Canadian-US borders as early as spring. About 17,000 people in Canada are trafficked every year. I read that hundreds of thousands of people have been trafficked in Russia as well as in other Asian, Central and South American countries. Many of the traffickers and victims have made their way here via northern and southern borders as well as all seaports."

He drew in a deep breath and sighed. "We have our work cut out for us but for now, Brooke and Cheynne, I would like for you both to work together to do some research on a nonprofit organization called Priceless Alaska. This organization assists trafficked victims. Also, check into Covenant House Alaska and Canada. If we work up there, we may need safe places to bring the victims to if we run into situations where the local authorities aren't immediately available."

Brooke got up to find a notepad and sat back down next to Cheynne. She glanced at Dakota. "I wonder what Sarah has up her sleeve. I bet she is planning some significant scheme of her own. Her RV is still up in the Yukon at Grace's Hope Ranch, which of course is a perfect place to bring girls that we rescue on our routes in and out of Alaska. Maybe we should work with her on this. She is very good as we have witnessed, in locating these heinous criminals and is from Canada."

"You're right. We'll have a talk with her. I think Sarah and Grace are planning to fly back later today. I really don't think Sarah wants to be here when Dirk arrives. I don't know if Jake is going with them or not. I'll talk with him about his plans. In fact, if he is going back today, maybe I can have him begin scouting around with Sarah. They could meet with PACT Ottawa, ACT Alberta and other organizations up there to find out what regions are experiencing the most trafficking.

Dakota sipped his coffee. "I read that Alberta and Saskatchewan have also been facing a rampant trafficking issue. Jake, Sarah and Grace are from Edmonton, Alberta, so maybe they could accomplish some ground work. I'd like for them to figure out how traffickers are getting across the Canadian-US border and how often they are being smuggled in on ships. I'd also like to find out what border crossings traffickers are moving through. Jake will be a lot of help, since he has traversed many of the border crossings for years."

Dakota said, "I think beginning in May, even though the weather can still be quite frigid and stormy, we might be venturing up there. In the meantime, running near the border crossings state side and a few trips across the borders from Washington and Montana, could prove to be effective precursory work. I just have a feeling that we might be able to locate and track a ring or two up there while the authorities are focusing on the southern borders in and out of Mexico." Dakota had that look in his eye.

"Uh, oh," Mack teased as he walked into the room.

"There's that look again. Good morning." He poured a cup of coffee and sat down at the table. "As I was getting dressed, I was listening to the conversation. The border towns of Sweetgrass, Montana and Coutts, Alberta, Canada thrive on the trucking and rail traffic that traverses back and forth. That might be a good place to start hunting predators."

Rhys said, "It seems like those would be easier crossings, but recently an enormous storm blew through there causing extreme whiteout conditions. The last storm like that was about twenty years ago. We'd just have to be mindful of the weather but I agree, it would be easier than tracking into Canada from British Columbia, unless we hear that our assistance is needed there as well."

Mack said, "Aye. I was happy that we weren't having to roll through there at that time. I remember that storm. On another note, just wait until the Keystone XL oil pipeline begins construction. We'll be up to our eyeballs in work. The pipeline will cross into the U.S. from Canada in Phillips County, Montana. The project is on hold because of tribal disputes, but when it does begin, there will be something like a thousand workers camped out in and near Sweetgrass. I'm sure traffickers will figure that out fairly quickly."

Dakota sighed. "Yep, I do believe we have our work cut out for us."

Cheynne stood up displaying an exuberant smile. "Anyone hungry for blueberry pancakes?"

She received a bunch of "oh yes," and "that sounds really good," replies.

Brook sauntered into the kitchen to help her. They pulled out some fresh fruit and smoked bacon and began cooking. The delicious aroma of smoked bacon and pancakes wafting through the house enticed the others out of their lazy slumber. Dakota filled the others in on the previous discussions, reviewing each territory. Everyone was content with their assignments and ready for the meeting with Dirk the following day.

After a delicious breakfast, most of the group went out to enjoy cross country skiing and snow-mobile fun. The weather was frigid with slightly gusty winds, but the sun was shining and the group thoroughly enjoyed the exhilarating outdoor activity. The festivities and good conversation continued through the first of the year. Chevyo and Yamka enjoyed the company of Jillian, Autumn and Liam immensely and planned to spend as much quality time with them as possible. Yamka had fun working with Autumn on a beautiful quilt, giggling and sharing experiences.

Jillian snowshoed with Liam, Dakota and Cheynne, marveling at the serene beauty of the Rocky Mountains. Dakota couldn't stop smiling as he felt the years of guilt and shame melt away like ice in July. Spending time with Jillian allowed himself to feel whole again and he planned to spend as much quality time with her as he possibly could. They shared past profound experiences, which Jillian was excited to recall. While gazing at a remarkable view of the mountains, an impressively large raven, glided in the air currents above them, leaving Jillian momentarily mesmerized. She felt a spiritual connection with the raven, which seemed to trigger memories of her life as a teenager. She hugged Liam and twirled around with him, laughing and dancing as her memories began to return, as if the sky opened up with a deluge of blissful experiences.

Jillian was tremendously grateful, content and finally felt like everything was as it should be.

Jake, Sarah and Grace headed for the airport on New Year's Eve morning before Dirk and Kate arrived. Dakota discussed the plan with Jake and Sarah, to have them begin scouting around in Canada. Grace was also planning a New Year's celebration with the young women and employees at Hope Ranch, which she was really looking forward to.

When the three arrived in Whitehorse, about ten hours later, they were walking toward Jake's jeep when Sarah observed a suspicious plane landing at a bizarre distance from the airport. The plane stopped and a large SUV sped up to it. "Hey, look at that." She quickly pulled out her camera and connected her zoom lens. The door of the plane opened, stairs were lowered and a group of women were rushed off the plane and briskly shoved into the SUV by two sinister appearing men. Sarah filmed them. "Jake, call 911! Grace, call airport security!"

Bibliography

1. Wikipedia. (March 9, 1977). Hanafi Siege.

2. Polaris. (April 3, 2019). Sex Trafficking.

3. Dominguez, Catherine. (Nov. 6, 2018) Operation Cross Country Human Trafficking Prostitution Sting. Houston Chronicle.

4. Santich, Kate. (December 3, 2018). Sex Trafficking Bust, Orlando, Florida, Polk County. Orlando Sentinel.

5. Paris, Kendis. Head of Truckers Against Trafficking. (Feb 11th, 2016). TAT

6. Harris, Dylan Woolf. (July 18, 2013). Sex Trafficking. The Nevada Trucking Association was addressing truckers and the general public to be aware of the forced sex trafficking issue and how truckers could help. The Elko Daily Press.

7. Kennedy, Geno. Rollinsville, Colorado. (2003) Welcome to the Mountains – Now Behave.

8. ABC 27, WTXL. (Oct. 30, 2015). Operation Safe Haven. MGN Online.

9. Burns, Steve. (Oct. 18, 2017). Operation Cross Country. Atlanta Journal Constitution.

10. Wikipedia. MotorSchiff St. Louis

11. Blakemore, Erin. (June 4, 2019). MotorSchiff St. Louis, History.

12. May, Meredith. (Oct. 6, 2006). Sex Trafficking. First

of a Four-Part Special Report. San Francisco Chronicle.

13. ABC News. (Feb. 9, 2006). Teen Girls' Stories of Sex Trafficking in U.S.

14. Markon, Jerry. (Sept. 23, 2007). Human Trafficking Evokes Outrage, Little Evidence. The Washington Post.

15. President Barack Obama. (Sept. 25, 2012). The White House. Office of the Press Secretary.

16. ICE Newsroom Online. (Jan. 23, 2017) Washington, D.C.. Human Smuggling/Trafficking. ICE Arrests nearly 2,000 human traffickers in 2016, identifies over 400 victims across the US. ICE Newsroom.

About the Author

Deb D. Donohue lives in the Colorado Rockies, where she enjoys writing, reading, drawing, dancing and hiking. Her son and extended family live in various parts of the country.

She earned a Bachelor of Science degree in Architecture, at Gerald D. Hines College of Architecture at University of Houston and completed three years of Interior Design Studies at Design Institute of San Diego, California. She studied writing, poetry and philosophy at Mesa and Houston Community Colleges and has enjoyed writing and research work for over forty years.

She has an extensive background in the fields of architecture, design, sales, writing and commercial driving. Deb looks forward to writing full time soon.

While driving across the country, she observed the harsh reality of criminal behavior, particularly within large cities, prompting her to begin writing, focusing on concerning social issues within a fictional context. Jillian, A Dakota Hunt Novel Book One and Anji, A Dakota Hunt Novel Book Two are fictional stories, however, certain incidents and events which occur in both novels are based on actual circumstances occurring within the sex trafficking trade.

The idea for the books came about when she studied Truckers Against Trafficking, (TAT) materials and website. She wanted to get involved somehow in the fight against sex trafficking and hopes her books will help create more of an awareness that our world continues to struggle with modern-day slavery, human trafficking.

The books are meant to encourage hope for the young women who have been victims of sex crimes and for their families who have suffered tremendous loss.

The stories are also meant to encourage young people to be alert to suspicious behaviors of possible offenders and to protect themselves while in public.

Deb also hopes that many more people find ways to get involved in the fight against trafficking and in the rescue of young people from such a devastating plight.